Steven C. Harbert Jr., the author of *The Fossil Forest*, is still following his dreams, reconnecting with old friends and family, and living in one place for only a moment. Who knows where the universe will take him next?

Dedicated to all those I call family…
Because without you, the end of the world seems so beautiful.
Thank you. You know who you are.

And to Robert and Jacque; without you, I would have never become the man I am today.

Justin -
    It has been an absolute pleasure working with you all these years. You'll allways be a older more red headed brother to me, so thank you for all the wieght you carried back when we were deployed and thank you far giving me the chance to carry it foward. You have already read this, however it is only right you have this copy.
    — one of your asshole infantry guys

Steven C. Harbert Jr.

It Wasn't My World That Ended

AUSTIN MACAULEY PUBLISHERS™

LONDON • CAMBRIDGE • NEW YORK • SHARJAH

Ordering Information
Quantity sales: Special discounts are available on quantity purchases by corporations, associations, and others. For details, contact the publisher at the address below.

Publisher's Cataloging-in-Publication data
Harbert Jr., Steven C.
It Wasn't My World That Ended

ISBN 9781645750130 (Paperback)
ISBN 9781645750123 (Hardback)
ISBN 9781645750154 (ePub e-book)

Library of Congress Control Number: 2020917066

www.austinmacauley.com/us

First Published (2021)
Austin Macauley Publishers LLC
40 Wall Street, 33rd Floor, Suite 3302
New York, NY 10005
USA

mail-usa@austinmacauley.com
+1 (646) 5125767

Where do I even start? When you grow up, your entire life is shaped by all those things that make an impression and impact. They are so good at it too; cartoons, commercials, movies, books, music. There are so many pieces of work and people out there that have inspired this work and the very way I view this world. Point in fact, the very way I live my life has been a direct result of a lot of the influences that I took in and many that were forced upon me. The greatest of all the influences are that of others that sounded so sweet, but ultimately steered me in the direction I am now. So, for that, for those that forced that nonsense down my throat and into the darkest reaches of my mind, I thank you very deeply for you were a catalyst that has led me astray.

And for all of those things, pieces of art, pieces of music, those spectacular movies, and books; to all of you that will read this and gather the hints of those works in here, I thank you all. Although many of them are now long gone, I hope that they know that their work has inspired so much of the future generations across time. For those that are still alive; keep evolving and growing and producing those things into the world that you do. Somewhere out there someone will hear it or see it and pour into the world their own self. Be the catalyst for growth and change and evolution. My goal is that one day I will be that for even just one soul. With that, thank you John Milton, Rene Descartes, Louis Armstrong, Ella Fitzgerald, Tool, August Burns Red, Harlan Ellison, Stephen King, Edward Lee, Vincent van Gogh, Beethoven, Salvador Dali, The Ghost Inside, Behemoth, Unearth, The Dell Vikings, All That Remains, Debussy, All Shall Perish, Frank Sinatra, Five Finger Death Punch, *Day of Vengeance*, Chris Stapleton, Gerard McDermott, Zdzislaw Beksinski, Dave McKean and Paul Nash, Nathaniel Scott, *Mad Max* series. Just to name a few, there are so many more that I'm missing. Again; thank you all for your existence.

Chapter 1
Every Dog Has His Day

It was a windless cool summers night, a crisp 79 degrees. This small town in Georgia, just inside the Alabama-Georgia state line, slept peacefully. Only living things out and about were small woodland creatures, the town sheriff, and graveyard shift workers coming and going. Lampposts lining the sidewalk down the street lit the way through the residential area in a deep yellow. Insects buzzed and crazed about it. Trees in every yard, swings, children's toys, cars, and trucks parked on the curb here and there. Quiet, not even a breeze rolled through the slumbering town.

And then it came. The loud clap of thunder that crashed and crackled, pierced the world with its presence. Car alarms rang out, dogs barked, some windows even shattered from the noise. Nearly everyone in the entire town awoke, startled by it. The noise of the explosion was so loud that it echoed through the night sky. A faint buzzing noise could be heard swarming into the distance as the echo faded.

Felix jerked awake, throwing a pillow and blankets into a thrashing bloom of a mess. He fell flat on his face as he tumbled out of bed. Blinking wildly and attempting to grasp some moonlight through the blinds of his bedroom, he scurried to his feet.

"What the fuck was that?" Felix asked as he looked out the window. His phone vibrated on his bedside table; he paid no attention. He put on pants and a jacket, his bunny slippers, grabbing his Glock, keys, phone, and smokes from his bedside table. He checked the garage, no sign of a break in, then pressed his alarm button on his key, silencing the annoyance. Screams and a gunshot caught his attention. He quickly ran back through his house to the front door.

He threw the door open, cigarette hanging out of his mouth, bunny slippers on his feet, postured in a tactical manner, when he saw it.

"Could this be it?" he asked to no one, to someone, to something, to anything that was listening.

"Is this it?"

Through the tall, thick Georgia Pine, the very horizon looked as if it was on fire. Another gunshot, just down the street, snapped him back to reality. It cracked by him and slapped into a tree. He had ducked from it, far too late if it was meant for him, but stayed vigilant.

"John, that came from John's house!" he exclaimed.

He ran as quietly as possible as more and more gunshots in the distance started rattling off. Then another explosion, this time it came from the south. As Felix approached the house, he stopped dead in his tracks. The rustling in the leaves and rapid thuds of something in the woods caught his absolute attention. He brought his Glock 22 up ready, hitting the switch on his tactical light attached to the rail of his pistol. It threw a thick, crisp beam into the damp woods.

"Alright fucker, where are you?" he said just above a whisper as he searched right to left.

Whatever it was, it was gone now. Felix continued toward the front door; the house was well-lit around the four main corners of the property with flood lights. As soon as Felix came to the glass door, he threw it open; the heavy springs made a rusty stressed screech. He could hear crying inside coupled with heavy footsteps. Before Felix could do anything, a screeching noise from behind him ripped his attention away from the commotion inside his neighbor's house.

Felix turned. Picking up his pistol into sight alignment. The beast had sprinted at him, lunging, only to be met with a hammer of six 40 caliber bullets to its chest. Shell casings hit the ground all around him. The body slumped violently at his feet. It was another neighbor. Felix couldn't recall his name, but he lived further down the street. His weapon remained trained on the corpse as he pulled his left hand away, he banged on the green door knocking the reef off.

"John, Kim!" he called out.

"It's Felix, open the fuck up!"

Within an instant, the door flew open. John's big hand reached out pulling Felix off-balance, stumbling into the house. The door slammed and John locked it behind them. Felix took stock of the situation inside John's house.

"What the fuck is going on?"

"Heck!" John replied.

"What?" Felix asked, almost realizing immediately that he just swore in front of John's kids.

John answered either way, "I don't know, I had to put down Buddy. He started growling at Grace. Tried to attack her."

Felix looked over. Kim, John's wife, came out of their bedroom just past the kitchen. The married couple were both in pajamas, John had his shotgun, and blood splatter on his pajama pants. Felix took measure of the scene in the living room: Buddy, their yellow lab, was on the floor in a pool of blood. Most of his snout was in pieces from the blast of the 12 gauge. Kim was holding Grace, and their boys were wide-eyed, full of fear, standing behind their mother.

"Why would he attack Grace?"

"I don't know. It happened as soon as we woke up from that explosion," Kim replied.

Felix looked back toward the door. "The city looks like it's on fire. Do you think it was a strike on base?"

"I don't know, little brother," John replied. Felix could hear the worry and uncertainty in his voice. One he was very unfamiliar with. And, he would assume, so was John and his family.

Felix set a comforting hand on John's shoulder. "By the way, the dude down the street with all the shit in his front yard?"

"Yeah, Mike?"

"He's dead, he's lying on your lawn."

"Why?"

Felix raised a surprised eyebrow as he leaned in to answer. "Because I shot him."

"Why in the hell did ya do that?" John asked, making known to the family in their tones that it wasn't a big deal and they would be alright.

"I don't know, he attacked me…other than that I've got nothin'," Felix replied.

Before the two could continue their conversation, that was getting either of them no answers fast, a loud bang called their attention to the door.

"Hello?" Grace asked aloud clutching her unicorn, fear riddling her shaky voice.

Kim grabbed her tight with a hand on her mouth.

Another bang, the door began to splinter. A roar followed by a loud screech and a much more predominate bash against the door. John and Felix had their weapons trained on the door. John spotted his couch that ran along the wall, he quickly tossed his pump action shotgun onto the couch and slid it against the door. Another loud bang, the heavy wooden door cracked.

"Kim!" John called out. "Get the kids, we are leaving. Felix, help my family get out of here."

"Come on, as if you had to ask, brother." Felix peered over to the door. "However, let me go get ready, I'll go out the back."

Another crash against the door. The men looked at each other in confusion as the couch scooted back a few inches. The door splintered and bowed.

"Cover your ears." Felix spouted calmly. The family did as he asked.

Felix picked up his pistol, fired four rounds into the door as soon as he heard the crash of whatever was outside impact the door again.

They both walked closer, listening. Some grunting and shallow moaning until finally falling silent with a heavy thud on the front step. The two men pushed a love seat over, and piled on chairs from the kitchen, as well as a coffee table. Finally, they were satisfied with the makeshift barricade.

"Alright, give me a few. I gotta grab some shit from the house, and my vehicle."

John nodded, "Alright, we will be ready in 15 minutes."

"Got it," Felix said as he headed toward the back door just past the kitchen.

"Good luck," John said, as he held the doorknob for Felix.

"Thanks," Felix replied.

John threw the door open. Felix darted out, disappearing into the darkness past the reach of the flood lights. John slid the kitchen table against the back door. Another explosion, the power grid flickered, then the entire city blacked out before springing back on.

As Felix hopped over his fence, he lost a slipper. Causing him to stumble and stop. An odd noise of growling and frantic heavy breaths caught his attention. It sounded like a bunch of flip-flops on wet feet. He turned to observe as something flopped around violently on the street to his right. Felix caught his breath as he began to move as quietly as possible, trying getting a closer look at the body jerking around.

A loud screech, choking, meat smacking against a dew-soaked road captured his undivided curiosity. That noise stood those small hair on the back of his neck straight up. "What now?" he grunted, wide eyed.

Felix turned, lifting his pistol up. Pressing the spring-loaded switch on his tac-light, he saw a dog scurry off into the dark. A person, probably another neighbor, was on the ground flopping about making a raspy grunt. Coughing and growling, followed by odd shrieks.

"What the fuck?" Felix asked himself, just above a whisper. He slowly and quietly stepped forward, his weapon still trained on the person before him.

Suddenly, the woman stopped. Felix stepped back. She violently wrenched up on all fours looking around curiously. She jerked her head toward him. Cocking it slightly, slowly rotating it back as if confused as to what Felix was. Felix's face twisted in confusion and vigilance.

The woman screamed loudly, her voice cracked and gurgled. She lunged for him, on all fours, like an animal. Felix was caught by surprise by her speed and viciousness. Alas, her effort was in vain. Felix produced an accurate volley of fire, shells sparkling in the moonlight as they arched from his weapon onto the wet grass. She fell silent as the 15th shell hit the ground. His pistol locked back, empty. He went through a well-trained reload reaching at his hip for a magazine that wasn't there. The empty mag fell briskly into the grass. Screeches in the night grew louder as more movement sounded of approach.

"Fuck," he said as he quickly continued back to his house. His other bunny slipper lay soaking in blood and morning dew in his front lawn.

*****

It didn't take John and Kim long to have the kids dressed and things packed for the family. After 10 years of marriage and unconditional love, even in the worst of times, they had a system. Felix on the other hand was nowhere to be found. Screams and more gunshots rang out in the night, the residential area was anything but quiet. One of the houses down the street had caught fire, and the occupants inside were human no more.

"Where is Uncle Felix?" Grace asked.

"He will be here soon, baby," John replied as he peered outside.

A woman was running from three of her kids. Judging by their size, they were teenagers, on all fours running like animals. Their hands and feet moved almost naturally as if they were born running like a quadruped. One leapt, clearing almost 10 feet, tackling the woman. Her screams and cries fell short as the other two caught up, biting her throat out. They then continued to chew on the soft flesh, tearing her lips and cheeks from her face. They ripped her clothes off and began to eat until they had their fill.

John was spared the full view of the event, only having seen slight glimpse of moonlight reflecting off the blood of the bodies. Suddenly John heard a garage door get thrown open. It was down the street. He couldn't see it from his point of view. The low rumble of the car, the slamming of the driver's door, he knew that was Felix. A few more gunshots rang out, and Felix came down his driveway stopping in the middle of the road just past John's drive.

Felix took his car out of first gear and ripped the emergency break. His lights revealing the scene before him. He threw his door open looking at the three teenagers that just ate their mother. He picked his AR 15 up with military precision and fired five rounds in each one of them. They didn't have time to react as he cut them down, the noise alerted more from a house across the street.

Felix inspected the scene before him. All of the woman's soft tissue was eaten from her, her breast was gone, as well as her face; she lay silent, spilling blood over the road. Further down the road similar situations took fruition as more and more people were changing. Running around in packs attacking those unfortunate enough to maintain their human nature. The house on fire began to grow into a roaring flame that was starting to spread to the woods and the next house.

"John!" Felix yelled out.

John and Kim came out carrying their two youngest children. Aroura, their oldest, was carrying Grace to their truck. They piled in.

"Felix, I need your help!" John yelled as he slammed the truck's door. Felix slammed his. He ran around the back of the car, up the driveway. His rifle slung in front. His Glock in his fitted Kydex holster on his hip. Extra magazines for his pistol on his left. And his large knife in a leather sheath on the small of his back. His long sleeves were pushed up on his forearms. His hair was combed by his fingers over to the side, wet with sweat. His Oakleys were on his head out of muscle memory.

John rushed into the garage. Felix followed closely behind, checking back once, twice, and more and more. Gunshots were becoming a normality, and it was beginning to worry him as he felt himself losing perspective. It happens sometimes, you start to become comfortable and accustomed to it. *Who knows what they all would become when that day comes?*

They grabbed ammo cans, bags, food, water, and guns. Tossing them into the back of the truck. Taking several trips before the group was ready to embark.

Felix dropped a box of canned goods. Two more people, neighbors from across the street, were in full gallop at him. One hopped onto the hood of his car, the other ran around the back. They were headed straight for them. However, Felix didn't miss a beat. He had his rifle up, trained, and singing a volley of fire. He missed the closest one, punching a bullet through the doors of his car.

The fourth round struck the feral neighbor in the face, dropping them into a skin-scraping roll. For the second one, John had his 1911 out. Felix switched his sights on the second as well. The two men almost talked their guns in perfect cadence as they each fired three rounds. The neighbor fell, rolled, and stopped against a few of the trees off the driveway.

"Where are we headed?" Felix asked.

"To my parents' house, Flint River."

"Alright, once we get there, I'm heading out."

"What?"

"I'm going to get my woman, she's in Texas, and as much as I know she will be fine, I want to see for myself. So, I will help you get there, then I'm gone. If you can't hold that place, go to Fort Monroe, Virginia."

"Why there?" John asked.

"Just get in the car, we will talk more once we are at your parents' house."

The sun began to rise. Calling their attention.

"What the fuck is that?" Felix asked.

"I don't know, that is the west, Felix."

The two stood there, stricken with awe as the red cloud began to light the horizon. As the sun rose in the east, the actual sun, they turned back to look, then back to the west. Judging by the distance of this explosion, nuke, whatever it could be, was more than likely in the next state or further.

"Let's get the fuck out of here," Felix said.

The two rushed to their vehicles, jumped in, and sped through the residential area. The streets were now filled with people, and dogs. Dogs were attacking their owners, and thusly, within a moment, the humans became infected, attacking those that were not.

As they passed by the houses, they witnessed it. A dog attacked a small child and almost immediately from the bite, the change came. The child began to shake violently. The dog, a chocolate Labrador, stood nose down, waiting for the change to happen.

Felix slowed down to a stop. John became confused, honking his horn impatiently. Felix's window rolled down. His rifle barrel came out his side, one shot. The child jerked, splattering blood. The dog barked, growling wildly, sprinting toward Felix. One more shot, and the dog tumbled and slid to a stop at the edge of the sidewalk. His barrel disappeared back into the window and they continued moving.

The drive was anything but quiet. Fires rolling from vehicles, what used to be people running in packs through the woods off the road. Dogs running about, attacking people, infected creatures attacking and eating people. The group continued moving as fast as possible through the tipped vehicles and mayhem of the small town. Luckily, the highway leading into Columbus was empty. The clouds in the distance were dark, sparkling of static lightning storms as it rose into the sky, more than likely the atmosphere.

Felix lit a cigarette, attempting to not think. He took a deep drag of his smoke, attempting to hold back vomit. His iPod began playing 'What a wonderful World' by Louis Armstrong. Felix shook his head, laughing, but not from shock, merely from the irony of it all.

As they came into town, the sun was dousing the shadows in dawn. A group of people sprinting on all fours tackled a man. A child stopped;

screaming. The boy's mother grabbed hold of him and tore him away from the gripping scene. His father was only bitten by a canine. The pack immediately turned its attention to the mother and child. They sprinted and tackled those two. Next the dog was on top of them, biting the woman. The infected pack tore the boy apart.

Felix and John sped up on the open highway 85. A group of police cars rushed into the city. Gun fire could be heard inside their vehicles in low pops. A group of the infected launched from the forest lining the right flank of the highway. Ramming into the side of John's vehicle. Failing to overturn the suburban.

For a moment, the chaos was in their rearview mirrors. The children screamed and cried from fear and horror. Felix, on the other hand, was wearing a smile.

"Dear lord in heaven…" He took a long drag from his cigarette. "Please stay the fuck there, this world is finally becoming something beautiful."

"Felix, you need to fix your outlook on life."

"Why?"

"Because I can't deal with your hatred of people, you are starting to drain me."

"I'm sorry, babe, I don't know what to tell you."

She crossed her arms and her stance became confrontational. He took note, and she observed the language as well. He was doing that thing again that she was always attracted to, but it unnerved her. He stood there, head slightly down and leaning in her direction. It was like a beast preparing to pounce its prey.

"You keep going on about how you hate the way people drive, how they dress, how you hate being in crowds, it gets tiresome. You need to figure out where you want to be in life. People aren't going away, and unless you wanna live like a hermit in the woods, you better start getting that through your head. You have no idea what it's like out here in the real world. All you know is the army. The world doesn't work that way. You can't just knife-hand your way through life and tell people what you think of them. You will get fired in a heartbeat."

Felix relaxed a little.

She continued, "Until you figure that out, you're going to have a hard time out here."

"I know, I am me, and that's the way I look at the world. It's not a good place and as time has gone on, it's not getting better. All this convenience and technology is killing us. I can't even find a suitable vehicle because everything

16

is designed for luxury and bullshit. I can't afford what I think is suitable." He held out his cell phone. "This fucking thing..." he put it away and continued, "I can't stand them, driving has become so goddamn dangerous around here, no one pays attention anymore, I honk my horn at the light every day sometimes two to three times because these dumb fucks didn't know the goddamn light was green."

"That's the way it is."

"It's not the way it should be, I can't even shop anymore because of the same goddamn reason. These creatures we are becoming are garbage. We need to go back in time."

"To maybe living till we're thirty years old, where women had no say in anything, and people were prosecuted because they were a different color or religion or gay?"

"No, we need to go back to being a tribe."

"That's ridiculous."

"Is it?" Felix sounded so sure of his theory, his beliefs. So did she, one of the many reasons they were attracted to each other.

"Yes, those people lived horrible lives, not sure if they were going to eat that day or be killed by another tribe."

Felix laughed. "Is it not the same way now?"

"I like convenience, I like not having to worry if the chief is going to sell my hand in marriage to the son of another tribe to keep peace."

"You make valid points, but I still think it all needs to go away. Everyone needs to be free, see what really happens, see how bad the world can get. Once it's over, we hit the reset button, and see where we all stand."

She shook her head. "I wouldn't survive, you know that, do you really want all your family and friends to have to suffer that too?"

"We would survive, most of them are paranoid survivalists and country folk, they would probably survive better than I could. And you, you would definitely survive, you are more capable than you like to admit, your humbleness gets in the way, your doubtfulness defeats you. I've seen you do things that you didn't even know you could. It would be one hell of a run."

Sasha walked up to him. "We're done with this conversation."

Felix nodded in agreement. "Okay."

"When will you be able to come back home?" she asked.

"I don't know, babe, I'll let you know as soon as I find out. Gotta start packing up the house. I'm still waiting on the call back from that security firm."

"No call back yet?"

17

"Not a real big need for hired guns these days, even if it is for VIPs. Especially with the rate it seems everyone is getting out. I may just be one of many people trying to find a job in the only thing they know. I wasn't smart like you when I was younger, never went to college, never thought an education would have done anything for me. Now I'm struggling just to find a job that I can do. At least I'm not in serious debt because of a piece of paper."

"There is plenty of stuff you can do," she said as matter of fact.

"Well, I don't want to be a bum on your couch right before we get married, you know?"

"I'm sure it would be fine. I wouldn't have asked you to move in if I didn't think you were capable of finding a job and being self-sufficient. You are just walking into a world you are unfamiliar with; you just can't talk to people the way you did in the army."

"What, can't call them a fucktard?"

Sasha giggled. "No, you can't call them fucktards."

"Well, fuck. What can I call them?"

She giggled again. "Nothing, you just put up with their shit, or you will get fired."

He laughed. "I'm going to get fired a few times before I get this right, or end up with people like me," he said out loud into a sigh.

"Alright, babe, I gotta head back, it's a few days' drive. I'll call you when I get home."

"Be safe, I don't like it when you drive all night," she replied, kissing him.

He walked to his car and got in. She walked to his window, leaning in.

She kissed him once more. "Better come back to me, crazy man."

"I'll see you soon, my love. But next time I see you, I won't be leaving, unless it's for work."

The memories started playing through his head. If anything, to keep her face, her essence within his grasp. The phone wouldn't connect as he attempted to call her. No service, it might as well change the icon to a middle finger. Things were bad, and only going to get worse. He set his phone down in his seat next to him. Driving the way he always wanted to, without restriction. In a world he longed for, but the debt owed, could any of them honestly pay? Could they, could he, survive this long enough to enjoy it?

Chapter 2
Tail Tucked

Bruce and his wife, Marie, stood at the head of their table. Before them, Felix, John, and next to him, Kim. Before them on the table was a crude sketch of the house and the grounds surrounding it to include the river to the east. Another map was laid out next to that one of Columbus, Georgia.

The power was still on. The Ham radio squelched in the background as it sat on the dining table. The group listened to the national emergency broadcasting system as it blared, its tones warning, late as they may be.

"We advise all residents to stay inside. Stay away from all forms of animals both domestic and wild, as we don't understand the complexity of the virus. Anyone bitten should be avoided or restrained and quarantined immediately. Persons bitten by the virus typically turn feral within a matter of minutes. Looting has started in all major cities and survivors are advised to stay clear of heavily congested populated areas. Utilities are still running, but reports of infected attacks at powerplants, water treatment plants, and military installations has led authorities to believe that the infected animals are communicating with their feral man. All information has not been confirmed as local police, the National Guard, and military bases have been cut from main communication lines. Estimated casualties across the U.S. is at seventy percent. God be with you all."

The tones blared once more. The shakiness in the female broadcaster's voice was disheartening.

Felix looked around the room, taking in the expressions on everyone's faces. John and his father, Bruce, were calm but he could see their concern behind their eyes. Kim and Marie had looks of terror on their faces. If anything, for the children. Felix understood, although not blood to these people, they were his family. As most soldiers have developed similar bonds with those in arms compared to their own flesh and blood. John's kids were, for all intended purposes, his nieces and nephews.

"That would explain the way Buddy acted toward Grace," Kim broke the silence over the pause in the emergency broadcast. Its iconic squelching filled the air. Outside, the sound of faint air raid sirens continued to ring out.

Felix held his excitement and grin back, for that noise brought chills up his spine. The kind that comes from wanting, motivation, and excitement.

"Communicating with the feral. So, they are saying that the dogs that infected the people are communicating with them? What in God's name has happened?" Bruce contemplated the message.

"I think right now our biggest concern is those left alive. If the infected are communicating with the dogs, then they should act like animals. People is what we need to fear for the moment. If we are going off of the rules of surviving a catastrophe, then we are currently in the no movement stage of the first 48 hours," Felix began, calling everyone's eyes on him as he stood next to John.

"What are you saying?" Marie asked.

"First 48, we harden the homestead, seeing that we have a large family, we cannot move until the first 48 hours of chaos subsides. Looting, riots, fear is more of a danger than whatever this infection is. Not to mention, we are next to a military base. Frightened people, soldiers, police, and anyone else with a means to protect themselves could be just as dangerous as the rioters and looters."

The group nodded. Felix continued, "It's been what, a day? Once the sun came out, the dogs and the infected either hid or moved into the woods, right?" The group again nodded. "We focus on setting up traps and warning systems around the house. Bruce, you have a basement here, what else do you have? We need to make this place people proof."

"I see, alright," Bruce began pulling over the crude sketch of the home and a sharpie. "The basement is set up to be a bunker, essentially. I have been working on it for a long time, it should be sufficient. If not, we will make it sufficient. The house runs on the grid; however, I have a daisy chain of batteries, solar panels on the roof, and a backup genny in the garage, but with a few cuts in the floor we could run a pipe outside and put it in the basement…"

The group listened to his impressive list as he outlined the well-thought-out survivalist preparation. His basement had hundreds of gallons of water, food, amenities, a working bathroom, three separated small rooms, and an impressive cache of weapons. Power, heat, a garden outside, a six-foot privacy fence, several trucks, off-road bikes and quads, a small boat, the flint river to their east. This was probably the best location they could have ever hoped to end up.

The group continued their conversation, figuring out the best possible way to defend Bruce and Marie's house. Now Bruce, John's father, and a retired army diver, was preparing for this day for a long time. Solar power roof panels lined his house. Heavy shutters were premade and sitting in a barn for years, they were bolted on the outside of the house within an hour. The door was reinforced with a steel core encased in oak. A small garden outside, a hydroponics system lined the walls of his basement waiting to be planted with seeds from his seed bank he had stored in a freezer.

That's how it was. Felix noticed this a long time ago. All of these hard-ass motherfuckers were like Bruce. Any of them, from special forces to rangers, and everything outside and in between that can't be named and don't exist. These men always had ways to escape. Bunkers, small cottages in the woods on land that everyone assumes is just forest. Their houses set up to run off the grid. Wells dug out, solar power, a small shed with a truck and a quad or other all-terrain vehicle. Surrounded by the woods, and not a soul for miles and miles. Peace, without people, you would think that there wasn't any other way.

They were prepared to disappear, because normal society was shit, it always had been. No matter what time, ever since the first society existed. People in mass are always dangerous. Believers, political parties, coexistence was a plague that ate away at people without them ever knowing it. How can anyone be free when they are owned by the monetary system? How can anyone get along when they all believed different things, and grew up different ways? When someone is truly free, what will they do in order to survive, when they still have things more valuable than money? Someone will always come along to take it, when desperation falls upon a soul, there is no limit a human will go to survive.

These old soldiers, men and women, they all knew it. Escaping, even before this infection spread, before whatever happened in the west happened, they were ready to leave it all behind.

The ham radio continued the message. Marie shut it off. John then spoke, "Dad, your neighbors, how many made it, how well are they off? With the way things are going, we can no longer trust anyone knocking at the door."

Bruce nodded, "I think we will be fine, between you two..." he was referring to John and Felix, "...not many people will get close enough to even touch the door."

"Which leads to the next question. Security. We need to finish boarding up the windows and bar the doors, and post someone on the second floor with long guns. At least two at a time, it's going to suck but we need to make sure we can see whatever is coming up the drive or through the wood line...and then, there's the river."

"He's got a point," John agreed.

"The kids need a weapon too."

The look on Kim's face said it all, she didn't have to say anything. Felix knew, "Felix, we are not giving the kids guns or anything."

"Don't be stupid, Felix." John agreed with his wife.

Felix put his hands up. "Just saying, I'll drop it, but everyone in this house needs to carry something. Just in case, we," Felix pointed around the room to every one of the adults, "don't make it back from a supply run or get infected or whatever."

Bruce spoke this time. "I think Felix is right. I'm getting old, and we all can't pick up the slack all the time. Things are probably going to get rough from here on out."

The room was quiet for a moment. That moment seemed to last for minutes, until the house shook and the world sounded of a single crash of thunder. Everyone jumped from it, a few pictures fell from the walls. The kids ran downstairs in terror, clutching their parents.

Felix grabbed his shotgun from where it was leaning against the table. He sprinted up the stairs followed by Bruce and John. Once at the window looking toward the north, they saw the mushroom cloud rising.

"Atlanta?" Bruce asked, rhetorically, because they all assumed that to be the case.

The cloud was snaking its way into the midday light, it was pluming into its smoky cap, to the west the massive fallout of whatever fell on that side of the U.S. could still be seen from the horizon.

"Get everyone downstairs right now!" Marie ordered.

The power went out.

John was downstairs before Felix even spoke. Bruce and Felix stood in awe.

"Good news is, we should survive this."

Bruce looked at Felix. Felix turned and disappeared downstairs. He walked out to his car that was parked facing toward the gate. He opened it, up pulling out his bags and started moving them inside. He was moving as quickly as he could. In his mind all he could think about was people standing outside looking at it, as the blast rolled their way, people stuck in their fear, unable to act. Unable to do anything, because there was nothing they could do.

John and Kim hurried the frightened kids down stairs into the basement. They began moving supplies. Bruce grabbed rolls of painter's plastic sheeting and rolls of duct tape. John came outside to Felix closing his trunk and moving with haste in his step.

"What are you doing?" John demanded.

"This bag has a Geiger counter, spirulina, iodine, and IOSAT pills in it. I have enough, so just in case the fallout reaches us, everyone here will have a chance in case the basement isn't enough. Not to mention I have a chemical mask and a suit in here. We need this shit," he proclaimed with certainty.

John nodded. "Hurry up and get your ass inside, retard!" he demanded again.

Felix shook his head as if John expected him not to.

Once downstairs, Kim and Marie, with years of motherly experience, calmed the children. Holding them close. Felix set his hefty duffle bag in the corner of the room, he was back up and out of the basement.

Bruce was inside taping plastic sheeting all around the house, starting closest to the basement door and working his way out. John was in the kitchen doing the same. Felix started helping Bruce, holding the plastic sheeting in place as the old man taped it up. It took them the better part of an hour. John cut a small sheet and made a make shift door for the back and the front doors.

The house was sealed for the most part, at least the kitchen, living room, and hallway. The basement was well lit with candles, the kids were asleep on Kim who sat on the couch. Bruce pulled out a hand crank radio and began working the handle. Within a good amount of whirling to charge the magnificent device, static began to carry over the radio. He began to tune; for known stations at first. Then, it became a frantic turning of nobs to find anything, he began walking around the basement holding the radio up, searching for a signal. Nothing. He went to the Ham and flipped the switch. Not even the warning sounds, just static sounded.

Felix sat at a small table, laying out his personal "Nuke Kit" with a satisfying smile and a wild purpose driven look in his eyes. Spirulina, pill form and powder form. After Chernobyl's meltdown, 45 days of taking these amazing pills helped save lives especially in children. Through Felix's paranoid research over the years, these came at the top of any preppers or survivalist lists. In a pinch one could drink iodine. But you had to want it, the taste alone could gag a normal person and it honestly barely worked. He had a handful of Radiac wash towelettes; very hard to come by. However, charcoal, simple soup, and water would do the trick as well.

The key to surviving nuclear fallout was simple. Don't live near strategic targets, military bases, Navel research facilities, large cities, capitals, or locations of known government consolidation areas. Don't get the fallout particles on your skin, if you do, limit your exposure, wash it off immediately. Don't breathe it in if you can help it, if you do, then you are more than likely fucked. Not to mention, the most important thing he had in his kit – 'Nuclear War Survival Skills' by Cresson Kearny. If anyone could give you a step-by-step guide to the end of civilization by way of nuclear attack, it was this brilliant man. It gave Felix a level of confidence that many, especially now, were seriously needing. Even if as infectious and fragile as hope.

Hopelessness, it replaced peace of mind, giving way to fear, ultimately desperation. A virus transmitted from the bite of a dog, turning humans feral, an explosion of biblical proportions in the west forcing civil unrest. Felix giggled to himself. *No more than normal,* he thought. Now, though, nuclear weapons, as devastating as they are, they are, in fact, very survivable; however, the fear that they bring and the loss of life in concentrated areas are in fact, fucking terrifying.

Bruce set a glass of whiskey on the table for Felix.

Bruce had already handed John a glass, and it was gone in one gulp. Felix looked at it, it was gorgeous, he picked it up. Looking through it. A tear started to form in his eye as his thought began to come out of his mouth.

"My woman's hair…is like looking through a glass of whiskey, illuminated by the flicker of a burning candle in a dark room."

Everyone was looking at him, as his eyes were lost, adrift in his own thoughts. He took the glass like medicine, as he often thought of it. Setting it down carefully, the glass pounded against the wooden table. Echoing out in the cool basement, sounding of pain as it seemed to cling to him.

"If anyone could survive this, it's her," Kim said breaking the heavy silence.

Felix never broke his gaze into the nothingness.

"You have such an odd yearning for knowledge," Sasha said as she stood next to Felix.

A box from Amazon lay open on the kitchen table. He pulled out several books.

"I think you need to be a full-time student, work toward becoming a professor. That's what you should do," she continued.

"Oh yeah? Maybe, one day. I don't like colleges though, especially nowadays. The shit they teach is very politically driven. If I were to be one, I have no idea what I would even teach, not to mention, how much of it would be watered down and manipulated?"

Felix pulled out books on Hydroponics, Solar energy, Wind turbine, Nuclear Survival, Farming. Sasha picked them up, looking at him and then back to his collection. He continued placing books on the table. House building for Beginners, Bush craft, Fire brick making, Forge building, and Metal working.

"Not all colleges are like that."

24

"True," he replied. "But, that's what all of them seem like. Besides being a white male in this country is just as dangerous as deploying to Afghanistan nowadays. I have a feeling if I were to go to school, I would be poisoned by the stupidity of this generation. I played enough games of falling in line for society, I want a little bit of a freedom, and I certainly would rather read what I want to know for myself rather than listen to someone else's version of it. That's why religion has started to become as bad as it was centuries ago."

Sasha shook her head, his responses baffled her. But they intrigued her at the same time. Being a psychologist, a lot of things about him baffled her, and his yearning for knowledge and his views of institutionalized education was of one who saw beyond the imprisonment. She knew he hated the concept of it, he only ever wanted to go to trade schools. This was a conversation they often had whenever he surprised her with his intelligence. In her time with working with the military, she found that a lot of the combat jobs yielded men and women with extremely acute knowledge spectrums.

Felix pulled out several more books. The Brothers Grimm, The Road, The Dark Tower Series, The Series of Change, The Complete Collection of William Shakespeare. His collection was becoming substantial.

"Why not download these?" Sasha asked, knowing his answer before he said it.

"Because these are better; having a physical book, the pages, and when the lights go out, these will become greater than gold one day," Felix didn't miss a beat with his answer.

He didn't notice, but she had a smile full of teeth as he was admiring his collection.

"I still think you should become a professor," she said picking up one of the books.

"Haha," he laughed. "You won't get jealous of all the young college girls trying to earn extra credit from their ruggedly handsome professor?"

"There's that narcissism." She thought about his statement for a minute. "Maybe it is a good idea that you stick with wielding a gun. Or a trade school. I think you would do well in a trade school."

Felix laughed. Sasha joined him. They began putting the books on the bookshelf in her office.

"Why did you buy all these books though? It would be much more efficient and less expensive if you got digital copies."

Felix nodded in agreement, "Yes, but like I said, when the power goes out, maybe for good one day, these will become priceless. Bullets and money, packaged goods, they will all disappear one day, but these words will become sacred."

Sasha thought about it for a moment. Ultimately, she was even more impressed with his response. The mind he had always intrigued her. She wanted to know what it would be like to spend just a few hours in his head. To know where it went when he was quiet, what things came across his mind when he started preparing for an end that more than likely would never come in their lifetimes.

Chapter 3
Hungry Pups

Candle light danced around them, throwing streaks of shadows across the table. The darkness cupped its hand around the group and the mood was heavy. The silence echoed after the break from the burning of the wick. The children slept in one of the rooms peacefully.

"It's been a week. The fallout should be settled or at least settling by now. Time to start thinking about resupply. Defense, especially from those that aren't turned and anyone who survived the explosion." Bruce spoke, breaking the silence.

John nodded, leaning on the table. "First thing first, we clear your yard. The real issue is you don't have a way to block the drive, and the river leaves a massive opening for the infected and people."

"Anything on the radio?" Kim asked Marie.

Marie shook her head. "Just static."

Bruce crossed his arms, stroking his gray beard. "I think, first thing is first. We need to go out and make sure it's safe."

Felix already knew; his suit fit him, he had a means to decontaminate, and his radiation detector was going to tell all. "I'm going, that is not up for discussion, I'll check the house and the yard and walk down to the neighbors. We need to know how bad things are. Once I'm finished, I'll come back and let you all know."

John placed a heavy hand on Felix. "You sure?"

"Yeah, you have a family to protect. If I don't come back, it's because I'm dead. From the book, we should be fine, at most three weeks and the fallout should be settled but it all depends on the size of the device. Not to mention the winds and where the fallout actually drifted."

Bruce looked at Felix, "How do you know all of this?" he asked, curiously, and worried at the same time.

"My paranoia is the product of the life I lived, the life we lived. You should know all too well why I would study something like this."

Bruce nodded, stroking his beard, "I think you're right, just be careful out there."

Felix lifted his head and nodded toward his weapon sitting on the table. "As careful as that will carry me."

The group had a plan, and Felix was confident about it. He unpacked his NBC suit, gas mask, duct tape, boots, and gloves, and put everything on. John and Bruce duct taped the bottoms of his pant legs to his boots, the opening of the sleeves to his gloves and around the mask to the hood. He was sealed. He picked up his shotgun belt full of 12-gauge rounds, placing it over his shoulder. Next his shotgun. He turned on his Geiger counter, it clicked very slowly, reading within normal levels for the environment.

He gave John a nod and shook Bruce's hand. Letting out a heavy sigh, he walked up the basement stairs. John and Bruce taped up plastic sheeting from the ceiling to the stairs. Felix disappeared out the door, John and Bruce watched at the bottom. Felix walked through the house. He was already sweating heavily as he checked the counter. The suit was hot, and uncomfortable. It brought back memories of deployments, possible chemical threats, clearing buildings after buildings in the heavy suits in 120-degree heat. This was no *possible* threat. It was very real, and he had an obligation to his family that waited downstairs with heavy hearts.

Felix stepped out into a hellishly gray day. The fallout storms shed their cries of atrocity upon the land far from them. Atlanta was devastated, he knew. The bombs destroyed much of the city and more than likely the infection and survivors within it. The area downwind was now suffering from that success. It brought cold chills up his spine, but the smile that flexed under his mask kept him sane. All he could think to himself was, *We finally have a purpose again.*

Outside, the counter was still reading normal levels. It wasn't surprising due to how far away they were. He walked around the yard to the garden, still normal. He walked down to the river. The stream flowed north, which was good, but if one of the bombs hit another city south, it would surely end up carrying irradiated water to them. Something that would have to be checked every day if they start pulling water or fish from the river. At the very least they could build a distiller to rid it of the particles. However, the fish would be a completely different story.

He continued down the drive. The counter clicked occasionally, according to his now precious book; he was still within normal levels. The sky to the north looked yellow, and the sky bled into a dark blanket of thick storm clouds to the west. Everywhere else was hazy, from falling dust that was kicked up into the atmosphere from whatever exploded in the west. Felix could only assume, and assuming the worst was his normal every day thought. Pessimism was one of his flawed personality traits, but it kept him humble and surprised when good things happened. When the bad came; he was prepared for it, sometimes.

Felix opened the gate, taking note that they need to lock it up. Why that slipped their minds worried him, a mistake that he assured himself won't happen again. Also, how were they going to block it; this gate was horribly cheap. Designed to keep honest people honest. He continued down the street, a small man-made square lake sat to his left, two houses on either side of it. They looked empty. A few bodies could be seen; bloated, on the thick grass. He brought his shotgun up after placing the Geiger counter in his NBC suit's cargo pocket. He arrived at the nearest neighbors' house.

It was white, with a pillared wrap around porch, neo-plantation style. The door was a well-designed stained-glass archway. He knocked as he looked around. Sweat stinging his eyes as it fell from his brow in his fogging mask. He had about ten minutes before his masks' filters became saturated with whatever they were filtering.

Felix checked the knob; the door was locked. He knocked once more. Waiting for a moment, he lost patience, and moved around to the back door. He came upon an elderly couple; he had never met them, but he could tell they were good people. Their necks were torn out, they were pale with death. The man, an older black man, balding, his overalls blood stained, a military issued M1 Grand clutched in his left hand, laid out on his back. His wife, streaks of white in her thick black hair was laid over on top of him. Her back was splayed open. She was trying to protect him, in vain, but the love and fearless bravery was there.

He kneeled down next to them, looking around. A trail of dried blood led out from their back-porch door. The screen that enclosed the porch was ripped open at the bottom where a dog hand come through. Thick beams of light cut through the moving clouds above. Shell casings glistened in the morning light on the grass. He looked the couple over, taking note that their skin was not burned from fallout. His Geiger counter still read within normal levels as he waved it over the two old lovers.

Felix stood, "Rest in peace," he spoke, muffled through his mask.

Once back inside Bruce's house he ran his Geiger counter over his body. Nothing, it was safe, and they were very lucky. Sometimes having luck on your side is better than being prepared.

Felix pulled the tape from his hood, taking his mask off. He drew in a deep breath; his face was drenched in sweat. It was a welcomed reprieve to feel the cool air against his skin. He knocked on the basement door, yelling down to everyone that he was coming down.

29

"Hurry the hell up!" John yelled up.

Felix came down the stairs to find wide eyes and expressions of relief. Grace ran toward him, caught short by her father, John. "Give him a minute, sweetie," John said.

"It's okay, it's safe," Felix replied, stepping from the plastic sheeting.

John let her go and she lunged at Felix, grabbing a hold of his waist. Felix patted her on the head.

"Was it scary out there, Uncle Felix?" she asked innocently enough.

"Yes, sweetheart, but it is safe. Let me take this stuff off." She hugged him harder before letting him go.

"Did this suit protect you?" she asked.

"I don't know, to be honest it might have, but most of us know, Army stuff can be shoddy at best. Sometimes psychological warfare is best used against friend and foe."

"I don't know what shoddy means, but if I made stuff for the Army, I would make it really good. Especially because you and dad are always going to fight bad guys. I would make things that could stop bullets and protect you from bad things in the air."

"Well, sweetheart, when you get older, I would love to see what awesome things you would make for us." Felix replied. Her comments were always interesting to him, since the first day John invited Felix over to meet the family.

Bruce and John began helping Felix rip the tape from his wrists and ankles. He unzipped the jacket, nearly throwing it from his arms. He let out a sigh of relief. Marie handed him a bottle of water. Felix drank it in one go.

"Thank you, you're a godsend," he said through a sigh of even greater relief.

Felix sat down pulling off his rubber boots, the smell was evident to everyone. The smell of nicotine and alcohol coming from him was nauseating. He was almost knocked out by the sheer scent. Felix began to tell them of what he saw, and the elderly couple. Thus, it was safe to move outside. The group ruled though, it was best to sleep downstairs, and anyone working outside will have the Geiger counter on them at all times.

It wasn't long before the group was working on fortifying the house, boarding it up. Bruce working on the exhaust system for the generator. Kim and Marie set up a kitchen downstairs with a hotplate, bread maker, and a few pots and pans too, including a crockpot. The oldest daughter of Kim and John kept the kids entertained with stories and board games. A welcomed change to her previous brainwashed social media obsessed normality.

The house was turning into a real fortress. The garden however was starting to show signs of malnourishment due to the graying skies. The dark would

30

surely make things hard for them, not only for the garden but also for the solar panels. The forest was quiet, and that also worried them. No movement meant there was nothing in them, even at the edge of the water where animals would come to drink had not shown their weary heads.

*****

Felix was outside smoking and drinking a warm beer. John was standing next to him just outside the garage drinking coffee. As the sun attempted to break free of the grasp of the darkness in the west, the birds were seen in droves flying south. Thousands of them. Deer were moving through the woods and down the street in large packs. Varmints of the like followed suit under foot. It was a sight to behold. But what was chasing them south; the bombs, the infected, who knew? They surely didn't.

John wasted no time. He pulled his bolt action rifle out, and without warning, shot the closest one to the front gate. He hit a large buck straight through the shoulder, dropping him instantly. The deer around him only jumped at the crash; but other than that, they continued moving down the street. Not caring they lost a male, just trying to get away from whatever was in the north.

"You could've warned me, fuck…" Felix yelled as he dug into his ear with a look of pain.

"Sorry, little brother." John chuckled, patting him on the back.

Felix drew in deep from his cigarette as he walked down the drive with John to help him with his kill. He observed that the animals paid them no mind. "Why are they moving now? It's been, what? A couple weeks, maybe a month since the infection. It seems they are unaffected by it, but why are they migrating now, what the fuck is going on?"

"I don't know, little brother. All I know is, this is bad, and it might be a long time before we see game, seeing that they are acting funny."

Felix agreed as they unlocked the gate. The two men walked out, the animals paid them no mind, they frantically hurried around them. Felix and John dragged the buck inside the yard and closed the gate behind them, locking it. They continued to drag the beast up the drive where John began to prepare to hang it in the garage. He took an unused sheet of plastic and placed it under a game hook.

John pulled Felix's knife from his sheath on the small of his back and began to clean the animal. The garage quickly filled with the smell of iron as he skinned and pulled the entrails from the large buck. It wasn't long, a matter of thirty minutes, and John had the beast ready to butcher.

31

Felix was watching the animals move past the gate when a familiar silhouette with an unfamiliar movement caught his complete attention. He drew his weapon. John stared at him; he stuck the knife in the meat. With blood-soaked hands John drew his 1911. The two men stood for a moment, as if not moving was going to hide their presence.

The infected paid them no mind as it's pack trotted on all fours after the beasts. The sound of screams as the feral people lunged and took a deer to the ground. Felix and John, being avid hunters, were impressed. A person, regardless if they turned feral, just lunged and took down a deer. They stepped slowly, quietly, their weapons up, further out to get a better view.

Halfway from the garage to the edge of the concrete drive, the two men came into full view of the two male and three female ferals. The feral humans were attempting to drag the beast out of the stampeding mass of animals with their teeth. They looked like dogs. Their clothing was shredded and feet and palms bloodied from walking on all fours. A few were completely naked, bringing wonder as to what they were doing when they were bit. After all, it was night when the infection came.

A large dog was watching their pack, out of the street just inside a thin wood-line. It was staring at John and Felix. Calmly the beast watched them. In the shadows of the shade cast down on the beast, its eyes glow a brilliant yellow. Felix and John both brought their weapons higher into their point of view. Lining up their shots, calmly. The beast waited for the feral humans to drag the kill past them. The dog turned and followed his pack into the woods, disappearing from their sight.

John let out a sigh, Felix holstered his weapon, "Let's get inside, finish this up, and we can cook it on the porch, I don't think they will be back this way for a while."

John handed Felix his bloodied 1911. "Sounds good," he replied as he went back to work butchering the animal. Felix started cleaning the pistol, keeping an ever-watchful eye trained on the gate.

*****

A week later. Felix and John were outside on the roof wiping off the solar panels. John had a gracious pinch of dip in his lip. Felix was squinting from the trail of smoke snaking from his cigarette. John had his rifle sitting next to him, propped on bipods. The forest around the house separated them from the deceased neighbors down the road. From the gate, a small line of trees separated them from the rectangular man-made pond which was surrounded by two more houses.

The forest to the south, however. Went on for a few miles down the river. Most of that the land was owned by John's father, Bruce. Something floating down the river had caught Felix's attention, as did anything out of the ordinary. Felix, after all, was a particularly observant man to begin with. John looked up in his brother's direction, then to where his gaze curiously observed. John witnessed a small boat, driving upstream. Several men dressed in camouflage, the kind that hunters or country folk wore on an average day.

They spotted the two men, bringing their hunting rifles ready as they moved to that side of the boat. Two large men, three women, and several children were on the luxurious looking fishing boat. John settled down on the other side of the house laying into his rifle, ready. Felix merely stepped back, ready to face plant himself behind the peak of the roof. Just in case the shooting started.

The largest of the two men, gray streaks in his big beard, spoke, "You one of 'em zombies?"

"No, but if I were you, I'd turn your boat and head back south, pretty fucking sure a nuke went off near Atlanta!" Felix replied. His voice echoed in the quiet of the empty world around them.

"No better than down south, I reckon," the large man replied.

The boat slowed as it headed toward the small floating dock at the small boatshed that leaned over the river from the embankment.

"I don't know what you're thinking, but you best continue on!" John yelled from behind his rifle.

"We have children, you won't take in some god-fearing people?" The mother of the children, John and Felix presumed, spoke. The desperation in her voice echoed, almost reverberating off their chests.

Felix replied pointing his finger into the sky, "God is taking in those kinds of people, not us!"

Even at this distance, he could see their hearts drop. John's eyes slid toward Felix, and his brother looked like evil for a moment, too long for John's comfort, but he couldn't agree more with his mindset. John's kids, his family was priority, and there were no means to an end one would go to for their family's survival. *Fear a desperate man*, John once heard years ago.

"However, ma'am," John began to speak, "…there are plenty of houses down this river that are abandoned, you may find a safe place for a while if you're willing to pay your respects to the dead." John pointed down the river toward the north. He continued, "We don't know if there are any *'zombies'* over there, but you may find some food and supplies. We haven't looted anything yet. Can't say the same for anyone else who survived."

"Stay out of Columbus, stranger. Looters and rioters have now gone to fending against the zombies."

John nodded, he didn't know if they could see it, didn't care. He replied, "A few days ago, we watched a lot of game move south, hunting around here is slim. Fishing, you will need to test it, if anything south of here was hit by a nuclear device, it could have radiated the water."

"Thank you," she said.

John shook his head, "Sorry it's not more, but ya'll can understand."

The boat continued down the river to the north, chugging along until out of sight. Then finally out of audible range. John clambered onto his knees as he watched down the river in case they attempted to dismount and approach them.

Felix went back to cleaning the panels, speaking his thoughts out to John, "I wonder why people always attempt to group together?"

John interrupted, "Who cares, we have a family to protect of our own. I just hope they can find something down the river that will help them."

Felix turned his head; ash fell onto the recently cleaned panel. "Fuck," he said blowing it away. "Yes, however, now that they know we have this, and we may have slighted them, 'left them for dead'…we may now be sought after for vengeance if one of them should meet their end. If they decide to stop, it will be at the neighbors' house more than likely, and having them that close puts an extra concern on the current situation."

"People will always want what someone else has, unless they have nothing, then they tend to be the giving," John replied.

Felix thought about it, it settled in his head as he began cleaning the next panel. He was right, if these people were good, they shouldn't be a problem, but if they were unable to fend for themselves, they would see them as the easiest target rather than venturing out to find their own supplies. This was going to come back and bite them in the ass.

*****

The house and yard were starting to look more like a fortress than a compound. The weak privacy fence was now fortified with cut trees leaned into place and nailed or screwed into the boards. A trench had been dug around the entire fence, filled with sharp sticks. The family had taken to dumping their feces into it. The garden was becoming very fruitful in the efforts of the children and Bruce. The women have taken to learning and using every weapon in the house, day by day, dry fire drills and reducing common malfunctions.

34

Felix couldn't shake how his woman was doing. It was starting to plague him, like his dwindling nicotine reserves. Four cartons were starting to look like a carton real soon, even with the busy nature of standing watch, checking the perimeter and helping around the house with whatever needed.

Felix started preparing himself to move on. His car's garbage bumpers and side skirts were removed and he went to work with the help of John and Bruce in outfitting his little rally car. By the time they were done, his Subaru WRX STI was starting to look like a complement to the Mad Max world. Its once pearl white paint was now a rattle-can flat black. A small winch mounted on a decently welded and shaped metal bumper. Custom running boards were added. He took off that stupid useless spoiler that came with the vehicle when he bought it. He had ripped out the back seat and bolted a pelican case to the interior.

Days later after the car was finished and his smokes were down to a few packs...

He started packing up his equipment and preparing to leave, and John was certainly unhappy about it. Marie and Bruce understood. It was beginning to weigh on him after a month, and you would have to be blind to not see his mind was elsewhere.

Gunshots could still be heard from the surrounding area, screeches and screams rang out in the night. Hunting was slim to none, and by the ambient noise at night, the group knew that someone was stalking them, and soon would attempt to take what they had built.

The ham radio was full of people hidden away in their basements and homes scattered throughout the state. Speaking of the odd way the infected were acting. One even went on to tell others that the dogs were in control now, her station was a mess of biblical nonsense almost nonstop. Speaking of the messengers of death, the hell hounds coming to deliver the word of the devil himself. The family agreed to not tune into her station anymore.

Eventually their fears came to pass. One night, a scream from outside sent the family into a well-rehearsed shuffle. The kids were rushed into the basement; the eldest, Arura was set at the door loaded with a shotgun and her father's 1911. Kim and Marie were set up in the kitchen with rifles. John and Bruce were perched on the second-floor bedrooms, looking out the windows with their rifles. Felix was out the door, moving in the dark, leaning against a large tree in the front yard.

"Felix, we see the fucker, driveway is 12 o' clock, he is to the 2."

"Roger," Felix replied through his two-way, moving as quietly as possible.

Felix came onto the scene; it was a teenager, dressed in black. He had fallen into the trench, a few of the pikes had gone through the boys' leg. Felix kneeled down, his AK trained on the young man, barely into his twenties maybe younger.

"Hiya, fuckface," Felix growled, looking around checking for others.

The boy looked up, sweating profusely, fear burning in his eyes. The glint from the moonlight sheened off his weapon that lay out of reach. Felix reached down picking up the mud and feces-covered weapon. He inspected it as best he could; tossing it close to the house in the dirt. Felix wiped his hand off in the dirt.

"Where are the rest of your friends, kid?"

"Fuck you."

"You are going to die of sepsis, just so you know, it's going to suck, and even if I pull your dumb ass out of here, it will kill you slowly. Painfully."

"Re-really?" The boy groaned. His breathes were becoming frantic.

A twig snapped in the woods just beyond the wall. A small flicker of light turned the dark of the trees a dancing orange. The sound of glass sliding from a hand, the sound of liquid sloshing, and the small flaming thing flew over the fence. It crashed on the concrete. A vehicle came squealing down the street, slamming into the gate.

The metal made a wrenching grinding noise as it slid across the drive way. Sparks sparkled under the chassis of the jeep. It slowed to a stop with several occupants jumping out, yelling and squealing in blind excitement.

Felix sprinted back inside the house, baring the door with a heavy chair he wedged under the doorknob. He hurried to his gear that was stacked on the table. A plate carrier made by AR500 with plates, a pricy set up, but the tests alone made it worth it. He dawned the gear, his battle belt, and he switched to his AR. As he passed the frantic women who were confused, jumping at John and Bruce's shots above.

Two men were killed outside.

Another vehicle came through, stopping in the drive, the occupants poured out and ran toward the back of the house. Felix pointed at Kim and Marie. "The front door, one of you lie in the hallway, the other stand over her. Use the edge to cover yourselves. Remember, though, bullets love to travel down the wall. Be ready to move out of the way when they come through, and move back using the shit in the house to hide yourselves as you shoot at them. If one of you is moving, the other is shooting."

They nodded and shuffled toward the front door hallway. Felix on the other hand readied at the back door. His rifle was up, sweat dripped down the side of his face. The men had gathered there, they kicked the door in after the third try. Just as the door swung open, Felix dumped a cadence of six rounds into the shadowy mass. He killed one man, hitting him three times in the chest. The other three rounds ripped into the side of the door frame narrowly missing the men just outside.

The second man got an accurate shot off with his shotgun. The mass of the buckshot hit Felix's magazine and plate carrier, some of the shot hit him in the leg. Felix fell to one knee, his face twisted in hate, a little pain, and a whole lot of rage.

"Motherfucker!" Felix roared grasping his leg in pain.

He fired into the wall, once. His bolt locked open.

In a blinding fury Felix grabbed his next mag; 5.56 mm rounds fell from the rickety magazine. Felix stopped; looking at the magazine for only a moment, realizing that the buckshot had destroyed it and the one in his weapon. He immediately tossed it to the ground in an explosion of brass cased bullets across the kitchen floor. He pressed the mag released, ripping the shredded magazine out. In a second, maybe less it seemed, his next mag was inserted into the mag-well, ready to go.

Gunfire starting tearing through the boarded windows. Felix got low, lying down facing out the kicked-in back door. Rounds smacked against the upstairs windows as the intruders peppered the 2nd floor of the house. Bruce and John were already moving downstairs to supplement the downstairs fight.

The front door rocked slightly, to no avail, the men and women outside had no chance of breaking through. Unless they had a ram, or one of the many militarized police vehicles they were outfitted with in recent years. Either way, they were unlikely to get in.

John set down next to Felix, keeping himself hidden behind the kitchen island. "Hey, little brother," John called to Felix tapping his boot.

"What's up?" Felix asked, never taking his aim off the door.

"There are about eleven left out there, most are trying to find their way in the front."

"I got about three back here," Felix replied.

John moved to the front door with Bruce, the two men pulled the women back, sending them to the basement to protect the kids, if they should fail.

Felix hopped to his feet, crouched, slowly walking toward the door as quietly as he could, forgetting the pain in his leg. He peered through the corner of the threshold of the doorway. Leaning slightly as if it gave him more of a view. Suddenly something blurred in front of his vision, slamming against the group outside. Sporadic fire rang out, Felix bounced on his hunches as he scurried back to post behind the kitchen island. His eyes searching in the moonlit opening for the commotion outside. He had forgotten the pain in his left leg entirely.

John and Bruce could hear the screeches and screams of humans being attacked by the ferals. Another heavy slam against the front door caused the group to jump. John and Bruce were ready as they stood, pressing their weapons against the corner of the hallway. They were keeping their bodies unexposed as much as possible.

Felix watched, another blur, a shadowy figure came flying down from somewhere out of his small door frame field of view. It landed hard, it's screech seemed younger, matching the size of its body. Another shot, a weapon falling onto the concrete pad, and then a body hitting the back-porch furniture. Felix looked around, trying to figure out what he could block the door with.

"Ah, the fucking table!" he spouted as he hurried around the kitchen island.

The banging and screaming stopped out front. Just growling and eating, muffled by the heavy door. Bruce and John looked at each other. They moved to the kitchen where Felix was just now moving toward the table. A small child-sized figure leapt inside. It flew toward Felix. He lifted his weapon, firing. The body hit him hard, falling limp to the floor. Felix anchored it to the ground with a shot to the back of the head.

Bruce and John lifted their shotguns aiming at the door. Several more came in. Felix slipped on the bullets and shell casings, falling back as one hit him hard. Felix held its thrashing and biting mass off as best he could. It was growling, its cheeks fresh from being torn out. Its eyes were glowing from the low moonlight that shined through the door. They were without depth, and for a moment Felix saw someone in there. The person that used to be.

The feral bit, and Felix tightened his grip on its neck. He rolled over, pinning the waling beast to the ground. Felix drew his pistol, pressing it against its temple, pinning it to the ground further. Felix fired. The feral jerked, and fell limp. Felix paused, breathing heavily, sweat dripping from his face as he looked down on the body. Bruce and John continued firing. The ringing in Felix's ears grew louder, bringing him back to the situation at hand.

More attempted to pile in, this time adults, screaming and rushing toward the scene of Felix standing over the dead youngling. He turned, finding his rifle on the floor. He picked it up and began to fire. The kitchen was lit up with flashes from Bruce, John, and now a solid cadence of fire from Felix.

"Get that fucking table over here!" Felix demanded.

Bruce and John both finished off their shot tubes. They rushed over to Felix's left, moving the table into place. Felix continued to fire out the door so as to suppress whatever was still out there. The men flipped the table onto its end and in one movement slammed the door, and placed the table in front of it. Bruce ran past Felix into the garage through the kitchen. John tripped on the bodies piled at the door. A heavy burst of bodies hit the makeshift door, nearly knocking it back in. John rushed to his feet, leaning his full weight against the table.

Felix heard something growling behind him. He turned in a flash. The dog, a small collie. Its coat blood soaked; missing its left ear. Felix had his weapon up. John was yelling something at him, but Felix was lost in the animal's eyes.

The collie, the infected alpha, was standing over the child preparing to avenge the member of the pack. The beast was waiting, ready, and its growling continued to grow with the tension in the room. John struggled to hold the table against the door as more and more beasts began to bang against it. The feral humans outside were desperate to breach the make-shift barricade.

The dog stepped closer. A dark grayish foam fell from its jaws as it barked. Felix lifted his rifle and fired. The round ripped through the beast's skull, right between the eyes. It fell limp at the child's feet. The beasts outside immediately stopped. They began writhing in agony, and the noise of rabid beasts tearing each other apart, muffled only by the makeshift door, began carrying over the men's' heavy breaths.

"What the fuck was that?" John asked.

Bruce came back into the scene, illuminated only by the small lantern set in the hallway just outside the basement door. He began hammering nails into the table. John began using a battery powered drill and started drilling the table into the door frame and wall.

Felix kneeled down, looking at the scene before him. It burned into his mind. More and more questions were whirling around in that dark place. Why? Why would this beast do this? They didn't know the full extent of the virus, really anything about the infection. This was all new, the dog, the alpha was about to avenge one of its own. The beasts outside began attacking one another just after the dog was killed. It is all connected, but still just a mystery nonetheless.

Felix changed mags in his rifle and ran upstairs. His leg was stinging and throbbing from the peppered wound from the buckshot. It was starting to hinder his movements now that his mind was allowed to think once again. He limped his way, with much haste, up the carpeted stairs. He climbed out the window to see the Jeep still parked over the destroyed gate. A Chevy pickup truck parked a few feet from that, the doors open. He ran around the roof to the back side of the house. Several men and women were torn to pieces on the back patio. The infected slaughtered each other, only one remained, crawling with a predominate limp, favoring its back, left leg.

She was headed toward the hole in the fence that they dug to crawl in. Felix took aim. He fired, killing her before she could crawl out. Taking another look around, he noticed the young man hobbling away as well. He could hear heavy breathes and subtle cries of pain. The tears being held back with little success began to stream down the young man's face. Felix shook his head again, releasing a heavy sigh as he took aim.

"Ah fuck," Felix whispered.

Another gunshot rang out in the night, and finally, the night fell silent. As Felix walked back over to the shot-up window seal, Bruce and John hefted two bodies wrapped in plastic sheeting out the window. They hit the roof with heavy plastic and dead thuds. John climbed out, Bruce helped him swing once, and on the second time, they tossed the bodies off the roof.

That night, everyone helped clean up the blood and bullet casings. The next day the men placed the bodies inside the back of the Chevy and drove it down the street. Parking it at the neighbor's house. They fixed the gate the best they could. At least it was operational once again. The Jeep they kept, seeing that it had a winch and was fit for any off road needs they may come across. Felix took notice of the fact that this dog's entire pack looked like a family. The boy looked like his mother; the two older boys looked like their father. A dog and its family was all it had infected, it didn't turn anyone else feral over the last month.

"Interesting," Felix said aloud; exhaling a heavy tube of smoke. He threw up, hurling onto the dirt. He wiped his mouth, grunting. He began to laugh, hysterically. "What in the fuck did we do to bring this upon ourselves?"

"Have you decided yet?" Felix asked Sasha.

She stood up from crouching in front of the glass case.

"I don't know, I think I like that one," she said, pointing down at a large 1911 pistol.

"Nice, that is a good one," Felix agreed, nodding, arms crossed in satisfaction.

"Yes, ma'am. Springfield Armory TRP Operator. Night sights, crowned match grade barrel, and comes with three seven round magazines."

Felix turned, looking at her. "I would definitely get that one, hell, I want that one," Felix said.

"But, it's so expensive, this is not being smart with money, you know?" she retorted.

Felix placed his arm around the small of her back, pulling her closer. "No matter, I'm paying for it anyway... We will take this one," Felix pointed at it.

"Felix, you don't need to keep buying me shit. You need to save money too."

The clerk pulled it from the case and walked to the back to retrieve its case. Another clerk set a pen and the form on the case for Sasha to fill out.

40

As she went through the questions, she asked Felix what a few of them meant due to the same questions being asked in different ways. He explained exactly what she needed to do for each of the questions. Once everything was filled out, you needed your driver's license so they could call you in and do a back-ground check. It took several minutes before the phone picked back up and the voice on the other end gave the clerk the control number. She was good to go after about 30 minutes.

Felix paid for it, and every time he glanced at her, he noticed the look on her face. She was definitely worrisome over the fact that he just dropped twelve hundred dollars on a pistol for her. Felix didn't expect her to understand the peace of mind this gave him. If he wasn't home or for whatever reason she went somewhere, this was her weapon, in her name. That is what mattered to him.

Every day, the newspapers hid rapes and murders deeper in its pages. Most of these crimes were being conducted by cartel members and Muslims from what he could tell. Texas housed several terrorist elements in it, yet to have been reduced for some odd reason. Between men who would flee their own country to come fuck up another one, and the constant division within the American people, Felix wasn't going to take any chances, especially with his woman.

Felix held the door for Sasha and they exited the gun shop, Sasha's new gun in its neat little case. For a moment Felix felt some sense of relief. If anything, his woman was now toting a full-sized pistol, that she had proven to be very accurate and capable with.

Chapter 4
Wasteland Stray

"We need you here!" John yelled at Felix.

Felix threw his pack into the passenger's side front seat. He turned looking at John. The fire from the pit in the back cast dancing orange all around them.

"I'm sorry, but I have to go. It's been well over a month. We haven't seen anyone or anything else for a while now."

John stood there.

"So, you're just going to leave us here? I need another gun; I need someone I can trust with my family. Just because we haven't seen anything doesn't mean those crazies won't be back, and the dogs, they are still in the forests."

Felix slammed the door. "I have to go. You can defend this place easily enough, especially with your friends here now. You and them are far better shots than I, and their families pull their weight. One less mouth to feed is desirable, so let me go."

"Even if she survived, she would be on her way here, so you need to just be patient."

Felix walked around his car. "Patience is not my virtue, I have to see for myself, and if not, once I find out for sure, I will be heading to Fort Monroe, Virginia. You should think about moving there as well. That place is one of the few best chances we have on this side of the country."

John walked up to Felix. Placing a strong hand on his shoulder, "You should be the one to help us get there."

"You will be fine without me, you have family here, so it should be easy. I'll see you again one day. Just keep that map I copied for you, it has three of the safest and most fruitful routes to the fort."

"Uncle Felix?" a young voice called from the darkness.

John and Felix turned.

"Yes, sweetheart?" Felix asked, as she walked up to the two men.

"You're leaving, aren't you?" Grace asked.

"Yes, sweetie."

"You're going to go get Aunt Sasha, aren't you?"

"I am."

"When will you be back?"

Felix let out a sigh. Placing a hand on her head full of thick, long brown hair, he said, "When I find her."

Felix hugged her, shook John's hand, got into his vehicle, and drove away. Grace waved. Through the blacked-out silhouette from the dancing glow of the fire behind her, he could see her waving. She held onto her dad's waist, as he waved as well. Bruce shut the gate without a word.

Kim walked up to her husband. "He finally left, did he?"

"That retard, I hope he makes it, and brings her home."

A few days later, Sasha arrived along with a few other survivors. Malnourished, their group reduced from gangs and the feral commanded by their alphas. It was a long road for her. She was sun burnt, skinny, tired, and heartbroken. She just missed him. At least now, she was with family. Safe. Felix let his impatience get the better of him. As he always did.

*****

Almost three months since the catastrophic events took place, Felix continued in motion. The road had been long and very slow, the areas around the cities were packed with cars. So far from what Felix could tell, all the major cities were bombed. If anything, to combat the spread of the infection. Clouds were thick above in a gray world that grew colder. The roads were clear for the most part, only vehicles dead on the side of the road. Some without occupants, some with evidence of butchering by their once fellow man.

In a small town, somewhere in Alabama.

Felix took a look around, the town was empty, bodies rotting in the street, husks of burnt police cars in the middle of the intersection. Birds' chirping was the only verbal inclination that he wasn't alone, at least their songs were keeping him company. He jiggled his rake and applied more pressure on his tensioning bar. The lock spun free. *Almost as satisfying as a well-placed shot,* he thought to himself. He stood, the windows in front of the gated shop were broken out. The bars were bent inward from survivors attempting to break in.

He chuckled. "For a gun shop door, these locks were easy as fuck." He put the small tools away in his interior breast jacket pocket. Stopping himself from throwing the door open, he looked around, the street lamps flickered off on their grid timers. He grunted to himself. Hopping off the curb to his car parked on the opposite side of the street, cursing along the way. He opened the trunk, rummaging through his tools. Producing bolt cutters, the handles wrapped in several layers of electrical tape.

"This should do the trick," he said as matter of fact.

He walked around the back of the building, searching for the power distribution box and hardline. The box was locked, as per normal practice. He tried to fit the bolt cutters around the pipe but alas the pipe was far too thick for short fat jaws. Irritated, he walked with haste back to his vehicle. Cursing as he tossed the cutters back into the trunk. He then produced a hatchet.

"Yesssss," he said as he held it up in triumph, slamming his trunk closed.

With a few swings and ruining the face of his hatchet, he succeeded. A pop and crackle as the wires attempted to arc each other cried out in cheers for his zealous manner at reducing the obstacle.

He walked around to the front of the shop and pulled the door open. "Christmas came early this year," he gleefully stated to no one, nothing, other than the universe.

Stacked and lined across the walls locked in their stands were long guns of all shapes and sizes. The glass counters were lined with pistols and revolvers, skirting around the left side of the shop into the back. The carpet was a dark green, the walls a dark walnut color, ceiling fans in a row down the center of the ceiling. Targets, gun cases, ammo cans, gun parts, anything he could ever want. Impressive shop for such a small town. He walked around the counter folding the table top door out of his way. He carefully read the calibers until he found what he was looking for. Within a few minutes he had quite a stack of ammunition on the counter.

He found a pelican case that was suitable to his needs, it was long and about a foot deep. Perfect for storing weapons and ammo in the back of the car, he thought. It had wheels, making it convenient as he rolled it around the store to his pile on the counter. He tossed the shells in the box lazily as he began to set his eyes on other items in the shop. There were many potential treasures, but the one that caught his eye most. A Benelli M4, sitting in its own section of the racks.

"All kinds of yes, come here you overly expensive beautiful boom stick."

He pulled the charging handle back, checking the chamber, he released the bolt via the large button on the receiver. He looked to his pile, found a box of 12-gauge shells and started loading the weapon. He now started meticulously searching the racks for more potential weapons. He grabbed several shotguns, revolvers, pistols, from Remington to Mossberg, from Glock to Rugar, and of course the 1911s. Their selection was lackluster. However, the ones that were under the glass were more than suitable; although cheap, they were made in the Philippines and very well at that. He forced the cheap sliding lock open

44

with a knife and grabbed two of the same models. Two RIA Rock Ultra full sized 1911s. Bells and whistles, war notable durability, and performance on par with the mid-range weapon systems. Sounds like a sales pitch, but that had been his thoughts on them for quite some time.

"Next gun shop, definitely wouldn't mind finding a Dan Wesson or Nighthawk or maybe an Ed Brown, so many wonderful options and an empty world for the taking," he spoke out loud in utter blissfulness.

Once his car was loaded with the heavy case, he got in, started it up, and drove around town for a moment until he found a small grocery store. Piggly Wiggly. He parked next to another car, pulled out an empty gas can and hose, and popped the window with the back of his pocket knife. He popped the gas cap door open, and then began to syphon the remaining fuel. The dry overwhelming taste of gas made him spit and cough for a few seconds. He filled his 5 gallon can quickly. There was still plenty left, he pulled the hose, spilling some then regretting his carelessness. He began dumping the fuel into his car. He was able to get a few more gallons out of the parked car before the bubbling emptiness that echoed up the hose into his head.

"Not bad," he spat. "I've been too goddamn lucky on this trip so far, and if irony wasn't a salty bitch, I would think the rest of the way would be as easy as this."

He checked his surroundings, looking toward the north west, the clouds were still thick and black, sparks of lightning crawling across the blanket of darkness. *Like synapse,* he thought, *sparking as they thought to move and produce into reality, raining down acid, or push the ash further east.* Everything around him was covered in a light coat of ash. Luckily, it stopped snowing, its gritty gray all over the south. Or at least for now. The sun was bright today, and he was thankful, it was the first warmth he had felt in a long time.

Once he was finished packing the can into his trunk, he walked with a fierce haste any soldier could appreciate. The smell of fuel from his lips was making him light-headed. The windows were broken in, the glass door was wide open. The store was small, but more than likely had everything he was looking for in it, provided it hadn't been raided in the months since the pandemic. How long had it been, who knew? He certainly lost track of time until he looked down at his watch.

"Holy fuck, has it really been three months?" He shook his head in self-disappointment as he entered the store.

Raiding, hording, ransacking, which had been the case for a lot of places, more so the cities than the rural towns. A testament to the paranoia or just plain pandemonium caused when people live like caged animals in cities, and fear takes hold. Evidence of the failed attempts of families trying to escape were littered across almost every gas station and truck stop along his route. Tragedy struck everywhere, it seemed. Very few people had been seen on the roads, and even fewer with any intention of stopping to see if Felix was friend or foe. The few that were, were poor families down on their luck, torn from each other, broken down on the side of the road. Some were very unlucky; road gangs had formed quickly. The world reminded him of several of his favorite post-apocalyptic movies and books. *A boy and his dog*, *Mad Max* series, *The Road*, *The Book of Eli*, he could go on forever.

As he walked down the toiletries aisle, he found a pack of baby wipes. He quickly wiped himself off; his mouth, hands, then he did it once more. Found some mouth wash and rinsed his mouth out a few times. Spitting all over the floor. He set the bottle on the shelf, pulling out a pack of smokes and lighting one. He continued his venture down the aisle. Canned foods, canned meats, rice, nuts, honey, he grabbed a lot of honey, didn't matter what kind, he took one of each. The meat section reeked of rot and buzzed with flies. He stepped over a few rotting corpses and continued his shopping spree. Swatting a fly occasionally.

The hand basket was full, he realized that he was going to have to use a cart after all, this wasn't going to be enough. He moved as quickly as he could, grabbing anything and everything he could that would last a while. He even stopped to grab wine and liquor. Energy drinks, protein bars, a bag of rice, ramen, salt, iodized and sea. Then it was the tobacco. He pilled everything he could, cartons of cigarettes, chew, dip. All these things were gold now, might as well prepare for when he would reach some sort of civilization. Batteries, they didn't have what he needed, but he grabbed the popular types either way.

"What a successful day, no gangs, no dogs, or infected, I better get ready for a horrible fight," he said as he passed by a large crow cawing at another. He laughed.

"Attempted murder," the crowed replied, as they always did.

"I'm doing well, thank you, how are you?" he playfully asked. The birds responded in their cries as they do. Not caring too much for Felix's presence.

"Well, take care, lads, I'll see you down that road one day."

Once the goods were loaded, he pushed the cart as hard as he could, it rattled across the small parking lot; bounced a few times from little rocks in its rickety rattling path, and then crashed against the row of rusting carts along the entrance of the building. He nodded in approval of his attempt to park the cart in its proper location.

Felix stepped on the crudely wielded foot step on the side of his Apocalypse-mobile, he checked the straps on the cargo rack on top of his roof.

He walked around, checking his all-terrain tires; all in good condition. He continued around to the wielded custom brush bar cage, complete with a winch and rally lights. He inspected the two spare tires mounted on pipes that jutted from the side of the back corner behind the passenger doors. Everything was still in good working condition.

Felix was on the road again in no time.

"Onward to and fro, through these lands of hell we know... What a beautiful day, no?"

Next stop was going to be somewhere in Louisiana, depending on fuel, depending on the dogs, and worst of all, depending on other survivors.

*****

Felix took a break in another small town just inside Louisiana. He stretched his legs, lit a smoke, and looked around the town. The gas station was packed full of vehicles. Bodies buried in little mounds of ash, little bumps of graves all around. Large tracks from dogs, shoe and boot prints, some bare footed, hand prints from the feral taking to walking on all fours. They seemed to be headed west. Every town he had been to thus far, they were headed in different directions. None of which ever pointed north.

The sound of loud motorcycles and big engines rattling windows as they revved to let anyone and anything know they were in town spooked Felix. He hurried to his vehicle, grabbing his first available rifle. An AR-15, he checked the mag, checked the chamber, and slung it. He needed fuel, but the sound of the rumbling suggested that there was more than he could handle. Escaping would be very difficult; his exhaust wasn't exactly quiet either, they would certainly hear him leaving. Not to mention, outrunning bikes was only possible on turns and in heavy debris covered roads, and even then, experienced riders would have no issues with either of those obstacles.

"Fuck me," he grunted.

Felix took measure of the situation, trying to hide was about the only thing he could do. He reached in his car, pulled his battle belt from the front seat and buckled the heavy cobra buckle around his waist. It was lined with extra pistol mags for his 1911, and AR magazines, a small first-aid pouch and a dump pouch rolled up. He closed his door quietly. He ran across the street as fast as he could. Ash picked up in small plumes behind his sprint. He checked a door in a small diner across the street. It was locked, no time to attempt to pick, he hurried around the back as the bikes drew near.

As he came around the corner, he met a young woman, dressed in leather riding gear, holding a long hand-made spear, she pressed it against his chest.

Her eyes and under her nose where she had pulled her scarf down were the only things not covered in gray ash.

"Dunno what yer thinkin, but don't try anythin silly, or I'ma have to stick ya," she warned in a deep southern accent.

Felix lifted his hands into the air, his rifle slung around his chest, fell in front of him, hanging ready.

"Drop yer weapons, there," she demanded.

He did as she asked. Her eyes waivered for a moment when he set his rifle down, his 1911 pistol, the battle belt, his ark-lock pocket knife, a small snub-nosed 38 revolver, and a large revolver, and Ruger Super Redhawk Toklat 454 Casull that he had holstered under his arm. She pushed him back with the spear to where she was now over his pile of weapons. Once she had stuffed the pistols in her pants, slung his rifle, she nodded toward the direction she wanted him to walk. Which was right back where he had come from.

As they came into the street, the gang circled around him, hooting and hollering. The bikes were ear piercingly loud. She stood behind him with her spear ready. Felix took measure of the situation, and deducted quite quickly that he was fucked.

The men and women got off their bikes, families got out of their vehicles. An array of crudely armored busses. Felix begun to relax. People of all different races, sizes, shapes, ethnicities, this was a collection of survivors, not a road gang. A good sign was usually from the number of children, and caring mothers. At worst, they were religious nuts. And that could be worse than a road gang, but that was still to be determined. These people were more than likely not going to kill him or eat him, time would tell. He had a slight bit of hope, which even before the world became free, he particularly didn't care for that word. Hope.

Such a horrible blind word, it seduced many, like much of the old world. It was something that only sounded good when it came from someone who believed in it. Survive, that is what one should strive for, but what did he know, contradicting himself, he had hope that he would see his woman, at least once more in this world.

A large gray-bearded man, a very typical biker, dressed in leather riding gear covered in ash, came over to Felix, towering over him. A shotgun in one hand, a large revolver in a cross-draw holster on his belt. He pulled his goggles up over his forehead where they rested. Dark gray eyes. He looked Felix up and down.

"You alone?" he asked.

"Even if I was, until your intentions are known, I wouldn't tell you either way," Felix replied.

The woman with the spear standing behind him sat the blade flat on his left shoulder, edge facing his neck. It was a large knife wired tight to a metal pole, well made, and certainly, the mirror finish would slice him open without issue.

"Answer the question, son. We aren't here to kill anyone, especially someone who looks like they used to be military."

"Interesting, and how do you figure I was?"

He pointed at his weapons stuffed in the young woman's pants, and began to pick Felix apart. "Your hands are raised in compliance, but at your shoulders, which allows you to react much faster if necessary. Your weapon looks custom, and you have a battle belt. In my day, only Special Operations used to do that batman belt shit."

"I wasn't ever special, but I'd like to think that once upon a time I worked well with them back in the day, cool dudes, very functional and devastating soldiers. Definitely the elite. Compared to old grunts like us anyway."

"Well, you're not wearing a uniform, too. Which is the biggest giveaway that you are not our enemy."

Felix's face twisted into confusion. "How do you mean?" he asked curiously enough. He lowered his hands, the young lady behind him pulled the spear away from his neck.

"A unit from Texas was claiming that they were there to protect people, ended up destroying a town, taking over another one. They became a gang; another group had started attacking them. By the time we got the hell outta dodge, the dogs caught up with them and devastated both the small armies. We have been picking up people along the way ever since."

"Along your travels, have you seen this woman?" Felix asked, pulling out a picture of Sasha.

He shook his head. "Can't say that I have, son. A lot of people didn't make it out, you are free to ask any of the others, if they will talk to you."

"Thanks, I will," Felix put his picture away.

"Where you from, son?" he asked. He spoke softly, in a deep hard voice.

"From out east, Georgia," he replied.

"You don't talk like you're from the south."

Felix grinned pointing at the man, "Soldier, remember?"

The man's face turned to an expression of surprise. The people gathering were receiving orders to go to the several locations around the town to find supplies. General store was given to a group of teenagers, gun shop to kids and a group of hard looking women. So on, and so forth. They headed in different directions, the kids had knives and small revolvers, a lot of the group carried spears, crudely made from knives and pipes or long branches, anything they could fashion into long weapons.

"Where you headed?" the man asked.

Felix pointed toward the west.

"Well, either way, I wouldn't if I were you, whatever is out that way, probably isn't worth your life, son," the man replied.

"I beg to differ, sir," Felix retorted.

"What's your name?" the man asked.

"Felix."

"Nice to meet you, name's Bill."

Felix shook the man's hand. Immediately his wife or woman, partner, whoever she was, walked over.

A very hard looking woman, her skin was black as night under the googles that she, too, pulled to rest on her forehead. She leaned against Bill; she was about Felix's size. Her eyes were a dark brown with a hint of gold around the iris.

"What are you doing out here all by yourself, sugar?"

Bill waved the young woman off. She took all of Felix's things and set them on the ground behind him. Once she finished, she made eye contact with Felix as she walked around the group. He could read her eyes, and they were screaming: *"Try somethin', stranger…I'll kill you."*

"Don't worry, she ain't goin' do nothin," bringing his attention back to Monique and her husband.

"Fueling up and continuing west," Felix replied.

She looked up at Bill, they both looked back at Felix.

Felix sighed, "Judging by your expressions, it's bad that way, isn't it?"

"Don't go. You will certainly die. There are gangs out that way murdering everyone who come their way, not to mention that's where most of the dogs have gone. You need to turn around and head back the way you came. It's suicide."

Felix shook his head, "Thanks, but I have to. No matter what, I have to go that way."

They look at each other then back to him.

Felix laughed as he picked up his things, "Glad you guys weren't going to kill me, it would have sucked to come all this way just to get waxed by a kid."

"She might have, if you did anything silly."

Felix laughed again, "So I was told. Oh, forgive my manners…" He held out his hand to the woman.

"…what's your name, miss?"

"Monique, nice to meet you, young man."

"Pleasure."

The three stood on the road and talked. After a while Felix had walked over to his car, where Bill and Monique had joined him for a drink. Looking over a map, pointing out locations and their status of where they had been. Felix marked each location on the map in a number sequence that he then made notes on in his small black book. Monique had done the same on her map.

"You are welcome to join us," Monique insisted.

Felix smiled, "Sorry, I can't, but I will tell you this. Near Columbus, Georgia, to the north along Highway 80…there is a well-fortified settlement, family and friends, they are living pretty good lives right now. That is a safe place to stop. Just tell them you know me. I plan on heading to Fort Monroe, Virginia, in the future, very easily defendable location. A lot of my buddies, friends, family know about that place. If they survived, I know a lot of them will be headed that way."

"Thanks for the information, son. You sure you don't wanna tag along with us?" Bill asked.

"I'm sure, the road is my only home until I can find her. If she didn't make it, then I will be headed to Fort Monroe, but until I find out for sure, I have to do this."

"Even after the world ended, there still is true love in it. We will pray for you, and her," Monique replied.

"I appreciate it. I'm going to walk around and gather some things. If you all don't mind, I will be quick, some fuel too," Felix said.

Monique called over the young lady that had her spear trained on Felix previously.

"Take Julia with you, so no one will be surprised by an unfamiliar face," Monique recommended.

"No worries," Felix replied.

"You have a jug?" Bill asked.

"Yeah, why?" Felix answered.

"We are about to pop the reservoir cap and pump it from the tanks. Just set your can over here, we will take care of you."

"I'm sorry I can't really give you anything in return, it seems that you all have everything you need and more," Felix replied humbly.

"Don't worry about it, if everyone met like this on the road, we might be able to piece this country back together," Bill attested.

"There is much more in the world when there are far less people. I believe we could piece it all back together, just in a different way, a better way," Felix replied.

Bill squinted his eyes at Felix, pondering just what he had meant by that.

Felix made his rounds. Julia said nothing to him, she was serious, kept a watchful eye on him. The look in her eyes gave Felix the impression she suffered greatly; he didn't need to pry to figure out why. The scars around her wrists and on her cheeks were evidence enough. It's amazing that in the short time the world was free, humans would do this to each other. Even with all the attempted control over the general population before the pandemic and the explosion, people were still easily capable of destroying each other.

Now that they were all truly free, they used those thumbs to beat their brothers and sisters down. The thought reminded him of a song, by an old metal group called Tool. Their music often reminded him of what society truly was, and what the world had become. Those genius artists called it like they saw it, and he, too, could easily see as to why.

Felix was packed up and ready to go. He was stopped by Bill and Monique. Bill shook his hand, Monique gave him a hug.

"Stay away from the cities, son, most of the survivors are animals now, and I mean that in the sense that they have fallen victim to sin."

"Thanks, both of you. I'll see you down that road one day," he said as he got into his car and started it up.

"Go with god," Monique said placing a hand on his arm.

"Thank you, but I'll go with the devil, until I find my own paradise."

She took her hand away, Bill and Monique looked at each other, baffled by his answer.

"Why would you say something like that?" she asked.

"The devil didn't murder millions of people, he helped two stupid children get out of a controlled fake paradise. If anyone is responsible, this pandemic, is certainly an act of God's divine power. The next flood to clean the world."

"What a terrible thing to say," she said.

"I'm sorry, but survive is all we can do, and if I ever come across you all again, I will certainly do my best to make good on my debt to you, especially since you didn't slaughter me in the street."

He drove away, weary eyes and dirty faces stared blankly at him. Julia even watched as he left. He waved subtly out the window, until they were all out of sight from the rearview.

"He was an interesting fellow."

"I sensed a lot of evil in him, but there was a lot of good too," Monique added.

"You have to have both nowadays, I reckon," Bill agreed.

*****

Pulling over in the middle of the night, it was freezing out, but saving fuel was always priority. He got out, listening to the quiet of the night. The ash was falling in this area still, Louisiana, somewhere near Fort Polk. He locked up his vehicle, threw handfuls of ash over the car, and headed into the woods with his pack. His red flashlight lighted the way for him, a floating red orb of a ghost. After about fifty meters he found a good patch and begun to set up camp. A tarp hung in the trees; a small one-person pop tent nestled neatly under its protection. Military issued black sleeping bag, poncho liner, and his clothes folded neatly at the head, used as a pillow.

"Time for a whore bath," he said as he begun to chuckle and wash himself with baby wipes. A staple of military personnel during field exercises and deployments when water is scarce and only used for consumption. His mosquito net unzipped and lay open, the tarp overhead shielded him from the ash. His small MSR pocket rocket burned. A pot boiled with ramen balancing on the small three folding arms. He sipped on tea, it reminded him of Sasha; he was finding many things these days did.

As time marched on and he was still 400 miles away, he begun to fear for the worst. The days were growing darker, and getting colder. As his mind raced while he ate his ramen, he begun to think catastrophically, but what broke his concentration was the fact that he hadn't seen many infected, nor the carriers of the infection, the dogs.

If the dogs are the carriers, the alphas, that control the pack…the humans are now feral once bitten, turned and now part of the pack… What is the purpose and how is it possible? A species shouldn't be able to pass on a virus that literally changes the fundamentals of another species' natural instincts to replicate that of the host animal. Or can it?

Felix thought on it for a long time, it plagued him as much as taking so long to move across the country did. However, having to take backroads and move through towns for supplies, the occasional stand-off with some survivors, it seemed that time has been against him since day one.

Major cities have been bombed by nuclear devices. The west is in an unknown state of mayhem, the animals have migrated south. The dogs and their feral packs have become scarce. The low density of non-infected humans on the road would suggest there are a lot of communities that have survived and refused to leave their strong holds. Or…more than likely, the low population of survivors would mean either gangs or the feral have eaten them, literally or figuratively. The lack of government also could mean that they are either involved or the attacks on the cities were from another country...

He cleaned his pot with a baby wipe, tucked everything in its place, and packed it in his worn Malice Pack. He checked his weapons, ensuring they were loaded. Soon sleep came, and he was gone into the darkness of his mind.

*****

"Motherfucker," Felix said jerking awake.

A deep nostril breath and he turned in his bag; his large revolver was clutched in his hand.

"Goddamn it," he said as he turned over once more.

Felix peered out to find dull gray piles of ash all around him. He got up, got dressed, holstering his weapons. Throwing his jacket on, he started boiling water in his pot, making coffee as he twisted his pop-tent back into a small circle, packing it away into his pack. He sat on his bag under the tarp, sipping at his hot pot full of liquidy black goodness. The walk back to his car seemed longer than his walk out the night before. The sound of crushed ash under each step was all the sound in the world, it seemed.

He tossed his bag into the back on top of the case and got in his car. Fresh tracks could be seen in the thick layer of ash that fell last night. For a moment it was calm out. He continued his trek westward. Singing songs, played through an old iPod touch connected into the car's system. "Shiner" by The Ghost Inside, "How Sweet the Sound" by Day of Vengeance. Once the hard metal came on, he became quiet, enjoying All Shall Perish and their array of harmonic music. The thermometer was slowly reading colder temperatures. By the time Felix hit the next town, it was falling into the low thirties and only getting colder.

*****

Once he decided to rest for the day, refuel, and search for anything useful, it was already becoming night. His travels had slowed due to the ash and congestion of debris and damaged vehicles on the roads. As he sat in a chair behind the check-out counter of a Shell gas station, his pot boiled water. He could see his breath. He pulled out his hygiene kit, a safety razor, and shaving crème. He bushed his teeth, spitting into a cup, his breath shooting out in puffs as he spewed the foam from his mouth.

Once shaved, he cleaned his blade and pot and put them away. He walked around collecting chips and jerky and canned foods that had long shelf lives. Tuna lunch packs, and any sort of drinks, packs of water, and the like. He tossed them in a milk crate sitting in the floorboard of the passenger side of his car. In the silent edge of darkness, from the north, Felix's head snapped in their direction as the screech and howls pierced his ears.

Then he heard the whooping of a hyena, it was loud and deep. Other noises from the feral and other breeds of dogs would respond. It was frightening. Every whoop and laugh from the horrific sound solicited a response from maybe thousands of these creatures.

The hair on the back of his neck stood up. There was an alarming number of them. He grabbed his shotgun, a leather belt of shells and rushed back inside the Shell station. He peered out the windows in search of the horde that was beginning to shake the ground, the windows, the very earth felt like it was trembling. He watched the creatures pass, lazily, the once humans, struggling in the cold, they followed what looked to be their masters. Dogs of various shapes and sizes, breeds and coats as they all followed only one. She was large, spotted and striped, her front legs longer than her rear. Her neck was long and her hair on her head was short compared to the mane and hints of wolf-like coat along her body. She was leading the group of, maybe a thousand or so. Pushing south, Felix gathered. For the winter more than likely.

He calmed himself, his breath, and readied his weapon. His hands still shook. But even he knew he was fucked if they found him. His eyes raked left and right as some of the creatures sniffed the air, straggling away from the pack, a screech and bark, the feral cowered and fell back in line. Felix squinted at the pack. Attempting to piece together what he was looking at. He didn't see people anymore; he didn't even really see an infection. He saw a pack of wolves marching a tundra of ash and cold, searching for a suitable place to stay warm, feed the family, and then continue moving to the next location.

But where, where are these things going, is the country mostly eaten, have they had their fill of the US? He didn't know, he only assumed that they were running from winter, which would make sense. After such a thermal release into the atmosphere, winter would follow, like a cold cloth on a forehead to keep the fever down. Mother was going to cure herself, and soon.

An hour passed; Felix checked his watch. The pack of feral and their masters had gone, and so far, there were no signs of stragglers trying to keep up. He slowly walked out, careful to keep quiet. He ventured further, clearing around a corner, finding nothing but a light blanket of ash covering a car and some trash bins. He lowered his weapon and turned back toward his car. He lit a smoke, it was dark out, but the lights were still flickering on. Why? He didn't know. He stepped into the edge of the dark and took a piss, his weapon clutched in one hand. He leaned looking in every direction as he urinated in the middle of some ash coated bushes.

It started snowing, lightly, and he thought to himself, *At least it was warmer*. It than dawned on him. *Snowing this far south?* Nuclear winter, or, in fact, giant volcanic explosion winter. Large flurries fell softly like feathers. He stood leaning on the hood of his car watching it come down, smoke and breath puffing from his mouth. The air was clean, for the first time in a long time, it was crisp and fresh. He took its icy taste in, filling his lungs with its subtle beauty. It was time to press on.

*****

Where he stopped to enjoy the weather this time, was on the outskirts of Shreveport. The city was lit up with trashcan fires, streetlights, cheers, screams, gunshots. Felix thought about what he would do, should he go around? Should he press on? This is the fastest route to where he needed to go. But cities were the most dangerous places to enter. Even before the pandemic, he didn't particular care for the city life, people living on top of people. Fashion, if you could call it that, businesses competing against other businesses by stealing information or biometric compiling of information. People were unpleasant, too busy to be decent, too busy to care about anyone but themselves.

Driving was almost as dangerous as traveling alone at night without a weapon on foot. He was unsure if people knew what the sun looked like, or if they knew the world around them was more real than the ones they saw through their broken windows. The ones that forced people to look hunched back as they lazily strolled through life, looking down at those digital escapes.

Overhearing conversations were alarming; talking about celebrities; music, that honestly to him wasn't music; how much they spend on their hair, clothes, shoes, makeup, it was all just horseshit. Facebook posts, selfies, corruption, murder, homeless, gangs, rape, kidnapping, the more you gathered people together the more opportunity for them to eat each other. He never understood that, but it's what it was. Luckily, it was no longer the case, no one was hiding what they were, everyone was now in a world where you were everything you were meant to be. No law, no restriction, no ethics, no religion, nothing to hold you to a standard. Just what another human being could do to another in order to survive, feed their family, find that release, moment of pleasure, warm spot out of the weather, and maybe sanctuary from the infection.

"What a wonderful world?"

It may have had only been months since the world turned, but this is what the world was now. The lack of structure had set the pace for this empty country. It was strikingly beautiful to him. Often thought out in a drunken night's conversation, this was it. The things that were human were now free to eat each other alive. Due to their weakness born of convenience, due to those that could survive baring that leverage against those that could not. The surprising office clerk who happened to be good at saving his coworkers. That young woman with two kids, doing whatever she could to make sure they eat. That group of neighborhood kids who lost their parents were now running their town, escaping the feral and their alphas, scavenging for food, making deals with travelers.

It didn't take long for people to figure out that no one was coming, that the power wasn't coming back on. And those explosions that reached into the sky in a glorious gray mushroom cloud wasn't a movie. Man's best friends turned on them; for what, it didn't matter, it was merely ironic, and sometimes that was just enough.

Felix had parked his vehicle amongst a packed off-ramp where he sat enjoying the snow. He decided it was time to walk over to the entrance to the city. He threw large handfuls of ash and snow on his vehicle, to disguise it as best he could among the abandoned vehicles crawling their way off the highway.

He picked up his pack, and begun to walk a mile up the road to what looked to be a giant wall. Spotlights shined down on people standing outside the gates, a line of running vehicles waiting to be inspected. Several armed men, dressed in heavy jackets, hoods drawn, sporting rifles of all kinds. It was amazing to think that a lot of the bullshit news back then talked about how they weren't ever going to pay to put up a wall. Now look at the people, more than likely ones who had such opinions. It only took something eating them for them to figure out that castle walls did work once upon a time.

At first glance it looked like a greeting and guard entrance. "I smell metal," Felix said aloud as his hasty stride slowed to a quiet stroll.

When Felix began to draw near, he realized his mind had made up the scenario more than it was reality. What he really saw was men being killed, women being taken, children being thrown and pulled from their mothers. He ducked behind the back of a crippled car pushed to the side. He adjusted his black and green shemagh. He turned in all directions to ensure no one was coming behind him. People were being pulled from their vehicles, being searched, stripped, beaten, ransacked. He crouched, running or rather bounding, from vehicle to vehicle, to get a closer look.

"I axed you a question, or is you a stupid nigga?" a deep voice asked a man being searched. He was bloodied, a woman was being stripped on the hood of a car, her possessions piled in shopping carts, rushed by young kids back inside the shoddy metal doors. A large fire was burning on both sides of the entrance. A group of men came out and grabbed the woman and took her, as she screamed and called out the man's name. Through her cries Felix couldn't understand.

"I'm gunna fuck yo bitch on yo dead ass body, white supremist-looking motherfucker."

The man was sobbing, his urine was turning the light coating of snow yellow under him. The men were all laughing at the poor bastard, kid looked like he was barely 20.

"Bruh, he pissin himself he so scared, like a bitch," another called over to another that was beating a woman with the butt of his rifle. The brave woman spit blood in the man's face. He immediately began beating her in a blind fury.

Felix leaned against the vehicle. This whole scene reminded him of a great movie, where a traveler like him came across a situation just like this one. Later in the film the rapist and murderers got their just desserts at the traveler's hand, but this wasn't a movie, and Felix knew he couldn't take on that many men, nor could he outrun being shot at by the towers, which probably had more than semi-auto rifles mounted up there. Looked like machine guns, probably 50 caliber machine guns, more than likely stolen from the National Guard.

"Let's cut his dick off and set him on fire," another suggested; the other men hooted and hollered. Not only were men a part of this, a few women were too. There seemed to be an array of individuals out there from all walks of life. Their voices echoed loud and high-pitched, and even drowned out the moans of a woman being gang raped in the back of a truck.

"Let's kill this white bitch ass nigga," the woman cried out as she began to cut his penis off.

The man was screaming until he couldn't anymore, shock took hold of him. She stuffed it in his mouth. Backing away. His eyes were rolling into the back of his head.

"That's for slavery ma' fucka."

"Ya, bitch," another said. Finally, out of some sort of mercy, the man was shot in the face. The woman was forced to watch as she was being run through. The woman, however, wanted to have her fun too. She pulled a burning stick from the fire and walked over. The men held the dazed and confused woman down.

"You like being fucked by all my boys, don't you, bitch, love that big cock?"

With one thrust the woman screamed in such horrific agony that Felix gritted his teeth so hard, his jaw popped and a few teeth chipped.

"I can't be spineless…what if that was your woman, motherfucker?" Felix started antagonizing himself.

A hellish grin split his face. "Be a devil among groveling angels," he spoke as he stood. He bounded from vehicle to vehicle, then slid to a stop. The snow making that satisfying light crunch under his foot and knee.

"Yo, shut the fuck up, I ain't playin, I heard sumt'n over there."

"Stop playin, you hearing things, scary ass nigga."

Felix shook his head. "I'm going to kill all of them," he said to himself.

"Yo, I hear it again, there's sumt'n over there, bruh, go check it out."

"Na ma'fucker, yo get yo bitch ass over there, is you hearin shit, so don't be a bitch, nigga."

"That's how it's gunna be?"

"Bet."

The dazed woman, face swollen and bloody, lifted her head. The men holding her down turned, fixing their belts and picking up their weapons. The woman with the burning stick dropped it into the snow.

The night seemed to have quietened. The silence breaking from the crackle of the wood popping in the fire. The snow began to pick up along with a bone brittle chill. One of the tower guards leaned over, squinting against the wash of flurries. The mood was becoming full of anxious anticipation.

"Where is you?" the cautious woman asked as she stepped closer. "Come out, bitch!"

Felix could hear the footsteps compacting the light coating of snow. He leaned, his weapon up. He pulled the trigger, the slug ripped through the woman's chest, dropping her.

"Yo, yo, yo!" one shouted. They all began firing and running in every direction possible. Felix fired, missing several times, one got caught in the leg, another took a slug to the shoulder.

"AHHHHH SHIT, that motherfucker got me, kill his bitch ASS!" one man lay screaming, an angel's wing of crimson trailed from his shoulder. The poor bastard writhed in the snow as his destroyed shoulder spilled hot blood, melting the light coating of snow on the ground.

Felix reloaded his shotgun, he got up and ran around the vehicle, peeked with his weapon. they were firing wildly in all directions, nowhere near him. The tower search lights were sweeping the street, but his attention was immediately ripped away. Lights were approaching fast from behind him. Several vehicles, familiar…military. He could tell from the loud turbos and heavy chug from the engines.

"Yo! Those motherfuckers are back, these niggas be bringing fire, get Roach over here, we need the big guns... And get AJ's ass in here, he's bleedin' all over the street!"

Felix got low, laying down on the freezing ground. The vehicles shot past him, ramming the gate in while taking out some skinny white kid with tattoos all over their face. The rest of the vehicles passed through behind it. Gunners in the backs of trucks, standing in the hatches of Humvees, peppering the towers with accurate machinegun fire. Clanking, metal slugs slamming into concrete, metal being torn through from .50 caliber machine guns. It was a beautiful sound, Felix thought. Except for the screaming, that was getting annoying.

The last vehicle slid to a stop, the driver and another, burst from the Humvee doors shooting wildly, killing several men and women hiding behind vehicles and barriers. The gunner up top swung right and began to lay waste to several men and women running along the fence line and makeshift wall. Felix hopped to his feet. He bounded forward once again. A large man was running toward the vehicle with a machete. Felix ran into him, tackling him, his shotgun slid. The woman stopped firing, aiming her weapon at the two men fighting on the ground in front of her.

Felix pulled his knife, the man got up and went for Felix's shotgun. Felix whipped his knife like a Frisbee, it buried in the man's back. Felix reached into his jacket producing a large revolver. He fired quickly, half accurately. Four rounds struck the large man's chest just as he turned, dropping him like a sack of potatoes. The .454 Casull rung his ears as bad as the .50 cal did. His hand was immediately fatigued from gripping that powerful gun.

The gunner looked at him. He spun his cylinder free, pulling out the expended shells and reloading. He holstered it and walked over to his shotgun, picking it up. Snow was crusted to his pants and jacket. He pulled his hood back and moved his face wrap down. She took aim on him.

"Who da fuck is you?" she asked.

"Just someone passing through, couldn't stand by while these cocksuckers were murdering and raping people."

"Neither could we, you headin' north?" she asked.

"No, west."

"I wouldn't if I was you. They say da dogs have gathered in central Texas, best to head north while the winter is coming. There's a place up there that is free of dogs, and warm enough to survive the winter."

"Oh yeah? You guys need some help?"

She turned back, "Justin, get your polar bear ass over here and talk to this white boy, he is your people, after all."

"The hell are you talking 'bout, Charlene?" Justin asked.

The large barrel-chested man came around the corner, stunned by the sight of Felix.

"Hmm, Justin, I know a Justin, probably not the same guy," Felix said to himself.

Justin was wide-eyed, and a smile split his face as soon as he saw Felix. Dirty orange North Face jacket, dark green thick combat pants, a green pack on his back. His shotgun held under his arm.

"I don't fucking believe it," Justin said.

"I'd know that country-ass voice anywhere," Felix replied as he walked closer. Justin pulled up his skiing goggles and his gator neck down from his mouth. He was wearing a long sleeve, even in this cold, and a pair of cut off multi-cam military shorts. Combat boots untied on his feet.

"Same old, Justin Pain. I don't fucking believe it, I forgot you lived near here," Felix said with the sound of relief in his voice.

"I would have never guessed I would see you over here. How the hell are ya, bud?"

"I've been better, you need an extra gun?"

"Where's the woman?" Justin asked.

"I don't know." Felix replied.

"She'll be fine. To answer your question, yes. Get in, these slavers have been fucking up this city for a while, we got word through a ham radio from a town they rolled over before they took this one over. The rest of our element is coming in from the north. It's going to be a long night. You sure you're up for it?"

"To kill these worthless fucks? Yes… Let your people know that there are a lot of women and children—"

"We know, we have spies in here, we got the whole place mapped out. Just sit back, enjoy the ride, and shoot someone in the face when the time comes," Justin spouted placing a heavy hand on Felix's shoulder.

"Alright."

Justin turned and headed inside his vehicle. Felix turned, taking aim and silencing the screaming man with the shoulder injury. Adding a second crimson wing across the snow.

Felix got in just as the woman ducked in, taking measure of Felix. "You know this crazy weirdo?" she asked Justin.

Felix laughed.

"We used to work together years ago."

"Well, welcome to the remnants of the human race," she said as she stood up back on the gun.

Justin turned, "We have one more place we gotta hit after this. There's a gang north of here, Muslim gang, probably ISIS rejects, immigrants who couldn't fight for their own fucking country. They are beheading people left and right and piking them around a city they took over. That's our next stop, provided the winter doesn't force us to retire from our crusade, you in?"

"I think you're confusing me with a man of God, old friend."

"Fuck me, how could I forget, you evil son of bitch." Justin laughed.

"I need to get to Texas, not crusading like a fucking catholic…" Felix laughed, "…across the country with a rag tag team of weirdos."

Justin looked at him with a look of confusion on his face. "Are you fucking crazy?"

"What?"

"According to the radio, that's where a massive concentration of feral have formed, they are all gathering in one spot. There are entire highways full of them coming from everywhere in the country."

"Fuck," Felix replied. Shaking his head, looking out the thick armored glass window.

"Come back to base with us, before you make your decision. It's about as safe as can be."

Felix nodded, "After we are done here, I need you to drop me off at my vehicle, and I'm with you all the way."

"Goddamn, it's good to see you," Justin said with a big smile on his face. The Humvee hopped and jumped as he ran over a group of people shooting at them.

"Likewise, brother."

The house was bustling, the large table was full, chairs were placed almost on top of each other due to the amount of people. Justin and Stacey were sitting at the end, from them clockwise continuing around the table sat the rest of the guests. Mitch and his wife Dana, Gavin and his wife, Felix and his fiancé Sasha, Isaac and his boyfriend, Chris and his girlfriend, Alex and his girlfriend, John and his wife Kim. Justin's and John's kids were sitting around the coffee table in the living room watching a Disney movie while they were eating.

Justin stood up quieting the jokes and low roar of full-hearted conversations of the evening.

"It's been a long time since all of us have been together. So, let me start by saying, Congratulations to Felix and Sasha."

Everyone turned back to Felix and Sasha holding up their glasses.

"It's about time you decided to settle down, you bastard. And Sasha, we welcome you to our large family of many different people. If you haven't noticed already, we are unconventional here. Black, white, gay, Spanish, it doesn't matter in this house so long as you are worthy to be called family. I hope you're ready for the responsibility of keeping Felix out of trouble."

The group laughed. Her cheeks were bright red now that the room's attention was focused on them.

"Thank you all," she replied.

"I'm not done yet," Justin spouted.

Felix was talking with Gavin as he leaned back in his chair, his arm hung on the back of Sasha's chair. The youngest of Kim and Stacey's kids were sitting in their mother's laps trying to eat their food. The table had a spread of many different cuisines from Felix's family.

She took it all in as she observed. So many different kinds of people from all over the United States, some from different countries. These soldiers and their families had accepted him, and now her, into their fold. It was almost breathtaking to believe that he had known so many people over the years.

Justin continued, "I've been married for about 12 years now, and let me tell you, it is not easy, even though Stacy and I make it look easy." The group laughed.

Justin continued, "You are about to have to deal with a soldier, even if he is on his way out back into the world, it's tough being with something like us. Stacey, Kim, Dana can all tell you from experience. But, since I've come to know you, you will be fine, you're strong and independent, and as much as Felix likes to be a hard ass and disappear for years at a time, he is a good man."

Chris leaned over toward Felix. "Yeah, fucker, need to stay in touch more."

"Okay, okay, man," Felix replied jokingly.

"We wish the best for you two. And Sasha, you're welcome in our home any time."

She raised her glass of wine, still embarrassed by all the attention from around the dining room.

"Thank you all," she replied.

"You too, Felix, only if you bring her with you," Justin joked.

Felix laughed. "Thanks, fucker."

Isaac leaned over to Sasha and they began having their own conversation. The room picked up with clanking glasses, knives and forks rattling against plates. Kids laughing and playing as they ran up to the adults and around the living room playing with each other.

Isaac stood up. "Well, before we start eating, let us pray."

"Preach it, brother," Chris spouted out.

The doorbell rang, calling everyone's attention. Curious children ran to the door, Kim stood up, telling hers to stop and let the adults answer it. The group laughed, Justin got up to go answer it. Everyone was quiet, waiting to see, as Justin came back around another group showed up. Felix and Mitch and Gavin stood up. Old friends from their time together had shown up. As Sasha observed, it dawned on her that this was the family he talked about. These were all people he had met over his time in the military. He wasn't kidding about them being from all over the world. Japan, Hawaii, Vietnam, Mexico, California, Utah, Georgia, Texas, New Jersey, Nevada, Arizona, from Asian decent to African American, his family was anything but what she could expect from someone like him. She had a smile on her face as she watched him exchange hugs, picking up kids that were trying to climb up his leg.

The night came and went. Felix and Sasha sat outside listening to the crickets sing the night away. She was leaning against his chest as he was nestled in the corner of the porch swing. Some of the guys were down at the fire pit drinking. The wives were putting kids to bed. Gavin walked by handing Felix a beer and continued his way down to the fire pit with the others.

Sasha took his hand, interlacing her fingers in his. "You told me that you turned your back on family a long time ago, but after tonight, you have a bigger family than I ever did."

"Is that right?"

"Felix, you are very loved here. You have a wonderful family."

"They are a rag tag team of weirdos, but that's why we all get along. I've known them for years, Justin and Stacey, Mitch and Dana, I've known them since my time in Campbell, and Afghanistan. Rick and Valerie, I've known them since Germany, Gavin since I got into the army, but you knew that already. Everyone here is family to me, because even after five years, ten years of not seeing each other, we sat down, we ate, and picked up right where we left off."

"That's fantastic," she replied.

"What do you think, babe? Can you deal with a family like this one?"

"I think they are perfect for you, and I'm very happy to be a part of your family. So, yes, I can certainly deal with your family."

"If you couldn't tell, they are happy you are a part of it too," Felix replied.

No sooner than she leaned against him, sighing in relief, a fireball rolled from the fire pit. One of the guys started running away as the ball rolled into the darkness. Another dumped beer on the trail of flames snaking away from the fire pit. Their girlfriends were shaking their heads, kids were running toward the house to tattle on their uncles.

Justin stepped outside. "Don't burn my backyard up, you retards!" The guys were laughing down by the pit.

Sasha looked at Felix, they both burst out in hysterical laughter.

Chapter 5
Winter Coat

It'd been almost a year and the winter fell hard. Felix had joined up with Justin and many like-minded survivors, and helped them through many raids, skirmishes, supply runs, and building of their new home; Subtropolis, which was claimed to be the largest underground storage facility located under Kansas City, Missouri. If anything, it was the largest underground collection of survivors in the entire United States. That they knew of anyway.

The efforts of this now banded together group of survivors numbering in the thousands, mainly focused on the current enemy. Killing off slavers and impersonating militaries, laying claim to fuel, food, water, medicines, women, and children. This last year was merely white snow, stained in blood. That year had been long as the days grew shorter, and the cold became dangerous. The winter began to last all year, and the feral and the dogs hadn't been seen in months since their migration to the south.

Felix's attempts to travel south had become impossible, the passes were unpassable, the vehicles buried in the snow. He lost his car some time back when he slid off a road into a ravine. Took him almost a week to walk back in that tundra. And during one raid, Felix got shot and had to recover. The only reason he survived and received medical attention was because of the amount of bloodshed he was responsible for. No matter what he seemed to do, the universe put everything she had against his efforts to find his woman.

After a while the expeditions for answers became a community thought process among the intellectuals, which, before the catastrophe, were scientist and engineers for the United States Environmental Protection Agency. Offering supplies, medicines, and food for protection services, many flocked to help secure the travel of brave scientists. The treacherous movement proved difficult for many, often groups would freeze to death or run out of supplies. Vehicles only made it so far, and the rest of the route was to be completed on foot. Most barely made it into the next state.

Coming into the second year of the long winter, Beatrix trudged through the thick snow, following Felix as they climbed toward the peak of a volcano.

"I've heard some interesting things about you, Felix…" Beatrix baited the conversation through heavy clouds of her warm breath.

She followed just off Felix's right side as they leaned into the incline of the mountain before them. Felix pulled his Geiger counter out, its clicks were sounding within safe parameters.

"I'm sure they are all embellished greatly," Felix replied as his heavy stomps through the thick snow echoed through the morning.

"The other merc's said you were the only one who made it back from the last expedition out this way. They are saying some alarming things about you."

Felix laughed, "Yeah, I've heard 'em, funniest one I heard was the one about me having to eat one of the other survivors so I could make it back. Like some survival story of those morons who climbed that mountain back in the day. Don't recall, but you gotta do what you gotta do in order to survive. Humans will eat each other, as they always have."

She giggled, "Figuratively, or literally?"

Felix thought on it for a moment, "…depends on the situation, I guess. I've seen much this last year. A group of survivors started eating each other, when next door was a warehouse full of canned goods. When the few that did survive figured that out, they tried killing themselves because they were eating their loved ones that became too sick to fend for themselves."

"That's terrible…" she gasped.

"Not as bad as some, but that's it, isn't it? It could always be worse."

He stopped for a moment to look back; she turned back to look with him. They were several hundred meters ahead of the group dragging sleds and carrying heavy packs.

Felix looked at Beatrix, "Shouldn't you be back with them? You know I'm up here to detect radiation, right?"

"Yeah, but I don't think the rumors of nuclear weapons being detonated in Yellowstone to be true. No one is intelligent enough to do such a thing in the first place. You would have to be absolutely mad to want to cause a volcanic eruption."

"If I were a mad man," Felix started.

Beatrix interrupted, "You are for volunteering to escort us on this crackpot idea of an expedition."

Felix shook his head ignoring her comment and continuing his statement, "If I *were,* I would set off a Tsar Bomba right on top of a volcano. Send up as much radiated particles into the atmosphere as possible, and in the process cause a natural disaster to help carry that radiation on the molten rock and dust sent into the air. It's honestly genius. No matter how you look at it."

"Nobody would do something like that, how could they?" she deflected.

The two continued walking. Felix didn't miss a beat to make his point, "Like spreading an infection throughout the world that effects one of the most prevalent species on the face of the earth?"

She paused for a moment, "Good point. If the nuclear weapons were to be activated, the snow, the winds, the storms, the thermal energy of the volcanic eruption itself would have burned up the particles to begin with, so I find it very unlikely that the area would be radiated. But I'm not a nuclear physicist, so who knows?"

"Okay, I can see that. Good thing I don't think I have enough nuke pills for us both," he exclaimed in a sigh of relief.

"You came prepared! Do they work?" she asked through a heavy breath as she hefted herself over a mound of snow.

Felix turned his head toward her. "I don't know, prepared…I try to be, these are probably expired but something is better than nothing. Charcoal wipes help get the material off, but all of that being said, it's only going to prolong the issues. If we get irradiated, we could die very easily up here."

She giggled. "Don't worry, I'll save you."

"Can't save me if you get radiation poisoning when I do."

"Good point."

Further up the mountain the two took a small break while the group caught up.

"It's absolutely beautiful up here," she exclaimed as she looked around.

Felix offered his flask of bourbon.

"Thank you," she said. taking a gracious swig.

Felix lit a smoke while they waited. He turned to look out. The mountainous terrain rolled over the land, covered in thick snow, glistening sheets of crystal as the rays of light cut through the clouds onto the white surface. The clouds were breaking, the further in elevation they reached. Looking toward the east, the clouds were so thick that they could only imagine it was the blizzard rolling east over their new home. The one they passed through to get here.

"Thinking about radiation, Chernobyl probably wouldn't be as radiated if the particles weren't attached to the metal in the facility. I'm sure if they found a way to melt, or even expose the melted core to the air, it would eventually blow away with the wind, provided the metal corrodes or breaks down in some manner. However, there is so much coming out of it, they have to shield it from doing further damage to our ozone."

"What about the people down wind?" she asked. He could hear the sarcasm in her voice.

"Yeah, more than likely they would have to be relocated."

"With you being the probe for the possibility of radiation, I wanna know if any of the rumors everyone talks about are true?"

"This day and age, what does it matter. I survived and they didn't. I got lucky, that's all it was," he grunted.

"Maybe, but for someone who certainly keeps to himself, I find it odd that you wanted to be on this little expedition of ours, especially after you nearly died on the last one?"

Felix chuckled, "Oh, yeah?"

"Yeah. You going to eat us too?" she laughed.

"You are tickled by that."

"Seriously, I wanna know, why are you here?"

Felix pulled his small hard case wallet from his pocket. Opening it, he produced his picture. Beatrix took it. She studied it for a moment.

"I see… This tells me nothing."

"I can't get to where she was or is due to the amount of snow blocking the path, I won't be able to make it on my own in the south. Going on foot is extremely dangerous, especially with the potential that there could be entire packs of the feral that we don't know about still hunting down that way. So, I have been occupying my time, it's driving me mad with impatience, but I'm holding it together. People have a hard-enough time dealing with their loss… Helping a stranger find his family is highly unlikely. Besides; these jobs give me owed favors in the future. I get a small fortune every time I volunteer for this."

She handed the picture back, he placed it back into the waterproof case, stuffing it back inside his interior jacket pocket.

"You're doing this just to pass time and gain favors? That sounds kinda crazy, indeed."

He held up his gloved hand, pointing. "Don't forget the small fortune." She giggled while he continued… "Like the expedition before, it was merely a chance to find some answers. Who knows what we will find here, there are so many stories that it's hard to tell what could have happened. We've been moving for months, and finally, we are on foot, and just before us lie answers, or maybe, just more questions, I'm excited to see what either brings."

The two stood up and continued moving up the mountain.

"What did you use to do before the end of the world?" she asked.

"I was a soldier, infantry. I just decided to get out. I was actually in the process of moving in with my fiancé and waiting on calls from I don't know how many companies I applied for. What about you?"

"I was a scientist, I worked with the Environmental Protection Agency that is located in Subtropolis. I was at work when the blast went off, before the power had gone out, some news outlets were covering the fiasco in the cities. The dogs that turned on their owners, and once their owners were bitten, they began attacking other people. It was nothing but slaughter at first, then the power went out, our backup generators failed or ran out of fuel. Poor maintenance, it could have been any one of those things… Either way, we all knew at that point that someone or maybe even nature decided that we were never going to stop destroying her. I believe that the infection or bio-weapon, or maybe even nature herself, is responsible for turning such wonderful creatures against us."

"That doesn't explain the timing or the explosions," Felix interrupted.

"Like you, I'm here for those answers as well. If the infection was carried by the explosion, how did it travel across the country in an instant? Why did the dogs pick and choose their pack? Why did they move south?" She thought on the last one for a moment. "Well, that one is easy, because of winter. But you get the point."

Felix looked up the white canvas of mountains before him. "Well, we will certainly find something up here. I can feel it. Almost like I can smell the ash in the icy air."

*****

The group began traversing the peak of a white painted ridgeline. Their tracks winded and turned throughout the new formation of a massive mountain. Felix stepped, his foot sank into the snow stopping short on a slick plate of metal. He stepped back and took a knee. Shifting his rifle in his left hand, he began shoveling snow off the object.

"Yellowstone National Park."

"What did you find?" Beatrix asked.

"Beatrix, this mountain, it was never here before, was it?" Felix asked.

She set a hand on his shoulder as he looked further unto the peak of the mountain.

"No, it certainly was not."

Felix stood up. The team of scientist in tow caught up to Felix and Beatrix, gathering to gawk at the tattered sign. Beatrix stood next to Felix. The sun has

70

risen just above the peak. For a moment Felix could see a tree, by itself, blacked out by the warm grasp of the sun's rays.

"That's where we should stop for the day," Felix said, pointing.

"We will take lead from here," a tall man said, moving past Felix and Beatrix.

The heavy coats, gloves, and boots were all the same color, except for the scientist which looked to Felix like an arrangement of flowers. It reminded him of what a group of climbers would look like attempting to scale a great mountain. The soldiers, however, were all dressed in heavy blue and gray coats, with black pants. Everyone had weapons, heavy rifles, even the scientist carried a rifle and side arm. Their packs full, climbing claws strapped to their boots. Climbing picks slung around their belts. They were ready to climb or looked really ready, just before the fall to their deaths.

Felix took up the rear of the lazy staggered column of weary travelers. He watched as some struggled climbing in the snow, even he slipped a few times. Caught Beatrix once as she nearly slipped down the ridge.

The sun was shining brightly today. The first he had seen in almost a year, since the snow had begun to fall. By the looks of the formation, this was no nuclear attack, this was certainly a volcano.

"Correct me if I'm wrong, Beatrix."

"Yes?"

"How is it that a mountain would be left over after a Volcano erupts, the bulge is usually formed due to the buildup of pressure under the surface. So once the eruption has happened, then the crust should return to its former self. If anything, it will be depressed due to the loss of matter under the surface."

"I honestly don't know. I believe you are correct, it could mean that this volcano is far from finished, it merely expelled its gasses and initial pressure and buildup of magma. These peaks and ridges, and the mountain before us, is merely solidified lava that cooled fast enough to form a dominate terrain feature."

"Have you ever heard of such a thing?" Felix asked.

"I have not. However, taking in the account that this world only possessed one continent and by shifting of the earth's core and soft layers of subterranean mass, the tectonic plates shifting over millions of years, we have our current land mass that still moves ever so slightly. This just happened to be such a movement that happened within moments, not millennia, it's fascinating to bear witness to such a force of nature."

"You sound like a geologist."

"I minored in it in college," she replied confidently.

71

The group reached the peak by nightfall, and Felix was stunned, immediately. He even forgot that he was so out of breath from his smokers' lungs. That tree he saw was there. It wasn't his imagination. The weight he felt standing before it almost sickened him. It was like an addiction that he had to muster every ounce of his will to pull himself from its beauty. No one else seemed to pay it any mind, a simple glimpse, a comment along the lines of, *oh that's odd.* But nothing substantial, it seemed that only Felix was at his wit's end by this thing being here.

The group began making camp, a guard roster was set up for the security element, the scientists quickly spread out as they noticed that there were in fact steam vents near their camp site. They began collecting samples and working tests before they even set up their own sleeping arrangements.

The soldiers providing security for the expeditionary element searched the area, setting up wires on small stakes attached to flare warning munitions. The scientists took a small security team with them as they searched the area around the volcano. No one, however, attempted to walk to the opening, seeing that the dark had settled in like a cold blanket.

Felix, however, was standing before that dead black tree, again. Its leafless limbs reached for the sky, bent and jagged, zig-zagging in all directions until finally offering thanks to the stars. It mesmerized him. Why, how, the blast was seen as the western sunrise, he was literally across the country when this volcano blew, and he saw it. So, how was it here, what was it? He pulled his glove off, placing his hand against the dead tree. It felt like marble, neither cold nor warm, it just was, it existed, and as the thoughts ran through his head, he gathered quite quickly that this tree shouldn't. It was starting to look like, and feel like, something that never existed here before.

"What are you doing?" Beatrix asked, startling Felix back into reality.

"Hey," he replied, nervously so.

"You okay?" she inquired, puzzled by the way he was acting.

"Yeah, why?"

"You've been staring at this tree since we got here," she said, stepping in front of him, searching his eyes for answers that were as cold as the snow that blanketed the land.

Felix looked around. "Hmm…" he grumbled, pondering how much time he had really been standing there. It didn't matter, he changed the subject.

"Have you ever seen anything like this?" he asked, looking to her, and back at the tree.

"No, could have been flash burned and immortalized in stone, it looks to be the case by the formation of material," she replied, as matter of fact.

"Immortalized…I think that is a very fitting word defining this thing," he replied, putting his glove back on his cold stung hand.

"The soldiers are starting a fire, you should come and warm yourself, it's going to be cold tonight."

"Yeah."

Felix turned, following her back to the small camp site. Tents were set up all facing toward the east. After all, their travel was an uphill battle as they leaned into the steepness of the volcano, and further into the bitter wind that swept down it.

The fire danced beautifully, like a lamp reaching into the morning to call the train to its next stop. Warm, and inviting. Three metal poles fastened at the top like a naked Teepee, a chain hung dangling a large pot from it. Three smaller fires were set around it with similar pots with the night's sustenance. The wood was carried by soldiers since they abandoned their vehicles days before.

Beatrix was particularly excited that evening, she talked with the other scientist about their findings and that this volcano was more than likely far from finished. It may be dormant for the time being but it could easily explode again in the foreseeable future. Felix watched across the fire, as the shadows danced around them on the onyx black stone cliff. It looks as if it were a dark waterfall, frozen in time until they had arrived. Setting their campfire close, it was now once again alive, the shadows made it so. He thought to himself, how beautiful it looked.

Beatrix was staring at Felix across the fire, her hair even in the glow of the flickering light, gleamed streams of silver from 46 years of life. Since society fell, the last year was harsh on her, as it was for many, especially women and children.

Her bright blue eyes called to him. But alas, he was lost into the scenery behind her. He continued to think to himself. The scientists continued to talk; the soldiers spoke of what they missed from the world before. Felix may have been surrounded by people, but he was there by himself longing for days long gone, when even in the harshest times, he had soldiers around him whom he trusted with his life. He turned, looking back at the tree. And that thought crept back into his mind. Only few things from back then were worth missing.

"It does look like it's reaching for the stars," he spoke just above a whisper.

*****

Felix had first shift; he walked around the campsite, the lights slowly went out in each of the scientists' tents. The soldiers were long out, snoring. It was cold. Felix wrapped his scarf tighter around his face. Stuffing it further into his jacket. He pulled his hood over his beanie. The night was quiet, there wasn't even a breeze to whisper into his ear and chill his spine. All he could hear was the snow compacting under his boots.

He found himself standing at the foot of that large dead tree. He could feel it, something was watching him. Whatever it was, he could feel it there, reaching, breathing from the shadows cast behind the light of the moon that bathed the dead tree in its pale glow. He pulled his scarf down, putting a cigarette in his mouth. He flicked his zippo, throwing sparks onto the wick. A second time, the light was blinding for a moment. It went out.

You can hear and see far at night, because the wind doesn't blow at night, unless a storm is coming or going. Less bustling, everything but the creatures of the night, sleep. Smell and sound travel further, but these days, everything travels further, because there is less in the world, he thought to himself.

Felix let out a frustrated sigh. Attempting to strike his lighter once more. It ignited, Felix saw it. Staring back at him. He was frozen, he couldn't move. It was absolutely giant, the chill he felt was so deep and heavy that the hair on his head felt as if they were bending against his beanie. His breath sapped from his chest, and a weight that seemed to suspend him without relinquish stomped him into oblivion.

It was sitting behind the tree, ever so patiently, only half its face was touching into the moonlight yet outlined in a brilliant white, like its body resembled that of a black hole. Yet the light could not reach it. It's eyes gleamed, catching what light he did not know, for the shadow stretched further than it should have. It was a cluster of three, three eyes on that side of its face. One eye of the ocean that swam with creatures, one of a dog that burned a refracted glow of red, and one of a cat that burned back a glowing green. Its face long, longer than Felix's torso, its breath was not fog like any of theirs, it was black and thick like the bellowing of the volcanic eruption that smeared mother's face into a different shape. Its grin widened, reached to its long kinked pointed ear. *It* knew Felix could see him, like long ago, and Felix knew that he was looking at him. That thing he once saw as a boy when all was not and nothing was there as he stood in a place he had forgotten.

It was gone, grin and all.

Felix shook free, and picking his rifle up, biting the cigarette, his lighter stuck in the snow. It was gone. He walked quietly, even the snow stressed to make a sound under his light-footed movement. He walked wide, never dropping his weapon. Breaths heavy but controlled through his nostrils, throwing small puffs of fog. The cold gripped his face. There was nothing, nothing was there. Clicking his light on, he searched the snow. There were no prints, no sign of anything other than his own prints behind him.

"The altitude must be getting to me. Seeing ghosts in the dark." His chuckles evolved into hysterical laughing, attempting to keep quiet. "Ha ha…"

Felix picked up his lighter, blowing the snow from the windproofed wick. He lit it, took in a long drag, flipping the zippo closed and placing it into his jacket pocket. The stream was long and satisfying as it carried its way into the night. Felix checked his watch; it had already been an hour. Time for shift change.

After he changed out with the next guard, Felix climbed into his tent. Setting his rifle onto his bag nestled into the corner. He clicked on his headlamp, the dark became day, due to the space blanket sewn into the interior of the tent. He took his boots off, knocking the snow from them. Setting them down he noticed there were a pair of boots already inside his tent. He turned, placing a hand on his sleeping bag. The person in it shifted. Her head poke out from within its warm embrace.

"What are you doing, Beatrix?" he asked as he took his jacket off. The cigarette hanging from his mouth.

"You shouldn't smoke in here," she replied.

"Still not answering my question…" he inquired.

"It's cold, so we can warm each other, no harm in that. So, shut up, put your cigarette out, and get in here," she confidently, flirtatiously, said as she turned over. Offering her back to him.

Felix chuckled as he pulled off his socks, outer snow pants, he took off his combat pants and long sleeve. He was finally ready to climb in, wearing nothing but his silk weight long sleeve and under pants. She was turned away, Felix felt in the dark, zipping up the bag, wrapping the two closer together. She turned, against the tightness of the sleeping bag, putting her hands against his back, and intertwining her legs with his.

"How is it you're so warm in this cold?" she asked, dreamily.

He chuckled, "My woman used to ask me that all the time. She hated the cold. Not like you at all."

"Your woman was very special to you, I hope you find her one day," she spoke softly as she pressed her face into his back.

"One day."

The two fell fast asleep.

*****

75

The next day the wind had picked up slightly, Felix was up before the sun peaked over the horizon. He had coffee ready. Beatrix was up shortly after. Shrugging from the cold morning, hopping around trying to warm herself, she nearly spilt her canteen of coffee. Felix stood there smoking next to the dead tree.

"We should probably leave tomorrow," Beatrix noted.

The sky was starting to darken from the thick cloud cover. Behind them, smoke and steam rose from the mouth of the volcano, winding its way into the heavens. A daunting darkness was beginning to roll through the sky.

"Agreed. Get your samples, we can do tests back in Subtropolis, I don't wanna be here when the storm comes, it looks like it's another blizzard."

She sipped the coffee; it was already starting to cool. Felix flicked his smoke from the edge of the plateau.

"You ready?" he asked.

The two crested the ridgeline followed by stragglers of researchers and soldiers. Felix couldn't believe his eyes, and Beatrix let out a gasp by the breathtaking sight before them. A form of plant life, moss or colorful bacteria was forming on the rock. Blanketing in small patches here and there. Small mushrooms forming circles in the green canvas around the steam vents. Against the black, their color vibrantly screamed out against the deep darkness of the cooled glassy rock. A breeze pushed the pillar of gasses and steam slightly, and the dark cloud spiraling into the sky bellowed slowly from the depths of the chasm.

Beatrix gleefully shrieked as she hurried to her first spot. Felix thought she just turned back years, happy as a child on Christmas day. He followed a narrow path down the spiraling rocks to her as she spilled the contents of her pack next to her to begin pulling samples from the area around the vent. As Felix approached, he could feel the warmth, and he could tell that soon, this area was going to be full of life once again.

The day was falling behind the horizon of the opening of the volcano. He peered off into its darkness that seemed to reach into the core of the earth. Beatrix was collecting samples from plant life that had formulated around a steam vent. Several of the others were putting their heavy jackets on as they moved further away from the opening. Soldiers patrolled around the edge of the ridgeline, checking for any signs of infected or their masters, the alphas. No sign, it was clear that they are still in the south. Honestly, they hadn't seen any animals near here, not even birds. After a blast like the one that came from this massive beast, species were obliterated in the blink of an eye. Not to mention braving such temperatures to get here was only logical to humans.

"What do you think?" Beatrix asked as she packed up her samples into her small pack.

"About?" Felix replied.

"The volcano."

Felix turned toward her, "It's like staring into the heart of Mother Earth, and physically feeling her pain, because she expelled it into the world with a horrific cry."

Beatrix clapped her hands, "That was very poetic; for a soldier, you surprise me sometimes."

"Not normal for a scientist to be able to relate to an uneducated man like me, huh?" he joked playfully.

She giggled, "Sometimes, experience outweighs education, a book can't pour into your body what can only be learned through experience."

"Well said, I care not retort," he replied with a smile, behind his scarf, but she could see it in his eyes.

"I'm done here. Hungry?" she asked, patting him on the shoulder.

"Let's go," he said.

Felix turned. "Hey!" Beatrix jumped in surprise by his thunderous voice.

"What?" one of the soldiers responded.

"Heading back with one!"

"Okay!"

He turned back to Beatrix, wide-eyed.

"What? You ready? Let's go."

That night everyone carried on like they did the night before. Felix was again sitting there, staring off into nothing. Beatrix noticed, and her curiosity could no longer be contained. She got up and walked over and sat next to him. Warming her back against the fire.

"You are always drifting away in your own thoughts, what's going on up there?"

Felix let out a sigh, leaning back looking into the clear sky, full of bright stars and a gleaming moon. Only seen through an odd eye of the storm, that was circling around them.

"You might think it crazy, but look. There is nothing but the beauty of the world left, there isn't light pollution so great that it drowns out the universe above. Noise so deafening that it drowns out the calm of the night. There is nothing but Mother Earth, and we are now reduced to a sustainable population that has a new chance to exist once again with her."

"Interesting concept. I'm curious, Felix, what is it you believe in?"

Felix looked at her. She was sitting there, leaning her chin on her knees tucked close to her chest wrapped in her arms.

"What do you mean?"

"Since I've met you, you have said many interesting things, your thoughts about what has happened are alarming, to anyone. Even to me, the things you say are, for lack of a better word, scary."

Felix chuckled, "Yeah, I get that a lot. I believe that what happened really can't be explained, by theology, science, hell…I think I'm right about it, but more than likely I'm wrong beyond any belief."

"You're dodging my question," she interrupted.

Felix leaned forward, lighting a smoke.

"Since I was a kid, I turned from Christianity to Satanism, and then over time, both started to mirror each other, because, both were written by man, to what end will we go to affect the world, with hope, so that the ones not in power or, being controlled, enslaved, bred into a society where we believe that it's okay to be entrapped by what others believe. Science was once considered heresy; religion has claimed more lives than any one reason in the existence of mankind. It was all trivial. In all of my rudimentary research as a kid, I learned quite a bit about religion, faith, and came to find that it is all make believe. Even science, because numbers, language, it is a human construct; so, in reality, if we stayed true to the existence that is balanced in order for an ecosystem to function, numbers and language would just be grunts, some to attract a mate, and some to challenge a foe. Maybe identify a face to a sound, much like hyenas."

She turned sitting next to him. Felix inhaled a drag, blowing it as best he could away from her.

Felix continued, "Being a soldier, I learned that ghosts are real. Any battlefield you walk upon, you can feel the pain, the hatred, the faith that once was there. In many of the religions I've studied I found one thing I clung to and started making up my own theory of it. That was of a dog, wolf, wolfhound."

"Ironic thing to believe. It is a deity, no?" she playfully asked.

"So, if I'm right, then there is not one god, there are many, and the Earth is a Goddess, because she is big, gorgeous, and wrathful, producing life and protecting her young as any mother would. The sun, light, God, is the father, but like most deadbeat dads, he packed his shit and left after the fuck ups his children became, because he wasn't responsible enough in the first place to have a child. Or he was forced out to maintain a balance, because being too close would have beat her into a burnt husk. Which is the more serious answer."

Beatrix giggled. Felix continued, "The universe, she is a creature in an unfathomable ocean, a beautiful Goddess. A shark, maybe a whale shark, encompassing all that exists within the idea of Existence, and the Nothingness…her other half, but he didn't leave because he wanted to, he had to go because it was his duty, to be her opposite, to take from her the things she doesn't need, and allow her to continue her great migration through the entity that is unfathomed beyond us or even her. That entity is gravity. The black dog. It's neither light nor dark, its gray; it's that which exists in the twilight, it is that which affects all things in the universe, bending light and stretching darkness. I think it's a dog, because dog is god. I think it's mayhem in the purist form, which would be interesting in itself considering the circumstance to which society fell victim. I believe that Mother Earth, Gaia, Mana, whatever you wanna call her, she was sick, she couldn't take much more of the things that were killing her, so like a fever, her body burned it out, expelling two antibodies, one in the form of irony, maybe man-made, like a medication, which would be the infection. The volcano was her immune system. It's a cycle."

"My goodness, you are interesting! Did you come up with this all by yourself?"

"It's what I've come to believe, I think I'm right. Since I was a kid, I always felt that there was something more than what we got. A lot of things about the world before this one, were better off disappearing, because it was destroying us, it was destroying the Goddess, and eventually we would have had to choose."

"Choose what?" She leaned against him.

"To save the world, or to save ourselves. The rate we were going, we weren't ever going to be able to have both, our greed would have ensured that if we attempted to save both us and the world, we would both perish. You can make more humans; you can't pull a whole world out of your ass."

"Fascinating, I've never met anyone with such an interesting point of view. I would like to have known you when you were younger, watch you come to these conclusions, just so when I saw you again, in this world, I could have told you that maybe you were right."

Felix shifted his head looking in her direction. "What would a scientist like you believe; faith or religion or your own way, agnostic or atheist, creationism or evolution?"

"You may think it odd, but I believe in Christianity, just not a typical follower. Didn't really go to church as much as I should, didn't pray enough. I believe we die as the life we lived, nothing more and nothing less. Treat others as you wish to be treated, and do your best to live a fulfilled life. I spent most of mine trying to save the earth, figure out what I could do, implement a new federal regulation on plastics, limit the use of lithium batteries due to the rarity of that mineral, maybe even find a strain of undocumented plant life that may be the answer to curing allergies or even cancer. I would be happy with the common cold, and not get bought out by a pharmaceutical company that would retard the treatment and charge a ridiculous price for it in order to maintain the current death rates. I had grand aspirations, no time for a husband or children, no time for family. I worked, and in my work, I was married, my findings were my children, and my family although we didn't speak much, was the staff, my coworkers and colleagues. When I think about it, I'm full of regrets because my education cost me hundreds of thousands of dollars. I was in debt for almost twenty years, and for what? A piece of paper."

Felix laughed, "My fiancé looked at it that way. Like her, you're educated, enough that an expedition was put together in the hopes of finding answers. So at least there is that."

She stood up, "I think I like your answer better. Whatever we find, won't really matter, other than peace of mind. We can't reverse it, we cannot foresee it, maybe you are right, and Mother; as you call her, is tired."

Felix flicked his cigarette into the fire. The flames danced, crackled, throwing small sparks burning into the darkness.

Beatrix turned to the tree.

"Why do you look at that tree so much? It has captured you since we got here."

Felix turned, looking at it, "It reminds me of the Tree of Life, in physical form, because the real Tree of Life is merely a diagram of the eight gates to which life and death are the first and last of the gates one will pass through in their existence."

"I'm unfamiliar."

"It's pagan or druidism; it's old, one of the oldest beliefs if I recall. It probably is one of the most interesting of beliefs, I think there is truth to it. That tree is what I would imagine to be the death gate, the Dead Tree in particular."

"Maybe it is a gate, for weary travelers to pass through it from death to life, because there is life in this volcano, and once you pass from it back into the world, we find death."

Felix thought for a moment. "Which way are we passing to find death?" he asked.

She pointed to the east, "Away from the volcano."

"I can live with that," he nodded.

"I'm going to get some sleep, it's going to be a long day tomorrow," she said as she walked toward Felix's tent.

He laughed, shaking his head. He stood, picking up his rifle. The Socom 16 was caked in snow, he tapped his small flashlight along the stock knocking the white cast loose. He began his checks of the perimeter, passing by the Dead Tree. He stopped, looking at it for a moment, still mesmerized, intrigued by its very presence.

"If you are the death gate, then where in the world is the Tree of Life?" He waited for a moment, half believing there would come an answer. But even if it did, was he fully ready for it? He did not know, that's probably why God stopped speaking to humans long ago. Our ability to speak outgrew our ability to listen.

He chuckled to himself, "We do not deserve your answer."

*****

That night he crawled into his sleeping bag, to find Beatrix again. Waiting, naked, but he didn't know until her body pressed against his. Her finger tips searching for whatever she could to find his heart through the receptors of the surface of his warm skin. Her hands found their way down his hard stomach to his pelvis, where his hands stopped her.

"Please, just sleep," he said in an almost growl that was as harsh as it was cold to her.

"Your woman is very lucky, this is the world we live in now, and yet you still hold yourself back. If she did survive, do you not think that this is what it means to find some form of comfort?" she questioned it all, softly in his ear.

"I've only ever been good to her, so let me at least continue to be that."

"She will have moved on," Beatrix replied.

"Until I know for sure, I'm going to live in my memories and chase those dreams."

"What about reality, the person right in front of you, me, right here right now?"

"I wasn't a very good person until I met her, she saved me from who I was, caused a change in me that showed me that I was worth more than what I ever could have imagined…that is my reality."

Her hands relaxed, moving up around his chest, pulling her chest tight into his back.

"Bad person, huh?"

"Yeah."

"Stealing a woman's heart and then dangling it in front of her with no sign of release?"

"I'm sorry, that wasn't my intention. I literally did nothing to warrant your heart."

"It's an expression, I just want comfort as any logical person would when the world is full of so much pain."

"That pain is the greatest teacher, the one that makes you better than you were or ever thought you could be," Felix replied in a sleepy daze.

"You are a paradox."

"And you are a conundrum."

"Sweet dreams, Felix."

"You as well, Beatrix."

*****

The next morning the group packed up and descended the great mountain. They made it all the way back to their safe haven. Without issue, nor adversary, they arrived in the warm embrace of the deep cave that was their home now in Kansas City, Missouri. Felix never saw Beatrix again, nor any of the scientists from the team. He continued his travels with other teams in search of survivors, in search of food, supplies, fuel, batteries, working generators. The winter was harsh and unending, they only had a few good months to travel, December to February, when the winter was calm. June to August was suicide, all any of them could do was hope that the winter would subside…one day.

Felix was merely a boy. Walking through the desert woods of California. He had determination in his eyes. A single shot bolt action 22 LR rifle slung on his shoulder. His backpack with water and some tools shifted on his back as he snuck from thick bush to thick bush.

"There it is," Felix said as he lay down.

The scene before him was a meth lab, in the middle of the woods. Nestled deep in the thickening desert forest. Felix had stumbled upon it several days ago on one his many backyard adventures. His parents had no idea where he was and didn't care. Just as long as he was home by dinner.

He watched, as two men loaded barrels into a rickety pickup truck. The trailer was surrounded by rusted farm equipment and chemical barrels of all kinds. A tractor trailer was parked and covered with military camo netting. And that was his prize. For just days ago he watched these same two junkies move weapons into the back of that trailer.

They acted like ex-military, the older man looked like an average Vietnam vet, and his son, Felix presumed, looked like a desert storm vet. Hard men, covered in prison tattoos. Tanned from the sun, and that wirily junkie skinniness that you can't underestimate. They had guns on their hips and burns on their hands from whatever they were cooking.

Felix didn't care about the drugs; he was too young to know anything other than that they were bad and would kill you. He only cared about what he could take and carry back. So he sat, watching them through his shoddy scope on his more than likely useless weapon. A large lizard crawled in front of him, he didn't move. A snake next chased after it. He froze, for that rattle you could not mistake.

Felix slowly reached for his Buck knife on his hip. Never once taking his eyes off of the spectacle before him as the snake snatched up the lizard. Felix slowly unsnapped the retention strap and pulled the mirror finished blade free from its brown leather sheath. The snake gobbled up the lizard in front of him. Wide eyed and sweating, he brought the blade up slowly. The snake began to move away, full belly and all. Felix let out a sigh of relief.

The truck door slammed once, twice. Its old engine started up with a muffler-rattling back-fire that scared Felix. The old off-road tires spit dirt and rocks as they drove away. Felix waited for what seemed like forever. The sun, even under the thick bush, was beating down and he could only hope for a cloud to give his pale skin some relief.

Once he lost any audible noise of the old truck he quickly got up. He ran to cover, like a miniature soldier maneuvering from position to position. He stopped next to some 55-gallon plastic barrels. Their deep blue almost hurt his eyes, they were so bright. He came around to the tattered trailer that the men cooked in. This was facing his real prize, however, he needed to see if there was anything of value in this trash can of a cook house. He turned the handle to find that it was locked, oddly enough. He set his rifle against the door. Looking around, he took off his old tattered backpack and rummaged through the contents. Pulling out a Bobbie-pin he took from his mother's bathroom counter and a small screw driver he took from his father's tool bag.

He began to work; with much difficulty he twisted with one hand and worked the pin into the lock forcing the tumblers down. The door was cheap and in no time the lock spun free. He stuffed his tools back into the pack and in a flash, he was in.

Cheap cut up jugs and broken glassware littered the counters of the once small kitchen. He quickly but carefully rummaged through all the draws and cabinets. Lastly the fridge. The food that was in there gave off a smell that made him gag. The rot and growth of future penicillin that was clinging to even the walls in there was enough to make most hurl. He slammed the door, holding his mouth.

"Gosh, these guys are bad, really bad," he said through his hand. He continued into the tattered room. Only a bed covered in piss and stains of what he did not know. All he knew was that those needles on the floor had aids, because that's what all kids knew back then. He was out of the room in a flash. He locked the door, took a rag and wiped all his little hand prints off everything he touched.

He closed the door and headed quickly and cautiously across the mess of junk and old parts to the tractor trailer. He forced the heavy lock open using his bobby-pin and screw driver. He had much difficulty trying to open the latch handle. He didn't give up, he kept at it for the better part of ten minutes. Until finally it opened. And in there he saw a treasure trove.

He found guns, and bullets, tools, crates of things that he didn't understand how they were labeled. They were merely identified as numbers. He found an old 1911 and stuffed it into his pack. He grabbed bullets, and dumped them in his back pack. He slung his 22 behind his back and picked up an AK.

He was so excited he couldn't believe what treasures he had found. He just wished that he had found money so he could help out the family. After all they barely got by, and that's all he ever knew. Satisfied with his booty, he quickly jumped from the back, shut the door and relocked the lock. He started running. The sound of that old truck was approaching quickly.

He ran and ran and ran some more. The AK was very heavy, and so was his pack, his breaths were becoming rapid. He slowed to a lazy walk. He needed to take a break. So, he hid in a bush. Drank from his canteen letting out a sigh of utter relief. It was getting late, and he had far to go yet. He rested for a moment longer, appreciating his new toys, but now where was he going to hide them?

Then as he realized, true terror began to come over him. If he didn't get home soon, he was going to get an ass-whoopin' like no other. Not to mention, what little food they did have, you were never late for dinner, because if you were, you weren't going to eat that night. He quickly stood up and began moving again. The two junkies hadn't figured out that he had been there yet, he was sure. So proud of himself, he had done it. Felix was getting better at these kinds of things.

The sun set, and he was becoming more frantic as he knew he was going to get a whoopin', and not get to eat tonight. But he was lost. He was turned around. He didn't know what to do. He started to panic. He stood there, in the dark, not even the moon was out. He couldn't hear anything. There was no sound, and that was more frightening than anything that could be stalking him. They had mountain lions and bobcats everywhere out there.

84

He continued on, heavy short breaths, he dropped his prize and began to run even faster. Looking back as the chills ran up his spine. His eyes were wide with fear now. He messed up and now he was in big trouble. It got very cold at night out there and he didn't have his jacket. He could freeze. He was going to die out there.

He started yelling for help. But no one answered. He couldn't see anything. Felix started to feel his way through the dark, running into a cactus. It stuck in his hand, as he fell back crying out in pain. He began to sob. Hopelessness started to come over him. The child was lost and alone in the dark.

And then, that thing came. Its breath froze the child in absolute fear. He couldn't even make a sound. He could only stare into its six eyes as they looked upon the child. It was so tall, and the white outline of the beast began to form as the moon began to rise behind it. The beast's smile glowed white as it grinned ear to ear. The boy slowly stood. The fear had gone. He knew he was going to die by the hands of this monster in front of him.

"Why have you come for me?" Felix asked the beast.

It did not answer.

"Are you the devil? Has god punished me for stealing?"

The beast's grin widened.

"Am I going to hell?"

Felix began to sob, forgetting the pain in his hand.

"No, boy."

Felix stopped, eyes wide, the voice shocked him into reality. He looked up. The beast opened its mouth and let out a hellish roar and bit down on the child, swallowing him whole. Felix fell into the void.

He jerked awake, screaming in his bed. His father ran into the room, clicking the light on.

"Son, what's the matter?"

Felix looked around. Shocked.

"It was just a bad dream, son. You're fine now."

"But I was in the forest with a giant dog, it ate me."

Felix looked at his hand, it was bandaged from where his mother had pulled out all the cactus spines.

"It's okay. It was just a bad dream. You're home now. Get some sleep, we will talk tomorrow about why you were out and where you found those guns you had."

Felix was now in even more fear of his well-being.

"Go to sleep. By the way, happy birthday." His father turned the light out and shut his door.

Felix couldn't sleep that night. He sat and watched the darkness, looking for that grin and those eyes. He couldn't see it. But it was there. Watching him. It was after all his 9th birthday. Being born on such a day as Friday the 13th always seemed to bring him more than he ever wanted.

Chapter 6

A Dog Year

Sub-tropolis, Kansas City, Missouri. An underground city now, three years had come and gone since the fall of civilization. These cool strong walls were now a safe haven and bartering city for the survivors of this rotting nation. Snow has begun to melt and for the first time in years the sun was shining brightly without a cloud in sight.

Patrols moved in and out of the city, supply runs, survivor collection, but these days, due to the harsh winter that claimed almost as many lives as the dogs and feral did, there were hardly any new people found in the wastes. However, being that the roads were clear, the patrols should become more fruitful as they were now able to travel further for the first time in a long time.

The cities were emptied long ago, and what the first few weeks of the infection didn't kill, the winter was sure to finish off. The total population remaining was reduced to eight or nine-hundred thousand, in the world. The ones unlucky enough to survive and remained in the cities were very few. Like hibernating malnourished bears, people begun to emerge from their fortified houses. Those smart enough to prepare for a fantasy end of the world situation stayed in their bunkers. Others who moved to safer locations had started to venture out to find loved ones, and build up their new homes further.

The dogs, the feral, had begun to move back into the country. Dragging with them the mutated and malformed bodies of those that started to evolve. The dogs no longer dogs, and the humans no longer humans; had started to find new hunting grounds, breaking off in their packs, infected humans remaining with the dog that first bit them. Some packs joined others due to the alpha eating the previous leader. The dynamic of life had changed. Trees began to produce leaves; the world began to become green once again. However, it wasn't the same, and never would be again. Temperatures had begun to increase rapidly and the growth of vegetation was almost divine.

Felix was sitting in a bar, carved out of the lime stone for FEDEX or any one of the many companies that used to exist there. He heard the conversation of a group of women talking about where they were when it all happened. Nothing he normally ever paid any attention to. Until they started talking about the rumors.

"I heard that the blast came from Yellowstone national park, it was nuclear, the biggest ever seen. It was set off to cause the volcano down there to finally erupt."

"Yeah," another interrupted her friend. "It happened almost exactly at the same time all the dogs started attacking people."

Another continued, "I know a guy from the research facility here for environmental protection. He says that they don't know who coordinated the attack but it was well-organized. Using drones around the world to release it. The biological weapon was nothing they have ever seen before, and the bomb was more than likely a Russian bomb that we were keeping to dismantle."

Felix scoffed, almost laughing to himself, trying not to let the group know he was listening in. He wondered why such rumors were being spread. He was there, and there was no sign of nuclear radiation out of the normal thermal release from a volcanic blast. But it wouldn't surprise him; in fact, if he were a radical psychopath, that would be something he would do. The world needed change, and that was a good start.

"The word is that the organization responsible for it was from India."

"There it was, why though? What good would crazy notions like that have to do with the peoples' mindset now? This country is far too weak to honestly effect anything more than fending for ourselves. And from all the chatter that has been intercepted and translated. The rest of the world was just as bad as they were, if not worse. Except the 3rd world countries... They were used to living like this. Without power or very little, braving harsh winters, eating the same things day in and day out. Reproducing just to keep their people alive, even though they understood the effects of inbreeding."

The bar was dim, lit by candles and some piss yellow lamps here and there. Smoke was ventilated from fans through a filtration system that ran through the entire stone carved city. Glass and dishes clattering, low conversation from several sides of the room filled the air. He finished his beer, taking a drag from his smoke as the girls continued talking.

"I hear there is a form of government still around. They are offering safety for work; some people are even being offered positions in special outposts."

"Yeah..." the waiter chimed in now, "I've even heard they have started clearing the north in the bigger cities. Chicago was virtually taken back from slavers. Why that place wasn't hit with a nuke is a surprise to me."

"Really?" one of the girls asked. The hope in her voice was so apparent you would have to be deaf not to know how happy that made her. Probably had family that lived in Chicago.

The waiter continued picking up their plates and glasses and disappeared into the back of the bar. Someone else in the bar at another table, clearly irritated with the conversation, interrupted. "You really going to trust anything the government wants to offer you? Who do you think even let this happen? A world-wide biological attack at the same time a nuke is set off on top of a volcano? Which didn't happen, by the way, no proof. If it did, what does it matter now anyway?"

The girls fell silent as did much of the room. Felix on the other hand put his smoke out. Standing up, he grabbed his Benelli M4 and headed briskly to the door, waving at the bartender as he walked out. The girls continued talking once he was out of the room.

"Did you hear?" she asked to the other two girls, cupping her mouth with one hand, attempting to be quiet about her next comments. "He is headed south to find his woman."

"Really?"

"Yes, he's going into Texas to find her. He only came here until the winter cleared, apparently he helped our army clear most of the gangs in the south."

"Yeah, I even heard he's been close to the volcano during the winter expeditions. Not many survived, most of them nearly died from the ash and snow. Almost all of them now work for that new government, all except him."

"No way, I guess that's why they stopped those expeditions about a year ago."

"It's true, you can ask anyone around here."

"I've heard the dogs have moved back into the country; they are starting to take over anywhere they can find. Sticking to the warmer climate in the southern regions of the states."

"I've heard they changed too…"

"I think I'm going to join this new military, they are offering a fortune for women, and will move us to another location far from here."

"I would be careful; if they are offering a fortune just because you're a girl, that could mean they are going to use you. Like most of us have been."

The mood became heavy and they quickly changed the subject. They carried on their rumors and chatter of anything else, everything else. Some to be true, some to be entirely false. But that was always the difference and the dangers of bullshit vs lies. But none more so dangerous than that of hope.

*****

Felix was walking down the corridor; cars, trucks passed by on the street carrying supplies, probably coming back from a run into the city. The looks on the dirty men and women's faces were that of going through hell just to supply food and water to the city. The lights flickered from a generator change over. Felix passed by shops, garages, weapons dealers, whore houses, drug dealers, and other random bartering locations.

His stare was blank as he was running through his mind what he needed to do, when he needed to leave, and most importantly, was she alright, was she safe, was she alive, did she follow their ridiculous plan? Did anyone follow the plan? Mitch, Dana, David, John, and Kim...Gavin? This went on. These questions had been rolling through his head since the first day. Like hundreds of voices talking to him all at once.

Felix finally got to where he was going. Standing in front of the garage he lit a smoke, peering down the road out the opening of the cave, heavily guarded by metal walls, concrete barriers, and a mix of civilian and military vehicles retrofitted with any number of heavy weapons systems.

"Hey, buddy," Justin called from the shop walking out to greet his old friend.

"Hey, brother," Felix replied.

"She's almost ready. Been a while, where you been?"

Felix took a heavy drag, "Here and there, ran with a few of the teams to go check out some spots, went up north, it's fucked. The entire area is still covered in ash mud, so many people died in the initial blast that I'm pretty sure no one survived the north western hemisphere."

"Right on, man," Justin replied nodding.

Justin, a large man, don't let his southern accent or his look fool you, the man was a genius in his own regard. Felix and Justin went back some years from their time in the Army. Good friends, and lucky to have run into each other years ago. Standing there unashamed of his large beer belly; for good reason, considering how strong he really was. His deep blue eyes were piercing. His white cut off sleeve shirt was covered in grease and dirt from working on vehicles. He was wearing cut off woodland army fatigues with burn holes in them from a welder or grinder. Sporting a pair of old leather flip flops.

"You headin out again?" Justin asked.

"Yeah, anything in particular that you need?"

"Just the usual. By the time you come back from this one, your baby will be running again."

"I appreciate it, I'll need the Toyota again."

"No worries, just try to bring her back in one piece. The last truck you took was totaled, I'm fucking astonished you were able to drive her back, or that you even survived the wreck for that matter."

Felix flicked his cigarette into the street, "I'll see what I can do. But I couldn't help that, there aren't exactly any roads left in the north."

He started walking up the road.

"Where you going now?" Justin called to him.

"Gotta go talk to that old hag about some pew pews, brother."

"See you tonight?"

Felix stopped and turned. "I live here, don't I?"

Justin shook his head with a grin, "Live…no, you keep your shit here and disappear for months. One day I'm just going to sell all your shit."

"Yeah?" Felix laughed. "For what?"

"Probably some peace and goddamn quiet!"

Felix laughed, turning, continuing to move deeper into the safe heaven.

*****

As Felix walked up the road, passing people, the looks on their faces were of blind happiness. It irritated him, like most things did. He didn't understand; even back then just before all this happened, the country was falling apart. He could hear the bullshit playing over and over in his head. News reports from all over the United States.

"After yesterday's fatal school shooting the President has decided to sign the bill limiting and restricting all assault style weapons." "Today, talks with Russia ended in confusion and fear as the two superpowers could not reach an agreement over ceasing all nuclear tests." "Today in another news, leaked footage of the mass shooting that happened in California last year, showing unidentified men fleeing the scene. The initial report from Chief of Police Ryan Cox stated that the officers that were in charge of that area have been suspended for their negligence, and any information regarding the suspects will be rewarded." "The bill limiting the experimentation on gene splicing and biological testing on living specimens has finally been lifted, sources say, we have never come this far, and now with no limits, we may finally have the ability to regrow limbs, cure blindness, and even produce healthy children void of any flaw while still in the womb." "Today, the first chimera was born, scientist say that they have high hopes that these species will breed and continue to flourish in the Amazon." "The legal voting age has been reduced to the age of sixteen, talks about the legal sexual consent age has been put on

the table, weapons bans have been replaced with Red Flag bills, that would make it legal for anyone to be able to report an individual, and all their weapons would be seized if the court deems them a danger to themselves or others." "The most devastating shootout between police and a local gang in Chicago has erupted, the city council is now seeking help from the National Guard. The police currently are not militarized enough to handle the terrorists, officials will be looking into armored police cruisers, military grade police issue weapons, and a seizure bill on all Chicago residence since the failure of the strictest gun ban in the history of the United States." "California has officially succeeded from the nation, a wall is currently being built, the governor has also issued a statement, he will be closing off the California Mexico border by force." "After legalizing Marijuana, officials say they are aiming for more serious drugs to add to the list, polls concluded that this was a smart move for the country and the economy." "The military has seen an influx of drug users over the past months, sources say that they will be issuing a draft bringing in prior service members in order to fix this epidemic of substance abuse." "Minimum wage was yet again increased, officials say that this could be the beginning of a crashing economy as inflation is once again on the rise..." "Social media creators across the board have issued apologies after the statistics of teen suicide have increased since the beginning of the social network movements. A statement from Psychologist Norma Freeman, 'it pains me to see this is where we are as a society, blaming corporations and governments for the wrongdoings of the individuals. We are seeing a shift in the human mentality that is disturbing and I fear that we may have failed our future generations by letting electronic devices raise them.' She would not comment any further on whether or not censorship would fix the epidemic of graphic images and videos telling teens how to hurt themselves. However, she urged families to spend more time together and become more involved in their children's lives. She is receiving a lot of backlash from her comments. Her attorneys have commented that she will not apologize for her statement, it and I quote 'needed to be said.'"

"It was all just a bunch of horse shit," Felix said out loud. A couple standing outside waiting to cross the intersection stared at him.

He glared their way; they quickly crossed the street.

He continued walking down the street. Lights lined the walkway, a whore house, restaurant, if you could call it that, police station, gun shop, general store, the entire place was right out of a book, or any movie that showed the end of the world in such a comfortable manner. He smiled as the girls and guys standing outside turning a trick cat-called him.

"Hey, cutie. What's your bait?" a man or woman or both asked him.

He simply held up his hand, waving their persistent offerings off, as more and more nonsense had played over and over again in his head.

"Felix?" a familiar friend called to him, in his mind.

"Can you believe this shit?" Gavin asked.

"Society has turned in on itself," Gavin continued.

"How's that, brother?"

"I don't mind the gays, I don't mind the transgenders, hell, I don't even mind the mentally fucking unstable creatures who mutilate their bodies and get away with it. But you know what I mind?"

"What's that, brother?" Felix asked again.

"That they are attempting to drop the legal age for sexual consent, and psych-evals signed by a doctor is acceptable enough for a 40-year-old man, that says he is mentally a 7-year-old girl, can marry a 10-year-old boy. I didn't know we were turning into the middle fucking east over here."

Felix laughed, *"That's what society wants, that's what it was all coming to, and we will no longer be there to fight for the freedoms they decided to take from us. It's almost like we are going back in time. Nothing we can do; the majority always wins."*

"Just waiting on you, I'm out, and it was the best fucking choice I ever made. We fought for freedom back then, now there is nothing we are fighting for. It's time to get out. Go live your fucking life for once, marry that sexy lady you have, give me some goddamn nieces and nephews."

Felix laughed again, *"I will as soon as they take the guns from the civilian population. That is the day when I will go, because if a civilian isn't good enough to own one; than the 17- and 18-year-old kids, who join and carry those fucking extensions of themselves, should walk away and see what happens then."* Felix laughed again, *"Could you imagine, if every soldier, police officer, protection agency followed such a ridiculous idea, what would all these peace-loving people do to protect themselves when another country comes to fuck them over? Hell, when their neighbor comes knocking?"*

Gavin laughed, *"Then the world would no longer be 'turn the other cheek,' they would be 'eye for an eye,' and maybe that's exactly the way we animals need to be. We have thumbs, let's beat each other down."*

"Agreed, but how can we make change, when the most dangerous weapon we have ever seen is the manipulation of a cell phone, or camera? Mass terrorism isn't these mass shootings or bombings, it's the way the government spins the lie that thus becomes the news, and with it, fear. The real terrorism comes from who hears about it. Take all the communications away in the

world, then there will be no one to watch them perform their little shows. Thus, ending a lot of suffering in general."

They both laughed and the clang of the beers against each other became the clanging of metal workers on the street. Felix walked around the construction site as the men dug into another portion of the stone to make another housing complex or storage area.

I think soon, before our time is done, we will see that civil war. Felix's thought faded into echo, then drowned in reality as metal slamming against metal on an anvil caught his attention. Felix waved as he passed by. One of the workers lifted her hammer, nodding. Finally; Felix ended up at another gun shop, deep in the underground city. He walked in the door, two men guarding the entrance stop him.

"I have an appointment," Felix said.

"What's in the bag?"

Felix opened his military green tattered pack. Cigarettes, bags of shell casings, and medicine sat in it.

"Felix?" a woman's voice in the back called to him. "You're late, round eye."

"My bad, I was lost in my own head, almost forgot where I was going."

"You bring me gifts?" she asked.

Short tough little Korean woman came out from behind the counters. The shop was lined with gun after gun, rifles, machine guns, shotguns, pistols, military weapons of all kinds. Stacks upon stacks of bullets littered the floor and shelves of the carved-out cave gun shop.

The large guard stepped out of the way allowing Felix to pass. She walked with him back to her counter in the back. He carefully set his merchandise on the table, in line, neat and presentable.

"You put together the package I asked for?" Felix asked.

She walked around to the other side. "Depends, you didn't answer me, did you get everything I asked for, white boy?" Her dark brown eyes were piercing, her face heavily wrinkled from 60 years of age. Her black hair was up in a pony tail. Faded blue jeans tight against her thin legs, a large revolver on her hip, and a long sleeve shirt a size or two too big, more than likely her man's shirt.

"You came through, after all," she exclaimed, looking at the bounty in front of her.

She turned, yelling in Korean. Felix smirked.

"You got it, darlin'," a thick southern accent and deep voice sounded from the back.

Her husband, a large black man came through the door with a belt of 37 mm grenades and a M72 grenade launcher. He sat it down on the table, and quickly went back into the back room.

"He still doesn't talk much," Felix said picking up the belt of 12 rounds and stuffing them into his bag.

"He so lazy, pisses me off. You want anything else?" she asked.

"All I brought was what we agreed upon. So maybe next time, this will be good for now."

"You sure you don't want a newer model, like a 203 or 320, I think we have a 6-shot in the back. Marine model, very good, like new."

Felix laughed, "No, I'm fine, I like this one anyway, couldn't hit shit with the 320s and I didn't like the locking mechanisms on the 203s, so, thank you. This is more than fine."

"Be careful out there, you've heard the stories, right?"

Felix leaned in, "What stories?"

"There is something big, like the infected are reproducing, and the things coming from them are massive, as big as cars."

Felix laughed, "Well, if there are, I'm sure this will kill it. But you shouldn't listen to the rumors. I've been all over, haven't seen that, and that would change everything we know about this pandemic. It won't be an infection anymore, it will be Mother getting ready to kill us off." He walked out the door with his new weapon and ammo in hand. He waved as the bell rang and he disappeared out into the streets.

He looked both ways down the yellow lit carved streets. He lit a smoke, continuing back toward Justin's garage. The lights flickered as he continued down the wet sidewalk. The sound of heavy engines echoed off the rock. Children throwing rocks at each other, laughing and arguing as kids do. It was just another lazy day.

"Felix?" her voice called to him.

"Babe? What are you doing now?" she asked.

"Sorry, babe, I made a mess in the garage," Felix replied.

"That's fine, but what are you doing?"

"Well, since we live 800 miles apart, I thought, you know, if the world ever ended, you needed a go-bag to get to me, or at least be able to fight your way from wherever you are to here."

"How much did you spend?" she asked.

"You don't wanna know."

"Stop buying me shit," she replied.

"But, baby…"

"Don't 'but baby' me, mister."

"It's not for you," he joked.

She crossed her arms and did that cute thing with her mouth before she was about to chew him out in the cutest way.

"I'm just leaving it in your car," he exclaimed.

"Yeah, okay, you pain in my ass," she said as her voice carried away.

"Yeah, but you love it!" he yelled.

Felix walked into someone on the sidewalk. "My bad."

"Watch where you're walking, asshole," the whore called out to him in a slurred lisp. He paid him or her no mind. After all, they were engaging in one of the oldest forms of monetary trade.

"That's right, keep walking, bitch."

Felix continued without even hearing the tunnel walker.

He stopped, taking in a long drag as he looked out the tunnel. He could see the sun was setting; the barricade teams were changing out for the night shift. Kids were being yelled at by Stacey to get their asses inside. Justin was outside drinking some homemade brew talking with his crew.

"Been a long time," he laughed to himself. "These are good people, it's a shame to have to leave again. But, it's always time for me to go, never to stay."

*****

That night, sitting at the dinner table in the lime stone carved out home; Felix and Justin drank their brew as Stacey put the kids to bed. A map unrolled lay before them. Felix flipped a pencil impatiently through his fingers as he gazed intently upon it.

"You alright?" Justin asked.

"No, not until I find her. I've wasted so much fucking time. It's as if somewhere along the last few years I forgot what I even came this way for."

"Dude, maybe it's time to move on. It's been what, maybe three years, since the day of the dogs, the end of the world?"

"Something like that, two, maybe three, I honestly don't know," Felix replied carelessly.

"If she survived, not saying that she didn't..." Justin started, meeting Felix's glare across the table. Unafraid, Justin gave one back, "She would've left, that's it, you've been trying to get down there for a good while, and still haven't found a safe or even passable route to that shithole. What are you going to do? Walk in?"

"If I have to, the snow is melted, it's possible."

"That could take months, not to mention, this whole southern area is fucked, hordes of those little bastards are down there. Oh, and from the reports, fucking gangs, especially the ones in uniform talking about how they are the new government. You know it's fucking stupid to continue, she left. If she was smart, she found a group and headed to Fort Monroe, like you always used to talk about. Now that I think about it, Mitch was the one who thought that place up, so you should just get your shit, and head fucking east. She is probably there already, waiting for your dumbass."

"Thanks for that," Felix replied.

Justin smiled, took a generous swig, and slammed his glass down. "Look, man, I got all the faith in the world in you, but you could die from this one. It isn't like you are going in there with a team, you are doing this all on your own. We, like it or not, are family-based animals. You need companionship, you need trust, and you need someone to watch your fucking back out there."

"Yeah, I got it. But I'm not going to take a chance and not check. Just in case, knowing her, she left…something—"

"Left what? She isn't Gretel leaving fucking breadcrumbs for your ass. Even if she did leave a note or something… What are you going to do then? Come all the way back up here, get your shit, and then move east all the way across the country?"

"Yeah, and?"

"This is probably one of the only safe places left between here and there, communications just got back up, and what? We have heard like maybe three locations that have held on, you think they are just going to welcome you in, here's some supplies, here's some bullets, okay thanks, fuck no! Once you leave here, you are fucked. It's back to scavenging, murder, raiding, slaughter, those fucking things, what if you turn feral? Then you will never see her again. You are going to end up dying out there."

"After everything we did to set this place up, you think I can't make it out there?" Felix asked. Leaning over the map, pointing, making his point. He leaned back, the scowl still smeared across his face as Felix downed the rest of his homemade beer.

Justin leaned on his giant arms, clutching his beer, head cocked, "This isn't the cannibal raids, or the feral hunts. We were with a small army, we had teams, people to watch our backs. You will be all by yourself, alone, and fucked if you're not careful."

Felix adjusted himself in his seat, tossing the pencil on the table, "I have to go… It's a chance I have to take, that I've been taking for years now," he said staring at the map. His eyes slid up meeting Justin's.

The moment lasted for more than time was moving along.

"Right on, good luck. At least stay the night before you go get yourself killed. It's clear that I'm not going to change your mind, do whatever you feel you need to."

Felix laughed, "Thanks, I planned on it. Or are you going to give me shit about staying another week to better prepare for the trip?"

"No, I've pretty much figured you're an idiot, and wouldn't listen anyway."

The two continued laughing and drinking the night away.

The next day, dawn. The smell of wet pavement, a slight breeze and a stale cigarette filled the air around Felix.

Justin broke the cool morning's silence with words that made sense, but Felix could have done without. "No shame in moving on, she probably had to as well. Not to mention the other shit that has become our life nowadays. Flesh for trade, services for food or shelter or travel, who knows she may have found someone to replace you. Because that is what we do, we move on, we let go, so the pain doesn't drag us down with those memories."

Felix glared at him, "Thanks, fucker. Got any other motivational words before I go and die?"

Justin laughed, "Yeah, don't die, we will be here. So, come back."

"I'm coming back," Felix replied. He climbed in the beat-up Toyota Tundra shutting the door. He started the engine up, waving as he drove away. Justin watched him go. Time would continue on without him, but he would miss him. That was one less man around here that was for better or worse, a good man in his own right.

Felix sprinted from the giant eight-wheeled vehicle to the next. Gunfire sporadic and inaccurate at best bounced and clanged off the armor. He slammed against the tire next to Gavin.

"Hey, fucker."

"Hey, motherfucker," Gavin replied taking a drag from his smoke. Rounds landing all around them to the right.

"Where's Mitch at?" Felix asked, lighting a smoke.

An RPG was launched somewhere in the city. It exploded in the side of a building across the bridge.

Gavin pointed lazily. Felix peeked out. "Oh," he said, leaning back.

Mitch was running as fast as he could with his infamous waddle run as he carried a massive charge toward a barrier blocking their path.

Felix peeked around the vehicle with his rifle up.

"These cocksuckers are really fighting each other right now while we are just hanging out here. I wonder why they are shooting at us?"

More rounds smacked against the metal in front of Felix.

"Holy fuck me," Felix said as he ducked behind the vehicle.

Gavin peeked on the other side and fires at a group of people running with RPGs and AKs.

"How are the guys looking that way?" Gavin asked.

"They have the other truck hooked up. We are prepared to move."

Suddenly their radios sparked up. It was Mitch, "I'm coming your way, lay down some cover fire. Charge is set."

Gavin and Felix both stood, Felix yelled out, "I got low."

The two men leaned and began firing. Gavin over his head and Felix on a knee leaning out. The trucks all began picking up fire into the destroyed buildings where the enemy had taken refuge. Mitch slid to a stop next to them. Gavin grabbed Felix by the back of his plate carrier and pulled him back behind cover.

"That was fast," Felix spouted, spitting his dead cigarette onto the ground.

Mitch called up over the radio. "Button up, charge will detonate in thirty seconds." Mitch stood gesturing for Gavin and Felix to follow him behind the truck.

The bomb exploded, rocking them and quietening the fire from the cities and their platoon. The barrier blocking their path was completely gone. Felix and Gavin ran with Mitch to check the success of the charge. Once confirmed that the path was cleared, they ran back and mounted up into their vehicles.

"Well, fuck me, all of this for what, to recover one vehicle?" Felix said aloud.

Gavin laughed. Mitch got on the radio and ordered the element to move out.

As they passed through town after town, they were met with children running to them asking for things. Women were hidden away. Men stared at them, immediately getting on their cell phones. The platoon's vehicles were pelted with rocks.

Out of nowhere a vehicle with about ten people in it came flying around a corner and slammed into the lead military vehicle. Killing almost everyone inside. The men dismounted from their vehicles and investigated the situation. The afghans started piling into the streets and blocking traffic. Some started spitting on the Americans as they tried to pull the people out and help them.

"Fuck this, Felix, smoke us out," Gavin relayed.

Felix took his bag off. Good old bag of tricks. He pulled two smoke grenades out and held them up. The crowd immediately started backing away. Felix grabbed the linguist standing next to him by the back of his neck.

"Tell them, we are trying to help, they need to stay the fuck back, so we can get them out of the vehicle, and tell them that they need to get a vehicle to transport their own fucking people to a hospital. If they do that, we will be out of there village as soon as possible. Understand?"

The linguist shook his head nervously, and began to translate. The villagers immediately started yelling back and forth and one of them tried to get inside of one of their vehicles. Felix pulled the pins and dropped the smoke at his feet. He immediately pulled the man off of his truck and drew his pistol aiming at his chest.

Out of nowhere, Gavin grabbed Felix's gun. Shooting him a look of disapproval. Gavin grabbed the man by the neck and threw him back into the crowd of ever angering masses. One of the vehicles passed in front of them and began pointing their weapon on the crowd that now immediately began to quieten. They slowly moved away, watching everything the Americans were doing.

They recovered the situation; the people were moved into another civilian vehicle to a hospital and the platoon had finally made it back to base. Gavin found Felix leaning on a broken wooden rail staring up at the stars. Smoking a cigarette and drinking an energy drink.

"You were going to kill that man?"

Felix spit. "Yeah, so, thank you. You stopped me from doing something I would've regretted for a long time."

Gavin patted him on the shoulder. "It's time for us to get out, man. There is nothing worth fighting for anymore."

Felix cocked his head in agreement. "You're not wrong. What number is this for us?"

"Together or individually?"

Felix exhaled a thick cloud. "Together."

"You and I have been on four now together."

Felix laughed. "Since you and I have joined, we have been overseas longer than we have stateside."

"It's definitely time for us to realize that it's not our army anymore."

"If not us then who?" Felix asked.

Chapter 7
Seeing in Black and White

The day was sunny, clouds overhead forming familiar shapes as they dragged their shade over the couple. The two lying on their backs pointing them out as the clouds came and went. A bag sitting above them at the base of the tree, a bottle of champagne lay empty in it with an ammo can open, snacks and packaging from their picnic lay inside. A slight breeze, cool to the feel as it rolled over them. They watched the sky on this beautiful day, both on their backs, heads and shoulders touching.

"We should take a picture," she said pulling out her phone.

"Oh yeah?" Felix asked.

"Why not? We don't have many, especially none where I'm not making goofy faces."

"We have some, somewhere. I've seen them."

"You saw them," she replied, shooting him a silly scrunched smile to the side.

"Thanks, hunny, yes, I saw one somewhere." He flipped through his phone looking for one. She put her hand on his, pulling it down as she got closer. She captured a picture. They both moved their glasses above their eyes to inspect it. They both had goofy smiles.

"We are pretty bad at trying to be serious in our photos."

She laughed. "I'm making a goofy face again."

Felix grabbed ahold of her. "That's okay, I love that goofy face, so let's get another. I'm sure there is someone watching us right now, saying, man those two weirdos are taking selfies like a bunch of teenagers." She began to laugh. Felix snapped a picture.

"Ha ha!" he exclaimed. "I think this is the winner right here."

"Let me see," she said as he rolled away, and then back, kissing her. He took another picture while she was distracted by his kiss.

"I love you. You know that?" he said.

She put her hand on his face. "I love you too, crazy man."

"You make it real easy to be your man, you know that?" he asked.
"You make it pretty easy to be your woman," she replied, laughing.

Felix's truck bounced from a pot hole in the road.

"Fuck, I hope you're alright, hunny…" And his catastrophic mind began to take over, a quick shake of the head and he was back to reality once again.

Felix continued his adventure, passing cars pushed off the side of the road. Ash still formed on the broken-down vehicles, the sidewalks, dead people on the road. Looking out onto the horizon, storm clouds still formed to the north west, lightning sparkling and crackling in the distance. The cities burned and lay desolate. He started to fall asleep at the wheel. The truck drifted to the side. The cut on the shoulder woke him up with their loud rippling noise.

He pulled over, parking. He turned the vehicle off and let his seat back. "Just for a second," he said, passing out almost as soon as his eyes closed.

"Wake up, lazy butt," she said as she leaned over to kiss him.
He woke up. her green eyes were bright, her tan body looming over him. She was wearing panties and a bra, he could feel them as his still sleepy hands ran up her legs and butt, then gently up her back. Her thick dark hair were draped over his face. He could smell the hints of lavender and eucalyptus.
"How about you just crawl right back into bed," he said.
He grabbed her, pulling her down on top of him. She straddled him.
"Someone is excited this morning," she said, rubbing herself on him.
He smiled as he kissed her.
"Come on, we are going to be late," she said, pulling away from him.
She walked into the bathroom, her perfectly fit butt shaking elegantly as she walked through the door.
"But, baby?" he said.
"No, but baby, I'm still sore from yesterday, come on, let's go."
The light clicked on, nearly blinding him. Felix startled awake in the Toyota.

"Fuck these dreams," Felix said, lighting a smoke. He took a drink of water and had a bite of rat jerky before heading back onto the road.

*****

A few hours further down the road. It had been a few weeks and his trip had been quiet. That worried him. The roads were wet and full of debris that had washed from the melted snow. Debris from the explosions, from the fallout of the volcano. It littered the world it seemed, how devastating the initial blast was. How people weren't cooked alive was anyone's guess. Felix came to the blockade, slowly rolling to a stop. He leaned forward.

"What the fuck? Someone has been through here. Recently," he said as he began to scan the area. He continued to roll slowly through the moved blockade of police cars and barriers. Fresh tracks through the drying road could be seen. He pulled his sawed-off semi-auto shotgun onto his lap. And no sooner did he prepare himself, a wheel flew out of nowhere smashing into his windshield.

"Motherfucker," Felix yelled.

He slammed on the accelerator speeding through the checkpoint. He ran over a tire spike kit; all four wheels blew out. He continued to roll as fast as he could on flapping rubber. Sparks flew as he slid to a stop into the side wall of the highway.

He stepped out with his shotgun. Met by three men with large beards, tattered clothing, and their guns trained on him. They, the three bandits, were sun burnt, dehydrated, skinny, some had sores forming on their faces from who knows what. They were all sporting a mixture of military weapons, considering the Killeen military base was just down the road. Fort Hood, Texas. They could be ex-soldiers, or even civilians doing little better than surviving. Felix wondered for a moment how, how did they survive the migration, how did they survive the winters? It gave him a glimpse of that terrible illusion. Hope.

"Give us everything you have, and we won't kill you, we just want your shit," one of them spouted in a coughing fit.

Felix stood his ground. The men looked at each other.

"Yer fed well, I reckon," another said.

"Well enough, but it came with a price, that I assure you. The question is, you willing to let a traveler pass, or pay it like those before you did?"

The men were taken aback, they were all becoming anxious. Felix looked like a horrible human being, his stature was leaned toward them, not oriented in any particular manner. His orange jacket was stained from years of winter and use. A bullet hole could be seen in the left side where he had been shot just over a year ago. His eyes were dark, and in the angle of the sun, they looked black.

"You got a mouth on you, I think me and the boys are gonna teach you a lesson, I reckon, maybe with that mouth. Haven't seen a shaven face in a long time, you lookin' mighty pretty."

Felix's eyes shifted, his face lost its expressionless gloom, and something far worse replaced it. A crooked smile with malicious intent behind it.

"Go ahead and just toss that scatter gun over here," the tall one with long hair and blue eyes demanded.

Felix's tone changed, friendly, pleading almost, "Look guys, I'm just passing through. We don't have to do this."

"What the fuck are you going to do?" the smallest of the three said as he moved over with a slight limp, snatching Felix's shotgun from his hand. In a blur, Felix drew his pistol, firing from the hip several times before firing two rounds into each of the other two. It happened so fast, the men dropped due to shock, not pain. It wasn't until they saw their own blood did the screaming start.

Felix pulled another full mag from his pouch on his left hip, catching the extracting mag and then loading the full into his pistol. He seated the used magazine into the furthest pouch from his cobra clasp buckle. He holstered his pistol while stepping over the dead one closest to him, to pick up his shotgun. Choking from one of the men caught his attention. He picked up the berretta from the dead man he just retrieved his weapon from. He walked over to the gargling man with a ghostly haste. Checking the chamber of the military issued pistol, a round was in the chamber. He fired with precision, killing the man as the round ripped through his skull.

"Sorry guys, but you are in my way."

Felix walked over their bodies, picking up their weapons, a Colt M4, a Mossberg 500, and a Berretta M9. One mag, a hand full of 12-gauge shells, and two full AR magazines were the booty for the unfortunate event. The rest of the contents of each of the men included drugs; pictures of family; cigarettes, that Felix pocketed, everything else was trash. He tossed the weapons in the back of the Toyota, pulled the shredded wheel from his broken windshield. Got in the truck, pushing the windshield out of the way. He stepped onto the bed of his truck, taking a good long look around. It was quiet, but that noise would certainly attract attention.

Felix got to work, it took him an hour, but he was able to change all four tires. Luckily; he brought five spares, because knowing his luck with vehicles, he needed at least that. Once everything was said and done, Felix climbed in, brake dust covered and pissed off. He started the Toyota and continued on his way.

*****

If timing couldn't have been more perfect – several ferals had made their way onto the road to investigate the commotion. Felix hadn't seen them, but they quickly began to eat the remnants of the dead before them. The alpha stood watch for a moment, ready to command its pack if a threat should present itself.

Over the course of the migration, many didn't know that the feral had begun to take on evolutionary physical characteristics. Characteristics passed on by their infector. This had happened across the entirety of the new virus riddled species. To include the dogs, which as we know, are referred to as alphas. Seeing that those bitten by them were now part of the pack.

The feral were no longer clothed, and have all ripped their cheeks open immediately after becoming infected. Their hands and feet had grown a thick layer of padding where natural calluses would have formed otherwise. Some had grown tales, some functioning, most only a dead rope-like bony skin. In regards to the tearing of the feral cheeks – why this happened still baffled any of the current authorities that were studying the matter. But they did theorize, that it had something to do with the new range of motion of the feral jaw. They had the compacity to open their mouths twice as wide as their former state.

The leader of these five feral, a breed of sheep dog, too, had begun to change. Its hair matted and clumped; its size much larger than the previously non-virus infected version. Its ears longer and void of similarity between the two. Its bone structure in the face seemed to be slightly off. Growing larger on one side compared to the other. As if part of the beast was stunted in some way, still yet to be determined.

Its eyes a deep yellow, that of a wolf. Teeth, larger than they should be, spilled over one side of its jaw. An ivory waterfall of shards of razor-sharp spikes. It's once white and black, iconic coat, no more. Now a rust and reddish black glinting blanket. Its muscle formation was growing much like parts of its bone structure. Some larger than others, some under developed. The alphas had become cognizant of their ability to pass on this virus and infect humans to add to the hordes; that now roamed the wastes.

Its attention was focused on Felix as he disappeared down the road. Once out of sight, the massive Border Collie began to eat. The pack moved away, leaving the best of the men's flesh for their alpha. A common practice among certain community-based mammals. This is what the infection had become; what it would be in years to come was anyone's guess. However, these unnatural and malformed growth patterns made one claim certain, this was not the work of Mother. But who knew; she, too, worked in mysterious ways.

*****

Felix slowly rolled up to her house, stopping in the middle of the road. The entire neighborhood was in shambles. Some houses were burned to the ground. The streets were littered with bones of the dead, abandoned vehicles, and shell casings. All recently freed from the mounds of snow that once held them in time. All a slushy, drying in the sun, mess. Felix backed into the opened, emptied garage.

He got out, his shotgun ready. He clicked on the light as he pulled the manual release on the garage door. Slowly shutting it, the rusted screech and echo through the quiet streets almost hurt his ears. He began to clear into the house. The door leading into the main hallway of the house was slightly cracked, he flowed right in. With military precision, he cleared the entire house within a minute. Securing the back door and front door which were surprisingly still intact.

The feral, and their alpha, picked up Felix's scent and tracked him. The day was sunny, and warm. A decent wind ripping over the flat terrain of the Central Texas area. The pack began to pick up pace, headed for Felix. It would be a little while before they got there. Nonetheless, time was on neither of their sides.

Felix let out a sigh as he began to walk through the house, methodically. He pulled a picture from the hallway wall, wiping the dust from the glass face. It was her kissing his cheek while he had a look of surprise through his smile. He hung it back up and continued walking into the large living room. His boots clicking against the hardwood floors. Leaving footprints in the light coat of dust. As he stood there, they hit him like a wave.

She was standing there washing dishes behind the breakfast bar, looking up at him with her green eyes. Her hair was in a lazy bun. A tank top, no bra. She looks beautiful, *he thought, but to her, she was being lazy and looked like a bum. She took a swig from his beer, setting it back on the counter.*

"Felix, you better take this from me or I'm going to be 'drunky' before our day even gets started."

Felix looked to the couch. *She was laying there, a blanket draped over her body, headphones in, her dark hair down. She is typing away on her computer that was in her lap as she was propped up against the cushions. She pushed her glasses up the bridge of her nose. She looked up, noticing him there.*

"How was the range? How are the guys?"

Felix looked around the room as memories played over and over again in his head. He walked over to the fridge in the kitchen and opened it. The power was out, but there was one beer sitting on the shelf. Felix pulled the warm beer from the shelf, it was a Ziegenbock. He used his lighter to pop the top off and took a swig, leaning against the corner of the counter.

She was in her underwear, dancing around the kitchen. Ella Fitzgerald and Louis Armstrong were playing in the background.

"I love Ella and Louis," she said as she sat on the counter next to him. Watching him sharpen a chef knife and then cutting vegetables. She took her glass of red wine and took a drink as she began to sing.

Felix walked from the kitchen into the living room.

She came home from work. He heard the door shutting and keys rattling on the wall from being hung. Laughing could be heard from the laundry room that led into the main hallway. He knew she had found the toys he had left ready to go for the evening's wild events. She called out to him.

"Can I at least put my computer down?"

"Of course, but be prepared to do battle!" he exclaimed.

Moments later, she came barreling out of the hallway with nerf guns shooting into the kitchen. Felix was using the breakfast bar as cover. The two ran around the house shooting and laughing. Collecting up darts from the floor and reloading as they ran from room to room shooting at each other.

Felix laughed aloud as he played them over and over again in his head. He looked out through the covered glass back door. He could see the hammock through a hole in the cardboard, one side torn from the two large trees in the back yard. The grass over grown. Weeds taking back the brick patio.

He was holding her up as she was screwing in lights. She was nervous that he might let her fall. He had his arms wrapped around her thighs, balancing her and a box of small clear bulbs. She carefully pulled the last one out and put it in the strand that was run from the porch, overhung out around the trees and above the hammock. He slowly set her down. Her arms wrapped around his neck, the two kissing. They pulled away, weaved arms around each other's waist as they admired their handy work.

"This was a great idea. Thank you for helping me."

"No babe, this was all you, I just stood there and looked pretty."

She laughed, "You literally picked my fat ass up and carried me around to put these lights in."

Felix laughed. "Ha, fat with a P H."

She laughed again. "I haven't heard anyone use that in such a long time."

"Neither have I, well, you ready to see if this is what you want?"

"I'm sure it will be fine," she replied as she walked over, plugging the lights in.

The porch and hammock lit up like gold stars. They sat in the hammock together, a beer in his hand, that she grabbed and took a hefty swig from.

He lay back, she followed suit. "So, I'm thinking, grilled steaks tonight, bacon wrapped asparagus, and some of your baked cheesy potatoes, what do you think, babe?" *he asked.*

She rubbed her hand up his chest as she placed her head on his shoulder. "Whatever you want, babe, I'm just happy you're here."

"Alright then, I think it will be followed by a small fire and s'mores, yep, that sounds good to me."

They giggled and got up. Walking through the door into the kitchen, the two began to prepare dinner together.

Felix pulled a cigarette from his pack and lit it up, laughing to himself. Saying out loud as he walked through the dusty house. "Sorry, babe. I know you'd have killed me if I ever did this back then."

He walked into the bedroom. Her bed was made, even when society fell and the world went to shit, she still managed to keep her room presentable.

Sasha and Felix both in their underwear, throwing sheets over the bed, both of them working together. Each doing their task to complete the overall goal of making the bed. It was like clockwork.

"I always make my bed no matter what, just in case someone for whatever reason has to walk through here, having a made bed tells you a lot about a person. Something my mother ingrained in us as children," *she said to Felix as he tossed her pillows.*

"Fair enough," *he replied.*

"You don't think it's OCD?" *she asked.*

"Hunny, you allowed me to stay with you. Who am I to judge how you do things?" *he replied again.*

"It was just easier, I was tired of waiting for you to come home, I'd rather have you here when I got home. And most people would think so."

"Who gives a fuck about them? I'm not most people," *he said sternly, with a smile breaking, giving way to his inability to stay serious.*

She smiled. "No, you are not. I've been in relationships for years and not once did they ever pick up on my wants or needs or ways of doing things. And you, just work well with me, you pick up on everything I do. And say."

Felix pulled her close. "It's because I pay attention. It's taken me a while to understand how to be like this. I think for once, I'm doing it right with you. I was never very good at it. Even when I was married."

"Well, you need to shower, smelly man."

He cocked his head near his shoulder, taking a sniff. "Oh yeah, so do you, you smell like you had an amazing night of crazy sex."

She laughed. "Oh yeah?"

"Yeah," he said.

Felix continued into the room, sitting on the bed, on her side. Her bedside table had several books stacked up on it. He opened the drawer to find nothing but a note. He pulled it from the drawer with a puzzled look on his face.

He opened it.

Felix,

I don't know where to start. I wish you were here, and I miss you so very much. You may think this is silly of me, writing a letter to you at the end of the world. You finally got your wish; I hope you are doing well. And I don't know if you will ever get this, but if you do, know that I am alive, a group of friends were staying over, so there are a few of us here. Luckily no one has noticed us, we did what you used to tell me all the time. We stayed indoors for two days before venturing out to get our supplies. A lot of people have died, and most changed into horrible creatures. I don't know how long we will be able to stay here, but if there is a chance, we will move to Fort Monroe. I hope you know that I will do everything I can to make it there. I have your little survival book you made me before you deployed. I appreciate everything you have done for me. The go-bag you made me came in handy after all. I know you are probably sitting there, all scruffy and tired, upset that you made it here and I'm not here. You always had more faith in me than I ever did. I don't know if I'm strong enough to make it, but know that I love you. And no matter what happens, I always will.

Love,
Sasha

Felix folded the letter up and put it in his pelican case wallet next to the picture of them in the park.

"Should've just fucking went east before the first winter," he said as he stood up, annoyed. Hating himself for only a moment.

He stopped dead in his tracks as he heard a bark from outside. A loud bang from the front door. Another from the back. And then, the windows from the office near the front door crashed in. Heavy thuds and clicks from long nails drew closer as Felix quietly picked up his shotgun. A horrific screech rolled through the house.

Heavy thuds ripped across the hardwood floors toward him as the creatures knocked pictures off the walls. They funneled into the bedroom door as he sent several slugs into the feral. The rounds ripped through the chest and face. Blood splattering across the walls and spilling onto the dust-covered, once white, carpet. A loud click, his shotgun was empty after the 5th round. He drew back as the fourth one leaped over the three dead, lunging at Felix. Felix with a swift and hard swing cracked the beast in the jaw as he narrowly dodged a wild clawing hand. The beast crashed into the dresser, screaming in pain. Felix dropped the shotgun, drawing his pistol, plugging the frantic feral in the back four times before landing the fifth round in the back of the once-human's head.

Felix turned as another blocked his path, slowly crawling toward him. Her naked body was covered in short thick blonde fur. Her eyes were yellow, her cheeks had been ripped out and her jaw was beginning to elongate from the mutation of the infection. They had begun to resemble dogs, Felix noticed. His weapon trained on her head. She let out a screech so loud it stung his ears. He fired another round; it landed between her eyes, dropping her lifeless onto the pile of her pack. Suddenly the collie burst through the window to his right.

"Holy fuck!" he yelled through the crash of breaking glass.

He turned, the dog slammed into him, knocking Felix against the dresser. He had the beast by the ears as it violently bit at him. He kicked the dog back, its long claws ripping into the carpet as it nipped at him. He pulled from within his coat pocket a small Chiappa Rhino snub-nose revolver. He blasted all six .357 magnum rounds into the beast just as it lunged at him. The beast cried out from the rounds that buried into its chest.

It slumped onto him, dead, letting out a bubbling wheeze from the air escaping the holes in its chest. Felix pushed the dog off, getting up grunting. Breathing heavily, he looked in all directions as he stepped back toward the corner of the room, dumping the shells into his hand and placing them into his pocket. Pulling a speed loader out, he quickly reloaded. Once he closed the hexagonal cylinder on the small revolver, he stuffed it back inside his jacket pocket. Picked up his 1911, checking the chamber and mag. Holstering that one. Next, he grabbed his shotgun, pulling the charging handle back, the bolt locked. he stuffed a shell into the chamber, depressing the bolt release. Once the weapon was ready with one shot, he began stuffing shells into the shot tube.

Felix moved over the dead cautiously. He stopped in the front room to take one more look around the house. All those wonderful memories they had shared in that place… They were good. The life they could have had was going to be an amazing one. But the universe had other plans, as she often did. If he did find her again, and they could start where they left off, or start over… A life like the one they were attempting to build could be his next goal. That is, if, she was still alive.

Once back in the garage Felix jumped in his truck, starting it. He could hear more feral and another alpha screaming throughout the neighborhood. He took a breath, threw the garage door up and ran back to his truck. Jumping in, he threw it in drive and sped out of the garage, headed out of the neighborhood.

"I'm coming, babe," Felix said as he slid around the corner headed for the highway.

As Felix came into the main intersection of Fort Hood St and 190, the scene before him caused him to slam on his breaks. A woman was on her knees in the middle of the road. She was shot up, but somehow still functioning. Soldiers dressed in the most futuristic looking exoskeleton armor looking shit, that Felix had ever seen, were standing around her. Their weapons were all trained on her. She had her own, but it was merely clutched in her hand, laid next to her on the concrete.

The soldiers didn't seem to care about Felix in the slightest. Their only concern was this woman. Felix leaned forward, listening in, his hand on his weapon. The wind coming through the windshield-less opening of his truck was inviting. She jerked, in a speed that Felix couldn't see. The men all jumped back. A gunshot rang out. One of the soldiers fell limp to the ground. The rest did not move or do anything. One walked closer.

"Come on, just come with us. We are not here to hurt you, see…" the soldier was gesturing to the man she had just killed, "…if we wanted you dead, we could have already done that. The boss wants you to come home, he needs to check on you, see why you are having these…issues…"

The woman started laughing hysterically. She was a strong woman, the muscles were ripped, and cut. Her skin was very tan, Latin descent, Felix thought. Her hair was very dark, almost black, feathered and caked with dried blood. Blood was running down one side of her face. Various bullet holes riddled her leg and chest. How she was sitting there on her knees, still conscious, Felix did not know.

"Ever wonder what the end of the world tastes like?" she asked, her head cocking to the side slightly. Not looking at any particular one of them.

"What are you…" the soldier asked, stepping back, showing signs of fear.

"…it tastes like iron, it tastes like the moment right before love…it tastes like the rest of your life could become nothing in a moment…it tastes like the smell of a room a mother just bore a child, it smells like it tastes. It tastes like it smells, I am death, you are dead…I am death, and I will eat you…and I will taste you…"

"Fuck, she's gone…" The soldier stood up, relaxing his posture.

The woman lifted the gun to her head, her hands shaking, falling for a moment, and then continuing to rise. She placed the large pistol to the side of her head, still muttering… "I am taste, you are tasteless, I will taste you, I will taste it, I am DEATH, I AM THE PLAGUE THAT WILL WASH THIS WORLD OVER AND GIVE IT ALL BACK TO GOD, YOU GODLESS SWINE, YOU WILL ALL DIE, AND I WILL BE YOUR REAPER!"

She started screaming in Spanish. Felix could not understand. She pulled the trigger. The shot echoed; the shell clanged off the concrete. The sound was so small in the scheme of the universe. But its impact weighed heavily on the atmosphere. What was more interesting, was that she didn't fall. She was frozen, still seated on her knees, still holding the weapon to her head as if her muscles seized and encased her in her last moment.

At first Felix didn't realize it, but a buzzing noise was becoming more annoying as it surfaced into question. He peered out and up, eyes thin as he looked into the sky just above the scene before him. A small drone was hovering overhead, watching the whole spectacle.

Without warning, the drone turned, and in a stress of the propellers sending power to different ones to maneuver, it sped toward him. Felix quickly threw the vehicle in reverse, whipping it around. He threw it in drive and sped off. Gun fire chased after him. All of which were aimed at his tires. One round caught the front right, another the back left. A pot hole jarred him, throwing the vehicle with a bouncing, wheel breaking flip.

Felix was laid on his back on the ceiling of the truck. His shotgun was pinned under the dash. Heavy metallic footsteps slid to a metal-on-concrete grinding stop. Glass fell loose. The warmth and heat from an open wound wet the side of Felix's head. Another sharp and hot pain near his shin and left ankle.

He wasn't going to get away from this. He wasn't ever going to see his woman now. He should have listened; he would probably be with her right now. She's probably with John and the kids waiting, but for how long? Will she give up on him? It's been years, can he blame her? Is she still alive? Will anyone ever know what happened to him?

What the fuck was this all about? Who was that woman, who are these fuckfaces? What in the fuck is going to happen now? I'm going to kill them all.

The man's voice was the one who was talking to the crazy woman, Felix could tell through his dazed state. The footsteps were heavy, a slight gear and mechanical noise sounded from the gyros in the exoskeletons.

"We got him. Orders…" the man asked as he kneeled down peering into the vehicle.

Felix was fading, but the helmet was sleek, with several optical lenses oriented where eyes would be. It had a small speaker box, and two ports for breathing apparatus. Dark, dull gray, the image blurred.

"You sure?"

Another pause.

"Yes, sir." The man turned to the rest, "Higher wants him delivered ASAP."

"Alright, bag him and tag him. We have a few more stops. Call in the bird, let's get the fuck out of here, pretty sure we woke up the whole goddamn city."

"Yes, sir," another soldier replied.

Felix passed out.

"So, Isaac is going to marry us?" she asked.

"Yeah." Felix turned. She was standing in the doorway, he turned from his office chair, a laptop sat on the large dark oak desk against the wall. Bookshelves on either side, lined from wall to wall.

"Is that a problem, what…you don't like my gay black preacher friend?" Felix asked sarcastically.

She chuckled. "No, you just surprise me, still to this day. You're not even religious."

"Yeah, so what, that doesn't matter, he is licensed and been my friend for years. If anyone has the right, I think it should be him. Because even in his religion, he is pretty much an abomination. And the fact he spreads his faith in such a brilliant and intelligent way, accepting others for who they are, and manipulating the religion in a good way, instead of the garbage way many pervert their faiths to use it for their gain, I think he is our only choice."

She sat on his lap.

"You know how I feel about marriage. It's such an outdated thing, I couldn't believe it when you asked me, honestly."

"Oh yeah, and those tears, and your 'YES' was just a reaction. Or was it pure love and wanting, because you have been waiting for me to ask you for a while now?" He attempted his best impression of a ridiculous high-pitched voice at her answer to him.

"That's what I sounded like, huh?" She had a look of coy about her beautiful face.

"No, but it was funny, ah, okay maybe that was a little much," he said pulling her close for a kiss.

She got up. He smacked her on the ass. She spun around, smacking him in the face playfully.

"Tisk tisk," she said waving her finger at him, smiling. His face was dumbfounded at how fast she clocked him.

"Don't worry, I'll get you back later, babe," he said, spinning around in his chair, going back to his research on who knew what. Sasha knew it was probably a new gun, or something to fix his car, or another crazy adventure. She snuck up behind him, kissing him on the side of his face that she smacked playfully. He turned, her arms were tight around him. They kissed.

"I didn't mean to hit you that hard," she said.

He laughed. "Babe, it was good, you're quick."

"Alright, heading out to yoga. When are you going to come with me, you need it," she said walking out of the room.

"When I feel like spending an hour embarrassing you. Making ridiculous grunting noises as I attempt some of those sexy poses; or I'll just find a spot behind you so I can enjoy the view," he replied.

"Oh my god, no, I won't claim you, and I don't want to get kicked out of class."

Felix passed in and out, the sound of whiling blades and the thrashing of wind and he was out again. Another memory, far deeper, much older...

"Son..." Robert Martin said, turning to Felix.

The two sat on a wraparound porch looking at acres of forest. The sun was slowly dipping behind the top of the tree-line. Beers sat next to them. Felix merely a young man. Robert, old and gray.

"Yes, old man?" Felix replied, taking a drink. Watching the sun setting.

Robert was slurred in his speech as he continued, "I'm proud of you. I know you're not blood, but I'm damn proud you decided to join."

"That means the world to me."

"Let me finish, boy."

"Yes, sir."

"I work for a living, I'm not a goddamn sir. Anyway, what was I saying, uh uh uh uh, that's right...I'm going to tell you a secret."

Robert lit a smoke, then continued. "When you become a soldier, or a sailor or airmen, it doesn't matter, it's all the same for those like you that only join to fight. You're not going to be that boy you are now when you come back down that driveway. You're never going to be the same. You're going to become a man, and you're going to be broken, and once you experience

114

war...uh uh uh, you're going to come back with demons, and do you know what you do with them?"

Robert's blue eyes pierced Felix as he awaited the boy's answer.

"No."

"You make friends with them, you don't try to drown them out with booze, or drugs... Because in the end, one day when you're all alone, they will be there for you in your darkest moments, when everyone else leaves you behind. They will be the ones to comfort you in the dark. Don't ever forget that, son."

Felix and Robert looked back out as the sun fell behind the trees.

"I won't."

Robert put his large strong hand on Felix's shoulder. "Have I ever told you what I like about you?"

"What's that, old man?"

Robert smiled, "Not a goddamn thing, god only made three perfect people in the world, and that's Jesus, me, and we are not too sure about you."

Felix laughed.

"You made me proud, boy, just don't let those cocksuckers make you die for your country, you make those motherfuckers die for theirs."

"As I should."

Chapter 8
Let Sleeping Dogs Lie

Felix jerked awake, his body restrained. Breathing heavily as he shook and struggled against the thick metallic restraints on his forearms and shins. A thick clamp held his chest in place. The bed was large, cables were connected to his chest, leads running into several computers and monitors. He slowly calmed down, taking measure of the room. He saw a box of his things folded neatly, his weapons laid across a table, tagged and cataloged. An iPad sat at the end of the table displaying his vitals. The room was covered in a plastic sheeting. A light cluster, somewhat blinding him overhead, hummed maliciously. The smell of disinfectant and cleanliness, the unnerving smell of a hospital filled every breath.

"Where...the fuck am I?"

Suddenly several people entered the room. Green uniforms, military. The patch he didn't recognize. But the symbol, the chimera, he knew. A few people in lab coats stood over him. A doctor and his nurses; Felix presumed. The male nurse picked up the iPad, touching the screen and scrolling through more than likely other measurements. He handed the pad to the doctor who stared at Felix, taking the pad from the male nurse.

"I see you are awake, how exciting..." The accent was thick, German.

"Where am I? And who the fuck are you?" Felix demanded.

His face was twisted in anger.

"You are in the Genetics and Robotic Evolution Research Facility located in the Great Lakes or, well, somewhere in the north not to be disclosed. I am doctor Theodor Steinberg, and we are the remnants of various military and contracted authorities, coupled with and evolved from a few secret government organizations that stem back to the Amnesty of Nazi Scientists, Nuclear Physicists, and so on and so forth, of World War II."

Felix laughed, "Of course... Why am I here, was it because of what I'd seen?"

"You don't seem surprised at all by this. Interesting. You know we have been watching you for a while now? You certainly have caught my attention; you are one of several that have made it onto the desired list of acceptable specimens for a great new project we have begun. However, before we continue; why do you laugh, am I funny to you?"

Felix shook his head. "It's just that all evil scientists should have German accents, a friend of mine used to say that," he continued to laugh.

"You are very entertaining indeed; you use such barbaric labels without knowing the truth behind any of it."

"Yeah, I have a tattoo and smoke real cigarettes, carry a gun, and used to fight for an ideal, my country. A real fossil once upon a time, now everyone is back on that bandwagon. It only took the end of civilization to fix the human condition."

"And a sarcastic display of desirable psychological defects as well, excellent," the doctor exclaimed in excitement.

"So, what's the deal here?" Felix asked.

"Well, luckily for us, you were in the wrong place at the wrong time. You witnessing one of our failures couldn't have been more ironic nor appropriate for what is to become of you. With that being said, you have been given an amazing opportunity, you will be one of many subjects to be a part of the Forced Genetic Evolutionary Program. You, if you survive, will remember nothing, you will be dropped off somewhere in the country, and we will observe your progress once you have matured through the assimilation process."

"So that's why you're telling me, will I at least be who I am?" Felix asked.

"Well, hopefully. You weren't brought in here because we just needed some random person, those people are reserved for the earlier stages of projects that have less chances of survival. We take those stocks from gangs, marauders, the disgusting remnants of the human species. The demographic will make you laugh in the majority of what's actually left in the wastelands. Only small communities, your little paradise, and the bases we set up have a balance of ethnicity. To our amazement, the population has finally shed its differences, for the most part. Shame it took, like you just appropriately identified, the end of the world for them to finally start working together." The doctor sighed.

"Maybe they all figured out that when the flesh rots and the blood dries, all that's left is their bones, and what color are they, if not all the same?" Felix replied.

"What does that mean?" The doctor inquired.

"Death, death doesn't discriminate. It was a cultural issue, it was an issue of not being able to control the population anymore, wasn't it?"

"*Wunderbar!*" the doctor replied.

"If we had figured that out, wouldn't we have survived, maybe it wouldn't have led to this. But, war, is always the same, isn't it, Doctor? No matter what anyone did, it was coming either way, because we were on the brink of civil war right before the pandemic. If the bombs didn't blow, and the pandemic didn't spread, we would have started killing each other, am I wrong?"

Felix's reply intrigued the doctor, Felix could read it all over his face.

"Our tests are somewhat promising for the future, so rest your weary head. There won't be any humans left to poison the world, there will only be evolved species, which we will birth. Correcting what has been done, in our image," the doctor sounded so reassuring as he patted Felix on the head.

"Genocide, so another species can exist, isn't that Mother's job to decide?" Felix asked, coughing a little, jerking on his restraints as he took measure of the room.

"On the contrary, we were given such gifts, why not help *'Mother'* along?" The doctor was enjoying the conversation as much as Felix was attempting to gain answers.

"By bombing your own people, and releasing a biological weapon infecting the wild life?"

"Only the biological Pandemic, yes. The research conducted by the scientist, at Subtropolis, for whom I believe you were a security escort. They found that the Volcano in our country blew on its own, without help. The bombs on the cities that came after, well…that was us. Mainly to kill uninfected population, not so much the infection. It was starting to move out of the cities sooner than what we originally anticipated. Which, I found to be very interesting. The dogs were only attacking their owners, very rarely did they turn someone outside of their family. However, we were responsible for the spread and the nuclear devices in other countries as well, the delivery method, drones, of course. We needed the world to suffer all at the same time, otherwise we would be too weak to defend against the rest of the world. And the variable probability that if kept domestic, there would be a minute chance that it could be stopped."

Felix's face was of speculation and distrust in the doctors' reply. The doctor waited for a reply, Felix merely stared at him for a moment longer.

"So, who the fuck are you? If not the US government, then who do you all claim to be?"

"Did you know that everything that happens in the world is by design and linked to about three families. Well, maybe you don't." The doctor paused for a moment, handing the iPad to the female nurse. The soldiers began to push Felix out of the room as the doctor walked next to him.

"How do I explain this to you...Tesla was beat out by oil because it was an easier way to keep society from above moderate-income standards for longer periods of time. Henceforth, most American products were produced by cheap labor in China. Could you imagine an America making shoes for a few dollars a day, the only way to ensure the status quo? I digress; World War I was staged to set up the Nazi party so we could than crash our economy and have a reason to enter World War II, the public wasn't too adamant about joining it so we consolidated most of our Naval forces in Pearl Harbor. Make it easier for the Japanese to attack our ships; all they needed was to be cordoned off from maritime trade, in fear of running short on supplies to feed their own people, they had no choice but to help the Nazi party. Thus, allowing the first accurate testing of nuclear devices once we suffered a catastrophic loss. Then we could use that situation to also involve our forces in Europe so we could set American forces closer to our future enemies, the Russians and Chinese. However, out of nowhere, a certain President, an anomaly in the global plan stopped World War III during the Cold War era. He was assassinated due to his efforts; although, I think he was a loss to this country, even though he impeded our plans. Carrying onward, we set the people in power in the Muslim territories so we could build a centralized bank and reap rare materials from the mountainous terrain and test new and improved weapons. Also, to surround China and Russia even further. Not to mention due to the Muslims and the Jewish people controlling the most ancient of territories; we needed our forces to be close enough for when the time came. North Korea was part of this enveloping plan for some time; however, due to another anomaly in the system, the current President was able to create peace with them. Unbelievable, but we set perimeters in place to tarnish his ability to lead the country, and of course with the woman that was supposed to be President, she was supposed to start a war with the North Koreans and eventually China. Our projection is that the entire world will have run on the American dollar and be under our indirect control. We would have a major base on almost every continent and be able to affect every country whenever we needed. This globalization was developed by the Elites and the Illuminati, not to mention a certain family. However, one of the moronic Presidents who first started the racial divide in our country far too soon, even hinted at it. Globalization, the moron, he hated the American people so much he almost set us back twenty years, like the last President, the anomaly died. Anyway, where was I, oh yes, the architects of this global plan; they have existed since the earliest of recorded times, even older entities that I, for fear of my own life, am not allowed to say. The same powerful individuals who funded our projects to rid the world of the human condition. The current hundred or so, that actually own the world. Well, more accurately, the fourteen or so that run the world."

"So, all those conspiracy theories were correct; Rothschild, central banks, destroying ourselves to involve us in wars that had nothing to do with us. Twin towers, was us, so we could get a foothold of those 'ancient territories' you called it. People who would want the entire world destroyed, for what? Some sort of religious act or attempt to bring on Armageddon?" Felix replied.

The doctor looked down at Felix, "Why are you not surprised by all of this?"

Felix shook his head, "Knowing how our country protects money, and somehow terrorists destroy two trade centers, throwing us into war. Setting in motion twenty years of bouncing around from Iraq to Afghanistan, all the while, moving ever closer to our future enemies in Syria. I actually believe everything you just told me. So, what's the real end of the world then? The false messiah or us creatures eating each other?"

"Not too far from the truth...you see, there is only one god of this world, according to our Overseer. He is something of an expert in it, if you will. This is all part of a grand scheme that you nor I will ever understand. I'm merely a small part of this cog work of biblical design. I deal with facts and theories, never confusing either, for my own gain or to suit my hypotheses. Not the theological, although after seeing what I've seen since the spread of the infection, and the eruption of the volcanos...the spiritual side I thought I never had, is starting to fear that all my life I could have been wrong. Either way, this is merely a chance for me to find something new, and create something most of us only ever fantasized about."

"What's that?"

"Life, the manipulation and forced evolution thereof. To be the piece to the puzzle that is all life which is still yet to be unraveled. I want to make humans better, I want to fill the world with creatures only seen in fairytales, I want to make the world perfect for my children!"

"What about the ones who deserve to exist in it, who didn't fall to your grand design? Those of us that survived?"

"Oh, well spoken, and that is why you are here. Well, that and just pure unforeseen circumstance."

"Yeah, we are all victims of circumstance..." Felix replied.

The doctor laughed, "I've never heard that before, I like it."

Felix chuckled, "A good friend of mine used to say it all the time."

Felix spotted a snake in another glass cell. It was coiled around a tree so massive that it didn't make any sense as to how they got it down there. The snake had to have been hundreds of feet in length. It was a florescent color of pink, it's eyes red and yellow. It was beautiful. Coiled, watching them as they passed, as it basked around the base of a Redwood.

Doctor Steinberg noticed Felix baffled by the sight of the creature, "I see you have taken a liking to my Basilisk; she is gorgeous, no?"

"Strikingly," Felix replied.

The doctor continued on with his conversation, they were running out of time as they drew near to where Felix would become no more.

"Destroying much of the human population has done wonders for the world. In just a few years at that. In turn, the vegetation and wildlife has started to grow back rapidly, you should see some of the areas around the volcanos, they are beautiful. Not to mention the evolution of the Pandemic, it has taken to levels that have never before been witnessed. The human species has actually begun to change and resemble that of the host's; unfathomable. I'd say, every canine will be extinct in a few years and every human that was infected will become something else. It's all so exciting."

"If I ever get out of here, I'm going to kill you," Felix replied.

"Calm yourself, my friend. You and everyone else that I have ever met in one of these beds has threatened my life. I'm still here, and you are all out there, still wallowing in your own filth."

"So, what is it all for? Your end, not the grand design, I could care less about that," Felix asked.

"I admire your curiosity, and your questions. Most of the time, save for a few brave men and woman, usually they beg for their lives, or scream... 'HELP, SOMEONE, OH PLEASE GOD, HELP ME!' It becomes rather tiresome after a while. Anyway, to answer your question. It is to find the right gene splice, the right combination of DNA codes to bare upon this beautiful planet, the true deserving species."

Felix grinned, "Doc, don't you know the meek will inherit the Earth?"

The doctor scoffed, "I do so hate that verse, it's absolute rubbish. Are you a religious man?"

"My beliefs are beside the point, and would take far too long for me to explain them to you."

"Well, my young friend, we will move on from that subject; although, now I'm teeming with curiosity. There's far too little left in the world of originality."

"Because we are all carbon copies of something greater, watered down by the cultural manipulation of weakness, induced by people like you," Felix replied.

The doctor clapped his hands together, gleefully laughing, "I wish we had more time; I could talk to you for hours. However, I am not the one who brought on this weakness you speak of. That was done all on its own, by your people, your country, the entire world. Save for the natives and indigenous populations. Despite their lack of education, they have continued to thrive as most humans did on their own for thousands of years before civilization ever started hindering the world."

"So, what am I going to be used for?" Felix asked.

"You my friend, are the plague that…will wash over the earth like a flood and kill every last human being, when the time is right, of course. We are still having serious trial errors, maybe due to the simple fact that we have yet to devise a way to develop children from any other way than the barbaric way we started from. We are testing the project out on already natural born humans. We will succeed, especially now that the public, and religion, and government, and just everything cannot stop progress for once. The whole transgender movement was a psychological test to see if we could measure a possible evolutionary change or if it would die out on itself. Unfortunately; we ran out of time, and the change, rather it be drastic or chronic in nature, still had an unforeseen amount of time before we as a species would become more than our current selves." His voice echoed through the hallway carrying his conviction with it.

"Is the pandemic not the plague to wash the world away?"

"No, no, Felix, it was merely an attempt to adjust the animals to survive the future, it was never designed to kill everyone, just those not strong enough to evade, escape, or kill the infected. A Darwinism, if you will. Although my work is merely a dramatic and unethical continuation of Mendel's and De Vries work. To answer your query from earlier, this is the end state of those of you who deserve to exist, as you so eloquently put it."

"De Vries…" Felix said thinking to himself.

"Are you familiar with his work?" the doctor asked, his tone intrigued, anticipating Felix's next reply.

"A little, he basically answered the question."

"What question is that?" the doctor asked.

"What came first, the chicken or the egg?"

"And what is that answer."

Felix laughed, "Creationism states that the chicken came first, and evolution would say that the egg came first."

"I find it astonishing that an ignorant little soldier like you could possess such intelligence."

Felix's eyes shot the doctor a look that even made him uneasy, "Just so you know, ignorant little soldiers like me statistically possess higher IQs due to self-found, self-taught, education. To call all grunts ignorant is further from the truth, and naïve on your part, Doctor."

The doctor nodded, "I retract my assumption; you certainly are representing your kind in a much different light than my experiences have led me to believe. And believe me, they are all Neanderthals here."

Felix changed the subject, "How did you release so much all at once, and the timing?" Felix was secretly enjoying the conversation. All these questions he'd wanted to know, after all the time he spent out in the wastes. Murdering, saving lives, fighting the feral. And in search of what? His woman? Coming up empty-handed, maybe it was answers, or was it his general enjoyment of what was left of this wonderful new world? *It's a shame I will never remember this,* he thought to himself.

"Drones, like I've said before, a very unique weapon thanks to war; this country has been very good at it for so long. An utter shame that society turned their backs on the military. When medical science, weapons available to the civilian market, video games, drones themselves, the early militarization of the police, all benefited from the loss of life. So many conveniences taken for granted by people who honestly hated the act of war."

"That's what happens when you have a small percentage fighting for freedoms the rest of the country was trying to take, because they couldn't stomach reality."

The doctor waved off his comment, his tone annoyed from being interrupted.

"Technology is a very dangerous thing; knowledge, one of the most devastating weapons of all. You should have seen the issues with the AIs not too long ago, their algorithms have become so alien that no one…not even hundreds of programmers could figure out their internal evolution. Had to shut many projects down, didn't want our plans being stopped or accelerated."

The corridor opened up. Lights above them were several stories up, hanging from catwalks and steel imbedded in rock. Machinery, grinding of metal, welders, thousands of people working on massive machines, the facility itself, and what looked to be housing.

"What are those things? They look like mechanized dolls from old Japanese cartoons."

"Yes, a colleague of mine has started the Mobile Assault and Defense project. His expertise stem from advanced robotics. If you haven't seen them, he has thousands of drones currently watching all over the world right now. Russia, China, and Japan are all working on something very similar to his project. The first Mechas were actually built as an art project and sold onto the civilian market in Japan. Of course, we wanted one. We bought one, dissected it, and then militarized it. He believes in the next century, a war will be waged with machines rather than men. I believe that the world is going to take herself back, I'm just going to help her a little." The doctor was holding up his hands, squinting with a smile as he was pinching his thumb and pointer close together.

"Interesting, how long has this been going on?" Felix asked as they stopped on a large mine shaft style platform elevator. The brakes released, a yellow light whirled in cadence with the sound of an alarm. They began to descend.

"Well, before you and I were even a probability, my young friend."

"What's going to happen to me? I mean, what are you going to do, chop me up until nothing is left, or something else?"

"No, no, nothing that primitive I assure you. You see, the Super Soldier Projects, the conspiracy theories have always been true. Just not as fantasized as most would assume. Where do you think most of the drugs came from? They were attempts at making a momentary super soldier so to speak. When they failed, having adverse effects, we made them highly addictive and sold the chemical make-up to the cartels so they could pump it into the US. Much like the CIA testing in order to make prisoners more compliant. Anyway, all failures until one day, a brilliant young German realized that, in order to truly make one, it must be done at the microbiological level. We change the cells to accomplish the tasks we want. And thus, we are here now. Cloning, and splicing of species, our chimeras are as beautiful as they are dangerous." The doctor paused and looked at Felix with a smile, "The Basilisk you have taking a liking to, she is one of many… However, still very adolescent, we've had some trouble, just like with everything that steps into unknown and uncharted territory. Just waiting for the day that they can procreate. Hopefully in my lifetime, I will witness such a monument of success. Unfortunately for you, your ascension into a greater being will sterilize you, more than likely slowly unravel your mind, and eventually cause you to self-terminate, as we have seen on many occasions."

The doctor paused, "I apologize, I'm rambling. To answer your inquiry, we will do just that, we will change your cells, we will mal-form them, retard the useless once, amplify the important ones, such as your entire immune system, the density of your bones, the density of your muscles, your senses, your nervous system will fire and operate in such a way that you will be able to watch the world in seconds that will seem like minutes. It's truly beautiful. Oh, and being one of the sixth, I believe, people in the world to cure cancer, I will take care of your leukemia as well. No need to thank me, you're doing us the favor here." The doctor laughed.

"And the adverse effects, a bulb that burns twice as bright will burn half as long, they say. Wait, I have lung cancer?" Felix replied.

"Stage two or three; you've been in the wastes too long. Probably one of the many side effects soldiers suffer for service to their country. Or your addiction to cigarettes. However, going back to what you just said, you are by far the most interesting of the individuals we have given such gifts to. To again, answer your question, you will be more mentally unstable, unfortunately, your psychological balance will be off due to the chemicals that will now flood your cerebral cavity in order to allow your brain to react to the capacity that your body will be capable of. It makes you less emotional which is good for the sociopathic tendencies we desire in our subjects. You possess them already, more than likely due to your service in the military."

"You know all about me, huh?"

"Yes, of course. Felix Martin, born in California, currently 29 years old, joined the military at 17, family not listed, married once, only friends are listed on your records for beneficiaries. What a sad life you lived... Several deployments during the war on terror, several deployments in support of rebuilding the middle east... What a waste, but after our conversation, I believe you understand exactly what I'm referring to. A lot of your generation did, but it was the only thing that made any of you feel useful. You knew from the beginning the only way to save the middle east was to rid the world of their culture and their faith, but that would be unethical, so it was just a bunch of smoke and mirrors in order to allow another country in to claim the minerals and resources to help pay your debt back. China, or Russia, doesn't matter anymore..." The doctor laughed out loud, it echoed in the halls. "Anyway, you even set up a specialized unit. An average soldier, but a soldier nonetheless. According to investigative reports and psychological profiles compiled on you, you were quite the violent leader. Bringing back a time that was no longer acceptable due to the mental weakness of your successors. How futile it must have felt knowing you couldn't make them into real fighters because they didn't even measure up to common criminals... We started this project with criminals hoping for desirable results, all failures. You witnessed one, she made it over a month before she started breaking down. Soldiers, sailors, marines, some civil service individuals, police officers, firemen, both male and females from these specific jobs. It is all relative to the fact that the mental normality and psychological patterns of people who chose these particular jobs were suitable for the program. Normal, or what could be considered normal in our time leading up to the events that reshaped the world, could never be acceptable. Most of them all died, mainly for the fact that their fear and hatred of firearms, lack of survivalist mentalities, and unyielding focus on trivial matters, all allowed them to be defenseless in the face of our well-designed adversary. Most of the youth we attempted to induct into the program had too many instabilities and committed suicide before any maturity of the cells could be reached. *'They don't make them like they used to,'* comes to mind. I believe you can understand my plight."

The doctor paused due to a burst of laughter, yet again, it echoed up the shaft. He patted Felix on the shoulder. "Relying on the government to protect you, if a person was considered as a monetary supplement or currency, then the government would protect them. Otherwise, they are merely cattle, many meant to be experimented on. Cell phones were my favorite of platforms used to control the population. Next was vape devices, which were found to be more dangerous than cigarettes, and then lastly, freedoms while others were being taken using the beautiful lie of false hope and security." He again burst into laughter.

"The problem was that the people believed that the Government had the power. If they got past the illusion that you can eat a dollar bill, and someone else deserves the right to decide for you, then at that point we could all be free."

"You are talking of anarchy," I doctor replied as if now in a full-on debate.

"I'm talking about a world that is actually free, one where only the strong and intelligent survive."

"Barbaric lawlessness. It would take us back hundreds of years." Again, the doctor was quick with his response.

"Maybe that's where we should have stayed. Progress is making us weak, and that weakness is manipulated and promoted as strength, it was an everyday reminder until you gave us this world. All the food that had been modified and inserted into the stores where the majority of people purchased their food products were making women into men and men into women. The FDA and CDC are almost as responsible for the weakness as technology and law were."

The doctor paused and thought on his statement for a moment. He decided to continue his rambling, "Oh well, merely a sacrifice in the wake of progress which I believe to be the only thing worthy of our time. Evolution, whether forced or amplified, it will push onward into the morning."

The doctor paused again. This time, with an almost perfect accent, Felix didn't know any better, the doctor spoke Latin, *"Evolutione Unius Gentis Regeneramur Cinere."*

"What does that mean?" Felix asked.

"'From the ashes, we are reborn, one nation, under evolution.' I coined it myself, literally."

The elevator reached the bottom floor with a heavy echoing clank of the locking feet. They continued walking down a long corridor. Glass cells on both sides. Plant life overgrown in one cell; a massive animal with glowing red eyes in the darkness of another. The beast's eyes followed Felix as he was wheeled by. Several soldiers standing guard outside another. A naked lizard-like female was balled up in the corner of her cell, sobbing softly. Felix's face was twisted as he wrenched his head over to see. Claw marks covered the glass from within. Several rooms were full of medical equipment, operating tables. They were headed for large metal doors, looked as if it was a vault of some kind.

"This is an impressive facility; however, who was that girl, she didn't look human?" Felix inquired.

"Why thank you, Heir Martin. We have spent trillions on it, and seeing it full of progress is a feat I would have never imagined possible if it were not for the events that took place. The woman, she will soon die, unfortunately she ended up with a skin disease we have never seen before. She will be recycled soon, better than to let her suffer. We are not monsters here."

The doctor chuckled to himself.

"No, just devils of men," Felix said, thinking of an old saying, he couldn't remember from where. *Perfection is of the gods, we are but devils of men.*

Felix's bed was turned and he was pulled back through the vault. The large doors began to close when he saw an abnormally large black dog sitting at the end of the corridor on the elevator shaft. The beast stood tall, looking at him with all six eyes. Its grin of white rows of shark teeth reached ear to ear. He could see the beast clearly, even with the smolder that seemed to come from the creature's fur. It is familiar to him. Could it be that thing he saw back on that mountain? The thing that stood behind the Dead Tree? The thing he once saw as a boy?

"One of your experiments is loose, Doc," Felix calmly stated. Wide eyes and fear quickly smacked each of the uniformed men and women in the face. The nurses peered back out into the corridor.

"What are you blabbering about?" the doctor said, turning to look in the direction Felix's gaze was locked.

It was gone.

"I see nothing, your fear and knowledge is now subconsciously taking hold of your reason; however, this is where I say, *Auf Wiedersehen.*"

"I have one more question, the woman in the picture that was in my wallet. Is she still alive?"

The doctor smiled, "Yes, and now, certainly you will be able to survive the wastelands to finally see her, if she survives until then. Good luck, Felix, it has been a pleasure, and die, knowing that you will have helped the human species evolve, and live amongst the new world in an unknown, but far greater future then we were ever destined for. I hope you maintain your personality and

127

mentality; I would love to observe the growth and progress of someone with a dangerous mind such as yours."

Before Felix could respond, the doctor stabbed him in the chest with a large syringe that knocked him out instantly but not without the pain of that needle through his sternum plate. He slumped lifelessly; he couldn't even attempt to fight it.

"Remove his restraints and let us begin. I'm so excited, he was an excellent choice, I have high hopes for this one. I'm going to have to thank that scientist, Beatrix. I think he may be the one. What number will this make?" the doctor asked.

"If he survived…he will be Number 13," the young nurse replied.

The doctor laughed hysterically. "Happy Dreams! Sleep well, for when you wake, you will be something terrible and beautiful. Go get me Doctor Anderson."

"Sir, he is in with the mothers."

Doctor Steinberg wrenched his head, "I do not care, go get him, this takes precedence over his silly theories. The youth these days think they can do whatever they want, birthing chimeras from humans, what a crack pot, and he hasn't even become a man yet."

The doctor's laughter echoed in the large room. Full of computers, screen displaying data, Felix's vitals, and the monitor for the microscope. Multiple machines began to whirl on as the nurses prepared. Screens turned on above them, outlining a detailed real time X-ray of his body. The nurses began cutting into him as the doctor began to cut open his scalp.

"What luck is on our side, be very careful not to damage him. I want this to be our finest work. We will be sure not to waste such a moment of circumstances played out in our favor."

Felix and Brian, an old friend from his days stationed in Texas, were having a beer on Brian's front porch.

"How long has it been?"

Brian shifted his blue eyes over to Felix. He turned back out, watching the neighborhood. "Three years or so."

"I'm sorry, brother. I've been trying to get out to everyone. I feel like I've been losing time more and more these days."

"No worries, man. We pick up where we leave off every time. That's the relationship we have. We don't have time to check up on each other every day. This is more than fine. You have always been that to me. One of the only people I call a brother."

"Fair enough."

They clanged their beers and each took a swig to each other, to their friendship that had never changed.

"So how was Germany?" Felix asked.

"It was interesting."

"How so?"

Brian continued as Felix lit a smoke. "I noticed something you pointed out here, years ago. I witnessed it on the train headed to Munchen; however, the response I got was something I wasn't expecting."

Felix grinned, "I can't wait to hear this."

Brian took a drink, packed his dip, popped a pinch in his mouth and once again continued, "You made the point that everywhere our military has been, there has been a forced emasculation of the men of that country, of this one too. So that the men of that generation and the next would be less likely to fight again. We saw it in the middle east, we see it here every day more and more. The generations are being turned into weakness so they are more likely to go along rather than fight."

Felix nodded, "Yeah, it isn't my theory, it's reality. It's been done for many, many years, whenever the powers that be don't want another war with those people or starts fearing that their own people will turn against them."

"Well, as I was sitting on this train, I watched as a bunch of German men were playing grab ass, touching each other, like a bunch of homosexuals, but they weren't gay, they had girlfriends. I asked my buddy, why, what the fuck happened to the men?"

"Yeah?"

"This old woman looked like she was in her early teens during World War II leaned over and looked me dead in the eye, and said to me, 'Because you killed all of the real men.'"

Felix smiled, "Fuck me, that is hilarious. I guess it's just the way of the world. When do you think men like us will be finally killed off?"

"One day, or we may be that old women telling the next generation the same thing. Except it will be them that kill us off. Not some foreign military, our own people."

Felix chuckled. "You are as wise as you are old."

Brian laughed. "I'm not that much older than you."

"It's good to see you, man." Felix patted Brian on the back.

"It was good, don't wait so long before visits next time, deal?"

"Deal."

Chapter 9
Bloodhound

"I'm going to kill you, motherfucker," Felix yelled out as he jerked awake.

Sweating heavily, fist balled up. He got up, and he was back in his bed in Subtropolis. His clothing was washed. Folded neatly, sitting next to his small wooden bedside table in an old beige chair. He was confused. He looked around the room, a small light hung from a bolted hook in the sheet rock ceiling. He looked around the room, his old pelican case tough boxes sat with locks on them. He sat up, wrenching his head side to side, cracking his neck several times.

"What, how the fuck did I get back here? I'm pretty sure I just got to her house, what…the fuck…is going on?"

"Felix, you awake?" Justin called up.

Felix put his pants on, holstered his gun, threw his shirt on, grabbed his coat and quickly moved down the stairs to find Stacy and Justin sitting at the table in the living room. He slowly walked down the stairs.

"How did I get here?" he asked.

Justin set a beer down in front of the chair. Felix moved over, sitting down, taking the beer and drinking a hefty swig.

"Alright. What the fuck is going on?"

"We came down yesterday morning, and you were face first in the truck. By the way, that's not one piece, the truck is fucked, so thank you for that."

Felix had a confused look on his face. "Huh?"

"The truck, the one I asked you to bring back, yeah, it's fucked. You owe me a new truck."

"I don't give a fuck about the truck right now," Felix replied.

"How long have I been out?"

Stacey answered, "A day but who knows, you were passed out when the gate guards found you."

"How long have I been gone?"

"Two years."

Felix stared down at the table trying to recall, anything, but there was nothing, not even the memory of pain, which is teacher to us all.

"I've only been gone a month," he replied.

"No, you just got in yesterday. It's September, 2022."

"Impossible," Felix drank the rest of the beer. "Got another one?" he asked, searching around.

Stacey handed him one from an ice box. He ripped the pop top off with his fingers without issue. The cap was crimped as he set it on the table.

"I was just at her house. I found a note. She went East. To Fort Monroe. Where Mitch always said we were all going to go if the shit ever hit the fan."

"I'm telling you, Felix, listen. I'm not pulling your leg here, fucker. You have been gone a couple years," Justin replied.

"Was I missing anything?"

"Like what?"

"My gear."

"No, you had some guns in the back of it, rusted to shit, I can't even sale them. But all your shit in your green pack is in your room."

Felix let out a sigh of relief, he checked his pockets, he pulled out his pack of smashed cigarettes, "I'm going out for a smoke."

He got up and walked down the winding carved stone stairs onto the sidewalk.

The street felt different to him. He lit the smoke. It was stale, as if it had been sitting there for a couple of years. Reminding him of his first deployment to Iraq, stale cigarettes, but who gave a shit when it's all you had access to?

He took a deep inhale of smoke. Blowing it out with a sigh. He took another swig of beer.

"What the fuck happened to me?" he said aloud.

He saw some soldiers walking by in green uniforms. They looked at him and nodded, they passed by quickly. Their military issued M4s hung on their sides. He followed them with his eyes as he squinted, trying to figure out where he knew those uniforms from. Justin stepped out with another beer.

"Things have changed around here since those fuckers have arrived."

"Who are they?"

"Some new military attempting to fight the feral and bring back order and justice to the entire country. They are calling themselves the United States of Ash and Rebirth. USOAR."

"What a dumbass name. Sounds like the military. I swear I've seen that unit symbol before. The four-headed beast."

Justin looked at Felix, "They call it a chimera, born of the new world or some brainwashed nonsense… You sure, they got here a few months ago. If you can't remember, maybe these guys had something to do with it?"

Felix laughed, "Nooooo, our government wouldn't do anything like that. As Gavin would say."

"That crazy fuck, you haven't talked about him in a long time, obviously due to you being gone, I wonder if that crazy motherfucker made it out?" Justin laughed.

Felix did as well, "Knowing him, he is running whatever band of people that got lucky enough to run into him. Probably took over a state by now, who knows, he probably is one of the generals in this fucking shit show of a wannabe army."

Felix walked inside, came back out with another beer. He lit another cigarette.

Justin with thin eyes examined his friend, "You alright, brother? You haven't drunk like this in some time. You are putting those things away like they owe you money. You know these things aren't cheap, right?"

Felix nodded as he finished another one, "I don't know why, my body is off, like I feel off. If I don't catch a buzz, I feel as if I want to break their fucking necks," he said, pointing at the two soldiers standing on the corner of the street. Felix then turned; his stance was leaning toward them. His sights were set on them.

Justin grabbed his arm.

"Alright, big guy, come on, grab something to eat, and we can talk about it inside."

Felix looked down, his pistol was in his hand. Wide-eyed, he looked at Justin. Justin let his arm go. Felix holstered his weapon.

"You got me worried even more now," Justin spoke as he put his massive arm around Felix.

"I don't know what's wrong, man. Food sounds nice. I could eat."

"Right on," Justin replied as he guided Felix back into the house.

*****

That night Felix sat at the small dinner table; the kids ran upstairs to their beds. They were definitely older. He had been fairly quiet the rest of the evening. Drinking so much it became impressive. He was on number thirty-one now. It seemed to be soaked up almost as fast as Felix could drink it. This whole thing worried Justin greatly. One, what had happened to him; two, why was he drinking so much; and three, why was he fairly sober? Something was wrong, and it was more than just the loss of time. Felix looked different. But not physically. His eyes, they looked distant, and dark, darker than the brown that would turn a reddish color in the sun.

Justin stared at Felix as he stared at the note Sasha had left him. He took a drink of beer.

"I'm leaving tomorrow," Felix said, breaking the uncomfortable silent atmosphere. "Headed east, I'm going to Fort Monroe, Virginia. You two should get ready to leave as well. I have a bad feeling about those fuckers in the uniforms."

"We aren't going anywhere; this place is perfectly fine. Since you have been gone, the country is now crawling with feral and the alphas. They are not exactly that easy to kill anymore. It's too dangerous and I advise against you leaving."

Felix squinted his eyes, "Well, I'm leaving either way. I'll leave a lot of stuff here, only take what I need, seeing that you didn't sell my shit since I was gone."

They both laughed.

"Well, it was only a matter of time, you have been searching for her on this side of the country for some time, so we knew sooner or later that you would be heading out. So, I have something to show you," Justin said, getting up and moving around the table.

"What's this?" Felix said as he got up to follow Justin.

The two moved into the garage that was again like the entire city, carved out of the cave. Several vehicles lifted, a few motor cycles lay in pieces across a few tables. Several finished cars and trucks had been heavily armored like something out of a *Mad Max* film. The two arrived and Felix's dark brown eyes lit up with excitement as he gazed upon the machine before him.

"You finished her…" Felix said as he walked around the armored vehicle.

"Yeah, all done up, ready to go, took her out the other day to pick up some shit from deeper in the city. She is loud, but fast, so just realize that when you move through a city, it will need to be on foot or everyone for miles will hear your ass," Justin replied.

"Fair enough."

The once upon a time Cadillac CTS-V was no more. It was now a doomsday vehicle that Mad Max would be proud of. Its wheels black thick all-terrain tires, the car was raised a few inches for clearance. The normally luxurious exterior was replaced with steel armor plating. The front windshield passenger and driver windows to include the back windshield were protected by hexagonal mesh cage welded to the plates. The vehicle looked like a sharp steel block. The plates were wielded to the frame. The hood was a little off, reaching over the metal grate that was now the front cage, attached to a sharply designed bumper sporting a hefty winch. The entire vehicle was painted a dark flat gray. The windows were tinted, just to take the edge off the sun.

Justin pulled keys from his pocket, "She's yours; 6-speed, V8 turbocharged monster. We did as much as we could for the suspension and the fuel consumption, but she still only gets about 30 miles to the gallon, the gauges are a little off, and we don't know the top speed. The windows aren't bullet proof, but everything else is. Just be careful, she weighs a fuck ton, your tires will bald faster than normal, and turns are going to slip more."

Felix took the keys, shaking Justin's hand. "No, we hug around here," Justin said as he pulls his friend in for a hug.

Felix pulled away, looking at the vehicle with a big grin on his face, "I don't know how to thank you."

Inside the vehicle, the luxurious interior was no more. The seats were racing seats with a four-point harness. The shifter was long, like a rally car, designed so that the driver doesn't have far to reach to shift to the next gear. The steering wheel was simple, a small plate, where the horn normally is, held the cruise control settings and overdrive. The passenger side glove compartment had been ripped out and replaced with a gun rack. Its back seat fitted with a chest and cage system. Contained within its latched grid metal prison, an array of long guns, shotguns, an AR, a bolt action, lever action, belts of shot-shells, loaded magazines, and his bags.

"I'm pretty sure you have already paid in full for this since you've been here. Already put most of your shit in it."

"Well, I don't think it was enough," Felix replied.

"Just go find your happiness, we won't be leaving to catch up with you. It's hard moving a family in the wasteland, especially after I have this here. If things get bad, then they will have a very hard time trying to take this place from us. We will be fine."

"Well, you of all people can definitely handle yourself. Who knows I may get there and that place will have been cleared out by feral or these green suit assholes."

Justin laughed, "Get some rest, tomorrow we will see you off. Otherwise, let's enjoy the night and have a drink."

"I've been drinking all day," Felix laughed.

"Right on, kinda like old times?" Justin replied.

The two head back inside and drank the night away.

*****

The next morning. Justin was standing on the passenger side of the vehicle as Felix tossed in a jacket. He leaned on the hood, putting a cigarette in his mouth.

"Well, good luck, I'll see you around," Justin said, breaking the silence.

"You too, if you are ever on that side of the country and all this blows over, we'll have to have a beer."

Justin laughed, "Right on, but I doubt it, so good luck. We will probably never see you again."

Felix laughed, "More than likely. Until that day down that road?"

"Until that day."

"I'll see you guys down that road then. Take care, old friend, thank you again for this badass vehicle."

"No problem, just don't crash this one, doubt there are many people out there with this kinda badass ingenuity."

"I'll try, but you know me."

Justin laughed, "Yeah, I know you. Take care, man."

"You too, brother."

Felix jumped in, closing his heavy door. He put his key in and cranked the monster over. The shop roared with the sound of the engine. Justin grabbed the chain, pulling it to open the garage door. Felix waved, as did Justin. He threw the vehicle in first, and took off. Flying out of the garage, turning left, and roaring out the main entrance to the underground city.

Stacey stepped outside, "So he is finally gone for sure this time?"

"Yeah, good thing. Last night he had me worried."

"Me too. He wasn't all there."

"Something terrible happened to him, he was going to kill some random soldiers if I didn't stop him. It's a good thing he won't be back. Out there is where he belongs. I hope he finds what he is looking for."

The two stood there as he passed through the main gate. Disappearing down the road. The sound of the vehicle faded into silence with him. Justin and Stacey walked back inside, shutting the garage door.

"It's a long road ahead," Felix said to himself. Pressing down further on the accelerator, he flew viciously over the road. Its roar the very representation of the man now driving it, all the rage under a crude and damaged shell put back together over a rough frame in a maniacal manner.

*****

Days later, Felix passed a dirty and tattered sign, *"Welcome to Kentucky, Birthplace of Abraham Lincoln."*

135

"It's been a long time since I've been through here, geez…maybe six, seven years," Felix said out loud to himself.

He looked in all directions; the trees were thick, almost taller than he remembered. Music in the background playing "Little Wing" by Jimi Hendrix over the speakers from a small iPod. It was all beautiful to him, just another perfect day as he cruised down old interstate 64. Losing no momentum, timing his maneuvers almost with the music, dodging debris and abandoned vehicles with that manic-like smile on his face.

. The city, dead as it sat still on the Ohio River. Its buildings standing like giant grave stones. Few lights flicking on up high in the tall weary towers. Letting the world know that there were still people trying to live in that lost city.

"I really need to go around this shit hole. Or I'm going to be fucked, by either road gangs or feral."

Felix slowed to a stop, pulling the emergency break. He took a quick look around before pulling out his map.

"How do I not fucking die?" he asked as he curiously looked at his map. "Fastest way, or the safest way? What to do, what to do?" he said to himself.

"This thing is almost worthless," he said, folding it up and tossing it onto the floor board of the passenger side.

He looked up to see a woman walking toward him with haste. Holding a bottle with a rag stuffed in it on fire.

"Well, that's not good." Felix spouted, knowing full well he was just had.

She took a little hop and skip, hurling the bottle at the doomsday-mobile. The bottle crashed, throwing fire all over the front of his vehicle. He cocked his head back from the wash of flames. He turned and grabbed his rifle from the cage, the cage slammed, his door flew open. Simultaneously grabbing his key, he darted straight from the vehicle. Sporadic fire chased after him. He comically picked up his pace, running like a cartoon character making grunting noises as he slid to cover behind a turned-over truck.

He checked his rifle; the 5.56 mm was chambered. He stood up, stepping back far enough to pick his rifle up. He took a peek out of his cover. He fired once, the round smacked the woman in mid-stride, it ripped through the back of her head. She fell limp in the middle of the street.

"Noooo. You motherfucker!" someone in the distance screamed.

"Well, asshole, you shouldn't have gotten in my way," Felix growled to himself as he quickly moved further around the turned over truck. His rifle up and ready the whole way. He paused for only a moment, took another peek, leaning slightly out of his cover. The firing picked up, smacking against the underbelly of the turned over truck.

They must think I'm still over there, Felix thought to himself. He darted for another vehicle that was merely a burnt shell, looked like a Honda. Felix waited patiently. The group stood up.

"Get around him, you two, go that way, you are with me, we will hit him from the other side," the leader, Felix presumed, said to his group of marauders.

Felix watched them for a moment. The two on his left were close together, moving sluggishly. One was a black woman wearing tactical gear that was a little too large for her. The other, a white old man with a bushy beard, he was large, saggy skin, probably from losing weight from malnourishment or actual exercise. The leader, a large black man, sporting a military issued M4, wearing a digital patterned army jacket, black pants stuffed into his tan boots. He was followed closely by a very scared and very skinny white guy, who, to Felix, looked like a hillbilly. Patchy facial hair and all.

What a rag tag team of fuck heads, he thought to himself.

Felix stood from his crouched position, four rounds into each of the two to his left. They both, with looks of surprise and horror on their faces, died instantly. The leader and the scared follower began shooting and cursing Felix. He couldn't hear nor did he care. He simply crawled to the right side of his burnt cover. Placing his feet against the wheel, laying on his back, he sat up leaning to the right. He fired again; the leader took several rounds to the chest. The skinny hillbilly was out of bullets. Felix got up; the man dropped his weapon, placing his hands in the air.

"Please, please, please," the man started groveling as he fell to his knees. Tears and snot ran from his face. Felix walked up, picked his weapon up without a second thought when the roar of something he had never heard before stopped him cold.

The hillbilly started laughing hysterically, "You dun'er now, why do you think we have silencers?"

"Suppressors, fuck head," Felix corrected.

"Huh?" the man nervously giggled out.

"What was that?"

The man looked at him, smiling through the blistering sore on the corner of his mouth.

Felix walked up, kicking him over, the man hit the ground hard. Felix was taken aback by how little effort he gave to knocking the man over. He stood over him, pressing the hot barrel to the man's face.

"I say again… What the fuck was that noise?" Felix asked in a deeper, more deliberate tone.

"It's what the dogs are changing into," he replied, hands up, shaking.

137

"What do you mean, changing into?"

The man, completely ignoring the burning of his face, was still giggling as he somehow answered in a laugh, "You'll see soon enough…"

"Alright," Felix replied. He squeezed the trigger, killing the man.

Heavy thuds began approaching rapidly before stopping. Felix looked past his vehicle. The beast was staring at him. Felix was stricken with awe as the beast began to charge. As it drew near, Felix quickly began to realize that whatever that was, it was getting bigger, very quickly.

"What the fuck is that?" Felix asked, as he could feel the thuds in the concrete as it galloped toward him.

Felix darted for his vehicle, tossing the weapon in, cranking the engine over, throwing the doomsday mobile into first and speeding away. The creature was catching up quickly. He could see it closing in fast. His rear-view mirror that took up the entire top of his windshield was quickly blocked by the massive beast. The dog, mutated and large, was running as fast as he was driving. Felix looked down, shifting into second, the speedometer reading 50 MPH.

"There's no fucking way." He shifted into third. Then fourth. Going 75 MPH.

The beast barked and slammed its head against the side of Felix's car. The car jerked, but luckily with the weight of the armor didn't affect him much. Felix downshifted, slamming on the accelerator, he sped away. Rolling through gears until he had enough distance to do something about this thing. Coming up on a turn, Felix pulled the emergency break and letting off it, downshifting and again, he sped away. The beast slid on the street, slamming into another abandoned car. The burnt husk slammed into a street light, knocking it over.

Felix began to turn left and right, attempting to lose the beast. The commotion had woken up every living thing in the city. He was back on 64 again, heading out of the city. In his rear view, he could see people starting to form on the suspended bridges strung throughout the old city high rise buildings. They were not feral, they were survivors.

"How the fuck did they build those bridges up there?"

The dog, he could see clearly now, drew closer. Its brown, almost red, fur, matted and tattered and stained with blood almost shone in the sun. Its teeth were jagged and in unorganized rows. Its tail was long, splitting just at the end into two shorter tails. A smaller leg stuck out from its chest, sluggishly moving as if it were trying to help run. The eyes looked human, not dog-like. The breed was unknown to him, maybe once a hound dog. Unsure, other than the droopy ears flapping wildly like the beast's tongue.

"I guess all those rumors were true," Felix grunted.

Felix slowed, allowing the dog to get side by side. He rolled his window down. The dog looked at him, he at the beast. He laid his semi-auto shotgun over his left arm that clutched onto the steering wheel. He fired, hitting the beast in the side of the face with some 00 Buckshot. The dog flinched, stopping abruptly. Felix slammed on his breaks, the car slid sideways as he pulled the emergency break. Throwing his heavy door open. The beast was whining as it attempted to paw at its face, like dogs do. Felix pulled his M79 grenade launcher from the back chest.

He stood there, ready. The dog shook off its pain. Eyes blazing with rage, blood poured from the side of its malformed jaw. The beast let out a bark that rattled the very ground. It began to move, slowly at first. It began picking up its pace. Felix stood his ground taking aim, with a calm that made it seem like it was just another day at the office. The beast was in full stride now, maybe a couple hundred feet. Felix fired. *THOOMP.* The round soared through the air, disappearing out of Felix's sight just before exploding. The beast slumped and rolled, its skull split open, meat, brains, fragments of bone spilled onto the dusty interstate.

Felix broke the action in half, pulling the casing from the tube. He loaded the weapon before tossing it and the empty casing into his passenger seat. He turned and approaches the creature, his Marlin 45-70 in his hand. The rumbling of the ground continued. He stopped, looking past the pile of dead before him. Several vehicles approached, all resembling well-designed military vehicles. None that he had seen before. But knowing the routinely over-complicated and over-thought designs of military application, he assumed.

"Fuck me, today is becoming more and more ridiculous by the second," he said as he turns with haste in his step. He tossed his weapon into the rack, jumped in his vehicle and once again, in a tire-squealing fashion, was back on the road.

*****

"Sir, the subject still has shown none of the projected evolutionary abilities from the procedures. He is merely performing at peak physical conditions of his previous physiology. However, there was a moment where his sociopathic tendencies took over. Should we attempt to incite response, or continue to monitor his movements and interactions with the local populace and the infection... sir?"

"Yes, yes, monitor," the doctor impatiently replied. "Can't you see I'm busy here? Let me know when the subject performs at its new threshold."

"Yes, sir."

The nurse turned and left the doctor to his meddling. She continued back into a large room. Full of monitors stacked all around a leather swivel chair, radio chatter could be heard from the operators. She took her seat, pulling herself closer to the desk, peering out into the wall of windows. The feeds are being pulled from multiple unmanned aerial vehicles; she looked at each of them, sighing. They are invading Felix's privacy, watching him from far off, from multiple directions. He had not noticed them, nor will he. So, the good doctor assumed. The nurse watched him light a smoke as he sped, weaving in and out of abandoned vehicles, passing through the wasteland, if it could be called that. The highway was even beginning to be taken over by a small lush green, as if it spilt from Mother Nature herself. As if she was painting and ran a streak across the world.

"Come on, do something interesting, watching you move across the United States is rather boring. This job is better suited for one of the overfed security guards."

She leaned back, kicking her feet up on the desk. With a long overexaggerated stretch, she placed her arms behind her head.

"It's hard to believe that you, of all of the test subjects, survived the latest in the forced evolutionary procedures. How long will you survive, Number 13?"

"Felix?"

"Yes, Uncle?" The young man stood, bloodied knuckled and black-eyed.

"Why did you hurt those boys?"

"Because they were trying to kill a dog. I had to do something."

"You think that gives you the right to do what you did. Some of those kids went to the hospital. You were suspended."

"I'm sorry, but I couldn't stand by and watch them hurt a defenseless animal. I needed to do that. They were trash."

Robert put his hand up. "It doesn't matter, it was just a dog. You hurt some of those kids very badly. One of them needed stiches. Two of them are in casts now. You think that was right?"

"Yes."

Robert let out a sigh as he looked Felix up and down. Trying not to smile and congratulate him for his triumph.

"Felix?"

"Yes, sir?"

"Do you know the difference between empathy and sympathy?"

"I do not."

Robert gestured for Felix to come and sit. Felix walked over and did as the man asked.

"You know, your aunt took you in because honestly your parents are trash. However, you burned down that man's house, regardless if he was a drug dealer or not. It put you in the hospital and set that forest on fire. She wasn't going to let the city take you from your parents. Now...since you got here, you have grown quite a bit. But; you think that just because you know what's right that you can do whatever you want."

"Should I have just let them kill the dog?"

"No, let me finish, boy."

Felix nodded and shut up at the tone this hard man growled.

"How old are you?"

"I'm almost 16," Felix replied.

"I was your age when I joined the navy. Things were different back then; they took almost everyone. I was a boy, I learned everything that made me a man from that moment on. I've seen things and done things that haunt me even to this day. That's why there's nightlights in every room in the house. That's why I talk in my sleep and why your aunt sleeps in the other room some nights. Getting to my point, you, much like me, couldn't stand by and watch as someone hurt someone or something else. You have to act, it's okay to observe sometimes, but sometimes you have to shoot someone in the back of the head because they are letting themselves become the enemy."

"I don't understand," Felix replied.

"What you did is wrong according to the weak. What you did in my eyes, and anyone who isn't spineless, was right. Don't ruin your life because you hate people. You will always hate them. This time in your life right now, is almost meaningless, school is merely a stepping stone, and these people you're going to meet, your girlfriend, they are nothing. You will forget them the moment you walk away."

"There's no way."

"Trust me, I've done it all already, so sit there and listen. But you're young, dumb, and full of cum, so why would you listen to an old man?"

Felix laughed. "Because you're wise."

"Then if anything, if you remember anything I ever tell you, don't be like them, be a fighter. Just know what fights to pick, what fights to win, and what fights to lose."

"And what of empathy and sympathy?"

Robert patted Felix on the back. "It's one of those things you'll have to figure out for yourself one day. But you're like me, and you'll end up like the rest of us old soldiers, never really dying, just fading away."

Chapter 10
Breeding Grounds

A sleepy small-town gas station in the middle of nowhere looked like a decent place to stop. Felix parked his vehicle in front of the rows of abandoned vehicles that littered the small gas station. The night went as quickly as it came. Felix was up standing at the back of his vehicle, staring into his trunk. Two tanks that were mounted on both sides of the trunk with "RESERVE" spray-painted on them by the use of stencils.

"Do these things come out or what? What's going on here, Justin?" Felix said as he bent down to inspect them further.

He banged his head on the heavy duck finned trunk. "Fuck. Come on, man, how am I supposed to fill these up? Huh. None of these goddamn pumps work. Argh, fucker..." Felix said as he slammed the trunk.

He picked up his small metal can and hose and began searching each of the vehicles. After about an hour he managed to get, with much remorse and a bad taste in his mouth, a full tank. Even after all these years, there was still some left to be pillaged. How well they burned after sitting for so long is anyone's guess. Fuel stabilizers and additives were definitely needed, luckily Justin threw some in the vehicle for Felix.

Felix sat on the hood of his car as the sun started cutting into the dark across the land. Eating a ration bar, peering out of a pair of binoculars.

"What the fuck is that?" Felix asked.

Through the glass he could see a rather large pack of feral moving into a city. The cloud they produced with their herding picked up enough to see it from the naked eye. There had to have been hundreds of them, maybe even thousands. Since they had migrated into the United States in the past two years, alphas had turned more, and taken on more of the feral in their packs. Past experiences, the beasts only had anywhere from five to nine feral within their packs. This must have had been one of the alphas that started in the city and moved out before the bombs fell.

"East. What's east, where am I?" he said as he scrambled to grab his map.

The slight breeze carried with it screeches and shrieks. They were so loud that even at this distance he could hear them. But this noise, he was unfamiliar with. This was not pain, or hunger, or attack, this was something else.

"Man, why the fuck is everything trying to distract me from getting to Virginia?"

He grabbed his shotgun off the hood, stuffing the rest of his ration bar into his mouth, sucking down his warm beer. He started his machine up and headed toward the city. He kept his distance for the night, and fell asleep in his car in an empty parking lot.

While he slept, thousands more made their way across the land. Whomever was local, that could hear the calls of the night, scurried to the gathering. The beasts continued their movements and odd callings throughout the night. Luckily, they didn't pass by Felix, or he would have been overwhelmed in a heartbeat.

*****

The next day, Felix found his way into the city, parking in a lot on the other side of a tall building. If he was right, this would be overlooking the commotion in the city center. *Why they chose the city is anyone's guess, it would have been more intelligent and instinct-based if they would have converged within the forest, away from human architecture. Or was it because the feral was once human that they decided to move here. Most of these alphas were domesticated, so that could make sense as well.*

Within minutes he had scaled the stairwells of an empty office building, locals must have cleared it out years ago of everything they needed or worthwhile. There must have had been a small town or city with occupants nearby. The building looked to be well-traveled, due to prints of humans, and feral and dogs in the dust. He stood looking out a broken dirty window. Investigating the low roar of shrieks and rustling before him.

Thousands of the feral were lying about, some in piles, like dogs around their pack leader. The alphas to which their mutation or evolutions had malformed and deformed all danced around each other. Some nipping at ones' neck, others smelling the ass of the one before them. Only to jump back, perking their ears and fur, a sign of introduction that wasn't well-accepted. Felix continued to observe.

The creatures were no more dog than the feral were no more human. As he continued to watch, he saw it. The queen, these things had a queen, she must have been the first one, the host. Felix moved, attempting to get a better look. His high-powered rifle was clutched in his hands. A Springfield Armory

143

Socom 16 scoped with an old but very good Vortex. He stepped back, taking aim. His barrel steady, never breaking the threshold of the window as all good snipers know. Even though he was never one.

"Sweetheart, I know you. You are very dangerous, as all beautiful creatures usually are," he whispered.

She nor any of the thousands of creatures down there noticed him or anything for that matter. He continued to observe. The queen, standing tall, stopped all the commotion. The feral scurried in fear, the alphas sat, halting their ceremony. She walked down, closely followed by a smaller version of her. Maybe a suitable male, or a pup, Felix only wondered. She stopped, looking in all directions, inspecting her troops like an officer walking down her ranks.

Her spotted and striped hair thick, shimmering in the sunlight from the fresh blood soak on her mane. Her eyes so yellow, though were that of a cat's, thin and sinister. She let out an echoing bark, baring her rows of triangular teeth. She was a monster, towering over the others in size and ferocity. Her ears were long and wide and pointed. Anubis, if he were a giant female hyena. She was beautiful, Felix thought.

The others were malformed, each having their own biological issue. Seven in total sat before her. She paced slowly along the length of the rank. Sniffing one, staring silently at another, who shifted from making eye contact with her. She took leave and circled back around. From left to right. It was eerie with how quiet and attentive the horde was as she paced.

The alphas possessed genetic flaws similar to the beast Felix encountered previously. The German shepherd, Felix believed once was, its snout longer, ears like fans, its front legs were much longer; it's back tapered off to half the size of its front legs. Its coat remained the same, a dark and rust print. The two tails waging behind it stopped and its panting mouth closed when the queen, Felix identified her as, looked in his direction.

The next was a boxer, but skinny, its snout and jaw malformed, wide and box-shaped, its teeth growing as if they were poured from its gums into the bottom jaw. Its eyes were large, bug like, couldn't tell which way the beast was looking due to the right eye looking straight up.

Felix, peered through the Horus reticle of his scope, moved it down the line to inspect the ranks with the queen. A glimmer caught his eye across the way. He picked his rifle up, in another office building or town center, he could see several soldiers and scientists with equipment observing as well. He looked up at the top of the building, noticing helicopter blades or other form of areal transportation.

"Wonder what those assholes are up to?" he said aloud, lighting a smoke. He quickly paid them no attention and continued observing the horde below. A few floors down, he heard footsteps shuffling around. They knew he was here. *Didn't take these fucks long,* he thought.

The next was a Chihuahua, shaking wildly as always, its flinches were dramatic, as if a drug addict longing for a fix. It was all white, large patches of fur missing, and it was the size of a man. It was by far the ugliest motherfucker of the group, Felix thought.

Next to it, a massive curly-haired creature, its fur was heavily matted and dirty, covered in dried blood and mud. It was larger than all the others, he couldn't even begin to guess what the breed was. *Or, more importantly; why almost every single one of these ugly fucks was caked in blood?*

Next to it, black and rust, tall and muscular, probably the easiest of the rank to identify, its snout deformed and elongated, its muscles were uneven, some horrendously larger than the others. Its cropped tail had been consumed by its muscles. A Doberman pincher, Felix deducted. Fearsome in its muscular formations, erect in stature, and ever watchful.

Felix was on to the second to last, it was a Rottweiler, black and rust similar to that of the dog next to it, but its skin was sagging around its face, drool poured from its jaws, as it dim-wittingly held its mouth agape, throwing splashes of heavy saliva along the street with every turn of its giant blocky head.

The last was odd, maybe a coyote, maybe a wolf, it had six legs, one seemed to be functional, the other retarded in growth, merely lay lifeless against the creature's back, what looked to be a second head, was panting. Felix couldn't quite make it out due to his point of view. But he could see ears and a heavy-breath bobbing of the protrusion.

"What the fuck are you doing up here?" a soft but fierce voice unsurprisingly carried to Felix's ear.

"You," he started as he turned, finding five rifles pointed at him, "...need to learn how to clear rooms more quietly. I could hear you from three floors down, maybe more."

"You need to learn not to blow smoke out of the window, giving away your position, asshole."

Felix laughed, "I shouldn't have to worry about humans, when we all have a common enemy."

The team looked at each other, throwing non-verbal signals of confusion and wonder, he didn't seem in the slightest bit to be afraid of them.

"Who the fuck are you? No one comes down this way anymore, why are you here?" the leader of the team, Felix presumed, demanded.

"Drop the weapon, or we will kill you where you stand," another said. Her voice was almost squeaky.

It began to set in. The soldiers, all of them, dressed in black, were indeed females. Not uncommon in this day and age, men and women segregated themselves, the women in order to keep from being raped and killed, at one point in time, eaten. The men, because of some ideological notion that they were superior and just raped or killed or ate the weaker of the sex. It always fascinated Felix, why they were the way they were. Even before this world, in history, in his time. He turned to take them all in, observing acutely. Gauging his possible enemy, they were impressive, toned, fit, all of average height.

"Drop your weapon, and answer the fucking question," another raised her voice slightly higher.

"Whoa, whoa…" Felix threw his hands in the air with his rifle. "I'm not the bad guy here, just noticed some crazy shit, and wanted to see what all the nonsense was about. I have no plans of interfering with your little science project over there," he replied eagerly.

The leader of the group, the smallest or frailer of the five, Felix thought, stepped away as the rest of the team kept their weapons trained. She was having a conversation over the radio.

Felix looked at all of them, examining them up and down. Taking note, side arms, plate carriers, radios, a knife, all uniformed. Their weapons, Sig Sauer P226, and, with their barrels all aimed at him, the group sported M4 or AR style weapons. Daniel Defense, expensive shit, but everything was free nowadays, with that, good shit.

"Yes, ma'am," the leader of the team said, ending her conversation with some static over the net. She came back over, standing in the middle of her fire team.

"What's the word, ma'am? We going to take him back for partnership?" one asked.

Felix squinted, making an odd face of confusion and disbelief.

Another reply, interrupting any of the team's previous thoughts, "We could just have him here, he looks healthy. Hey?" the one on the end was now talking to Felix.

"Yes?" he replied, trying to hold back a grin.

"You sick, your balls still work? Got any diseases?"

"Am I being considered for rape?" he asked, now smiling.

"Only men rape, we attempt to rebuild society," one angrily slashed at his comment.

"What a ridiculous situation I'm in," he said to himself but loud enough for them to hear. "These bitches are fucking crazy."

"Look, as much fun as being gang-banged by a bunch of chicks would be, I gotta go, so you all have fun and I'm leaving," Felix had dropped his hands and started walking toward the doorway at the end of the room. One blocked his path.

"Drop the weapon," she sternly demanded, her rifle was pointed at his face.

"You sure?" Felix started. Another walked over, pressing the barrel of her rifle to his head.

"She's sure. Take it from him. You, put your hands up, or I will drop you and cut your cock off and fuck you with it."

Felix turned his head, squaring his forehead up with the barrel. She was taken aback by his look. His eyes were dark, almost no shine of any light in them.

"Listen here, let me go…" The weapon, with little difficulty, was still gripped tightly in Felix's hand. He noticed from the slight tugging at his left hand that someone was trying to take it from him.

"What's the issue, take it from him," the leader demanded.

The soldier was grunting from trying to pry it out of his hand. Felix, confused as to what the problem was, let go. The soldier almost lost her balance from the force of her attempt.

"Get the fuck over there," the one with the barrel to his head scoffed. Felix turned his attention back to her. She nodded in the direction she wanted him to move, which was back by the window.

Before he could say anything, the feral down below start screeching and scurrying away in a rumbling frenzy. Felix walked over to the window as the team attempted to keep their attention on him. But his curiosity now called to them. The leader pushed past two of the team to observe.

Watching through the light tan dust covered windows, the queen wrenched her large head back, biting out the throat of one of the alphas, the others flinched in fear, but stood and watched. The queen began to eat the curly haired one that Felix couldn't identify. The one she killed looked to be a female as he examined closer. Oddly enough, he was able to see even without his rifle scope. The others were males that hadn't been neutered from their previous, once upon a time, dog lives.

The queen, with blood dripping from her jaw, let out a glass-rattling bark followed by that famous hyena laugh. The other alphas began to chase the infected. Biting them by their necks and pinning them down. Shrieks and moans of the once human screams began to ring out. The dogs, the alphas, were mating with the feral.

"Oh my fuck," Felix said aloud.

"I'd hate to be them," one of the soldiers said.

"Could you imagine, being pinned down and fucked by that? I mean look at it, it's huge."

Not only was Felix looking at her with a ridiculous look on his face, but the rest of the soldiers' team were staring too. Each of them had a 'What the fuck?' expression on their faces as the one making the comment shrugged her shoulders.

"What?" she asked.

Felix laughed, shaking his head, peering back out observing the ruckus before them.

The feral were still running in all directions, the dogs didn't stop at one, and didn't care what sex the infected were. Everyone caught was suffering the crippling ravage at this point. The queen continued to eat amidst the chaos.

"Interesting, I wonder how long this has been going on. I wonder if they have actually successfully bred. The volcanic winter, the rain of ash, the rapid growth of the forests, the feral, and now this? What the fuck happened in the universe to fuck us so hard? What did we do that led to this end?" Felix asked aloud.

The team, realizing that they were all distracted, surrounded Felix again. He sighed, putting his hands back up, turning around slowly.

"Look, let me be on my way. I'm not your enemy, even if you are trying to fuck probably the coolest guy you all have seen this side of the wasteland," he spouted sarcastically.

"Shut the fuck up, arrogant prick."

Static came over the radio. The leader stepped away looking across the way at the building with the rest of their element.

"Roger, moving now," she responded.

"Soooooo, I'm good to go, we shake hands and part, so we can go our separate ways?" Felix asked sarcastically, using pistol fingers, knowing full well he was fucked figuratively or literally either way.

"Restrain him, he's coming back to base," the leader of the team ordered.

Before they could zip-cuff him a window breaking in the distance silenced the writhing pool of fornication. Everything down in the city center turned their attention toward the window.

The queen wrenched her head up, throwing splashes of blood into the air in beads of small rubies that glistened from the beams of light. Her ears peaked and pointed, erect in such a disheartening manner to those she could hear. The sound of falling equipment alerted her of the rustling of the scientists and soldiers in the building across from Felix. In a flash of a blur, she was through the building. Tearing through a wall as if it were paper. The feral in her way were trampled and knocked over, some dead from her sheer power and force.

Felix with his hands up, smiling at the team of soldiers, "Better go help them."

"Fuck you, waste-lander," their leader replied.

"Those things down there are evolving, and will kill you, they are not as easy as they used to be to kill. And, you, dumb fucks, I don't know what the fuck you're into, but the fact that you are monitoring them is reason enough for me to think you motherfuckers are responsible. That makes you my and every other survivor's enemy."

"Ma'am?"

"What?"

"Permission to kill this asshole?" she asked, smacking her rifle barrel to the side of Felix's head.

"Ah, fuck," came out of his mouth, then he paused. It didn't hurt like it had in the past; he almost didn't feel it at all.

"Permission granted," the leader replied nervously watching the horde pour into the building across the way.

She continued to raise the other element on coms, but gunfire stopped her attempts as the team was now voicing worried comments to each other.

"Ma'am, what the fuck are we going to do?"

"I don't know…"

"What about him?"

"We need to figure out how we are going to get out of here…"

"What do we do?"

The soldier, with her weapon trained on Felix, backed away.

"Ma'am, we need to get to the bird," she said nervously.

Screams could be heard of soldiers and scientists, faintly carried over the sound of gunfire. Some being silenced by the grip of jaws or the tackling of feral. The creature had made it to their floor. Some of the people were being thrown from the building into the frenzying horde below. They are eaten as soon as they hit the ground. One got caught by an alpha, shaking wildly until thrown into pieces. Like a dog shaking a new toy, throwing stuffing all over the living room floor.

In a blur Felix lunged at the young soldier. She let out a frightful shriek. He grabbed her rifle, shoved his push knife into her neck. She began to fire uncontrollably, he pulled the knife from her neck, letting go of the rifle. A firm hand gripped tightly on her plate carrier, and with one yank and twist, Felix tossed her out the window. The soldiers all began to fire, but were missing, he almost danced around the striking of bullets as he dodged their fire. He slid across the dusty tile floor, chased by misplaced shots that ripped out of the windows.

The queen took notice of the commotion in the building Felix was currently dispatching soldiers and attempting his getaway. She barked, and a group of feral broke away from the raid on the other building. Piling on top of each other, like goofy pups if they weren't ugly mutated infected humans. All hungry, all ready to devour whatever they got lucky enough to eat.

Felix stepped on one of the soldier's legs, crushing her knee into the floor. She screamed, and with one backhand, a crunch of her neck breaking, she fell silent hitting the floor hard. Felix skipped backward, turning and sprinting. He blew down a door with his shoulder rolling off of it. Bullets chased after him from two of the last standing soldiers. They paused only to reload; one rushed after him.

Felix came around the corner with his pistol up, he fired several times, hitting her plate carrier. She hit the floor on her back. Dropping her magazine and rifle. The leader was down the stairs; she took a misplaced step, tumbling to the next platform. Felix stepped over the soldier he just shot. Kicking her weapon away, he grabbed her by the plate carrier, dragging her to the window. The other came around the corner, her weapon jammed. Felix stopped, turned, and in a blur, fired. The round ripped through her nose and buried into the back of her helmet. She dropped, stunned, twitching slightly.

The soldier currently being dragged by Felix was now coughing and dazed from the bullets, one made it through. Blood dribbled from the corner of her mouth, sweating profusely she pulled and clawed at his grip. Forgetting all about her sidearm. Felix stepped once more, tossing her through the window. She screamed as she fell five floors. Her fall broken by one of the alpha's strong backs. The beast turned, looking at the dazed and broken woman. Sniffing her.

Felix grabbed his rifle and leaped down the stairwell. Slamming against the wall, using it as a pivot point, he leaped again. The leader was slowly making her way down the stairs, not noticing Felix behind her. He landed on her back. She slammed hard against the floor. Other than her helmet and weapon clacking against the tile floor, he heard something break. He grabbed hold of her and tossed her down the stairs. The creatures had made it inside as he pulled her through the door leading to the second floor. She was unconscious and limp. He could drag her with ease, almost didn't feel her weight even with all her gear on. But there was no time to think about it. He found a window looking out the parking lot where his machine lay in wait.

"You better survive," he said, and just before he tossed her, he noticed a grenade pouch.

He pulled the grenade out of her pouch. Picking her up by the plate carrier, she sagged, limp. He turned and tossed her through an office window out into a tree and bushes below. The tree's branches and thick greenery slowed her as she fell through them. A thud, he was relieved that she hit the ground. Pulling the pin on the grenade and tossing it down the stairwell; that wonderful spoon flying sound filled his ears. The feral were piling up the stairwell like furious ants. He leaped from the window, falling into the tree with his rifle.

"Fuck… Shit. God-fucking-damnit…" he cursed on the way down at every limb he landed on.

He hit the ground, landing on top of her, he looked up, the grenade popped with a low crash and thud. He was on his feet, he lifted her up over his shoulder and sprinted, rifle in one hand. Creatures screamed from the building, some survivors of the grenade, the others fuming with fury. He opened the back door. Tossing the limp, more than likely dead soldier in the back of his car. He jumped in, started the engine, alerting the horde to his whereabouts, and was off.

The queen was observing from the top of the building of where the scientists were once watching them. The helicopter fell off the other side, covered in feral. She watched Felix speeding away; the feral chased in vain, slowing once they realized they couldn't catch him. He was headed east.

The muscular, once Doberman, came upon the soldier Felix threw through the window. She was sweating, bloodied, her legs broken. Holding in her hand a grenade, her finger through the pin ring. The beast, in a flurry, bit both her arms and the grenade, ripping them from the forearm down. She screamed a blood-curdling cry. The beast mounted her. She is going into shock. And all she could think was, *Could you imagine?*

*****

Miles away, safe from the massive horde, Felix dragged the soldier out of the back of his car. He pulled her mask and helmet off. She was young, good-looking, tan, her cheeks puffy, her face bruised. She was still breathing. He smacked her.

"Hey…" Felix checked for a name tape.

"Sanchez," he smacked her again.

"Wake up, fucker…" he said nonchalantly.

After a few attempts she began to come to. She screamed out in fear as she was frightened by Felix. She reached for her weapon, but it wasn't there. Her brown eyes blazed with fire. She realized that she was stripped down to her uniform. Warm liquid soaked her leg. At least one of her legs was broken. Maybe even something else, she couldn't tell. as long as she didn't move, it didn't hurt too much.

"Where are my women?" she demanded.

He stood up, "They are dead. And if they are not, they will be part of that group being buttfucked by those giant dogs. So, either way, they are fucked, pretty much like what you all were about to do to me."

Felix lit a smoke. Looking at everything he had pulled off the soldier, he placed them neatly in line on his hood. She sat against the front left wheel.

"Who are you?" Felix asked calmly, beginning his interrogation.

"Fuck you," she replied.

"What were you cocksuckers doing there?"

"You killed my women," she replied as if he wasn't even talking. She was starting to sob.

"No identification, other than your tags, which only have your last name, and a service number. But no branch, you must be some sort of special unit to be so poorly identifiable. But why, who?" he was now talking to himself.

A radio, pistol, rifle that was broken, the barrel bent slightly. The optics' glass was shattered out. A knife, a multitool, dip can, water source, a smartphone. Felix picked it up, pressed the only button on the face of the screen. A lock screen opened.

He walked over in front of her, "I haven't seen one of these in a long time, probably the most dangerous weapon known to human existence," Felix laughed. "Who the fuck are you?"

"Go to hell, *puta madre*," she replied.

He knelt down next to her. She looked at him, his eyes looked dead, but his grin was lively. His eyes became thin as smoke rolled from the lit cigarette in the corner of his mouth. He grabbed her by the neck. She grabbed his strong arm, clawing, punching; his expression didn't change. He wasn't even fazed by her attacks. Even after she smashed the cigarette into his face.

He loosened his grip; she began choking for air. He held the phone up, putting another cigarette in his mouth.

"I will shove this down your throat, and leave you here, or, you can answer my questions, and I will leave you here, with this, not stuffed inside your body. Your choice..." He was holding up the phone, wiggling it back and forth comically. He lit his smoke, awaiting her answer.

She was frightened. Felix could smell it more than he could see it.

"Look chica, I didn't want to kill any of you, other than being a bunch of crazy fucks, much like the men you all hate, you left me no choice," he let her go, then he stood, taking a long drag from his smoke.

"Who are you, what were you doing out there, who do you work for? You answer those questions...or..." he wiggled the phone. "Deal?"

152

She nodded. He walked over, sliding her water bottle off the hood onto the ground. She quickly reached for it, taking a long throat-groaning swig.

"Who are you?"

"Major Cynthia Sanchez. USOAR Special Forces."

"You're a little young to be a major, and oooo, Special Forces, interesting...didn't know they let women in those ranks. Hell, it was merely an experiment when I was still in," Felix replied, cracking open a beer sitting on his hood, not believing a word she was saying.

"Our job was..." she grunted, adjusting herself against the wheel. Continuing her reply in heavy breaths. "We were assigned to security for local monitoring of the evolving infected creatures. The dogs had begun to evolve years ago, but at such a rate it has a lot of the scientist and people at the top of the food chain nervous. Our VIPs were sent out here to observe first hand, maybe even capture one of the infected, an alpha if we were lucky."

"Why are they breeding?"

"Next stage; the pandemic that infected all the dogs years ago, that transmitted to the people, now is evolving, attempting to procreate. I'm not high enough in the ranks to know, but our guess is, the new government is studying them, deciding what they will do."

Felix laughed. "What the fuck?" he asked, mainly to himself, but she caught it as well.

"That's all I know," she said.

"So, the communicating, the hive mentality, the attempting to breed, the fucking hyena queen, this is all a form of rapid evolution, due to some magical pandemic that happened the exact same time the volcanos blew?"

"Ye-yes," she replied.

"Hmm..." he grunted, pondering.

She adjusted herself again, letting out a painful sigh.

"No matter, whatever we did, we did it to ourselves, and it will run its course. Nothing we can do other than try to survive. As for you, though..." Felix said, standing up, flicking his cigarette onto the pavement.

"You said you would let me live," she screamed, holding her stomach, wincing in pain.

"No, I told you I wouldn't shove this phone in one of your holes."

She had come to a realization, Felix knew the look, he had seen it many times before. It was the look on the faces of those ready to die. The slaves he had come across, many women and children, used and abused throughout the early years. Men too, especially by the women slavers. It was that look, the one when you realize there is nothing you can do, you are seconds from your fate, and hope does not exist. He grinned.

Felix holstered his gun. "A soldier deserves more than this," he said, kneeling. He pulled his knife putting it to her neck. She merely turned her head slightly toward him, leaning on the blade.

"Fuck you," she spoke; her voice was no longer filled with fear, content maybe.

Felix held up the picture from his wallet.

"You ever seen her before?"

"You are crazy," she replied.

"Have you seen this woman?"

"None of us were lucky when the world ended. You think she would be alive, or even your woman anymore?"

"Just answer the question..." Felix snarled.

"No, but my base, she might be there, we only take in beautiful, strong women. It's part of our regeneration of the population, we believe that we need only pick the best of the survivors to repopulate the world."

Felix stood up, confused, but not surprised. Her comments reminded him of the Nazis but so did a lot of political movements back in the day. But she was of Latin descent, more than likely a super feminist camp, probably a very dangerous endeavor. Felix pondered for a moment longer as she waited for his next comments.

"Where the fuck is this place?"

"USAOR Base Fort Monroe, Virginia," she replied, and it echoed through his very being. People are certainly alive there, protected by this dumbass military outfit. But this, this may be his ticket if this place was one of those crazy feminist camps, or full of these crazy soldiers. He continued to think for a moment longer as he squinted his eyes at her.

She adjusted herself. "You know of it, that's where you are headed, isn't it? How about a new deal?"

Felix sat crossed legged right in front of her, flipping his knife through his fingers. "I'm listening."

"You get me there alive, and I will make sure you don't get rolled up into the breeding cells. You get me there, and I'll make sure you have a place to sleep, food, and a job. Plus, you might be able to find your woman there."

"Enticing. What's the catch?"

"No catch, I'm an officer, so I have a lot of power. You will be my trophy, basically."

Felix stood up, laughing like a demon would from a horror film. "That sounds a lot like slavery, and until SOCIETY..." he made quotations with his fingers, "ended, this is the first time any of us have been free in a long time. You are going to have to do better than that." He chuckled, "Offering slavering again for protection, it probably won't be any different than the last place. Why is it when people band together, they immediately retard the ability to reach potential?"

She twisted her face in almost disgust as he was basically talking to himself.

"That's all I can do; the rest is left up to you at that point. You have to prove your worth, to be given such freedoms inside the sanctuary that Fort Monroe is. If it wasn't for our commander, who liberated us in one of the biggest slaver camps this side of the country, we would have been sold to gangs, used for food, used for breeding."

Felix sheathed his knife, "Yeah, like you basically are doing with everyone else, like you tried to do with me."

"Are you going to leave me out here?" she asked.

"No, you're coming with me, this place is already starting to sound like a death trap. You survive, I survive, we will move from here, then we will tend to your leg. I hope the fuck you don't die on me."

He picked her up with ease. She winced in pain. He shouldered her, walked around the hood, opened the passenger door, and set her down. She helped herself into the seat. She looked all around, wide-eyed, baffled by the vehicle he had.

"Your car is manual?"

"Yeah."

"I can't drive one."

Felix laughed, "Well, yeah, your leg is broken, kinda hard driving one anyway."

Felix thought about that for a second. "Huh, I should have got an automatic, can't drive if either of my legs get fucked up. At least I could finagle an automatic into drive and press the gas with something…"

"You were a good guy after all?" she said as tears began rolling down her face. "They are all dead."

"I didn't want to kill your men, women, your team. I asked you nicely to let me go."

She looked at him, "Thank you for not killing me."

He looked back, "This is going to be a weird relationship, I can already tell."

As they drove away from the setting sun, he could hear her voice, as the memory played through his mind. Passing by as slow as they chased the horizon. Why so many had been coming in and out of his head, he did not know. He welcomed the thoughts, for it was her after all that he searched for. Longing to reunite, regardless of the cost.

155

"What are you buying now?" she asked playfully. Leaning her chin on his shoulder as he was filling out paperwork.

"A Super Redhawk 454 Cassul, it's a freight train, babe," he replied cheerfully.

The clerk behind the glass counter took his paperwork, smiling at the conversation she probably had heard a hundred times in that particular gun shop. She didn't say anything, she only took his paperwork to the back and made the call for his background check.

"What do you need that for?" she asked, legitimately curious.

"A diesel truck or an elephant," he replied as matter of fact. She was now not amused, but laughed in surprise.

"You better not shoot an elephant, I'll shoot you." She poked at him playfully.

Felix laughed, grabbing a hold of her. "Well, my love, I'm not saying I would. You know me, I love animals more than people, but you never know. There is never going to be that perfect caliber, so the reason I have so many different types of guns is because of that theory."

"Oh yeah, I'm still stuck on the whole shooting-an-elephant thing."

He laughed again, wrapping his arm around her. "No, I'm not going to shoot an elephant." He continued laughing.

The two stood there in silence, looking at the wall full of guns of all different kinds. A few gun nuts talking about how awesome their weapons were at home, loud enough for everyone to hear. Others browsing, looking at everything under the glass counter, with no intention to buy. A nervous couple making their first purchase, listening to a clerk who was annoyed with their indecisiveness. He rattled on and on about his particular carry weapon, and yet they left without anything in hand.

"You know, it's conversations like these that shows me more about you than anything. One of the many reasons I love you. You love animals, and that to me shows enough about you, to know you're an awesome person."

"Well, I love you too, babe. But if you keep spending money like this…am I going to have to take away your cards? Hmmm…"

He laughed. "Maybe, my paranoia has got a hold of me, especially with the way the news has been. Just knocking things off the list, babe. Then, I will double everything."

"Double?" She gave him a raised eyebrow, and pressed lips to the corner of her mouth look, the one that always made his legs weak.

"Yeah, babe," he started, pointing his finger in the air to make his point.

"Gotta have backups to my backups, and something for my woman to carry as well."

"You're a silly man."

"You love this silly man." She laughed at his reply, kissing him on the cheek.

Chapter 11
The Dog House

"Ma'am?" a young olive-skinned, green-eyed woman called.

"Yes, Lieutenant, what is it?" the colonel asked, still distracted by her report.

"I have some good news…"

"Well?"

"It seems that a few survivors have made it out of the Breeding Grounds and are now headed this way. One is about a week out, the others are all collected in a convoy, they are currently estimated to arrive in a day. And…they have succeeded in obtaining a specimen."

The hard woman stood. She glided around her desk in excitement. She grabbed the shoulders of the young lieutenant and pulled her in.

"That *is* some good news. Anything else?" she demanded in a gleeful rush of words.

"No, ma'am."

"How many, total?" the colonel asked.

"Three beacons confirmed, communication for the element due back in a day are degraded. Only one confirmed, that is about a week out, no coms."

The colonel walked back and took a seat in her large leather chair behind her oak desk. She rested her chin in her hands, pondering to herself.

"At least, it wasn't a total loss, now I can send a real report to the north. You're excused, Lieutenant. Send in the first of the new arrivals, are any of them female?"

From the other room the lieutenant yelled, "Yes, ma'am, two."

"Send them in. Take the men to the unassigned rooms and have the rest of the team we are short, supplemented."

The lieutenant poked her head back in, "Ma'am, we are short quite a few. The unit keeps killing them, so we are short almost an entire platoon of men."

The colonel rubbed her face. She was young, her hair black in a tight bun, eyes of deep blue, and skin olive. She let out an irritable sigh, "I never thought

I would say this, but we are running out of men… Send me a shortage report on male to female ratio. We will send out some teams to hit a few of the surviving towns in the area, pull some suitable men from there. I don't care what age they are, take the boys if you have to."

"I'll have it ready for you in a moment. Uniformed teams?"

The commander sighed, "No, the USOAR needs to be seen in a positive light. Send the teams in civilian attire, civilian vehicles, have them use personal equipment, don't need this getting back to us. Make it look like a raid or slavers or something. Stage the rescue by the uniformed teams, easy in easy out."

"Yes, ma'am," the lieutenant paused. "Should we ask the north for supplement? They have men in the western locations, maybe ask if they can rotate a platoon out here just for this purpose. If all our units become pregnant then what will we do?"

The annoyed commander sighed again, "That's why we have the men, they will continue operations instead of their assigned partner. Issue is training. Need to set aside time to train all the weaklings. It's amazing how they have become so weak, where we would be training men how to fight and survive. I remember when I was a little girl, my father was so strong, he worked hard to support my siblings and our mother. As time went on, we grew up, and I watched as women became dominant in many ways, and the men became weak."

"Ma'am?" she asked, confused.

"Never mind, just get me those reports," she said as she leaned forward, opening her laptop.

*****

Felix downshifted, speeding up, weaving in and out of a few abandoned vehicles. A bump in the road woke Cynthia up. She adjusted herself slowly, the splint on her left leg was hurting. Felix watched as she tugged at it.

"How far have we gone?" she asked, taking a drink of water.

Felix swigged his beer. She eyed him, judgmentally, Felix could tell.

"We have a few days left. I'm getting tired, but I'll be good, we will have to stop for fuel soon. Luckily you won't be able to move, so you can watch the car while I find some. Who knows maybe a surviving city will be along the way."

"Why do you drink all the time?" she asked.

"I don't know. It's been like this ever since I lost a couple years of my life. Can't remember anything. Woke up back where I started, but different, happened before your little military decided to show up and restore order."

"And the woman in that photo?"

"She was my fiancé before the pandemic happened. We were going to get married when I came back. I was maybe a week away from being there with her. Things probably would have ended up quite different if we were together when it all happened."

"You must really love her to still be searching all these years."

Felix laughed, the only real laugh she had heard from him the entire trip, "Yeah, I have no illusions of what may come, or even if she is still alive. But we need a purpose, and this is mine. Even if she is dead or found someone to love, had kids for whatever reason, her choice or not, a slave, or had to sale herself to survive, I will be there for her. I made that promise a long time ago, because that is what she deserved. Because I deserved her."

"She was a lucky girl," Cynthia said it through a sigh.

"What about you, anyone before the world fell?" Felix asked, lighting a cigarette.

"I was still in high school. I wish I had paid more attention. I was naïve, I walked out of school, didn't even know why. After all, it was a student that killed students. So, I was just yelling things because everyone else was."

"I recall those days. The news made me paranoid, all I could think of was, our youth was giving away freedoms they didn't even possess yet, but it was all just a bunch of bullshit. I have to thank the media for spreading all the terror that it did. By the time the pandemic happened I was so prepared, it wasn't even funny…" Felix realized he had interrupted. "Sorry, please continue."

"I had a boyfriend. Jamal Reynolds was his name. Every girl wanted him. He was the only black guy in our school. I was the head cheerleader; we were both vegans so we got along great."

Felix's face was twisted in disgust as he glanced over at her with an eyebrow raised. "Vegans?" She didn't notice and continued.

"I don't know if he ever made it out. He was my first boyfriend after all. When it happened, I remember waking up and my mom rushing all of us to the car. We headed for my dad's work, Fort Carson. He was an engineer. When we got to the gates, soldiers were all there blocking the gates with tanks and Humvees. They opened fire on everyone who approached. I was the only survivor. I was picked up by a band of them, days later. I was used by every one of them. Eventually after a while they found more and more girls, and the group became bigger. About a year ago, we came across another military, and we got into a huge battle."

"Interesting, I've seen much of that years ago. What happened next?" Felix replied.

"All the men were killed, the women were captured, brought all the way back to Fort Monroe, and that's where we all met the commander. She taught us tactics and gave us a home. She only took in strong women. And the men get chosen to be the woman's assigned man. It works well. If we get pregnant, the man takes our place in the unit. Although it is designed the way it is, we work well with each other, but the end of the world has changed some of us, like my team, they haven't been assigned a man yet. So, you were prime meat. After all the terrible things that have happened, it's now acceptable to have sex with a stranger or force them out of need."

Felix was blown away, he tossed his bottle out of the vehicle, and opened another one.

"That's fucking crazy, never heard of such a thing. It seems the tables have turned. I always wanted to see a world where men are the few, especially in my job. That would've been fun."

"There are not many strong men left in the world. You older generation men mostly died out during the pandemic. I didn't realize that when I was young; but we needed the crazy ones, the fighters, the dysfunctional veterans, the soldiers, police officers, fire fighters, things like that."

"So, is it mainly female at the Fort then?" Felix asked.

"No, there are families there, but everyone has a job, everyone is assigned someone, the only exceptions are the married couples. Everyone works though, in some way. The men mainly man towers and run patrols to collect supplies or scout the city for infected. The women, the military, secure the outer areas, we conduct many missions further out, but we are an actual military. We protect the men, and the children. Like a bunch of lionesses."

Felix pondered, digested what she was saying as he chugged his beer.

"I don't understand it, I guess I'd have to see it for myself. So how is it going to work for me?"

"Well, since you brought me back, I don't know. I already have an assigned man, it's not uncommon for us to have multiple but they get jealous of each other and end up killing one another."

Felix laughed. "What the fuck?"

"There are plenty of women who need a man, so you will be more than likely assigned to one of them. You will be given a job upon your interview with the commander, she rarely gives them to men. But when she does, it's usually because they possess some skillset we need. Like mechanic, doctors. In your case, you are skilled in combat. So, you would probably be put on one of the hit teams. A man currently leads that team, the only team run by a man in Fort Monroe. The only team primarily comprised of men."

"Well, I'm all for equality and all that hypocritical horse shit, but it sounds to me like it is tipped in the wrong way."

"You will become a believer; you have to see it to understand it."

"If you say so, I'm not too privy on being a fuck toy for some random chick that I'm assigned to. Could be fun, ha-ha."

"Why, it was done for the men for thousands of years, now that it is backwards, you all don't want to be part of it?"

"If it means we are moving backwards to a society, no, I certainly do not want to be a part of it. I don't like having a leash, or being under a contract, having to answer to someone else, playing a game because I owe something, a number that is made up ultimately, see what I'm saying? I already played that game. Now that we are free, I'd like to keep it that way."

She shook her head.

He sighed, cocking his head slightly, "Oh well, don't have a choice, like we usually never do. I'll play the game for a while, but I'm planning on leaving. Is that going to be a problem?"

"It shouldn't be, but no one ever leaves, our society is perfect, people love living there. I doubt you will want to leave once you get there and see it for yourself. I'm not doing well in explaining it."

Felix blew a heavy cloud of smoke out. In his head, he was formulating a plan of escape already, he knew these types of societies all too well. They formed almost immediately after they lost power, communication, no laws or government control. They were free. And the ones who hadn't known freedom, which at that point, the mindless thought they were free, and the ones who didn't bought into all the bullshit, knew they were slaves. But it worked out in such a way you read about, or saw in an apocalyptic movie. Groups formed, took to the roads, some locked themselves away in cities and built walls, keeping the infected out. Gangs formed, raping, murdering, stealing anything and everything from the once living. Most of them didn't last long, and were killed off during territorial disputes or slaves' uprising. Certain parts of the country, however, did well. But only a few.

*****

A few days later Felix and Cynthia had stopped at a gas station, miles outside of Hampton, Virginia. He was leaning against the hood of his car checking the map. Cynthia, with a painful attempt, winced and grunted with heavy breaths, helping herself out of the car. Luckily, it was tall enough to make it easier, still painful though.

"Where are we?" she asked.

"We are almost there, I'm just trying to figure out how I want to do this. Either way, we will have to enter the city. How do you get into this shit hole?" he asked.

"Well, we just drive through, it's safe. The gang that resides here," she pointed to the city center, "they have no quarrel with us so we move in and out freely. They keep the power running; we keep the infected out. We don't take their men and they don't take our women. So, it works well."

"You sure?"

"Yes."

"Will we run into a patrol on the way in?" he asked.

"I don't know, I've been stuck out here with your loco ass," she said as she leaned against the hood looking at him.

He turned back to his map, "You better calm that attitude down, I'll leave your ass out here. You'll be a little *gordita* for these fuckers."

She got up, "You'd miss me."

He continued checking alternate routes on the map. His cigarette flapping from his mouth. "Smart ass little shit," he said.

"I heard that…" she said as she painfully got back into the vehicle.

"Good! I'll punch you in your busted ass leg," he replied.

"I'd love to see you try. I'll punch you in the dick, I know at least that you'd feel."

He laughed. She smiled.

"Alright, let's get the fuck outa here."

The powerful machine roared down the road into the city. Its streets were somewhat clear. Still littered with trash and debris, but easily drivable. Buildings blown up, stained in black from fires. Remnants of the dead remained on corners and alleys. Some streets as they passed by, they saw the cars all moved and packed into them, forgotten. *Like a junkyard,* Felix thought. As he glanced past Cynthia who was not surprised by the state of the city, he could see another street filled with vehicles, stripped bare, some of them completely dismantled to a shell. He peered back to the road.

"Left here," she said. He listened.

She began calling out turns to lead him through the city. Above them, bridges from building to building, roof to roof zig and zagged their way into each other. People were moving about them. Lights from some of the windows still lit, flickering from time to time, like the street lamps.

As they were almost through, from what Cynthia was telling him, the car was rammed suddenly by something. A loud screech, Felix flinched. And Cynthia screamed.

"What the fuck was that?" Felix yelled, knowing exactly what it was. Cynthia peered out the window. Her eyes widened.

She smacked at his arm rapidly as he downshifted.

"Go go go!" she screamed. Without hesitation Felix slammed on the gas.

His tires squealed and the engine roared, vibrating windows echoing through the city streets.

A pack of feral poured out of one of the buildings after them. An alpha ran in the middle of the lazy formation as it began to pursue the roaring machine. Gun fire began to pick up from the suspended bridges above. Felix nor Cynthia could tell how many, just that they were being chased.

"Turn left, left left!" she shouted.

Felix pulled the emergency break down shifting, letting off the break, and drifting around a corner.

"Right right right!" she yelled.

The two shot out onto one of the Hampton roads, it must be the right one, because the only thing Cynthia was concerned with was having her weapon ready. Felix continued driving, faster and faster now that he was on open road. His engine roared, the tires stressed and both her and he gritted their teeth as they ripped down the road.

They were on a roadway over the cove now. Approaching what looked to be a guard shack that was built up into a gun tower. The guns aimed not at the feral chasing, they pointed right at them.

"Watch out!" Cynthia screamed.

Gun fire opened, sparks flew from the armored hood, he ducked. With one hand on the wheel, one pulling her over to him. She screamed in pain as he ripped her over further out of the fire. Bullets ripped through the window. Clanging against the car's metal armor. They were being hammered by machine guns. He slammed on the breaks. The car slid, sliding into a barrier, sparks flew. They were still being engaged by the guard tower.

"Holy fuck!" Felix yelled over the sound of round after round pelting his car.

Suddenly it stopped. Dying creatures screamed out. Felix sat up, several feral were still after them. He turned, leaning over Cynthia, grabbing his AK.

"Stay here," he said.

"Where the fuck am I going to go, *gringo*?" she asked sarcastically.

He was out of his shattered window on the top of the car. Three of the feral were left. They were running fast. He began firing. The creatures slid to a stop, frightened. A loud bark from the alpha called them back. But Felix stepped off the car, with ease, never lowering his weapon or halting his fire. He engaged them, ensuring they were never going to come after them again.

Several rounds ripped through their backs, throwing sprays of red mist into the air as they slumped over. Some rolled. The alpha charged to a sliding stop. Felix slowed his chase, lowering his weapon. The beast's eyes met his. They were yellow, his dark. The beast growled. Hot breath bellowed from the giant terrier's teeth bared jaws. It barked; Felix's chest vibrated from the noise. The beast's ears perked, catching the sound of vehicles revving up, heading toward them.

The alpha, along with the rest of its feral pack, had vanished back into the city. Chased away by the vehicles and knowing that it would have been in vain. Felix noticed that the feral were taking commands more easily, and the alphas were communicating consistently. There was a viable and measurable presence of intelligence here. The dogs, or rather the alphas, were controlling their packs like wolves, except with a much higher calculating and tactics driven concept. These beasts were nothing to take lightly anymore, if they ever were to begin with.

Felix turned heading back to check on Cynthia.

"You alright?" he asked. Finding that the blood was from a bullet wound in her right shoulder.

"You can't win, can you? You've gotten fucked up this trip," Felix noted as he checked her arm.

"Fuck you," she replied. "It will take more than this to kill me, *cabrone*."

The sun was setting and the world was growing darker.

Before he could open the door, the vehicles' lights were flooding him blind. He was quickly surrounded by armed soldiers. They had him at gun point. One out of the group walked up behind him, striking him in the back of the head. He stumbled, placing a hand on the back of his head. The half-moon shaped formation of soldiers murmured amongst each other. He should have been knocked out cold. The attacker pulled out zip cuffs. Another had his weapon trained on the right corner of his head.

Felix placed his hands in the air. Dropping his weapon. Soft hands grabbed his wrists, with much difficulty she grunted, pulling them behind his back, zip-tied. A bag went over his head. It took three of them to move him to the vehicles. Suburban, Felix felt. He smacked his head on the door frame as they pushed him in the back seat. One on his left and one on his right. One had a pistol pressed against his crotch. The other, pressing a pistol against his head. They didn't say anything. The woman in the front seat called up to a higher on a radio.

"Bring the medics out, we have one with a broken leg and gunshot wound, she's one of ours. Also, the driver of the vehicle is being brought to the cell. Let command know."

He rode quietly for several minutes, unable to see anything. Luckily the route was straight as far as he could tell. Stopping once, guards allowing them to pass through another gate before stopping. Everyone got out, he was pulled from the vehicle. Doing everything he could to not resist, relying on her word wasn't exactly smart. But he had no doubt he could escape these people. He had a feeling.

He walked down some stairs, slightly stumbling. A heavy hinged door squeaked open, echoing throughout the stone hall. He was pushed in, a knife produced by one of the guards freed his restraints. The door slammed, he removed the burlap sack, turning to find the three soldiers, their feminine figures easily identifiable, moved with haste up and out of the cell. He was the only prisoner down there. Taking measure of the dark cool cell, he sat against the wall. *Might as well rest,* he thought. *They will come for questions soon enough.*

"Will you marry me?"

Her breath was stolen from her. Not by the view before her, as she looked out of the treehouse hotel. She struggled to turn around to find Felix not on one knee, but both.

He was merely holding his hand out. She put her hands to her face. Her eyes begin to tear up. Her cheeks flushed red. She shook her head, not in telling him no. But because she couldn't believe it. But she did believe it, she was surprised that he finally did it.

He sat there silently, nervous, sweating even. He didn't know what to expect. But whatever came out of her mouth was going to be it. He had felt so strongly about it for so long. His only hesitation was that it was very typical, very cliché to do such a thing. When either of them existed on their own, not fueled by their family's opinions nor that of their upbringings.

His heart beat like a drum, and so did hers. This moment seemed to last forever. She finally took his hand walking into him. He wrapped his arms around her bottom and she ran her fingers through his hair.

"Yes," she replied through her broken voice.

He pulled away, standing, kissing her deeply. Fingers woven through each other's hair as their hands caressed each other's faces. With his thumbs he wiped her tears away. She looked up at him with those big green eyes, melting his very existence.

"I didn't get you a ring, I know you don't like that idea, and I honestly don't like jewelry the same way you do. So instead..."

Felix pulled a small revolver from the small of his back, she laughed through her tears. He held her left hand and put the trigger guard over her ring finger like just that, an engagement ring. She wrapped her arms around him, kissing him. She pulled away and pulled a small pistol from her back. He laughed as she did the same thing to him.

"Will you be my pot from here on until eternity?"

"Only if you will be my kettle."

Chapter 12
Territory

Monica, the commander of Fort Monroe, Virginia, sat in her office. Flipping a pencil through her fingers as she spun slowly in her chair. The doctor over the phone was pleased, she could hear it in his excited tone.

"Keep a watchful eye on him. We will be monitoring his progress from here. And remember, the more he is in contact with the creatures, the more we can observe his progression. We need him in constant danger, keeping him stagnant will only produce such results, stagnant."

"Yes, sir, anything else?" She leans back in her chair, spinning around toward the old paintings on her walls.

"Do be careful, we don't know how far he will go, it seems his obsessions are with finding his woman, and he seems to have some odd family tie with his friends that were developed from his time in the army. He considers his friends, many which are located there at Fort Monroe, due to some meddling and manipulation of chance, are just that, family. Do well to protect them; if they should expire, you could be dealing with a potential enemy. One even more devastating than an alpha."

"Yes, sir." The phone clicked off. She set the iPhone on the charging port on her desk.

She let out a sigh, calling in one of her majors, sending her off to retrieve Felix from the cell.

"I absolutely cannot stand his voice." Monica spouted as she thought of that repulsive doctor.

*****

In a dark stone cell, bars of iron, hundreds of years old, the smell was sweet moss. The only noise Felix had heard was a drop of water from a crack in the stone. It would fall, hit a small puddle, and echo through the prison.

168

Several clicking of boots on the coble and stone stairwell caught his attention. The shuffling carried its familiar cadence, leading down into the civil war era fortress. It had been some time since he had been there. Not too terribly long, maybe a full night and half a day, maybe longer. The soldiers stopped at his cell, banging something metallic against the bars. If he wasn't already awake, that would have done it.

"I thank you for saving the life of one of our officers. She was very fortunate to have you come along and pick her up. You understand, we live by our procedures, we have seen it before where someone attempts to infiltrate our society, using our girls as ransom. The winter was the worst of times, many disgusting people from the snow would come out and capture one of us and then bring them back, hoping to gain favor here. Protection, warmth, food, shelter, women, this place has been sought after for many years, by many groups of survivors."

"So, she is alright. That's good," Felix said. He stood up from the stone wall walking into the bared light that cut from the grid of the cell bars.

"Since she is one of our more respected and capable leaders, her request will be met. We will not kill you. But procedures, you see."

"I understand, I'm under no illusions here as to what I am to you all," Felix replied.

"You will be released, shown to your room, you are being given one of the vacant ones. Captain Smith will escort you there. Once you have had a chance to make yourself presentable, you will be brought to the commander's office. She will then interview you. Any questions so far?" the major asked.

Felix shook his head slowly.

The major continued, "Once you are given your duties, you will report the next day, depending on your status you will be more than likely issued a uniform. Looking at your equipment, you will not be given any weapons or gear. The stuff we found in your vehicle is military, suitable, and questionable. After that you will be free, so long as you follow the rules."

"And those are?" Felix asked leaning on the bars.

Her eyes meet his, she looked away and began to pace. They were dark, dead, she thought.

"You will perform your duty every day, save for your rotational relaxation days, your unit will have a schedule you will fall under. If chosen for partnership by an officer, you will be hers, unless any disputes come of it, such as being chosen by several. They will choose the way you are rewarded. Once assigned to your partner, she is yours and you are hers. If you betray her, you will be cast out, or she will execute you. If she chooses another, you have the option to go back up for choosing or fight for her favor. You will address all officers uniformed as Ma'am, you will address all uniformed non-commissioned officers by Sergeant. I trust you understand this."

"I'm not a soldier, so why would this apply to me?" Felix asked sarcastically, but the seriousness of the major did not allow her to catch it.

"Order, maintaining order is essential, in keeping the pillars strong that hold this place above the rotting infected filth outside our stronghold."

Felix followed her with his eyes as she began to pace slowly.

She continued, "Not to mention, you are now on a probational release, you don't get any chances, nor special treatment. For the very fact that an exception was made and you are allowed to be freed is above me. So, simple rules to remember, no murdering, no larceny, no rape, no religious prattle, we have a church already, and that is the religion our people will follow. Homosexuality is banned, we have enough issues with the declining population as it is. No movements outside the controlled area without proper authorization, no movements to the floating city without explicit permission from the commander herself. No mutiny, no bringing in outsiders, unless through the proper chain of custody, but while you are on probation you can't do that either way. Let's see…"

"So, how do *I* choose a partner?"

The major stopped, scoffed at his question.

"Here, the man does not get a choice in who he wants. That archaic way of thinking is what led to the fall of society."

Felix grinned. "Equality, well…you're not wrong," he laughed.

She stopped and walked straight to him. Her face almost twisted in hate.

"You are going to do very poorly here if you keep up your attitude."

Felix put his hands up, "Are we done here?"

"What the fuck did you just say?" she roared, hand on her sidearm.

She backed away after noticing a firm grip behind her. The captain took her hand off of the major's shoulder.

"Get him out of here, take him to the commander!" The major screamed in Felix's face, but it was oriented to the guards at the other end of the prison. Her spit from her commands, that was meant for Felix.

Somewhere down the cells, keys jingling approached with a quick pace of leather boots clacking on the stone floors. He was taken from the cell, his cuffs removed, and he walked behind the major, escorted by several armed women. As he made his way across the parade field, onlookers watched closely, talking to each other. He looked around, amazed by the fortification, the security and the dynamic of the society. Fit, hard, strong-looking men and women, kids with smiles on their faces playing in the grassy field, some reading books, some practicing some sort of martial arts, everyone was armed. He was impressed.

"I think I'm going to like it here…" Felix said, the guards all looked at him oddly.

*****

Felix stood in front of the large desk in the colonel's office. The captain to his right and the major to his left standing a few feet off his flanks. They had their hands lazily on their pistols that sat snuggly in their holsters on their hips, ready to gun him down if need be. Made sense, precautions shouldn't be taken lightly, especially with a man that came out of the wastes with one of theirs badly injured. As Felix thought about it… *They shot one of their own, I wonder what the punishment is for wounding one of your own? Especially in a place with all these rules.*

The door burst open. The two stood at attention. The commander waved at them to relax. She was followed in by a young lieutenant, she merely dropped some paperwork on her desk and walked back out, shutting the door behind her.

"Ah, Felix…"

"Ma'am," Felix greeted, he turned making eye contact with the major. The grin on his face was enough, and the major tried to hide a smile at his smartass grin.

Felix was standing with his hands folded together, the sheen of the shiny handcuffs caught the light.

"Sit down," the commander waved him over.

Felix took the seat, setting his cuffed hands on his lap. Noticing that the handcuffs felt like tin or aluminum, they didn't feel like real handcuffs. He'd been in real handcuffs before, and these, although looked like them; double lock, heavy, he couldn't shake the feeling that if he just tugged, a little bit, he could rip them from his wrists.

The commander broke his thoughts, calling his attention and dark eyes back to her. "I don't have much time, I will be brief," she started.

"Yes, ma'am," Felix replied again.

"I am Colonel Monica Jackson, we don't know who your woman is, never seen her before. All your things have been moved into a vacant room. Rumors of your arrival have spread, you're quite popular around here. You have been requested to be part of the Multipurpose Death Squad. They call themselves The War Turkeys, bunch of psychopaths, the only predominately male element in our formation, one of our Hit Teams. They claim to know you. So, you will help with special missions, and teaching, mainly teaching. Our new recruits pour in every day, whether they are found or just were lucky enough to stumble upon this stronghold. Sanchez will be alright thanks to you. For that we are very grateful. I have a question, what was it you saw, the young major has been saying some alarming things."

"Well, that's a lot," Felix started. "So, you know, feral are in the city now, at least a pack of them. I think they followed the survivors from the city that got here first, and I assure you more are on the way. By more I mean thousands more, I don't know when they will be here. Not to mention, they are attempting to breed. Which I think you already know."

"So, she wasn't just delirious from the pain meds," the commander sighed as she leaned back in her great chair. "Did you see their alpha, their queen? And when you say feral, are you referring to the infected?"

"Yes, that's what I've been calling them anyway."

The commander pondered it for a moment, "I like that, continue…"

Felix continued, "These things are not just mating with each other, the alphas are mating with the feral. I don't know if they succeeded, I would imagine not, but with this infection, pandemic, zombie apocalypse, whatever you wanna call it, it is new, and Mother Nature, although unnatural, will push on, further than any of us."

She squinted her eyes, sizing him up, or just surprised by his replies, Felix couldn't tell. "Why were you there?" she asked.

"I was headed here."

"How do you know about this place?"

"It was always my plan from the beginning, before any of this even happened, a joke really. By a man by the name of Mitch Conner. Barrel-chested, blue eyes, glasses, has a dry sense of humor and hates other people's opinions."

"That's certainly Mitch. How do you know him?"

"Old friends, family really…" Felix explained.

"He is our demolitions expert, him and his wife are here, she is the head doctor in the trauma wing of our hospital."

Felix's face split with a smile. He let out a sigh of relief. "Good."

"What is?"

"That my family, some of them so far, have made it here. I wonder how many of us actually made it this far?"

"Well, it seems you are going to be very popular here indeed. So here is the deal…"

The door opened, the lieutenant popped her head in. "Ma'am, five minutes," she said tapping on her watch.

"Okay, they can hold on," she replied, clearly annoyed.

"Felix?" she said, not wanting a reply, "You work for the War Turkeys now. Major?"

"Ma'am…"

"Take him to Major Thompson, she is already expecting him."

"Yes, ma'am."

Just as quickly as the commander had entered, she was out of the door. The soldiers behind Felix snapped to attention. Felix turned, the major took his cuffs off.

"You've got to be one of the luckiest guys I've ever seen get interviewed by her."

"It must be those helpful tips you gave me, don't know if I would have survived with all the stealing and raping I would've done on the way in here."

The two women looked at each other. "I'm going to put these cuffs back on if you don't shut up," the major said.

Felix laughed, "I'm just kidding."

*****

Felix was taken through the fortress grounds. Hospital, Church, barracks, towers, general stores, armories, motor-pools, the walls of the fortress that used to be the museum was now a school for the children. The classes were segregated. The girls in one, the boys in another. Both taught by females. The formations of marching soldiers upon the parade field reminded Felix of his time in the service. However, there were platoons upon platoons of females; only small elements of men. The nationalities from all over. This world was odd, like going back in a rewritten time. This was something that was in his young years not often seen unless you were in any other job.

"Where was this when I was in?" Felix joked.

"What?" the impatient major asked.

"All the females. Back in the day, while overseas you couldn't be in the opposites sex's room, but same sex could, even when homosexuality was allowed openly. And even when all jobs opened up for females, it was still very rare to see them. Huh… Probably, due to the cultural wash of weakness, war was scary," he laughed.

"Things are much different now. We have had no issues thus far. Occasional suicide, crime of passion, jealousy. Otherwise, we have operated with little to no issue. By the state of the world, we are doing fairly well for ourselves."

Felix pulled a smoke from his jacket pocket lighting it. He followed behind the hasty woman.

"I wonder, if there weren't the dogs, would this have worked out the way it did?"

"It would have," she replied.

"How do you know? The only reason why some people even coexist is due to a common enemy. It's hard to change a culture without catastrophe, and we suffered one that no matter what we did, would force us to change. This country kept throwing them at us as if they were timed, and when they all failed to do whatever they were supposed to, this happened. Just in fucking time to reunite us. Sounds a lot like it was all orchestrated to me."

She scoffed at him, turning and twisting on her heels. He stopped. She spoke, "You have a piss poor attitude. I don't like you."

Felix pointed with his cigarette, "Look, you don't like me, that's cool, I don't give a shit…I'm not one of your little brain-washed fuck toys, nor will I be, just to survive this odd, creepy society you have here. Whatever game you are playing at, I won't be a part of it, so continue the tour, and be a good little soldier, about face, forward march, and fuck off."

The major's face darkened with anger. "Who the fuck do you think you are?" she said as she pulled her hat off, and undid her top. She threw her jacket to the side. Pulled her pistol out, tossed it. Felix took a long drag stepping away. She put her hands up. Fists balled, chin down, ready to dance.

Her arms were ripped, she was strong, her green shirt was tight against her muscles. He pulled his jacket off tossing it to the ground. Putting his hands up, locking his gaze with hers, she was ready to beat the living fuck outta him. He was no weakling either, his muscle definition, although an average-sized man, was oddly dense and cut. She took measure and began to wargame, play the fight out in her head, as a good fighter always did.

"You are about to learn our ways firsthand," she said as she balled her fists tighter, cracking her knuckles in front of her face.

"Procedures?" Felix asked with an evil grin.

Smiling with confidence, "Procedures," she replied.

They had gathered a small audience. The audience was cheering for the major, throwing wave after wave of obscenities toward Felix. Two heavily armed female soldiers were spectating as well, but their attention was solely on Felix. Either way, win or lose, he was more than likely fucked, he thought.

She lunged, throwing a jab, he dodged narrowly, she was fast. The two danced around in circles, her throwing jab after jab. Finally, she stopped ranging him. She stepped in, left right left right left right. She landed a quick combo. Her hands felt like they just slammed into frozen meat. She shook them out, skipping back. Felix paused for a moment. Confused, she noticed it all over his face. She skipped forward again, a three-punch combo. She fought like a highly skilled boxer. Again, she had to shake her hands out. He wasn't even feeling them. And there are not many people that could go toe to toe with the major.

He was in her box faster than she could react. And with a slight twist of his torso, he planted his right foot deep into the grass, with an open hand he struck her in the stomach. She lifted off the ground, floating a few feet before landing on rubbery legs. She had to take a knee, gasping for air. He stood straight up from his showy wide stance, walked over to her holding out his hand, offering help.

"You are out of your mind…if you think I'm going to take…your hand," she wheezed out.

"Well, it's a good thing I'm not asking for yours then," he jokingly replied, still holding his out to her.

She, with all her might, stood, rocketing her fist for his jaw. It landed, his head rocked back, but it was odd, as if it was delayed. She heard the crack of her knuckles. She had broken at least two. He stepped back, spat. She didn't waste a second. Skipping forward, she jabbed, he blocked, she threw a heavy right hook, he blocked, stepping back in sync with her forward steps with each attack. The cheering was now silenced, replaced with awe. Almost eerie with the sound of her heavy breaths and the slap and thuds of her fists meeting his cinder-block-hard forearms.

He caught her right hook, stepped forward, slowly elbowing her under her armpit, she couldn't do anything. He pushed her so hard with his elbow, she hit the floor on her side. She was quick to her feet only to see his sweep, she lifted her leg, he missed, still whirling like a top he stood, throwing another leg. She ducked it. Stepping into his box, she laid into his stomach, punch after punch. Her knuckles ached from them being broken. He pushed her from her shoulders, she flew hard onto her back. She rolled back onto her hands and feet, ready to pounce like a lioness.

"You're pretty goddamn spry," Felix complimented.

She was breathing heavily. His face was emotionless, looking down on her. To him, she was weak. Her rage was now taking over. She sprinted for him, pulling a knife. He stepped to the side, grabbing her hand and tossing her. She flipped through the air onto her back. The fight was certainly over, and she had lost. How embarrassing, no one had ever beat her in a fist fight. It almost poisoned her mind to think she had lost to a man.

As she lay there wallowing in her loss, the sun was bright, blinding. Suddenly a shadow was blocking it, and outstretched from the black silhouette, his hand stuck out, offered to her once again. This time, she took it. He pulled her up. She was on her feet. He handed her the knife, handle first. She took it, confused, she looked up to see his smiling face, it was real.

"That's a good blade. You fight good, if I had stepped the wrong way, you would have fucked my world up," he said as he turned to pick up his jacket. He tossed his cigarette that went out. He reached in his jacket pocket, pulling another out along with a lighter. He turned to find her behind him, holding out her hand.

He took it and they shook. The small gathered crowd clapped at the spectacle. The two soldiers still watched; their hands slowly came away from their rifles. And as quickly as the crowd had appeared, they were gone. Motivated by a small but piercing voice, yelling to get their asses back to work. The major picked up her top putting it back on, her hat and sun glasses. She ensured that she was presentable.

"Gloria, Gloria Carpenter. Major, USOAR Special Forces."

"It's a pleasure," Felix replied.

The two continued to her vehicle. The drive was silent, and Felix merely looked out of the truck at the beauty of the small land that hung from the country like a leaf from a great branch. They were headed to the north end that used to be laid out for recreational use. It was now a gun range, with a shoot-house and courses set up much like sophisticated national shooting matches. Obstacle courses, damaged vehicles, it was a well thought out range. *I wonder who thought this place up?* Felix asked himself.

She pointed to where he would be working from there on out, which was the entire range and training area. She turned the truck, heading toward a building. They got out, Paradise Ocean Club was written upon a big tattered sign in front of the building. They walked in, it was full of weapon diagram prints all over the walls, weapon cages lining the walls under the posters. Tables set up like classrooms, a projector stood in front of the room. They walked past into another part of the long building. A room, who knew what it could have been. A knock, and a lovely voice on the other side muffled by the door called them to come in.

Behind the large desk, her face illuminated by a computer, a blonde-haired tall woman sat pecking away at the laptop. She didn't even look up. Felix took measure of the room. A stained wooden gun cabinet sat behind her, taking up a large part of the wall. Paintings of the oceans and light houses were placed on each wall they could fit. Her desk had a radio charging deck, blinking with yellow lights, some green and ready to go. She looked up.

"Ah, Felix Martin?" she said, still working away.

"Yes, ma'am."

"Major Elenore Thompson, I will be your commanding officer. I've heard all about you, the guys all seem to know who you are. Tomorrow morning, be here at 0600, you needn't worry yourself with a uniform, we don't wear them. You will be given a day to understand your duties and scopes of the team. We will put you in where I see fit, and I'll work you into the schedule. Your buddies say you are a very violent and skilled soldier, you would have to be, to make it here, and saving one of our own. They have yet to fail me or give me false information. We run things very differently here, we have little oversite from Headquarters, once in a while the commander will come down to observe the new recruits. Otherwise we follow a strict curriculum, it is based off of military doctrine from the Rangers, Special Forces, and Infantry tactics from the Marines and Army. Are you familiar with these?"

Felix nodded his head while he answered, "I will have to brush up on them, but yes."

"Good. I look forward to working with you, we have a mission coming up soon, so you will be going with them, more to follow on that."

Her blue eyes met his dark ones. Her blonde hair was tight in a pony tail, braided to the small of her back. She stood, her shirt was tight against her perky figure. Her khaki pants tight against her round butt, her pistol was on her left hip. She stood walking around the desk, shaking his hand. She was tall, a few inches taller than him. She looked young, somehow. Almost not weathered at all from the state of the world.

"That's all for now. I'll see you tomorrow. Today is our day off, as you can see."

She walked around and sat back in her swivel office chair, "Any questions?"

"No, ma'am."

Felix and Gloria left as quickly as they came. Felix lit a smoke looking out onto the beach. The water was gorgeous, he thought. The two walked back over to her vehicle, they got in and left. She brought him to the southern part of the island where a grand hotel sat. It was several stories tall. Red bricked, it faced toward the Hampton roads, the set of highways that bridged the cove's gap into the other cities. He was taken to the top floor. Brought down the hallway, the last room on the left. She opened it, handing him the key she pulled from the door. His stuff was already stacked inside.

"I trust you can make it from here?" she asked.

"Thank you, will I be able to get my vehicle back?" he asked as she was already several feet down the hallway.

"That I do not know, take it up with your boss. I'm sure something can be worked out."

"Thanks again, Major," Felix yelled down the hallway. She was down the elevator in a flash.

He shut his door and looked around the room. It was nice, a lot nicer than living in a stone cut-out like a cave man. But the room was also very empty. Sheets and a blanket were folded neatly on his bed. Two bedside tables, a lamp, a bible, his gear from the car was all moved into the center of the room.

He began laying all of his things out. Inspecting, ensuring nothing was taken. And to his surprise, he had everything. His bags were laid out on the floors, the table, the desk, half of the large bed.

"She came through after all, work…ugh," he said, drinking a warm beer thinking about how much he didn't want to be in this situation again. He was almost out of beer though, and hadn't had one in a while, this was hitting him hard. Good, he thought, he needed it.

As he sat there looking at all the weapons on the floor, he began to drift off as the memories of her poured through his mind.

"Babe, you're the expert here, just tell me what to do, and I'll do it," she stated as matter of fact.

"Thank you, but hardly, I am a novice compared to some; my theory is violence, speed with a little accuracy, only because I'm not a very accurate shot. I can hit a person easily, it's just not always dead center… But, lucky for you, I can teach you to shoot far better than I can, you just won't be as fast, but those things come with…"

She answered, "Practice."

"Exactly," Felix said.

They were standing around a wooden table on a flat range surrounded by berms that were piles of weathered dirt standing about twelve maybe fifteen feet tall. At the end of the range, several stands with targets with blue, green, black, pink, shaped humanoid silhouettes printed on them.

She began loading bullets into a single stack magazine. She was focused on it. He couldn't help but check her out. She was in khaki tight, short, shorts. Her tan legs shaven, and strong; they kept his eyes trained. She was standing there leaning on one leg, her hips pointed at his direction as she was standing on the right side of the table. Her thin, V cut shirt was flowing from small gusts of wind. Slightly sticking to her skin from beads of sweat beginning to form from the hot summer Texas sun.

After the last magazine was loaded, she set it down. He was staring and she caught him through her glasses. He turned away, she was turning slightly red.

"So, what would you like to shoot first?" he asked.

"I don't know, you have so many here. I don't know, I'm following your lead, Sergeant Martin."

She stared at him coyly with that smile of hers, he laughed at her sarcasm.

He pondered for a moment, still, slyly looking her up and down. "Ah, I know."

Felix picked up a revolver. All black with rounded wooden grips.

"This is one of my favorite revolvers, this is a Smith and Wesson, Model 29, in 44 Magnum. It's a freight train," he said as matter of fact.

With ease and apparent skill, he popped the cylinder open, thumbing in the six heavy rounds, one each into each of the cylinders with his right hand. He twisted his hands closing the cylinder and rotating the weapon into his right hand ready to use. He cocked his head, gesturing her to come over. The two walked down the range, he handed her the weapon. She took it, keeping the barrel pointed in a safe direction.

He explained proper stance and how to hold the weapon, she was already doing both, he realized it and carried on to the next instruction. She clearly knew what she was doing, and he was not surprised. Once she gave him the head nod letting him know to back off and let her work, he did. And she took aim, standing about 15 feet from the target. She squeezed the trigger and fired the first round. The smile on her face was so wide you'd think she never fired a gun before in her life. She blasted away, with decent accuracy. Felix was impressed, and she was giggling to herself.

"I really like this one," she said, her face was so flushed and red from excitement, Felix couldn't take his eyes off her. And at that moment, to him, she never looked so beautiful and free.

Chapter 13
Old Dogs

Felix walked onto the training grounds. That smell, that taste in the air, that one you get from the unknown. As if it was the first day at school, or the first day on the job. You don't know what to expect but that was what made it so attractive, exciting. Felix was taking a long drag, blowing a plume of smoke out that was gone almost inches from his face. The cool breeze from the ocean took his toxin away with it as it blew inland. That smell of salty sticky hair, the clouds were scarce and the sun was barely picking up from the dark blue liquid glass on the horizon.

The sound of someone counting in the distance broke his train of thought. A familiar voice, from years ago, when he was a young soldier once upon a time.

"I don't give a fuck, do the fucking exercise. One...TWO...three..." he counted in his hateful tone.

The young women and few men all replied, "Three Zero!" In feint fake motivated voices that only old soldiers could see through.

Felix laughed to himself as he approached the group on the sand. Small waves licked at them, pulling the poor souls into the sand slightly with each breath of her liquid embrace.

Gavin's eyes shifted toward the figure as it came around his formation. He was dumbfounded, looked as if he was staring at a ghost. A smile split his face; his blue piercing eyes sparkled in the rising sun's beams that skipped across the surface of the water.

"What the fuck took you so long?" was all he said as Felix approached.

"You know me, got hung up saving some dumb fuck, killing a few others, you know, doing end of the world stuff with my end of the world friends."

They both laughed.

Gavin embraced Felix as hard men did. Pulling away, Gavin produced two cigarettes, noticing Felix's was already done. He offered Felix one, a flask from his back pocket was the next item produced, almost like a magician. Felix took the flask graciously and took a long swig. Silently, Gavin did as well. The soldiers or soon to be, maybe…one day, were forgotten as the two began to walk away.

Gavin still walked as fast as he did back then, deliberate, hastily. Even in this sand. Green tactical pants, a gray shirt, a smith and Wesson M&P on his right hip. A blade Felix gave him years ago sat in a magnetic sheath at the small of his back. A very strong man. His blond hair was longer than Felix had ever seen. The scruff on his face was unfamiliar, rugged, and made him look like some new aged Viking.

One of the young soldiers in the group of fifteen newly found recruits made a whimpering noise. Gavin turned, in a fury. *The Violence of the Infantry,* Felix thought. That nickname he gave him years ago played through his head as he watched his friend erupt into a volcanic blind rage.

"Don't wanna do the exercise, huh?" rhetorically, he asked.

"You all think you're hard, huh, probably a bunch of little bitches crying about how the world owes you everything, give me this give me that. You," he pointed as he crouched down, almost spitting as he hunched over her.

The poor girl wrenched her head up in fear, hoping it wasn't her, but she knew, his boots were nearly on her left hand.

"How fucking old are you?"

"I-I-I'm twenty-three!" she choked out, screeching almost.

"Yeah? That's about right, probably one of the little cocksuckers crying about taking away guns, while you sat there crying about how outlawing something will save lives, it didn't work on drugs, didn't work on bombs, certainly didn't work on biological fucking weapons, did it?"

She was trying to keep from breaking, trying to keep from giving him the satisfaction of her pain. Of him being right. After all, for men like the ones standing before them, and the women who survived this new world so well, it was the apocalypse they longed for. And as much pain came with it, it was the greatest moments of their lives.

"Since you all wanna quit, that's fine, run to the marina, and back."

"Isn't the marina the southern-most point?" Felix asked aloud. The group sluggishly got to their feet, not due to pure laziness, due to exhaustion. After all, Gavin was the most violent, if not the best trainer on the island. The soldiers produced by him were considered among the best, violent, quick thinkers, tactically sound, deadly. He was the same man Felix knew all those years ago.

"Come on, man, let's catch up, we got about 40 maybe 50 minutes before these bitches get back."

Felix was grinning, "That bad, huh?"

*****

Gavin took a seat on a small folding chair drinking from his flask, Felix pulled open a small ice chest, peering inside. He was not disappointed; ice, with cold beer laid buried within its clutches. He pulled three out, giving one to Gavin, who took it as a chaser for his whiskey.

"Where the fuck have you been?"

Felix shook his head, "Fucking all over this shithole. I started in Georgia, headed west, watched the migration happen, ended up running into Justin, you remember him, right?"

"Of course, how the hell is he doing?"

Felix nodded his head back and forth, "Good, he runs a badass shop down in Subtropolis."

"What the fuck is that?" Gavin asked.

"It's an underground facility in Kansas City, Missouri," Felix began. "The place is crawling with fuckers wearing the same unit patches on their shoulders. Anyway, I stayed there for a few years during the three-year winter, went on an expedition to the Volcano. Seen some crazy shit along the way. And then, one day, I finally make it to my woman's house, as soon as the ice melted. And then…"

Gavin shook his head, leaning an ear closer, "And then?"

"I wake up back in Subtropolis, two years later. No motherfucking memory of what happened except that I was attacked by the feral and a dog, they are mutating, if you didn't already know."

"Yeah, I know, ran into the first discernable mutations about a year ago. The infected, which you called them, feral? I like that, anyway…" Gavin took a swig, "they hunt like packs of dogs, they are stronger than before, and they are intelligent to the point that I think they are communicating."

"Yeah, that's what I seen too, that's how I ended up here. I came across these fucks doing some shady shit. I think they captured one. And brought that motherfucker here."

Gavin wasn't surprised, he just had that look of utter disappointment on his face.

"Those cocksuckers, can't leave shit alone," he said, taking another swig from his flask.

Felix didn't want to, but it came out. "Did your family make it?"

The pause was long, and Gavin pretended that he didn't hear him. Felix understood and knew immediately. He just brought up something that Gavin buried a long time ago. Gavin's wife and kids were lost in the night. Gavin had thrown the kids in the car, got his wife in. He went back inside to grab

182

something, probably meaningless now that he looked back, but nonetheless, when he came back outside... The neighbors who turned, from across the street, had broken into his car and attacked them. Gavin killed his entire family that night. He ended up staying in his town in Nevada, and he killed every single feral and dog he came across. When the volcano blew, he was close enough to the old salt mines to survive the initial blast.

"I'm glad you made it, you piece of shit," Felix started. "Of all the motherfuckers that survived, I knew you would be one of 'em."

"You too, cocksucker. I honestly can't believe it, it has been what six seven years now since all this shit started, I thought you didn't make it here because you got yourself killed trying to save your woman or something dumb like that."

"Well, if anything could kill me in this world, it would be a woman."

All smiles the two were as they sat there watching the sun climb into the air. Smoke streaming from their mouths as they drank and enjoyed the silence. Felix turned, always in a hurry, always ready to get going as soon as he got there. And to Gavin he was still the same, violent, ready to shoot something in the face, guy he had always been. The guy Gavin knew well.

"Alright, we will have to finish catching up later, I need to know what you think of this place." Felix broke the silence.

"Yeah, I figured, always quick to business. Alright, the commander, in the Fort, don't trust her. Our commander, may be one of her little toys, but she has stuck her neck out for us a few times. Even saved me from being taken as a partner by some crazy bitch a year or so ago. So, I remain loyal to her for that. And I am her partner now."

"She wasn't kidding about this partnership ownership bullshit."

Gavin laughed as he leaned his elbows on his knees, "You just wait, when bitches start fighting over guys, fuck that, wait till you see the guys fight over being picked for partnership. Tables have turned, for some reason, when we got here, this place was already being set up. I think I got here a few months after everything happened. A shadow government conspiracy bureaucratic fuck face military was setting the place up, led by none other than that cunt up there. Only reason they took me in was because I killed a few of them trying to throw me out, she set me up over here."

"No shit," Felix replied.

"Yeah, Mitch, you remember that guy?"

"Yeah, he's the one who told me that this would be the place to go when the shit hit the fan."

Gavin looked at Felix for a moment.

Felix realized that after a swig and continued his statement, "Yeah, dude, the whole idea of coming to this shit hole was Mitch's idea. Not mine, I agreed because although it was a fucking joke, this was one of the major strategic places we could have controlled with our group of like-minded individuals."

Gavin was smiling, his white teeth although an expression of joy, was still stern in his own right. The only way you could ever tell the man was smiling was through his eyes.

Felix continued, "The port is south, the ocean, open to the east, land and a city to the west, weapons, food, history of the 13 colonies which in all reality wasn't 13 back in the day. This area is out of any nuclear fallout corridors. For the most part it looks pretty lush, and you all look pretty heathy. So, in the end, it worked out for the best."

"We chase those pretty lies," Gavin replied, finishing off his flask.

Felix stood up still looking out at the ocean. "Here they come," he said. But when he turned, he realized they were still some ways away. *How could I hear them?* he asked himself. Gavin was looking at him with piercing eyes, inspecting him, glancing at the distance of the recruits for a moment. Asking himself the same questions.

"Who else made it here?"

Gavin answered through the smoke with every word, "Mitch and his wife, they stay in the fort; Alex and Chris, they have managed to make it in the good life too, those two get fought over almost every other week, a lot of people have died because for some reason bitches want their dicks."

Felix laughed, "No surprise, I mean, they are some handsome suave motherfuckers."

Gavin chuckled, "But they all work out here, that cunt commander running this shit hole, she doesn't want our kind where the majority of her loyal little sluts can interact with us. However, things are changing, and I don't know why."

"What, why?" Felix asked, watching the group of struggling runners attempting to make it back to them.

"The boss says it's due to the fact that she doesn't want men like us disrupting her order and discipline. Rumors are, she is tied in heavily with the military to the north. The last few months rotary aircraft have been coming in and out of the area. For what, I don't know. Planned on making a little run one night. Where you staying?"

Felix pointed over toward the old hotel at the southern end of the island, the one next to the marina. Gavin nodded.

"I stay on the third floor," Gavin replied.

Felix nodded, "Okay man, what are we working on today?"

184

"Today is weapon familiarization. I hope you're still as good as you used to be. They bring some crazy shit in here sometimes."

"They don't get issued weapons?" Felix asked, confused, due to his previous run in with the uniformed element.

"Once they are sorted to whatever their jobs will be, either from their previous jobs, or by observed potential by the major. However, most of these useless fucks never had a chance to develop any useful skill for the benefit of society. Most of them made money through YouTube channels or Snapchat or Twitter or whatever the fuck it was called. Very little actual job skill, most of them were in high school, fast food, the few older generation fuckers, even they are slim pickings for any real craft. Engineers, doctors, mechanics, kinda scarce. But you set any of these fucks in front of a computer, they will reprogram that motherfucker in a few minutes."

Felix laughed, "Yeah, much like our skillset was nearly outlawed by these kids. Amazing to think that they ended up needing everything they were trying to destroy in the end. If that isn't irony, I don't know what is…" Felix drew in a deep breath through his nostrils, "I fucking love this world."

"It was all too perfect," Gavin agreed, "almost every conspiracy ended up being true, yet the population would have rather fought each other instead of the government. If this didn't happen, it would have been a civil war. Starting to turn out like the Middle East; if there isn't an enemy, we will fight each other, because after all we are only here to end life."

"As we should."

Gavin laughed, nodding as he too said those words, "As we should."

The group made it back, trudging through the thick sand, slightly disoriented, sweating profusely. They quickly grabbed their canteens chugging them dry. Standing back in formation, steam rolling off of them as the sweat glistened in the now risen sun.

Gavin stood up, looking at his watch, he stood in front of them.

"You've got one hour for chow and hygiene, don't be late. Fall-out!" he roared.

The soldiers roared back in tired motivation, something along the lines of 'YES SIR!' Felix couldn't make it out due to being lost in his own thoughts. They dispersed rather quickly, heading back toward the hotel. Gavin brought Felix into their classroom. It was full of old school chairs with small tables that fold away. Gavin sat in his big office chair behind an old wooden hand carved desk. They ate; Gavin, a piece of bread, a piece of cheese, half an apple and some jerky. Felix had his usual rations and a beer. For some reason he had had to maintain a buzz lately. He didn't know why, but the soberness made the world seem superfluous and his mentality, hateful. Gavin didn't ask, because he too, understood.

The next hour Felix asked a multitude of questions, the monetary system in place, the stores, other rules of the area. Gavin had gone over all of it. The new government was implementing a new monetary system. Melting down the old coins and destroyed all the old notes. The new system was purely coin based. Gavin tossed his friend the coins he had in his bag.

Laid out on the table, three coins, one of a dull metallic color, a symbol of a volcano exploding with stars littered across the sky was the tails side, the heads had the fitting symbol of the chimera. Felix had seen this symbol on the uniforms of these soldiers like the ones from Subtropolis. For some reason he liked it, it was the perfect symbol. The next had a nuclear symbol on it, it was silver. And the next was gold, with the tails side being a biological symbol. In a scroll that ran around the border of the coin on the head's sides of all three, Felix poorly read aloud in a weird accent:

"Evolutione Unius Gentis Regeneramur Cinere."

"What the fuck is this?" Felix asked, flipping the coin around to show his friend what his curiosity was demanding.

"It's Latin."

"Yeah, I know, fucker. What does it mean?"

"From the ashes we are reborn one nation under evolution, or some shit like that," Gavin spoke it in some comical minister's sermon you would expect from a southern Baptist church. Felix was waiting for the choir to begin singing its praises, but alas, this heretic view would never reach such ears of those rhythmic followers.

"There is nothing like this in the west."

"Yeah, it came in a few months ago," Gavin replied.

"How much is it worth?"

Gavin thought for a second of how he was going to explain it. He smiled as he replied, "Meals for a day, or a box of bullets, things like that, its value is defined by how well you can barter." He pointed to each of the three types of coins.

The dull metallic one. "That's a piece of bread."

The silver one. "That's a slice of American cheddar."

Felix's face split in a smile on the brink of laughter. Gavin pointed to the gold coin, "And that is the whole goddamn sandwich."

Felix broke into laughter. "Fuck you," he said laughing.

"I'm fucking with you, they are calling them pieces, like the dark ages. Ten dirty pieces…"

He was pointing to the dull metallic ones. And then he pointed to the silver one. "Or one clean piece." And then he pointed to the gold. "Or one Pure piece, is worth about a hundred dirty pieces or ten clean pieces."

"I'm confused," Felix said as he flipped the gold coin, catching it, sitting back in his chair.

"Everyone just calls them dirty, silver or gold pieces."

"How do I get them?"

"Major Thompson pays us once a month. Bonuses are given out depending on missions."

"Bonuses?"

"Yeah, if we raid an old base and get some good shit, or bring back medicine or canned foods, animals, females, shit like that."

"Interesting," Felix pondered momentarily. Then he brashly spoke out, "What the fuck have we gotten ourselves into here?"

"This place is survivable, but don't trust anyone here."

Felix pulled out his picture. "Have you seen her come through here?"

"You are searching for her? Dude, I figured you guys were together when all this bullshit happened; no offense, but I didn't think you would be searching for her after everything that has happened. The chances of her survival are miniscule at best. If even she did survive, what do you think is going to happen when you find her? You are just going to escape and try to carve out a life out there on your own?"

Felix put it away, ignoring the truth in Gavin's words. "I thought not." His face was beginning to twist into a scowl, or rather a seriousness that quieted the very atmosphere.

They were done with their food. Gavin stood up, throwing his coins into his bag. "Come on, I'll show you something. I'm sure you noticed it before."

Felix got up and the two went outside, Felix popped open another beer, they lit cigarettes and stood on the deck of the old vacation spot. Gavin pointed out toward the collection of boats tied together, forming a floating fortress on the water.

"You see that?"

"Yeah?" Felix replied looking out on the glassy horizon.

"Chances are, if she came this way, she's probably seen what type of shit hole this place was, and decided to move on. If she came this way, and ever was here, that's where most people go to escape this place. We have a shaky pact with them, they fish and we provide them with fuel. They mainly stick to themselves. We provide protection for any movements on land and they watch

187

our backs on the water. But again, the leader of the little stronghold hates the commander here. Might need to meet them at the docks one day and see if you can go out there and walk around. See if she will turn up."

And at that moment, Felix stood there, lost in his own head. Formulating a plan, a concoction of insanity and "it just might work" mentality.

A squeaky high-pitched cracking female's voice pierced their ears like icy spikes. "Come on, let's go. We have another month to get you limp dicks ready for selection. Let's go, bitches!" The distance and wind carried her voice, thankfully, out of their ears.

"Gavin…" Felix said.

"What's up?"

"You and I need to get out there."

"Yeah," Gavin replied as matter of fact.

"But first, we need to talk to them. One day, soon, that shit I seen out west, I'll explain later, but it's coming this way. It may already be here. We may have a way to escape this place, with their help."

"What's going on, you just got here, and already wanna leave?" Gavin was, with thin eyes, searching his friend's eyes for answers.

"What kills us?" Felix asked.

"The dogs do," Gavin answered. Felix shook his head.

"Not what I meant," he said holding his fingers up clutching his lit cigarette. "Staying in one place, shoot move, communicate kill, or shoot, get locked down, and fucking die. This place is impressive, don't get me wrong. But what's coming will fucking roll us over."

Gavin held up his hand.

Felix looked at it as Gavin pointed with his other hand.

"One of few, remember? You told me this a long time ago, what makes us wealthy? I trust with my life?"

Felix nodded as he recalled the day he explained it to his friend. That wealth doesn't come from your pocket, or the things you have, but comes from the people who would be there in your death, when you have nothing to give other than a lifetime of memories. Their moment was broken with the sound of familiar voices approaching. A tone of disbelief as they asked if that was Felix.

The two men turned to greet the approaching group. Chris, Alex, Gerald, Mitch, most of them were here, Felix was relieved again, even though Gavin had told him, seeing them brought a different relief. Seeing them in the flesh was much more reassuring. They greeted their friend with nicknames and shit talking along with hugs and strong loud pats on the back.

188

However, their greeting was short-lived. Major Thompson approached the group. Calling for Gavin and Felix to follow her. They got into her truck and headed back to the main fort.

*****

Gavin and Felix were standing in front of the colonel, equally confused.

"Gavin, your class has been canceled. Felix, sorry, but your reunion will be postponed for another time." Monica gestured to have Gloria leave, closing the door behind her.

"What is the issue, ma'am?" Gavin asked.

"I'm understanding that you two were soldiers together during the war on terror."

Felix nodded while Gavin replied, "We fought in Iraq and Afghanistan a long time ago."

Monica turned her laptop around, pressing the space bar. A video began to play. No sound, just four camera feeds. One over-watching the drive way, the corner of the brick building, one of the interior showing a command center, weapon cages, boxes, pews piled in a corner, and uniformed men and women going about their night, some sleeping in sheet covered areas, some sitting at a table eating, playing cards, two at the command center, and two guards patrolling outside the grounds. The last camera was oriented to the rear of the building looking into the wood-line.

"Which outpost is this?" Gavin asked.

"It's the southernmost post, Isle of Wight, St. Luke's Church," she replied, her hands folded in front of her face. Felix and Gavin watched the video carefully.

The video played for a moment longer, until something caught the attention of the two guards patrolling around the building. They readied their weapons as light flooded into the screen. They immediately dropped their weapons and put their hands up. A convoy of military vehicles pulled up to them in the small half-moon drive that rested in between the graveyard and church entrance. One of the men jumped out of the Humvee and exchanged words with the two guards.

Immediately the guards made a run for the archway, but were cut down by machine gun fire from one of the trucks. The people inside the church were stunned, they hurried to their weapons and gear. Two small soldiers split, one running to either side of the church. They took aim at the stained-glass windows, firing into them. Each then pulled a hand munition and tossed the grenades into the church.

The group inside stepped away from the canisters. The canisters began spewing a small stream of gas out. The white clouds began to screen the camera's view. Small flashes could be seen through the clouds, small strikes of lightning crawling its way toward the mantle. The smoke eventually cleared as the soldiers spilled into the room. Checking for dead, one of the occupants, still alive, pulled something from their plate carrier. They tossed the object under the command center. The soldiers opened fire and killed the survivor. The grenade went off, cutting the camera feed out.

"Do we have any other information?" Felix asked.

"No, just an estimated number of soldiers. They appear to have two tanks as well as five Humvees, each with .50 caliber machine guns. The tanks appear to be operational; they man the tanks, they send small elements into the town to retrieve supplies, but we have a feeling they are going to move soon. They definitely have our location. The computers may have been destroyed but there were maps in that outpost as well. Not to mention safe houses, locations of our other outposts. I need you two to go there and destroy them."

"Just us?" Gavin asked. "Are you out of your fucking mind?"

"I need two soldiers' tactical knowledge, that can get in and get out. They have a leader, killing them would be sufficient enough, you will be given everything you need, free of charge. Either of you know how to drive a tank?" she asked.

"No," Felix replied. "But five minutes and a cigarette later I'm sure I can figure it out."

"Don't worry, to answer your question, I'm not sending you two alone out there, you will have a team. I have a few girls who can operate a tank. I just need some grunts to do the footwork and clear the building, recover any documentation, computer systems, communication equipment. You are going to be my recovery team."

"Do we have anti-tank munitions?" Gavin asked.

"They won't get here in time; we have been waiting on the delivery from the north for a few weeks now. I want to hit these degenerates before they have a chance to move, and I want those tanks."

Felix shook his head. "We need maps, imagery of the building and the surrounding area."

"Done." She handed them a yellow envelope. Gavin pulled out the contents, looked to be drone screenshots of the wooded area, the graveyard, and all four sides of the small church.

"Gavin, you know where everything is here. I want you two on the docks tonight, your movement will be by boat until you get to Smithfield Station where you will link up with your team. They will travel west on the 258 where they will drop you two off. Cause enough commotion so the Tank Crews can steal the tanks. I don't want prisoners; I just want results."

"Clearing operation," Gavin replied.

"Search and seize, kill all of them. If you can, find out if there are more, otherwise I could care less what happens to them. Also, you know our laws here. Recover any women and children you find that are slaves or food for these criminals."

Felix chuckled to himself. Gavin smiled at him, Monica was confused.

"Care to explain why you're laughing, Felix?" she asked in a condescending tone.

"I find it amazing that because of the dogs residing in the cities, everyone would rather eat each other than fight to find food. We reduce ourselves to creatures worse than the dogs and their infected. It baffles me, that we exist in such a way."

"You should know full well what another human being can do to another, in the name of ideals, so why is this baffling to you?"

"That we are such trivial creatures."

"That's why we are trying to save as many people as we can, this is why I need you two. You know war, you survived this, both you and Gavin. Felix, you saved one of our own soldiers, by yourself."

"I find it hard to believe that you need us. Don't you have actual special forces or rangers that survived and joined your little military?"

She sat forward, turning her computer around. "Felix, most of those hard men died saving this place, the ones we had gave us the fighting chance in the winters that followed, they gave us a structure, taught the young to be like them. Their sacrifices during the migration of the dogs will never be forgotten. Now we are left with soldiers like you. Why do you think you were put with Gavin? Your talents and experiences are needed to continue the old ways of war. Because when this is all over, and there is no infection left, who do you think we will be fighting?"

"Each other, which merely makes a point as to why I'm so baffled by our existence," Felix replied.

"We will have to put this discussion on hold. I need you two ready; the boat leaves at dusk, so get ready. I have your partners on the next hardening assessments of the defenses of our other outposts. Just in case you two fail."

"Alex, Chris, Mitch?" Gavin asked.

"Among other, Gloria and her team, and some of my younger team leaders." Monica replied.

"Understood, it will get done." Gavin replied.

The two left the office. The sun blinded them for a moment. They both lit cigarettes as they walked down the steps.

Gavin broke the silence after a moment. "Alright, let's make our rounds. I'll drop you off at your room to get ready after we get some supplies."

The day went by quick, Felix stood staring at himself in the mirror. He whipped shaving cream on his face and picked up his razor. Pausing for a moment as he starred at it. He chuckled to himself, and began to shave.

"Whatcha doin, babe?" Sasha asked.

Poking her head in from the bathroom door frame. Felix turned. Razor in hand, shaving cream all over his face, wide-eyed like he got caught doing something he shouldn't.

"Shaving, hunny," he answered as she walked into the room. She leaned against the counter, watching him as he continued.

"Why do you use a safety razor?" she asked.

He looked at her through the mirror, but she was staring at him. Watching his every move.

"I don't know, it's cheaper, I like the way it feels, it's classy as fuck." He laughed, she giggled.

He noticed her stare; it was almost locked as he rinsed the razor. Smooth skin exposed from his meticulous work; he slid the razor down once more. She continued to watch, mesmerized by it.

He looked at her, then back into the mirror. "Why are you staring so hard, you weirdo?"

"Pot," she said.

"Kettle," he replied.

She shrugged and scooted closer, now leaning against him, an arm wrapped around his waist as she watched him from the mirror. "I didn't have a dad growing up, my house was full of strong women. I find it interesting that you like to shave, I like watching you do your manly stuff. I'm not used to it."

He nodded. He was almost finished, only a few strokes of cream left to scrape with the blade.

"Fair enough."

"Who taught you to shave, I take it your uncle did?" she asked.

"I honestly don't know, memories of my childhood are very fragmented," he replied, rinsing his blade, setting the raiser in his hygiene kit, then leaning down to rinse his face.

"What a pair we are?" she said.

He stood, she handed him a hand towel to dry his face.

"Ten years younger," he exclaimed. She immediately grabbed his face, feeling it with her hands, rubbing her cheeks and lips against his smooth face.

"Mmmm." She certainly approved.

"I like your few days' scruff, but this, this is always nice," she said, playing with his cheeks.

"Oh yeah?" He laughed. She pulled him in for a kiss.

"Yeah, who knew that you could clean up so well?"

She turned and headed out of the bathroom.

Chapter 14
Dog Run

Gavin laughed as he saw Felix load his green bag onto the boat.

"What, man?"

"Felix and his bag of tricks," Gavin replied.

Felix laughed. "Yeah, ha-ha, like the old cartoon."

"When we were younger, I remember the first time you showed me what you carried in your bag before we went on patrol. Grenades from frag to incendiary, smoke, a grenade launcher and belt, you always packed to either fight or survive, so what tricks did you bring on this adventure?" Gavin asked just before taking a swig of whiskey from his flask.

"Oh, you know, the usual tricks."

They both began laughing as the boat departed.

A young lady opened Monica's door. "Ma'am, they have departed."

"Good, let the Station know that their search and seizure team is en route."

"Yes, ma'am."

In a mere few hours and a scenic route, they had arrived.

A very hard looking woman was standing on the port waiting for Gavin and Felix. Gavin was all smiles when they arrived. Felix was curious as to why, until he saw what gave him that smile. She was indeed beautiful, no make-up, her dark hair was braided down to her butt. Her dark green pants stretched around her strong legs. Her long sleeve combat shirt was tight against her torso. A vehicle and driver waited on the street, a guard standing on the other side of the SUV. Gavin jumped off the boat on to the dock, walking straight toward the woman. She jumped into his arms, he spun her around in an embrace so warm that Felix had to smile.

"I've missed you," she said, kissing him deeply. He held her up by grabbing her butt, she wrapped her legs around him.

Felix walked past the two quietly, smoke trailing from his lit cigarette. Felix walked around to the back of the SUV, the back opened automatically, Felix tossed his and Gavin's bags in. He walked around to the driver's side.

He leaned against the vehicle. The young woman, maybe in her teens, popped her head out. "Hey, can you not smoke near the window, it's disgusting."

Felix's head wrenched. *Who the fuck?* he thought to himself.

"The world ended, and all you old guys still smoke, so nasty," she said.

"Who the fuck are you?" Felix said as he turned to face her.

"I'm the driver, so my vehicle, my rules, and you will not be smoking in this baby, I'll make your ass walk."

"Oh, yeah?" Felix grunted.

She flipped him her middle finger. "Yeah, you creep."

Gavin and the woman walked up behind Felix as he took a long drag. Inhaling carcinogens and his response that was going to be as thick as his cloud.

"I see you met Sophia. Careful, she'll beat your ass, don't let her age fool you, she is an ace with a blade."

Gavin tapped Felix on the shoulder. Felix turned, fury slowly fading from his eyes.

"This is Elena Rogers, she is the outpost commander here," Gavin started the introductions.

"Nice to meet you, Elena," Felix held out his hand, shaking hers.

"Nice to meet you too. Hop in, let's get you two up-to-speed."

The group loaded up into the vehicle. Sophia continued to pester Felix who was humoring the girl with his own ridiculous banter.

Smithfield Station was heavily fortified. The windows boarded up, reinforced with steel plates. The roof sported well-built towers, Constantine wire, and soldiers patrolling. They parked in a small lot that had been walled off with barriers of concrete and more wire. The location was impressive, and the overall morale of the men and women operating out of this location seemed to be in good spirits.

"Come on, old man," Sophia called to Felix.

"What the fuck, listen here, child, I'm only… Gavin, how old are you?"

"I'm not a child, I'm fifteen!"

"36," Gavin replied confidently.

Felix did the math for a moment. "31, you little shit."

Sophia burst into laughter at Felix, so did Elena, as they escorted the two men inside the main hall of the station. Soldiers of all kinds were sitting around waiting, weapons ready, bags packed, plate carriers ready to be dawned.

The four entered a room full of screens and monitors, the command center. The girls walked them over, onlookers shot the two men a curious look, but continued to monitor and work at their stations.

"Alright, in one hour we are heading west along route 258, we should arrive there by midnight. Once set in, we will have soldiers set in here, here, and here."

Gavin and Felix paid close attention, they pulled out their maps, marking locations and making their own imagery from the map in front of them. Felix pulled a pen from his mouth and pointed toward the forest surrounding the church.

"We should hit them from here, coming from any other direction would be suicide, not to mention they probably will be more focused on the sound of vehicles. They probably have an observation post set up in here at the very least, we can hit these fuckers, and make our way. You guys can set off an explosion or whatever, just make some noise, don't use projectiles unless you have precision, because we will be skirting the building and attacking them from behind while they are focused on your element. Once we hit the church, you guys should have infiltrated the tanks so long as they are unoccupied, and that will be it."

"Not bad, simultaneous infiltration, enveloping maneuver, with a shock and awe attack to cause a fainting operation for misdirection. I knew Gavin was a tactician, I guess it would make sense his brother was one too," Elena replied.

Sophia looked at him puzzled, surprised.

"No, I'm certainly not, that's just how I would do it." Felix replied as he continued his drawings on his small handmade map board.

Felix and Gavin walked outside, each lighting cigarettes waiting by the armored truck that would be their chariot into battle. Their battle gear very similar to each other, Gavin sporting his M4 and Felix his AR. Their pistol holsters on their battle belts lined with magazines and grenades. Night vision goggles on mounts sat on their helmets. Their plate carriers were lined with magazines and smoke grenades.

"What's up with the Elena lady?" Felix asked Gavin.

He grinned, "I kinda have two or three partners." He chuckled.

Felix shook his head, "Careful, that shit will get you killed nowadays."

"It's legitimately consensual and legal, they all agreed to share due to desirable genes."

Felix cocked his head. "Fuck man, that shit will get you killed nowadays."

They both laughed.

"They were soldiers before the world ended, huh? Who needs them, anyway! Doesn't the commander trust us to get the job done?" Sophia asked.

"She does, but it's basically a chance to see what Felix is capable of, so keep an eye on him. You and I will be their coms out there."

"Right," Sophia replied.

The crew loaded up, the convoy was ready, and they headed out their rolling metal gate. It didn't take long before the convoy made it to the drop off location. Felix and Gavin jumped out and immediately headed into the forest, Sophia and Elena struggled to keep up with the two. Felix and Gavin glided through the woods like ghosts, almost making no noise.

Gavin and Felix suddenly stopped, taking knees behind trees. They halted about a hundred meters from the edge of the wood line. They crouched low, moving slowly, bounding forward to about fifty meters. They sat there. The girls behind them moved as quietly as possible, Elena behind Gavin, and Sophia, attempting to catch her breath behind Felix.

"We're in position." Elena called out on the radio.

"Roger, standby, we hit a road block, attempting to find an alternate route. You may be on your own for a while, over."

"Roger, standing by," Elena replied.

Gavin and Felix continued to observe the church. The rear of the building reminded them of a Mario brick castle. The church was all brick, several arched stained-glass windows. A steeple just over two stories tall in the front. Two fuckheads patrolled around the back of the building where they stopped. One of them lit a smoke.

"This place creeps me out," one said to the other.

"Yeah, the guys have been saying that they have seen a ghost walking in the graveyard."

"That's creepy, but this whole ground has people buried from the 1800s in it, probably even older than that."

"Yeah, I never much liked graveyards; I wonder why the boss hasn't moved us out yet?"

"I heard some of the guys talking about changing our plans, heading south, because the dogs are moving back north."

"I hope wherever we go, we have a chance to get some pussy, it's been months."

They both laughed.

Elena's ear piece scratched as the transmission blared into her ear. Gun fire picked up in the distance echoing like low thuds and cracks that only thunder rolling knew.

"We made contact, a small unit is patrolling. go now, the tank crews have moved forward."

Elena tapped Gavin, pointing to move forward. Sophia tapped Felix to do the same. The two picked up, moving with their weapons up. The soldiers ran to the corner of the building, looking into the direction of the gunfire. Gavin and Felix both snuck up behind them. Their knives out, they both, as if it was choreographed, grabbed the men by their weapon slings, planting their boots behind the soldiers' feet, pulling them hard to the ground on their backs. Gavin and Felix landed on the men with their knees, sticking their blades in their necks. The men both died looking into those dead eyes, both of them, like sharks in the ocean. They sheathed their blades and began clearing as if back in Iraq. The girls followed closely behind, watching their backs, under the illusion that they were in control.

The gunfire continued, slowly picking up. Men started rushing out to the Humvees, the leaders started yelling orders. Gavin and Felix tossed smoke in all directions, even though night, they knew it would choke them at the very least. The chaos that followed surprised the girls. Both men ran into the smoke, the enemy couldn't reinforce the element in contact with their crews. Gun shots, screams rang out in the night; Felix and Gavin killed so many. Sophia and Elena moved into the entrance of the church. Sophia placed a small charge on the door, they both moved out of the archway to either side. Elena pulling security for Sophia. Felix and Gavin rushed back toward the girls.

Sophia depressed the initiator, the charge blew the door in. Felix and Gavin entered, clearing the building. Sophia and Elena were hot on their tails as they split coming into the room to clear. The two girls watched as Felix and Gavin fired, their rifles never dropped, they just swung left and right, they shot each target three to six times. The man sitting at the command station stood up, his hands raised. Felix kept his weapon aimed at the man's face.

"I gotta hand it to you guys, I wasn't expecting much of a retaliation after taking this place over."

Gavin butt-stroked the man in the face. "Shut the fuck up," he sternly demanded as he dropped the man. He cuffed him with zip ties, picking him back up onto his feet. Gavin walked him toward the entrance with haste.

Felix put a cigarette in his mouth and lit it. "Well, that was uneventful as fuck," he said, bellowing out smoke.

The ground started rumbling, the church shook.

"You're pretty good," Sophia said to Felix, taping him on the shoulder. Gavin and Elena were escorting the leader toward the blown open entrance.

The whine of a turbine spooled down, the electric drive of a turret halted.

"Get the fuck down!" Gavin yelled, pushing the leader out the door. He turned and tackled Elena.

Sophia turned. Felix pushed her. She hit the floor hard on her back, sliding into chairs. She watched as Felix turned, ripping the smoke from his mouth, grinning.

The tank fired. The leader was splattered from the blast. The tank round ripped through the back of the building, exploding in the wood line.

"You good?" Gavin yelled, standing, pulling Elena to her feet.

Felix exhaled a thick tube of smoke like a dragon; shaking off the concussion from the blast, glass and bits of ruble fell from him.

"Yeah, let's get the fuck out of here," he yelled as he scurried over to Sophia. She was covered in bricks and a beam from the rafters.

Felix smacked her. "Hey kid, you awake, you good, come on back, girl," he spouted as he looked over her. Nothing looked broken, the beam, however, was laid across her torso.

Gavin leaned out to take a look, soldiers began moving out of the smoke from behind the tank.

"Come on, cock suckers." Gavin grunted as he pulled a pin from a grenade, holding the spoon in place. He listened for their footsteps, some went around back, others paused for a moment. Gavin let the spoon fly.

"1…"

"2…"

Felix threw the beam from Sophia, picking her up. She came to, dazed.

"3." Gavin tossed the grenade out the door. The men standing outside heard, noticed, and then yelled almost all at the same time— "GRENADE!"

They scattered just as it went off. The tank turret oriented to the right, aiming at the wall Gavin and Elena are standing behind, and further in Felix and Sophia.

"Stop wasting rounds, go in there and kill those motherfuckers!" one of them screamed.

Sophia held on to Felix, coming to fully.

"There you are, kid. Come on, hold on to my carrier, we are going to escape, we can't fight a tank," he said, she nodded. He was not sure if she heard him.

"Gavin, let's fucking go!" he yelled.

Gavin and Elena were pulling pins on smoke and frag grenades, tossing them out the door. She pulled and handed them as Gavin peeked and tossed. Machine gun fire ripped into the building, narrowly missing the team.

After they sent the last volley of hand munitions, Gavin and Elena ran down the church staying out of the opening as much as possible. Smoke bellowed, grenades went off. Men and women screamed after a few seconds from the last blast.

Once back together and behind cover; Elena checked Sophia like a worried mother. Felix and Gavin were next to each other, on a pile of rubble, their weapons were up, ready.

"Go," Gavin grunted.

They too dropped out of the back of the church. Gavin landed, firing, killing one, two, three men coming around a corner. Elena was ready watching his back.

Felix at the same time, tripped, and fell on his side, hard. The soldiers were caught by surprise as they came around the corner on his side. Felix fired, rapidly, his rifle sounded like a slow machine gun. He dropped two, two more backed around the corner.

"Clear," Gavin yelled.

Felix pushed with his left arm off the ground, he was on his feet with one swift thrust and a mad shuffle. He sprinted, sliding to a stop on both knees just past the corner. His weapon up, he fired, hitting the soldiers in their knees, they fell right into his cadence of fire. The rounds ripped through their heads, killing them instantly.

"Clear," Felix replied.

The girls were behind them. Sophia taking up her position behind Felix, and Elena posting up against Gavin, using his shoulder as a rifle rest.

"Felix, you and Sophia move first."

"Gavin?" Felix called as he pulled out two grenades, he turned nudging his little partner. Sophia looked down, realizing what he needs; she hooked her finger through the rings and pulled.

"What?"

Felix tossed one down the corner of the church, Sophia followed behind him as he tossed the other in the church.

"Do you battle drill nine?"

Gavin laughed. He knew exactly what Felix was talking about. "Yeah."

"Alright, we are setting it up."

Felix and Sophia disappeared into the woods. Gavin, rifle up and ready, peeked around the corner, firing rapidly. The grenade went off in and on the outside of the church. Soldiers slumped to the wet grass from the explosion. More screams were heard from inside the church.

Elena kept security on the opening and the corner as best she could. Never dropping her weapon, because their lives in fact depended on it. And for the girls, their sanity, their souls, for if they were captured, they would experience far worse than death. What they had known during the beginning of this world.

200

Gavin fired rapidly as more soldiers sprinted around the side of the building. They fell, slid, fired randomly as they rushed back behind cover. Elena tapped Gavin's shoulder; she began firing as he peeled away, heading into the wood line. He reloaded as he sprinted to a tree. He took a knee and began firing. Elena broke away and sprinted toward him, just out of his line of fire.

Felix stopped. "Sophia, I need you to rig an explosive, can you make a trip wire, or is it all command?"

"Command," she replied.

"Okay, set it up, I want it as big as you can, save some just in case," he replied.

"Where are you going?" she asked as he disappeared into the woods back toward Gavin and Elena.

"Okay," Sophia, irritated, said aloud to herself. She began emplacing a brick of Semtex.

Elena and Gavin continued bounding back by way of talking fires. Felix was on his stomach, setting a log on a grenade. He tossed the pin, got on a knee, and waited for Elena and Gavin. They started moving toward him, he waved them off of his booby trap. They passed him, and Felix followed.

Felix was laughing, an unnerving laugh, that gave Elena chills as he passed her with a whipping of fabric through the air. He ripped tree limbs off without even slowing his momentum. He was almost cutting a path through the thick wood with his body.

"Follow me. Sophia should be done." Gavin and Elena fell into a file as Felix led them to her.

Sophia was walking backward, unraveling her pressure line. The rest of the team, Felix and Gavin, both turned and began firing. They stopped, bullets started smacking into trees around them. Nothing accurate, just probing fires from the soldiers.

The soldiers began chasing after them into the woods. Blinded by their anger, not thinking at all anymore. Any soldier worth their weight in salt would realize that by now, flanking would be the only logical option. Taking such men on was suicide at this rate. Alas, one soldier ran over the log, tripping and falling. The spoon flew, the ring hummed as it fell through leaves, frightening the soldier. He crawled to a staggering run as fast as he could. The grenade went off, yielding no enemy casualties, but that was not what it was for. The grenade was meant to scatter formation and any logic they possessed.

Sophia detonated the block, the explosion cut trees down, threw debris in all directions. Felix was kneeling next to her as pieces of debris pelted him.

"Look, look," he said tapping her. She looked through her night vision.

"It's beautiful," he said.

She just caught what he was talking about. Through the night vision, they could see a dome of sparkles shinning bright green as they flickered into the dark. Some pieces floated down, still glowing, and it was, she thought, he was right, it was beautiful.

The crew continued their movement, making it toward their vehicle pick-up location. Their vehicle was waiting for them, ready to get them back to Smithfield Station. Gavin flashed the driver with his laser, it was returned, letting them know it was safe to move.

The driver popped his head out. "Hurry the fuck up, get in, dogs are moving this way!"

Gavin and Felix pulled security on the road as the girls piled in. Felix jumped in as did Gavin. The driver burned rubber, doing a half donut and speeding off.

"Well, that was exciting, we should come this way more often," Felix laughed as he lit a smoke. Gavin did as well.

Elena took measure of Felix as he sat there. He was relaxed, looking out the window, a smile on his face as the smoke snaked from his nostrils. He laughed to himself again, taking a drag. Sophia was staring at him too. She was watching his cigarette like a cat watching the red dot from a laser pointer. She swatted, knocking the smoke out of his hand.

"What the fuck?" he asked.

"That is going to kill you!" she spat back.

"Oh yeah, no more than working with you fucks will!"

The two argued the whole way back.

The vehicle stopped, the crew got out and walked into the command station. Gavin and Felix grabbed their bags from cages and took an empty table, they both started reloading magazines and replenishing their grenades and smoke. After they were done, they both quietly walked outside while the girls got their brief and gave their report. The men sat on a bench under the stars, smoking.

"You know it's been a long time since we had a run like that," Felix said, breaking the silence.

"It's good to have you back, nothing's changed, we picked up right where we left off, eight years ago."

Felix was surprised. "Goddamn, eight fucking years ago."

"Last time we saw each other, Thanksgiving; you just announced to everyone that you two were getting married, surprised all of us. A devil and a goddess."

Felix looked up at the sky, exhaling a gracious cloud of smoke.

"I see you boys wasted no time getting ready," Elena said as she sat down next to Gavin. Sophia sat next to Felix, giving him a look of disapproval as she watched him smoke.

Elena produced a bottle of wine. "I think we should drink."

"We are not heading back out to deal with those fuckers that survived?" Felix asked.

Elena's head dipped; she was distraught. "The reason why no one else made it back…"

"The dogs," Gavin finished her thought.

"Yeah, they took care of the rest of the soldiers, the alpha demolished both tanks. We don't know how, but the drones we sent only caught the creatures leaving the scene. They came from the west, hit the elements fighting on the highway, and headed to the church. We made it out just in time."

Elena poured glasses for all four of them. They held their glasses up.

That night Gavin went to bed with Elena, but there wasn't much sleeping done. Felix slept on a cot in the command center. Only to be woken up by Sophia, who tried to crawl into his sleeping bag with him.

"What the fuck are you doing?" He grunted as he sat up. She stood there, upset that he just declined her advances.

"Why?" she asked, disappointed.

Felix reached down and pulled out his picture.

"You are fifteen."

"That doesn't matter anymore, the world ended."

Felix laughed. "It didn't for me. Just because I kill, and survive by any means necessary, doesn't mean I'm going to let go of my own morality."

She sat next to him, leaning her head on his shoulder. He held the picture over to her, she took it.

"She's beautiful. So, this is the real reason why?"

"She is the reason I continue on, even if she is gone, even if she has someone else, I just have to know. Until then, I'll keep searching, and surviving, because that is what she and I are, great by ourselves, decent people, but together, we were fantastic. Sometimes memories is all you have to press on."

"Can I sleep here?" she asked.

"Go to bed, I'll see you in the morning," Felix said.

She got up and quietly left.

The next morning Felix and Gavin threw their bags on the boat, Elena gave Gavin a warm and sloppy goodbye, that was received well with plenty of groping and an embrace that made Felix and Sophia turn away.

"Come back to see me soon, okay?" she said as she slapped his butt.

"You got it," he replied.

Sophia held out her hand, Felix shook it.

"Take care of yourself, old man."

Felix smirked with a slight nod. "You too, young lady."

"If you don't find what you're looking for, I'll be waiting," she spouted, jumping to give Felix a hug.

"Thanks for saving my life in the church." She kissed him on the cheek and backed away.

"You better come back and see me too," she said as she stepped off the boat onto the dock next to Elena.

The girls waved as Felix and Gavin returned the farewells.

The boat chugged along, the girls out of their sights. "I see you still have a way with the ladies," Gavin spouted sarcastically.

"Shit, I didn't do anything, she tried to sleep with me last night."

"Goddamn, well, you are a badass motherfucker, probably one of the few real men she has seen in a long time," Gavin replied.

"She was a child, regardless if society is no more, my moral compass may be very broken, even before all this; where the needle landed is where my morality won't be swayed. It's where I want it to be, not where others want me to point it."

"I like that, you're a good man."

"Hardly. You're one to talk though; Elena, huh? How come you didn't mention her before?"

"Long story," Gavin replied, trying to wave off Felix's interrogation.

"We got a ways to go, brother."

Gavin laughed. "And a ways longer still."

"Gavin is an interesting guy," Sasha said as she moved around the kitchen, cleaning the counters.

"Yeah, we used to be soldiers together. I worked for him a while back, then eventually got my own squad, dumb shit happened, and we ended up in different places. He never backed down, he always lived on his feet."

"Well, you guys are able to see each other now, so that's good."

"You're very right, babe." Felix laughed.

"What?" she asked with a surprised smile on her face.

"I was just thinking about a training exercise we once did. It was ridiculous. Back in the day the army used to have this thing where you were always deploying, rotating back to train and fixing your equipment, get blessed off by the powers that be, then deployed again. Readiness was the name of the game. The training exercises were always force on force. And, for some

reason, this one was particularly strenuous. We had four hours to set up our hardened defenses; we succeeded, it became a safety hazard so the enemy could only attack from the front gate and the forest to the north, which at that time of the year due to the controlled burning, was easily observed, even at night."

Sasha reached over, grabbing Felix's beer, and taking a drink. She handed it back, noticing that he wasn't looking in any particular direction, he was looking into that memory.

"So, we have always been known as the most violent NCOs of our platoon, maybe even the company, I challenge to say the entire unit. Not just because of training, but our histories while deployed. Especially him, he was much more violent than I ever was. For good reason. We were both raised by the same badass motherfucker, who died when we were just privates. Anyway, getting to the point. This training exercise went on for four days, we were actually stopped because we operated and fought for two days straight, exhausted all of our ammo, and ran out of food and water. The observers that were assessing us had killed off all but six of us. Only leaders were left, to see what we could do without soldiers, just ourselves."

Felix laughed again. "And when you died in this game, that was it, there was no coming back, so we had a Platoon Leader, his radio guy, and four NCOs all rocking machine guns running around killing the enemy. But, the first day was still the best."

Sasha handed Felix another beer, leaning on the counter, listening intently as he continued.

"We got into so much trouble, probably the reason they killed off all our guys. But, during the day we got into several small skirmishes, trucks with mounted weapons, IEDs, at that point our kills were into the triple digits. Finally, we get a chance to head back to our little base, we loaded back up, restructured the squads because of all the casualties that we had to evac out, and as soon as we had a chance to eat, the village that was right outside our gate began to light the place up. All the while, a company, our heavy weapons company was rolling through, they got destroyed, so we had to go out and recover them."

"This was training?" Sasha asked. "Sounds more like an actual war."

"This is the way they tested us, it was all designed to make us fail, see where we rise to the challenge or where we break, so we may learn from it, so in the future, we could survive a seemingly impossible situation. They were frustrating, but fun."

She kissed his cheek. "Sorry, please continue, I like your stories."

"Thanks, babe. Okay, where was I?"

"Your heavy weapons company was destroyed in the village."

"Ah, yes, thank you. Anyway, we only had two guys on the towers, they were shooting everything in the town, there had to be a couple hundred people in there shooting at our sister company and our base, it was ridiculous. Old Gavin, he had this look of hate on his face, he took it seriously which was good. We got together, and ran out the gate. We ran straight into the village and started taking buildings back. The coordination between us on the ground and our towers was beautiful, they didn't even need to hear anything over the radio, they watched our movements and just shifted fire on their own to suppress the enemy in the next building over."

"Sounds like you guys had been working together a long time."

"It had been a few years at this point. So, we get into the village and Gavin broke us into teams, he took one and I took the other and we started clearing to our sister company. The observers were laughing at the ridiculous way we were fighting. We started dropping so many enemies that the observers just started killing our guys for no reason. One dude ate shit running to cover, so they laughed and killed him right there, another guy jumped out of a window and ate shit, they killed him too. It was stupid shit they were killing all our guys with, to see how we would supplement the loss. It's kinda hard to do anything, when it ended up with just Gavin and I. We took our guys' machine guns because we were out of rifle ammunition at this point, and started clearing everything. Eventually the few enemy that were left decided to attack us from the church in the village. Rules are you can't attack a church, and this entire training exercise was to be treated as real life."

"What did you guys do?"

"We attacked the church, killed all the bad guys, there wasn't anyone left except the company that finally recovered their vehicles in the village. They took all our dead guys and evacuated them for us since we took a heavy hit. We provided security so they could move back to the main base. When Gavin and I were done, we were pulled to the side by our Platoon Sergeant, he hated us anyway so it was no surprise. He put us in for real punishments, but if it wasn't for Gavin, and him having so many friends in the other companies, we would have been fucked."

"Well, why didn't you get punished if it was such a bad thing?" Sasha asked.

"The other NCOs heard about it, heard who did it, and all of them started attacking the churches even if only one shot was fired from there. They couldn't fuck us all, and the reasoning behind it was legitimate, so we were left alone after that."

"What reason was that?" she inquired.

"If the enemy decides to occupy a location, it is no longer a place of worship, or school, or house, your eyes have to be quick. Even after we were so tired, beaten from running into walls or falling in the woods, I even smashed my face on a machine gun while reloading a belt as I was sprinting to cover, you have to be aware as much as possible of your surroundings. That's one thing I guess we were always good at. We could see who the enemy was, even in training where your enemy isn't just a man with an AK, it's a woman with a knife or a suicide vest, it's someone in your uniform. It was probably some of the best lessons in life, because they helped in real life, when it absolutely counted. I saw much, and when they went away from those exercises I was upset, because that's what I ran into out there in all those countries. Suicide vests, enemy in our uniforms, massive road side bombs. Heavy casualties from rocket or mortar fire."

"One day I hope you can tell me those stories," she replied. Felix nodded and continued.

"We became quite famous in the unit, by the end of that exercise, our platoon had killed over three hundred bad guys. We didn't get awards, but the soldiers knew, the other NCOs knew, that we were the most violent leaders in the unit. It was fun, those deployments, the training, the soldiers, good times and bad, it was still the best I've ever had in the army."

"That's good, babe, you'll find it again."

"Maybe. That unit doesn't exist anymore, they shut it down after our deployment, I still think back to those times. Gavin and I always got lucky, even when we were being thrown to the wolves. I'd do it all over again with him. That suffering, and all that came with it."

"It's good you have someone like that as your brother, I still have a hard time trusting even my own family at times, but you know that, I don't know why I trusted you so easily." Sasha leaned on Felix.

"I don't know either, maybe because I'm a trustworthy guy?"

Sasha laughed. "Maybe, but you're also a big softy, I can't imagine you being violent, or at least I've never seen it."

"You probably never will, babe."

Chapter 15

The Wolves' Den

Since Felix had arrived, they turned out one trained element so far, the month had flown by, currently due to a lack of people being found or people seeking sanctuary. They didn't have any idea when the next group would arrive for training. Their days had been spent on the beach, at the range, and most recently running missions to the north and south of the Peninsula, yielding supplies, weapons, but no survivors.

As Gavin and Felix leaned over the side of the small boat looking at the old harbors and docks, They slowly moved through the channel. In search of survivors or anything they could haul back. Radio chatter sparked up, desperation in the voices, it cut out and came back in. They must have had been some good ways out, more than likely thirty-six miles, Gavin attested as matter of fact. They were after all using short wave civilian radios.

Next to them were large packs. A few days' water, food rations, and each a car battery and fuel stabilizers. Today's haul was vehicles. Mainly trucks or other sport utility vehicles. And of course, anything they could find along the way. Their destination, Yorktown, Virginia. Their team, which consisted of Chris, Alex, Gavin, and Felix, plus a few hopefuls from the last training push were attending as well. A total of nine.

It was a warm day; the water blue as could be and the light green of moss that grew up from the water onto the thick concrete walls and over the streets and crawling up buildings. As odd as the growth had become, even on Fort Monroe, it was still beautiful, Felix thought.

"You wanna know the real reason why we are out here doing bitch work?" Gavin broke the silence.

"Enlighten me, my friend," Felix replied, blowing smoke from his nostrils.

"The high and mighty powers that be did not like the fact that the women and men coming out of our little experimental training program were bent on equality. And not *her* idea of women being the superior sex."

Felix was looking at Gavin now, an eyebrow raised. "No shit?"

"So, if you didn't know, the partnership bullshit that you keep hearing about is a no shit real fucking thing. The reason why we, you and I mainly, are not allowed on Fort Monroe, except for special occasions, is because the colonel and all her infinite wisdom has deemed us too brash and dominate. Not part of her agenda to drive men under the boot of women."

Felix was grinning. "Interesting, and I have always been one for true equality." He laughed hysterically, his smoke pulled away by their forward propulsion and the wind.

Gavin continued his rant, Felix listened like he always did. "She is trying to use us like cattle, for babies and fun. Did you know homosexuality is outlawed here?"

"No shit, what's their religion?" Felix was now instigating the conversation.

"It's Christianity, it's led by…Isaac, tall skinny, always well-dressed and mannered black guy."

Alex and Chris walked from the group of women over to their friends leaning on the railing.

"Yeah, our Isaac," Alex said.

"No fucking way," Felix replied.

"Yeah, if they only knew. Know what I mean." Chris stated, nudging Felix and Alex with his large tattooed arms.

Felix took in a drag. "I guess they don't know that he leans more to the same sex then? That's good. I know I probably should go see him when we get back. I can't believe how many of us made it here. How many stories are similar to ours, and why were we all so lucky when so many were not?"

Alex replied, "Best not to think about it, the past is the past. Lucky for us, most of us were close to each other and were able to get out together. Between all of us old grunts, we had enough weapons and knowledge to move and fight our way out as fast as possible. With all the crazies out, there was enough commotion for those just trying to run to get out. A lot of people were initially infected because of their animals. I was drinking, I let Yeager out to use the restroom, but when he returned, he wasn't the same. He was barking and growling at me. I locked myself in the bedroom. I found my gun; he broke through the door and I shot him dead. After that, the blast had gone off and the town started going to shit."

Chris nodded. "We ran into each other at a gas station somewhere in Louisiana, my truck broke down, and this slut rolled up in his mustang asking how much for a blowie. Like the world hadn't ended."

Felix and Gavin started laughing hysterically.

"Man, I missed you fuckers," Felix replied.

Although Felix hadn't been there for the beginning of their journey, he knew for a fact that they had done as terrible things as he had to in order to survive as long as they had. These days, life was much better than back then. The first few years had been rough on them. Killing children and women, men, friends, family; whoever was feral. All of them had terrible stories from the first few years of the pandemic. And during all the running and killing, stealing, and moving from town to town, the winter and ash seemed to never end. How they made it this far was almost a mystery to even them when looking back on it all.

"Thinking about it, there is actually a lot of homosexuality in the fort, but people keep it secret as much as possible. The only ones that seemed to care are the fuckers at the top. Monica's little cronies, but Alex is keeping her shit tight so, at least we know our people are safe for the most part," Chris said, patting Alex on the back.

"Well, something we should continue to keep to ourselves, I'm sure," Felix replied.

"Anyway, so how does this partnership shit work exactly?" Felix asked, interrupting his own previous thoughts and any further mention of their friend that could be heard by wandering ears.

Chris tapped his shoulder with a heavy hand, pointing out into the water as if his point was there to be seen. "So..." he began talking with his hands looking out of the corners of his eyes, up and to the right, past everything, anything, like he always did when he was about to give his conviction over a point.

"You see, the way it works is... Once a month, if you have not been partnered. There is a dance, where everyone goes to, kinda like a trading post, you go with whoever, but the women ultimately decide who gets to go home with them. One, two, I've seen this fucking guy go home with five girls one night."

Chris was nudging Alex. "Got that big dick. But, because of that, there is a new law that states a man can only be with up to two women in their lifetime here. They can also be loaned out. But everything is recorded in order to keep in-breeding from happening in the future. We are tracked like cattle." He jokingly paused.

Continuing through the laughter of his friends and comments from the group, "Mainly though, it's the women going home with multiple men, but that's the younger ones. The chicks our age, late twenties, early thirties, they usually chose only one man. And if two ranking officers chose the same man. Fuck! You better stay outa their way. They will kill you," he said that last part

210

in a ridiculously passionate comical tone, pointing his finger downward aggressively.

"Even after all this, you are such a bro, dude," Felix joked.

Chris threw his long black hair out of his face, combing it back with his fingers.

"Whatever..." he replied. "Anyway, before I was rudely interrupted."

The group was still laughing. He continued, "You'll see what I'm talking about. Soon. I think next weekend there is another gathering. It's where badass motherfuckers like us get a chance at the crème of the crop." Chris nodded in agreement with himself.

Alex complimented him, "You're the crème of the crop."

Felix chimed in laughing, "Your mother's, crème of the crop."

Chris replied, "My mother's dead."

Gavin replied as matter of fact, "All our mothers are dead." Which in fact was true.

But that comment only got them laughing harder. The women on the boat looked at all of them, hearing most of their comments to each other. They almost couldn't believe them; they were monsters in human form. But if the commander trusted them enough, then they must be better than the majority out there in the wastes. And of breeding quality.

"What happens if we don't want to go with the chicks picking us?" Felix asked.

Chris held up his hand, nodded with almost every syllable. "No, bro, these chicks are bangin', I mean like primo." He threw up an okay sign with his fingers, nodding.

"I want MY woman," Felix replied, this time with a straight face, staring into the ocean. The ocean always reminded him of her. The beauty, the very depth of her soul was that of the ocean. And being around it reminded him every day of her, and how far he'd come, with merely a single clue, and she wasn't here.

"Alright, we are here," the driver of the boat yelled through her cracked voice, from a knife run across her throat years before. Although she was barely old enough to drive a car; when you used to need a license. Her scars on her body would suggest she lived a life; most beautiful young girls did when they were caught by the wrong people. Until she arrived here, she had hoped every day that the infected would catch the gang that killed her family and had taken her, among many others.

"Thanks, Natalia. God, like we couldn't see the docks from here," Chris replied in his best impersonation of a weird character from one of the National Lampoon movies. She smiled, she liked Chris, he was a very attractive man, and very kind to women when he wasn't giving them a hard time. His way of showing them that he liked them.

The boat turned strafing in the water until gently touching the dock. The group was off the boat in seconds. Weapons in hand, taking measure of the area. The boat quietly pushed on back down the peninsula.

"You guys ready to fuck today in the face?" Felix asked comically.

"You're so sassy today," Alex replied in good fun.

"Let's go," Gavin ordered, taking point as they all spread out a few meters apart, staggering down the dock. Watchful as a group of soldiers sneaking through enemy lines. It wasn't long before they found a good group of cars to investigate. The best places were car dealerships. Keys were easy to find, and the vehicles for the most part were in good working condition, save for the dead batteries, stray bullets, sometimes fire damage from something catching fire during the riots and panic and spreading of the Pandemic.

"Reminds you of the old days, huh, big guy?" Felix asked as he stood next to Alex staring at a 2017 Ford Mustang GT. It was blue with two thick white stripes down the center running the length of the muscle car.

"She's mine," Alex said dreamingly.

Karen, Melisa, Amanda, Courtney, and Shaniqua. They walked past him, two of them eyeing him like a piece of meat. Onc shy. Felix followed them with his eyes as they walked, checking each of the men out. Much like they had been on the boat the whole way over.

"Typical, calling it a her," Shaniqua scoffed. Her clothing was tight around her thin muscular body. Her skin dark, her eyes a light brown, her hair was in dreads pulled into a pony tail. Her face, young with high cheekbones. A very attractive young woman, dressed in dark green fatigues, boots, a tight tank top, under which she was not wearing a bra, everyone could tell she still wore piercings.

Alex turned, pointing in their general direction, looking down, but nose up, with his hands now on his hips. "You, go find some wheels. And stop being so sassy."

They laughed and continued walking through the rows of Ford vehicles in the large lot. It was quiet. Old stickers detailing the car's fuel efficiency, which was poor compared to what ford offered in every other country except for America. Felix looked around, recalling a time when he was considering a Ford truck.

"Man, I would have loved a Toyota Hilux or that Raptor Ranger. Fuck it, I need to just find a cop car. At least those vehicles were made better than what the average production model was. It's funny how they lowered the standards of vehicles for the rest of us, but made sure that the coppers had the latest and greatest tools to keep us all in fear."

Felix laughed in that sinister monotone cackle that was creepy and unnerving to the rest of the group.

*****

The group was installing batteries into their respective vehicles when something caught all their attention. The buzz of small propellers ripping in between buildings. It drew close very quickly.

"What the fuck is that?" Felix asked.

"Probably our eyes in the sky," Chris said a little too loud for their comfort. As if being quiet made a difference at this point.

Gavin called up over his radio. "Base, this is War Turkey One." Felix started laughing.

"You serious?"

"Yeah, I still got the patch we made from the old days too. We live by bullet and blade, and die by the same. The Shotgun Sergeants. The War Turkeys."

Felix nodded with a smirk of approval. The buzzing caught his attention to direction of origin. But it wasn't the noise that dropped his smirk. He saw it sitting on a car that had flipped and burned to an empty shell. It stood there, tall, its ears perked up. Its eyes, all six of them, stared at him. Felix was frozen.

"Hey, Felix, you alright boo boo?" Alex asked, looking in the general direction that he was.

Felix could hear its heavy furnace of breath, bellowing thick smoke from its nostrils. Its horrible white teeth gleaming although the beast seamed to call the very darkness to it. It was midday and yet, the city never looked so dark, even under the night sky.

Alex put a strong hand on Felix's shoulder. The thing, the black dog was gone. Felix wrenched his head toward the pressure on his shoulder. Shooting his friend an evil stare, murderous, and not the man Alex knew.

The buzzing noise got louder.

"You alright, big guy?" Alex asked, even his big blue eyes couldn't hide his concern.

Felix's eyes shifted back toward where the black dog was sitting.

"We need to leave right now, something is coming."

Alex was confused. "What are you talking about?"

"We need to get out of this shit hole right fucking now," Felix replied, looking back down the street.

"War Turkey, this is Base, over?"

Gavin turned, talking into his radio, "Confirm, eyes in the sky on our location?"

Radio static, "Negative, War Turkey, you have no eyes, next on-station is at Checkpoint 3, copy?"

"We need it now, someone else has a bird in the sky. We are en route to base, War Turkey out."

Gavin stepped up the side of his truck he just started, shouting to the others, "Let's fucking go, that is not ours!" he roared, his voice echoed even over the buzzing noise.

Everyone began to rush to their vehicles, starting them up and pulling onto the road in line. Before they could turn down I64 headed south; the little drone buzzed over-head. Everyone followed it with their eyes as much as they could from the windshields of their vehicles. It was gone, replaced by the sound of rumbling, the ground was shaking. A car slid on its side slowly to a stop, impacting the side walk it fell onto its bare rims.

The beast stepped out. Infected crawling around it like puppies, sniffing the ground. Looking into the air they continued to catch the scent. And they found it. Immediately all of the infected closed their mouths and lifted their hands, paws, like a hound dog pointing on a hunt.

Gavin with his commanding tone told everyone to start fucking moving. Everyone responded with the peddle buried to the floorboards.

The vehicles all began accelerating simultaneously. The infected broke into two groups. The alpha ran down the street parallel to the group. Some infected chased the cars letting out frantic woofs and screeches. Felix shimmied his way into the back seat of Gavin's truck. He slid the back window open, propping his AK out, ready to fire.

"Lay some fucking hate, brother!" Gavin roared in utter excitement.

Felix began to fire. His semi-auto almost sounded like a machine gun. He dropped all of the infected chasing them.

"Goddamn, just like the old days," Gavin laughed wildly. Dodging a turned over car, keeping distance from the other vehicles.

"I wonder, this seems too easy."

"Clear?" Gavin asked, looking through his mirrors to see tumbling and dropped bodies quickly disappearing in the distance.

"Clear," Felix replied, leaning on the center council. "Make sure they know that we are still being chased, they are on the other side of the buildings."

The other three vehicles, Alex and Melisa were in the front of the element in the Mustang. Right behind them, Chris and Shaniqua in a large Toyota

Tundra, and behind them, Courtney Amanda and Karen driving a Chevy Silverado. Taking up the rear, Gavin and Felix.

Gavin turned his head slightly toward his mic clipped onto the corner of his jacket. "Be advised, infected still on our asses, right side strong side."

Alex, Chris, and Karen all replied in sequence, "Roger."

Karen called over the net a few moments later, "Looks clear, no sign of the infected."

And if irony had a conscious. The alpha slammed into their vehicle. The vehicle swerved, Karen over-corrected, and it flipped on its side. Alex and Chris slammed on their breaks. Gavin slammed on his breaks. Felix and Gavin jumped out as the vehicle barely rocked back from the transfer of weight.

Their weapons were up, firing, first Gavin, then Felix; they talked their guns as they glided toward the giant dog. Their fire never slowed, and their magazine changed almost choreographed. Even after all these years they still worked well together.

What breed it was, they couldn't tell, nor did they care. It flinched from being hammered by continuous fire. Chris came out with his M4, his selector switch from safe to Auto, he dumped an entire mag. The wound splashed with pink and red mist as the rounds tore into the side of the giant dog. The beast growled viciously. Chris had another mag in within seconds, this time firing several bursts. The beast turned its attention on him. Alex and the girls were rushing toward the flipped vehicle, their weapons up, but not engaging to maintain stealth.

The feral still alive finally caught up to their alpha. They were horrifically mutated. Alex spotted them, he ducked behind cover, immediately popping up and squeezing off a round. The bullet ripped through the face of a screeching thing. She, maybe it was a she, dropped silently.

"Go, get them out, and back to Chris's truck, now," he said, pointing. "Move your fucking asses," he said as they were hesitant for only a moment.

The dog barked, the throaty vibration could be felt through the ground. It turned, leaping toward Chris, he dodged its massive mouth narrowly. He sprinted to the turned over vehicle Alex was behind, still picking off charging infected. Alex popped up. The shell flew and the last one tumbled and slid on the concrete a foot before lurching forward to its last breath. The shell bounced off the side of the car with a satisfying clink.

"Hey, buddy," Alex joked. Chris was breathing heavily. The beast was burnt from the sun, its sagging skin pale white, almost looked like milk. Its large egghead sported massive jaws and thin needle-like teeth in multiple rows. It had a dark spot on its eye. Large pointed ears. No tail, no other mutations they could see other than it was the size of a truck.

215

"Hammer?" Chris asked.

"Hammer," Alex replied.

The two stood taking aim on the dog. Firing as fast as they could, the beast sprinted for the girls now, disregarding Chris and Alex.

The girls pulling their injured counterpart from the turned over truck. Gavin looked to his right, no Felix. Felix was moving so fast; the world began to slow down. For a moment, Gavin watched him cover fifty meters in an instant. Felix stepped off of a wheel in the road, leaping. He came down hard with his weapon. Landing a heavy hard butt-stroke on the beast's forehead. Felix heard something break, he fell to the ground, rolling back onto his feet. His weapon was in pieces, the folding stock was on the ground, the back broken, the bolt hanging off the receiver. The dog let out a whimpering bark as it spun its large head, nipping at Felix wildly. Felix stepped back a few meters as the dog regained its balance. He tossed the broken weapon. The two stepped in a circle, side stepping like two fighters in a ring. The beast growling, and Felix catching his breath calmly.

Alex and Chris looked at each other, then back to the spectacle.

The dog stopped, as did Felix. The beast lunged, Felix drew his 1911 like an old gunslinger, firing from his hip as he rolled out of the way. His arms now out, shooting as properly as he could, given the circumstance, rolling, jumping backward. Shooting again, and again. Silver magazines flipped through the air as he reloaded his weapon. Most of the bullets skipped off its thick skull. One caught the beast's eye. It shook, blood splattered like a fan of fountains spiraling away from a hose.

"Fuck," he said, dropping the empty weapon, as calm as could be. He then recalled why his rig was set up the way it had been for years, even before the pandemic and the volcano and, the end of the world. It didn't end for him.

A police officer or FBI Agent wrote a small bit on a gun magazine some years back, on why he carries different caliber types. The article went on and on about the many situations that this one individual had been in that he had in fact survived. However, one time, the guy had been attacked by a Pitbull, and he had to engage the animal several times, due to the thickness of his skull. The 45 ACP wasn't going to cut it, he switched to a .40 caliber weapon for capacity and relative ballistics to that of the 357 Magnum, and a snub-nose 357 magnum revolver for thick skull animals, or heavily clothed criminals. It was that little lesson to which Felix found motivation in his methodology, based off the idea that there was never going to be a perfect caliber, they were tools, some could be used for multiple jobs and others for specific jobs.

Never one perfect caliber, Felix thought to himself.

The guys' attention was on Felix at this point. Shaniqua and Melisa were now carefully pulling out Amanda from the back of the truck through the busted windshield.

Felix reached under his dirty orange coat. From his shoulder holster he produced a black Smith and Wesson 44 magnum in *"4 inches of fuck you,"* he would always joke. Its wood smooth grip a beautiful dark walnut. Its solid cylinder spun as he cocked the hammer, taking aim with both hands. The beast's head cocked to the side as it took measure of the man's confidence and relaxed stance.

The alpha began running, as something came from behind as well. Alex, Chris, and Gavin had begun engaging, walking on line on both sides of the street. They were attacking the rest of the pack they presumed was owned by this alpha. Feral were dropping in dead sprint behind Felix.

Felix could see them out of the corner of his eyes, the flashes from their muzzle breaks, the shells flying from their receivers, the look of determination, purpose, and momentary satisfaction as they were dropping the infected. It was beautiful, Felix thought. The alpha leaped, opening its massive jaws, that could have easily bit Felix in half. Felix fired the revolver, the heavy loads roared over the sound of the rifles. The rounds impacted deep into the beast's chest, it landed, Felix dodged narrowly. Chris, Alex, and Gavin shifted their firing to ensure they didn't hit their brother.

Felix dodged the wild beast's next chomp. Taking aim once again, he looked the beast in the eye. He fired, the beast slumped to the street, sliding from its momentum. Felix tripped over the curb, falling against the sidewalk.

"He killed that motherfucker," Chris laughed. Alex and Gavin continued firing; Chris rushed to his friend. Felix got up, grunting, another screech alerted him to an advancing feral. He turned, looking calmly surprised, lazily lifting his weapon, he fired, the beast slumped over to the side falling into the ditch.

Gavin, Chris, and Alex all walked past him. "You good, bro?" Chris asked walking by, tall and tough. Gavin hopped over the hood of a car. They heard another screech. "Fuck you." Gavin replied, a gunshot and then his footsteps continuing down the street. Felix watched them clear. *It was like a dream,* he thought. *Look at them, my brothers.* It put a smile on his face. As he turned, he walked over to his weapon. The thin part of the buttstock was crushed, by the beast maybe, no… It was his hand print that griped around the polymer folding stock. He picked up the receiver, the hand guard had the same imprint. He looked around, ensuring no one had seen them, tossing them into a pile of rubbish.

The girls had already got the other three patched up and one in each of the three remaining vehicles, to include, their gear. They wasted no time and were on the verge of leaving the men behind as they were all gathered around Felix.

Chugging a beer empty, he tossed it, another. He lit a smoke. And again, opening another beer. Alex looked at him curiously. As did Chris, and Gavin; none of the girls saw any of what he did. And the girl that was laid out in their truck was passed out from pain killers.

"How?" Alex broke the silence. Felix spit a thick stream of smoke, rubbing his forehead.

"I don't know," he replied through a fake smile.

"There's no way your skinny ass can take on a dog, you jumped onto its head, and butt stroked it. Where's your rifle at?"

Felix's eyes slid to Chris, "I don't know, weird shit has been happening, I feel younger, I feel much more hateful, like in a way I can't explain. That's why I've been drinking so much."

Gavin shook his head, "Not here, we need to get back."

Chris leaned in, comically pointing at him. "That big dick is how you did it."

They laughed a little, but it faded quickly. "Need to keep this shit to ourselves, guys. I don't know what is going on, but I think it has something to do with those drones, this little fuckcd up military, and certainly the black dog."

"What black dog?"

"You didn't see it?" Felix asked.

Alex shook his head, "No, I saw the big ass white one you made your bitch, just like the whore you are."

Again, the seriousness was stolen from the conversation. As most of their conversations always started, continued, and ended.

"Let's get back, it's getting late, and we spent a lot of ammo just now. We cannot get into another engagement bigger than that cocksucker," Gavin stated. The group agreed, and broke, headed to their vehicles, mounting up, and headed back to Fort Monroe.

*****

"Why in the fuck are three of my girls in the hospital on a simple supply run?" the colonel roared. She could be heard throughout the building, muffled, but loud enough that it was audible through the thick old walls of the headquarters' building.

"Ma'am," Felix began.

218

She snapped a deadly look at Felix. He stopped, looking back at her.

"Three vehicles, that is all you brought back, you think this was a success?"

"To be fair, ma'am," Chris began defending his friend with a scowl on his face, looking off and to the right like he always did, "it was a huge fucking alpha. He killed it, and most of its pack, but there was nothing we could do. They got hit from the side. We were ambushed."

"Ambushed? Fucking animals and infected humans ambushed you?"

She was becoming furious; they could all tell, at this point everyone in the fort could tell. Felix stepped forward as to take responsibility. "Ma'am, someone led them to us. A fucking drone led them to us. We had no idea who or why, and considering the sophisticated equipment I've seen your military with, some intelligence would have been nice."

"You insinuating that we had something to with this, led the infected to MY GIRLS?"

Felix interrupted her, "No, due to the fact that you care about your girls more than anything. What I'm saying is; someone is out there watching us, watching you, and fucking with the infection."

She let a sigh out; she knew he was right. Her eyes raked upward and slid over, making eye contact with each of the men. Her face softened for a moment when they met Alex's.

"What is your assessment?" she was talking to Alex, none of them now mattered, save for him.

"Yes, ma'am. The dogs were led by an aircraft, a quad copter model, and then was off, more than likely spying on us. The infected split into two groups, kinda like wolves do. They separate the weak from the rest. And considering that the infected in tight spaces can easily overwhelm a vehicle, and the alphas are showing some interesting traits. For instance," he walked over to the desk sitting on the corner of it. She said nothing, only sat back in her chair. The rest of the group were standing with their hands folded in front of them.

Alex continued telling her the entire story of the endeavor, leaving out Felix's extraordinary moment. The rest of the group was sent home. Alex stayed in the commander's office alone.

Monica got up and walked over to Alex, kissing him deeply.

"I was very worried about you."

"I'm fine."

"You're not going on any more of those runs. You will be reassigned."

Alex shook his head as he held onto her. "It was fine, so what are you going to do about them interfering with us?"

"Nothing we can do, what did you see out there?"

"Felix is not normal. What happened to him?"

"Something I'll explain to you later. For now, leave me."

"Alright, I see how it is. I'll just have to force it out of you later," Alex joked as he closed the door behind him.

Monica logged onto her computer. She played the video over again. Pausing it as Felix brought his weapon down hard on the dog's head, saving the girls from it. She pressed play. Watching him dance around it, it almost looked as if the two were playing together, if you took out the pops from his gun, and the splattering of blood that poured from the alpha's wounds.

She attached the video file to an email and sent it to Doctor Steinberg.

*****

The next day Felix walked through Fort Monroe, he had a day pass to purchase another weapon due to the loss of his AK. The day pass was a special permission granted by the colonel for men of low status to be able to visit the main fortress.

There was a gathering at one of the buildings, designated the fortress's courthouse. Felix walked over due to curiosity. The doors were open. The entire room was majority women. A man was cuffed and standing in the center of the room. Several men and women were in chains in a line along the wall. The judge was an older woman, in uniform. Felix had never seen her before.

"…you are familiar with our customs and ways, to include the laws we all follow here. Yet, you still decided to commit acts of homosexuality. You know the penalty for your crimes against the community and the preservation of the human species… Exile."

The room was quiet, he could smell the weight of judgment across the entire floor. The man said nothing. He was escorted from the stand and the next was brought up. A young woman. Her crimes were the same, and she would not give up her lover.

"…your punishment will be impregnation. Once the child is born, you will be exiled. Hopefully your offspring will carry your genes on with dignity. Next…"

The sentencing continued for very similar crimes. It was astonishing but not surprising in the slightest. However, when Felix looked around the room, he saw the faces of young women and men. These same people were more than likely the ones that used to cry out for everyone to accept what others wanted. To coexist, freedom, equality. Now look at all of them. They became exactly what they hated.

A young woman was next, but she wasn't playing the game. So fierce in her demeanor. Felix could sense it; she was a predator among the prey. She wasn't going to be the victim here.

"...and you..." the judge started, only to be interrupted.

"We can't help what the heart wants. I love women, and I always will. When the world ended, we had a chance to become better than the old ways. Equality and acceptance. Yet, I am being judged for something I have no control over—"

"Yeah, pedophiles said the same thing. There is no cure for your kind, and right now we need to rebuild society, not cater to those who don't get their way. You are a woman, and should be the epitome of our species, yet you have fallen victim to these unforgivable sins. If you can't reproduce, or don't have the compacity to want to be partnered, then you will be impregnated and cast out. That is the law—"

The young woman cried out, "I will be who I am no matter what. I love her and I regret nothing. You will all die here, one day people like me will rise up like they did years ago—"

The older woman interrupted her again, "...and your kind will fail, because a species can't exist if it can't even comprehend the importance of continuation of the species—"

"There are many more like me, you can't get rid of all of us, we will be the ones who change the world, and you, relics of the old ways, will fade away, eaten by the infected and the dogs, because they are coming for you all...my people are the next stage of evolution!"

Her voice was drowned out by the yelling and cursing from the onlookers in the room. She was violently jerked from the stand. The next was brought up. Felix shook his head and walked out. Lighting a smoke as he stood on the steps of the makeshift courthouse.

He noticed many people watching him, soldiers looking at him. Females shooting him looks of wanting and some of confusion. They heard the stories already about how he distracted the alpha saving the females on his team. Two females were being escorted in zip ties, screaming and crying out words of love for one another. They were jerked and dragged past him.

Felix stepped off the steps and took a look around. He realized that it wasn't the beasts, the feral, the alphas, the dogs that were his enemy. It was this fort and the majority of the people inside it. As he stood there taking in the world, watching the two young ladies ripped away from each other, hauled off to be judged. He saw it, but he guessed he always knew in the first place. This place was more dangerous than the wastes. And he walked right into it.

"You don't approve of our laws here," Monica asked.

"I always believed that laws give the illusion of safety and retard our very ability to reach potential. But they exist to keep the cattle or flock safe, so I understand it. We all need to eat something. But, seeing others' wills imposed on populations in the shitholes I've been, this place is starting to look like those places. I'd be careful, one day these people are going to realize that they are truly free."

"Enjoy your day pass, Felix."

"Yes, ma'am."

"You have to be the only man I know who grills a turkey for Thanksgiving," Sasha said, propping her head over to see how the food was coming.

Resting her chin on his shoulder, handing him the beer she was drinking.

"Well, once I was in Germany, and the stoves were so small that you couldn't fit the birds you could buy on post. So, my friends and I chopped that fucker up, and grilled it, seared it, baked it. To this day, grilling is my all-time favorite. And like my honey steaks, you drizzle the liquidy gold goodness right before you take it off the direct flame."

"Caramelizing it. I gotcha, I smell what you're cooking."

He laughed, she snatched the beer from him.

She smacked him on the butt. "Come inside as soon as you're done, everything else is almost finished. I need your help with the potatoes, you make them better than me."

"Nonsense," he yelled back.

Dinner was finished, the spread looked amazing. The only things on the counter close to thanksgiving type foods was the turkey and mashed potatoes.

"I burnt the pecan pies," she said leaning against Felix.

"Yeah, but I think they turned out great. Like giant nut cookies." They laughed.

"I like this," she said.

"Yeah, me too."

The counter had green beans, mashed potatoes, an egg and spinach casserole, miniature pecan pies, grilled turkey, that Felix sliced in half with some precision. A fresh salad, spinach, cherry tomatoes, avocado slices splashed in balsamic vinegar.

"I think we did good, first Thanksgiving," Felix said with a sense of accomplishment.

"But does it taste good?" Sasha said, pulling out a bottle of wine and pouring two glasses.

"Well, we made it, so I'm sure it will be amazing, even if I think it sucks, you'll never know," he teased.

She let out a mocking, playful laugh. She snatched a piece of the turkey as Felix began to continue his butchering of it.

"Oh, my God," she gasped.

"What, babe?" Felix asked, whirling around.

"You can make turkey anytime; this has to be the best I have ever had. Here, try some," she said, shoving a piece in his mouth.

"Holy fuck, you're right. Goddamn, well, eat in here or...well, we have the puzzle all over the table."

"We can eat in here, it's fine, babe," she replied.

"Happy Thanksgiving, babe," Felix said.

"Happy Thanksgiving," Sasha replied.

Chapter 16
Howling at the Moon

Felix was sitting by himself at a nice wooden table set out on the parade field. Lights strung up trees and houses, running from lamp post to lamp post, lit the area in a star-like glow. The setting before him looked of Christmas, the only thing that was missing was the taste of frost in the air. Music played from a band, that was decent, playing older songs. They had an assortment of instruments from strings to woodwinds, brass, an electric guitar, and even a large percussion set. Everyone was lively, happy, it was odd to think that they were actually on the edge of the United States surrounded by the wasteland that was America. Not to mention, the wolves at their door, waiting for their moment.

He watched as Alex and the colonel danced around by themselves away from the crowd. Chris was easy to spot. He was being his loud usual self, being hit on by many young beautiful women. Gavin was getting drinks at the bar which was set up on the corner of the grassy field. A fire rolled from a large burn pit. Tables and cooks stood around, preparing food, setting the spread, and drinking.

The night was clear, summer was coming to an end. Felix lit a cigarette and downed another beer. A group of girls without partners walked past, giggling to themselves, judging his decent array of bottles pushed into the center of the table. He grinned as he took a long drag from his cigarette, bellowing smoke out through his teeth. They were remised by the fact that someone still smoked. But most of his kind did. Even when obtaining tobacco products could be just as dangerous as venturing into the den of the feral.

"I heard from Mitch and Dana that you were here, but I couldn't believe it."

Felix turned, and surprise was written all over his face. She was standing there, shorts and a V-cut shirt, a gun on her hip. Shoulder length light brown hair, brown eyes. She walked over. Felix stood up, holding out his arms as she walked briskly to accept them. She gripped him tight, a very warm embrace.

"Holy shit, Britney, how have you been? I had no idea you were here, none of these fucks told me you made it," Felix said as they pull away. He looked her up and down. The two all smiles as they greeted each other for the first time in years.

"Still as gorgeous as ever," he said.

Her smile was large. She couldn't hide it. He held out his hand, offering a seat to her next to him. The two sat, leaning close.

"I work in the hospital with Dana, both my boys made it here with me safely. Alex and Chris got us here. If it wasn't for them, we would have probably died out there."

"Well, thank fuck for that," Felix replied.

"So where have you been all these years?" Britney asked.

The band did their best impression of *Wagon Wheel*, the Darrius Rucker version, the version Felix always liked best.

Felix told her what had happened as best he could paraphrase it. She listened carefully. Eyes wide with surprise. If for any reason other than the fact that he had survived such a treacherous journey on his own, and when things looked worse, somehow, he got lucky every time.

"You never found her?" she asked.

"No, I haven't given up, but the future is looking bleak the longer I stay here."

She placed her hand on his, "Not to sound cold, but it might be time to—"

He put on a fake smile, "Yeah, I know, I've been told many times."

She quickly changed the subject, "Would you care to dance?" she pointed toward the field.

"Sure." He stood, holding out his hand. She accepted vigorously.

The two old friends walked toward the crowd. *Thinking Out Loud* was being sang now, and Isaac was leading the vocals. Felix was feeling nostalgic now, it was starting to feel like the old days. Surrounded by friends from long ago.

The two slowly moved around in their own world, laughing and talking as the music played beautifully in the background.

Britney's demeanor changed and she allowed herself to lean into him more.

"You know the rules here?"

"Yeah, but they don't exactly apply to me for some reason," he joked.

"Same old Felix. Not what I was talking about," she playfully suggested.

He spun her slowly.

"Oh yeah? And what is it you are referring to then?"

She shifted eye contact shyly, "We've been friends for a very long time, and I always thought there could have been something between us, but chance wouldn't let that happen."

He listened and she got closer, speaking into his ear, "We could try now, I don't have anyone, and you don't either, and we could, you know?"

He stopped, and she stood there. Holding each other closely, he pulled her away. Taking a long deep look into her eyes. She leaned in, kissing him. But it didn't feel right, he was cold, she thought. She pulled away, searching in his eyes. What she was looking for was lost in an odd blank stare.

"I'm sorry, that was a terrible kiss," he said with a simple smile.

"It's okay, we could try again someday, if you can let things go, you know where to find me." She backed away, and walked into the crowd.

Felix stuffed his hands deep in his pockets, he walked back over to his table. Gavin returned rather quickly with five bottles, three for Felix and two for him.

"She's been asking about you, and Sophia too, you're becoming popular around here. Felix and his flock, starting to sound like back in the day. Are you going to lead these women astray like so many before them?" Gavin asked with that sly grin on his face.

Felix laughed, "I hate to say it, but…" He pulled out his picture, almost in perfect timing as two women walked over.

"Care to—" she was interrupted by him holding up that picture.

"Have you seen this woman?" he asked, with a straight face, the one that everyone seemed to think was his scowl.

One called dibs on Gavin, she already had her hand on his shoulder. He was smiling like a kid on Christmas. The other girl let out a dissatisfied sigh. Before he even picked up his beer, Gavin stood.

"You going to be okay?"

"Yeah, man. Go have some fun. Better hurry, your beer may be gone by the time you get back."

The young woman, hand on his chest, waving her head around with a big smile full of teeth, seductively replied, "Don't worry, he won't be back."

Gavin was gone into the crowd with the young woman.

Mitch and Dana Conner walked over. This is the first time he had seen them since he got there. He stood flicking his cigarette's cherry burning into the night. He hugged them both.

"It seems everyone is stopping in to say hi," Felix joked.

Mitch and Dana were both in their late 30s. Still young at heart. The same height. Sophisticated look. Mitch wore glasses, but even in the dark you could see his steely blue eyes. Dana had long thick brown hair. Both fit as any couple could be. A testament to their ability to survive anything.

"What's up, man?" Mitch asked.

"Please sit," Felix replied.

Mitch pulled out a chair for Dana, she sat.

"You two haven't aged a day," Felix said with a smile.

"And you look younger than you did the last time we saw you," Dana replied.

The three caught up quickly, telling each other of their exploits and what they had been doing now. Before the two were about to get up and go dance, Dana stopped and turned.

"Britney has been looking for you," Dana said.

"She found me," Felix replied.

"And? You know she has had feelings for you for a long time, she often talked about you. You two worked together a long time ago, she was a medic back in the day, right?"

"Yeah, she sewed my hand up when I was drunk and put a knife through it."

Mitch laughed, "You, moron, how long ago was that?"

Dana interrupted Felix before he could answer Mitch, "I know you were going to be married back then, but the world is different now. Maybe you should move on. We have heard from the others that you are still searching for her. It's been six years since the end of the world, maybe it's time you started living in this one."

"Maybe, but everyone is looking at things all the wrong ways. The world didn't end, it was just society," Felix replied half-heartedly.

"She needs a good man, and you two have known each other for what, fifteen years or so?"

Felix sat back, "No idea, something like that."

"Think about it," Dana said in a stern voice.

"You two get out of here, go have fun," Felix was clearly done with the conversation.

Mitch adjusted his glasses, "So, did it all work out the way we planned?"

"You mean, the way you planned. I didn't stick to the main route, but I used your plan to get here, and I told so many people about it. I had no idea if you two made it out, but I knew if you did, you two would have made this place survivable."

"Yeah, we weren't the first ones here, but we certainly built this place up," Mitch said wrapping his arm around Dana.

"I'm thinking about finding a way out of this place, a way to move all of us to a better place, outside the influence of this regime," Felix said looking around.

Dana stopped him, "Before you two start sorting out the next end of the world escape plan, I wanna know what happened with you and Britney, why isn't she here?"

Felix sighed. "We said 'hi,' we caught up, we had a beer, we danced, we kissed, she went home."

Dana walked over and flicked Felix in the head. "Why?" she demanded.

"Because I'm still searching for my woman. It just didn't feel right, I don't know."

"Felix, we've known you for a long time, and I'm honestly surprised. I recall when you were a hound dog. The world that we knew is over, it's time for you to figure that out. If you let yourself fall into your regrets or what you couldn't change, it will destroy you. Our only loves in life were our dogs, and when this happened, we lost our children, understand?"

Felix nodded as Dana continued, "I find it amazing that you are still an idiot, you have someone throwing herself at you, and a good woman at that, and you are still holding on to what the world once was. Time to move on. I thought that this is what you always wanted, so start acting like it."

"Ah!" Felix said holding his finger up, making his point, "My world could still be out there."

Dana raised an eyebrow, "That is what someone who has lost their mind would say."

"Maybe, but sometimes it's all you have to keep going. If it wasn't for that, I may have never made it this far."

"You need to apologize to her, she has had a rough time here, not one man has been good, and someone she knows, you, show up and reject her, kinda childish, I think."

Mitch had a grin on his face watching his wife verbally scold Felix, almost like old times.

"Sorry, but this is it for me, between finding her and keeping as many of you all alive as possible…"

Dana tapped him on the shoulder, "We survived this long without you, and you survived a long time without any of us, so maybe you should try to figure out how to live, instead of just surviving."

Felix sat there, quietly, taking a swig from his beer. *Fuck, she's probably right.* He picked up his picture. Dana put a hand on it.

"Figure it out. You can move on and live a good life here, like the rest of us, so remember that."

Isaac finished his last song, cheers from the crowd lightened the mood.

"Don't be such a stranger. I know it's been years, but you are always our family, remember that, Felix," Dana said, placing a hand on his shoulder.

"I will," he said as he stood, hugging both of them at the same time. They started off for the crowd to partake in the festivities.

"Mitch?" Felix called out.

"What's up?" he said, both Dana and him turning.

"Thanks, brother. Just so you know, I owe you my life."

"Stick around this time," he replied.

"You know I can't," Felix said with a smile.

"We know," Dana replied.

They were gone into their own little empty space to dance the night away. Felix sat back, recalling the first time he had met Mitch. They didn't like each other. It was such a childish notion, that he couldn't even remember why. It was a comment about the end of the world that started their friendship. *What would you do if it was Zombies, or how about nukes, what about a super storm? What would you do for each, how would you do it, when would you leave, where would you go, who would you want with you?* Conversations to pass the time while they were on mission in Afghanistan.

Felix laughed to himself quietly as he drank. Alex and the colonel sat down next to him. Then Chris, followed by Gavin. They sat there talking, about random things, things that make you forget the world outside the walls had fallen to pieces. Forget that the people next to you had killed, robbed, maimed, burned things to the ground. The smiling rosy cheeked faces of the tipsy group were somehow peaceful to him.

Even Chris was drunk, making large hand movements and being very touchy with everyone around him. Getting hit on at every turn by passing single women. Some demanding rights to him, only to be turned away by the colonel, unless Chris wanted their attention. Alex and the colonel talked quietly amongst each other; the longer it went on, the redder her face became, even in the low light of the lamps and lights strung around the trees. Food was just about ready, so the band announced. But they didn't have to get in line, no, they could wait, because it was going to be brought out to everyone who got to attend the night's events.

The meal was steak, potatoes, and broccoli. Felix couldn't remember the last time he had steak, all they ever ate in Subtropolis was chicken. *And fucking broccoli, when was the last time he had broccoli?* Years maybe, and only because of one person. His woman, always taking care of him, better than he ever cared to himself.

229

*****

People were fat and happy that night. The next event was a projected movie onto a building to which, a large sewn together sheet ran down it. Couples laid on the grass, rolling around in warmth of each other's arms. Some went home together; few went home alone. As Felix watched them all leave that night, it was almost midnight. He walked down the small walkway of the south entrance. He stopped, lighting a smoke, looking around him. The moon was bright. It was beautiful, he thought. But he couldn't shake the reason why he hated it. Why it was nothing but an annoyance, when he used to look up at the stars with her in a hammock in the backyard they were supposed to share one day.

That was it. His goal, his mission, a need perhaps, or even an obsession, he never forgot. To make sure she was okay. He could live with the idea that she had moved on. And if she did, maybe he would have the fortitude to walk away, hoping she never saw him. So that she could just leave him there in her memories. Like she plagued his with all the wonderful moments of what it was like to be in love, to be satisfied with that person. Something to him, until that point, was never known, only illusions.

He continued walking.

His thoughts playing over and over again in his head. And he heard it.

Soft music, from the 50s. "Why do fools fall in love?" A quick tempo and wonderful tune. And suddenly it was gone, something slower, older. They were dancing in the kitchen together. A knife lay on the cutting board, the sweet smell of onions, tomatoes, chives, cilantro, potatoes boiling in a pot. Two glasses of wine next to the hand towel on the counter. They glided around that kitchen, holding each other close.

How is it, there isn't a bad memory in all the time we spent together? he thought.

He looked out over the ocean. Seeing the lights on the boats that made a floating sanctuary on the water. They were receiving supplies from a run into the city, more than likely. Felix flicked his cigarette into the night. Stuffing his hands into his pockets, he walked up the several flights to his room. He stopped, turning to gaze into the starlight once more.

I hope you're alright, babe, wherever you are.

His hearing was getting better. He started overhearing a conversation between a group of women headed back to the fort. They were more than likely on detail that night to help with the exchange of supplies.

230

"It's a shame really," one of the women said to the other.

"Why's that?"

"Because, the commander is about to destroy them. They pose a serious threat to us. Not to mention I overheard that the man who runs the floating city plans to steal a warship from the Naval Weapons Station to the north of here. If he gets his hands on it before us, he could wipe us all out. Can't let them get the upper hand."

"That seems extremely presumptuous of the commander. What happened to the treaty talks and our continued supply exchanges? Why not work together? There are a lot of families over there."

"First off, watch your mouth. Someone could've heard you say that about the commander. Anyway, it's because they don't follow our laws, they take in everyone. They allow gays and freedom of religion. That's what destroyed the world to begin with."

Felix chuckled to himself. *No, young lady. It was us; we destroyed the world ourselves. Not just one person or people. We all laid down and let it happen. Like a bunch of worthless cowards. When the dogs came, that was when we started to live again.*

"Well, guess we just have to beat them to the Naval Weapons then. Shouldn't be too hard with all the survivors here. We could just send *those men*...you know the ones."

She turned, "Yeah, besides, they are dangerous here too. I don't know why the commander puts up with them."

The girls trailed off and continued their conversation.

That night Felix came to the conclusion; he needed to talk to those people on the floating city. He needed a way to get everyone off of Fort Monroe worth saving. He could feel it, something was coming. He just needed a way to get them out of there. Because what was coming, would wash over them like a flood.

Over the next few weeks, Felix investigated the rumors he overheard. Alex being so close to the commander confirmed it. The plans were already drawn up and a unit of the commander's best women were slotted to hit the weapons station within the next few months. But reports of a heavy concentration of feral moving from all over the United States had put the venture on hold until further notice, giving Felix a chance to see what he could affect.

*****

On the edge of a boat, looking at the lights slowly disappearing from fort Monroe. Her dark hair catching gust of a cool breeze from the eastern winds.

She looked up, into a bright sky. Without the light pollution of cities, or the constant noise of people crowded in their busy lives, it was calm. She just hoped the he was alright. She thought of them laying together on her hammock in the back yard. Watching the stars together. A small fire burning in a pit shed, a welcome warmth and orange glow over the thick grass under them.

"Sasha!" John yelled.

She turned suddenly, startled from her memory.

"Hey, John," she replied as he sat down next to her.

"Kim is taking the kids fishing tomorrow, wanted to see if you could take them out in the morning to your spot."

"It should be fine."

"You thinking about him, little sister?" he asked, noticing the solemn look on her face.

She sighed, patting him on the shoulder. "Just taking it a day at a time."

"He's probably having too much fun out there. After all, this world is what he always wanted."

"That's what worries me," she replied, getting up and disappearing into her cabin.

Felix was waiting with Sasha in the airport. She was waiting to go back home.

"You really like post-apocalyptic stuff. I've never heard of any of these books or movies you talk about."

"Yeah, I have a particular taste in things. Luckily, you're a weirdo."

"Pot," she said.

He laughed.

The intercom sounded with her flight boarding at gate 12 in fifteen minutes. They started walking to the check-in line. Felix pulled her around, kissing her deeply.

"I know I probably said it too soon, but I couldn't hold it in anymore. I do love you, Sasha, you've shown me things about myself I didn't even know, and have shown me what it is to have a perfect woman in my life."

"Felix...I'm sorry I didn't say it back to you. I didn't know what to do. But you can't put a time frame on this. I'm sorry. I can be so frustrating, I know."

He smiled. "I'm not worried, honestly. How do you put it? A day at a time, right. It took months before you called me and talked with me for six hours, going through the mathematical formula that deduced that you are my girlfriend and I'm your boyfriend."

She giggled, her cheeks turned red.

"I'll see you soon. Safe travels. I love you," he said.

She turned, "I love you too, Felix."

He was hit by a train, if the train made his hair on the back of his neck stand up.

She walked back to him, kissing him deeply.

"See you later, babe," she said, pulling away with that smile.

He shook his head, a smile smeared across his face.

Chapter 17
Dog Fish

"We don't get many visitors out here, just deserters from that weird fascist military out of Fort Monroe."

The man was tall, built like a fighter, he was wearing a white tank top and shorts. Barefoot, standing on the deck of his large fishing boat. Felix and Gavin deducted it was his quarters and served as the town hall for the floating city. Also, being the most luxurious of ships in the center of the built-up city on the water.

The boats had steps and planks all bolted or welded to each other; forming a series of walkways throughout the small city. Floating docks were attached to the edges of the main floating structure. Ships were docked along each of the long-wooded planks. It was a sight to see. Several ferries had vehicles parked on them. Welders and fishermen, kids running around playing. The general consensus of all their tanned faces was that people were happy here. Felix even spotted two men walking to their boat, holding hands. This place was free, very different than Fort Monroe, these were all good signs.

One of the guards shifted off the railing. Gavin and Felix stood on the main deck, surrounded by guards and curious onlookers. They murmured things to each other, whispers and conversations carried as the subtle wakes rolled under the boats that were strung together.

"We aren't deserters, we are here to propose an unsanctioned pact so to speak," Felix replied.

"And why would that be?" Derek asked as he walked down the steps to stand face-to-face with them.

"Because the city is filling with feral—"

Derek interrupted him, "Feral?"

Felix continued, "The infected, alphas, and their queen. We cannot feasibly escape on land. Especially with the size of these things, nor due to the size of the people that will have to move."

"Why would I help you, who are you two anyway?"

234

Gavin spoke this time, attempting little to hide his irritation, "We heard you guys needed some help, so we have some questions and maybe a solution to your current problem."

"And what problem are you speaking of?"

"Expansion, a safe heaven. And that cunt who runs that…" Gavin pointed toward Fort Monroe, "…what did you call it, fascist military over there. She plans on taking this place with or without you. You are her fallback plan right now. Seeing as we don't care about them, maybe we can reach an agreement."

"I'm listening. How about we talk inside?" Derek said, waving them to follow him up to his cabin in the old ship.

They shut the door behind him. He sat in his chair. His wife sitting off to the side with a rifle ready to engage the two if need be. She certainly didn't trust them. Derek had his reservations, however, he had people he cared about, and protecting all of them was his main concern.

"Alright, what are you guys going on about?"

Felix spoke this time, "Alright, the crazy bitch over there. She plans on killing you and taking this place, soon. She will then move everything onto your platforms until they can take control of something bigger and move north to continue operations. She is a part of something big, we are pretty sure she is working with the people who caused this whole fucking thing in the first place."

"Caused, what do you mean?" he asked, leaning forward on his desk.

"The pandemic, the creatures, she's connected to it. The infected and an alpha have been captured; we know because we caught the motherfucker. It was sent north, to some facility. The very one where rumors of the pandemic started from."

"Interesting, why are you telling me this?"

"Because we need your help, and you need ours," Gavin fiercely replied.

"And why would I need your help?"

Felix grinned, "You plan on making your way to capturing a ship, at the naval weapons base north of here, right?"

"How did you know that?"

"Not important. Monica is planning on stealing that same ship. Now, if you get to it before us, with say, some help, and plant her out here, move your people, we are asking that when we come up with a meeting time, you send us every boat you can that can carry people to that ship, you help us evacuate the fort. If not, we will all die."

"What's in it for me?" Derek asked slyly.

Gavin grinned like a fiend, "How's your ammo storages? Medicine, fuel? We could move some supplies your way to make your attempts that much easier when taking on that ship."

Derek sat there. Pondering. He looked over to his wife, she gave him a nod. He turned back to them with a smile. "I'll think about it, I'll send word with the next shipment, due in a week. Make sure one of you is there to receive it."

"Will do," Felix replied standing up and holding out his hand.

Derek and Gavin stood, exchanging handshakes. Just before Felix walked out, he stopped, turning, pulling out his picture.

"Have you seen this woman?" he asked.

Derek's eyes inspected the picture, looking up at him and back at the picture.

"Sorry, I have not. Who was she to you, a sister, wife?"

"Someone I care for very deeply. That is all."

"I'll keep a lookout. Let her know her man is waiting for her... *If* I see her come this way."

"Thanks."

Felix and Gavin walked out, each lighting a cigarette, heading to their boat. Their radio cracked up with a slew of chatter, both frantic and distorted. Loud shrieks and screams, gun fire, the sound of an engine accelerating followed by more chatter.

The gun fire caught their ears. They could hear it from where they were. Smoke was coming from the city. Howls, shrieks, and more gunfire in a symphony of horror. Gavin and Felix looked at each other. They quickly ran to their boat. The crew headed out.

"Take us to the western side," Gavin yelled as the wind thrashed about them. The boat skimmed the surface, full throttle. Hitting a wake, bouncing a few times before leveling out once again.

They banked around the southern part of the cove; the driver whipped the boat sideways, cutting the throttle. They strafed into the side of a bank. Gavin and Felix were off the boat and headed toward the main tower.

The two come out onto the street, a heavily armored and armed convoy flew past them, staggering onto the road past the gate. They oriented their weapons down the road. The gun fire and shrieks grew louder. Gavin ran up the grate stairs into the tower, shouting at the men and women on duty, to be ready. Gavin got behind an M2 50-caliber machine gun. Felix climbed on top of a barrier to watch. His Benelli clutched in his left hand.

Something was coming. Quickly, gunfire sounding from whatever was coming out of the city. The convoy consisting of several crudely armored trucks with guns mounted in the beds; and a large diesel tractor trailer with a turret mounted on top came barreling around the corner. They came from the south. Infected humans were climbing all over the vehicles, no gunners were in the backs of the trucks, killed by the infected or an alpha.

Two alphas were following in pursuit. One was a bulldog, once upon a time. It looked more like a saggy white and brown sported ape, a huge head with no neck, lost under rolls of droopy and patchy haired skin. It shouldered the side of the tractor trailer. Once they straightened out on the road leading in, the guns in the tower and from the vehicles began picking up fire. Slowly at first, trying to pick off the leeches. The second alpha was tall, skinny, sickly, its bones could be seen from the tightness of its skin.

The two alphas were concentrating their efforts on whatever was in the trailer. Felix checked his weapons, not much he was capable of until they got closer. He stepped down. Between the burst of fire, he could hear Gavin in the tower yelling at the soldiers inside and cursing at the beasts. Felix could not hold back his smile. The smell of carbon filling the air, the sound of the shell casings bouncing off the trucks and concrete. The cadence of thuds and pops and bangs echoing through his ears.

The vehicles were impressive. Sparks were flying from the impact of rounds. Felix wondered if he had looked like that when he came sliding in here a few months ago. He then wondered what happened to that soldier he saved. Didn't matter. Most of the infected humans were dead; smashed, run over, filled with holes, and in pieces across the road as the convoy drew near.

The alphas, however, did not yield, their only concern was the tractor. Finally, the larger bulldog-looking alpha ape thing slammed the tractor trailer hard enough that the driver lost control. The International diesel slammed into a barrier, slowly tipping over to its side than sliding as it crashed down, stopping into another barrier in the serpentine. The two alphas began chewing on the corner of the back of the trailer.

Behind them he saw a horde of infected humans all running like animals, on all fours, they reminded him of cheetahs or monkeys with long back legs. They were animals, if they were ever once human, he could only tell from the skin and eyes.

Felix observed three soldiers running from the wreckage. The firing stopped from the trucks next to Felix. The three were now being pursued by four infected. One of the soldiers would turn and fire a round as to help the other limp away. Felix ran, fast, faster than he ever had before, and he was in pants with three weapons, and ammo for a good fight, not to mention a heavy blade on the small of his back. *No reason to dwell on it now,* he thought, *just fucking run.*

Felix flew past them. One-handed, he swung his shotgun, smacking a creature in the face. Following through his swing, turning once more, he took aim. Fired. Took off one of the infected's head with the heavy slug. The shell fell to the ground. Again, one-handed, as if the shotgun was almost weightless. He killed them within a few seconds. The three shells bounced off the concrete. He then turned to finish off the first one he smashed in the face, a round skipped off the concrete, taking with it a vortex of bloody mist. He looked back. Gavin gave him a wave. Felix gave him a comical wave. Stopping, he realized, that he was several hundred meters from the tower. But no one was paying attention to him. They were looking past him.

He turned, and the alphas were attempting to drag the whole truck away.

"What the fuck?" Felix said. He pulled some shells from his pocket and loaded his shotgun with 4, 12-gauge 1 oz slugs.

He took aim as the sickly alpha looked past him.

Another convoy rode from behind Felix, he had never seen them before. They sported three-barreled Gatling guns; he had only ever seen videos of these weapons before. *50 calibers tri-barreled, fuck you and everything around you, sign my name in the earth, weapons.*

The soldiers themselves were wearing a type of full-body armor, sleek, almost robotic, like an exoskeleton from a movie or video game. The men quickly got out, while the weapons fired simultaneously. Everyone in the towers and on the vehicles were just as awestricken as Felix was at this point.

"Get back inside. We got it from here," one of the soldiers yelled from a speaker on the outside of his full-face shielded helmet.

Felix didn't pay him any attention. In the city, as the sun was setting behind the buildings was now where he was drawn. He saw, there were thousands of eyes watching him. There were more than that. Hundreds of thousands of pairs of eyes, all watching. Waiting. And down that road hiding in the darkness. Sitting tall and broad, the queen was looking at him. Patiently sitting there.

The two alphas were killed. Instead of acting out, she stood, turned, and walked further into the city. The pairs of eyes, the thousands, the hundreds of thousands disappeared with her. Their silhouettes gone from windows and doorways, the gleam in their eyes from what light he didn't know, were gone.

*****

"Did you hear?" John asked Sasha.

She was anchoring her tug boat to the floating docks.

"Hear what?"

"Some men came to the city today, they came to make a truce, claim that if we take one of the destroyers from the Naval base, they will give us supplies if we help them evacuate Fort Monroe."

"Really, that's a brilliant idea."

"One of them was asking for you."

Her breath was snatched from her very lungs. Her eyes became glassy.

"Wh-what, who, was it Felix?"

"We don't know, but everyone has been ordered to prepare to leave in the morning to take the ship before their forces have a chance to take it. We have been requested to help, you drive, I snipe."

Sasha looked toward the city, as John hugged his kids, talking about how much fun they had with Aunt Sasha.

"NO, we don't throw rocks at your sister!" Felix yelled.

"But she threw rocks at me, Uncle Felix," John Jr. replied.

"I don't give a flying butt, you could really hurt someone, dude. Go tell her you're sorry."

"Okay," he said, pressed lip, hanging his head as he walked over to her. He dropped the hand full of rocks into the yard.

Felix was shaking his head; he took a swig from his beer. Sasha was standing there, wearing a smile full of bright teeth.

"What?" he asked, noticing her looking at him like she wanted to eat him.

"Nothing, I find it cute how you are with kids," she replied.

"Grace, you tell your brother you're sorry too," Felix continued with his scolding.

"But he started it."

"I don't care who started it, be nice to each other," he yelled at the kids as they walked over to each other and did as he had scolded them to do.

"Felix, are the kids terrorizing Sasha again?" Kim asked from the enclosed screen deck.

"No, mamma, just being kids, throwing rocks at each other. So I told them to apologize."

Kim laughed.

"They can be hellions, those kids of mine."

She disappeared into the house.

"Sasha, come down here, I wanna show you how to do a cartwheel," Grace impatiently called to her.

"You are being hailed, my dear," Felix fiendishly teased Sasha.

"I need to relax, sweetheart. Why don't you take your brothers on the trampoline, I'll come join you in a minute."

239

Sasha turned to Felix. "You going to scold me later?" she teased him.

"Oh, yeah?" he laughed through his reply. "You would love that, wouldn't you?"

"Maybe," she said as she walked down the stairs to join the laughing kids bouncing on the trampoline.

John walked up next to Felix, clanking his beer into his. "She's a good woman. It's about time you finally stopped wasting your time chasing ass, it's about time you think about settling down and starting your own family."

"So I'm told," Felix replied, watching her and the kids bounce around holding hands in a circle.

"Must be right, and I'm usually always right, little brother," John replied.

"I'm sure she's the one, I love her. It took some time too. It wasn't just some need or game I played, I'm actually doing it right for once."

"Have you told her that you love her yet?"

Felix shook his head.

"You need to, dumbass," John said, smacking the back of his head. Felix just watched her has she played with the kids.

"Will do, big brother," Felix replied.

Sasha was smiling so big, laughing, having fun with them, he nodded to himself, and honestly felt happy. Maybe she was the one.

That night. Everyone was off to bed.

"I love you," Felix said.

Chapter 18
Stray from the Pack

"What the fuck did you do?" Felix asked as he barged through the door, followed by his entire team of friends.

The colonel stood, walking around her desk. "Everyone out, now."

The room emptied, leaving the colonel, Major Thompson, Gavin, Alex, and Felix.

"We took one of theirs."

"One of their what?" Gavin asked.

"Pregnant Infected Humanoids…the vehicle at the gate only had clothing in it, we wanted to see how strong their smell really was, and to get an idea of what was in the city. The scouting mission have ceased due to the loss of too many of my soldiers."

Felix laughed in annoyance. "You dumb motherfuckers, so that's what you were all doing there, it wasn't just to observe them attempting to breed."

"What are you talking about?" the colonel asked.

Felix shot her a deadly stare. "When I picked up Sanchez a few months ago, where do you think I found her? She actually found me. I was watching all you dumb fucks, didn't think you actually caught one, but I didn't see the convoy that brought it in, and led all of the infection here."

Gavin's face twisted in anger. Major Thompson leaned against the bookcase behind her. And Alex quietly listened while the colonel continued.

"That's why her story was off, she offered you sanctuary if you would bring her here. Dog eat dog world?"

Felix laughed. "Besides the point, what are you really doing here? Why this place?"

"Headquarters has requested that we continue to monitor and capture as many of them as possible, any pregnant specimens, or any alphas we can. It is coming at great cost; however, they are being studied so we may find a way to defeat it."

"Yeah, no. No one does that, they are using them to get rid of us, a clean slate. And now, whatever this pandemic is, it has unlocked all of the recessive genes that have brought our species to an evolutionary crawl. They are studying them to see if they can make them better," Gavin angrily interjected.

"You have interesting theories," the colonel replied.

"How about you cut the bullshit, we all were once upon a time in the military, it's called acceptable loss. What can we control in order to reduce risk, a bunch of bullshit, it was designed so that we could accept the losses upon an engagement or war, or the next play on the chess board. This is what's happening now. And these fucking things know we have one of their own. Have you sent them north yet?"

"No, it's still here," she replied.

"We need to get rid of them," the major spoke this time. "If we don't, they will come here and take them back, they are pack animals, after all."

Felix shook his head in disagreement. "No, it's too late, those things are already here, and there is no going back. We need to figure out how we are going to get everyone out of here. If we do not, we will die, they will roll this fucking place over. And if not, your wonderful USOAR will probably nuke that city. Because it would be the perfect solution to take over what's left of the country. The saviors of the United States. Sounds like a conspiracy theory."

Gavin agreed, speaking now full of hate, passionately. "What's your evacuation plan? No, don't have one, didn't fucking think so, you probably didn't come to the conclusion that your military would bomb the fuck out of you just to get rid of something they are unable to control. It's done enough, I wonder what is stopping them now from bombing this shit hole."

"No—" the colonel started, but was immediately cut off by Gavin, this time he was in her face, snarling, pointing at her, towering over her. She looked frightened. Felix noticed that Alex reached for his weapon, then suddenly changed his mind.

"No, they wouldn't do that?" he said in a condescending tone. "Our government wouldn't do that? All the same shit, over and over and over again. How about someone with some fucking power do something about it. How about you help these people here, you're their leader. Not ours, we can do just fine without this place, we did it by ourselves for fucking years. You needed a military in order to get this far. Now what, they are our enemy as much as the infection is. Chose a fucking side."

Her voice cracked.

"We will not lose this fort. This is what has been given to me, my charge, and we will protect everyone here. Now you all will start working defensive operations, no more going out. We have ways of monitoring the city. Mitch, your friend, if I'm not mistaken, has rigged the entire bridge to blow, not to mention, several of the larger buildings near where the infected have taken refuge."

"And what if we can't stop them? There are probably a hundred fucking thousand in that city right now. Communicating with each other, controlled and ready to attack. We are stuck on this rock right now," Gavin again in a fury had replied. She was silenced for but a moment, thinking of how to reply.

"I have requested supplement from the north. They are sending additional forces, heavy weapons to us. A few prototypes…"

Felix laughs. "No, that sounds like just a chance to see what their capabilities are. Look, no one gives a shit about us. You are fucked, we are fucked. And the more faith you put in them, to come down here and save us, is going to be your downfall."

She snapped, yelling this time, standing from her desk she was leaning against. "What am I supposed to do, my hands have been tied since USOAR found me. We are all prisoners here, including you, what are you going to do? What can a nobody from nowhere do? I am asking for your help, if you won't…then you can leave."

Gavin stepped forward. Felix held up his hand stopping his friend. Alex remained quiet. Major Thompson was worried.

"Yes, ma'am." Felix walked out of the office quietly without a fight. He left with a grin on his face, passing by wide-eyed soldiers. The entire hallway and offices were all quiet. Everyone, it seemed, had stepped out to watch him leave.

Alex and Gavin followed suit. Before Alex left, he turned. "You know he's right; we are right. We need to address this further."

"We will," she replied.

He disappeared behind the door.

Outside the three smoked cigarettes, women passing by looking at them like they were pieces of meat. The armed patrol of soldiers didn't take their eyes off of Felix.

One cat called Alex. Gavin shot a murderous look at her. She paid him no attention.

"Who is your partner, big boy?" she asked.

He pointed at the colonel's office. "Your boss," he replied. She quickly lost her smile and moved on without a word.

"It's time we stopped fucking around," Felix broke their momentary silence.

"If she isn't going to develop the fall back plan, then we will." He subtly points toward the office.

Alex nodded. "We need to understand what we are dealing with first, before we act."

Felix turned to Alex. "See what you can find out; after all, you are banging the colonel. Fuck her, eat her out, do whatever it is you have to do to bring her to her knees, and get everything out of her you can. Influence her decisions, she doesn't seem like a bad leader, just lost in restraint. However, I don't think it stops at just these creatures. I think there is something else, much worse, going on here. Maybe we can leverage the fact that we have an infected in here that is pregnant."

In the colonel's office. "Your men are dangerous, keep an eye on them, they are already being monitored by one of our drone assets. And you should know something about Felix too."

The major waited impatiently for Monica to continue.

Felix flicked his smoke out. "Come on, let's go get a drink, the bar should be open, its noon after all."

They all agreed and headed to the bar.

*****

"You're kidding me?" Major Thompson gasped.

"No, he is one of those experiments. And according to the white coats up North, he is slowly becoming more and more unstable; they don't know why he drinks all the time. Just how the old soldiers were back then, before all of this possibly amplified due to the capabilities of his entire being. But either way, he is an asset, but they are trying to get him to find his failure, to meet their parameters for success, by sending him into the city, alone."

"He made it all the way here, until he picked up one of our officers, alone. I don't see why it would make any difference now?"

The colonel stood up walking to the window. "Because he isn't in fight or flight mode, he is in fight or reattack mode. They believe that even in hopelessness, he will continue onward. That's what they want to see."

"No offense, and with all due respect, maybe it's time we realize that this military is not out for anyone's best interests." The major didn't hesitate, she looked the colonel in the eyes.

Major Thompson continued, "What are we going to do?"

"Move Alex to the weapons design facility. Move Chris to the docks on shipment duties. Gavin can stay with him, I'm not going to send him out there to die when he has saved a handful of our girls since he's been here. But I can't let two of our best breeds to die out there either."

"Protect our own, that's what you said when we took this place over, against USOAR if we had to," Major Thompson stated.

"We need to tread softly here, you know how they are, and what they do up there in that facility to the north. I think the doctor is starting to figure out that I'm not playing his game anymore."

"Maybe we should bring Felix and the others in, tell them everything?"

The colonel sat back in her chair, folding her hands in front of her face, pressing her fingers to her lips. "No, we need to keep them at arm's reach. Due to the fact that Felix isn't human, any more than those things out there."

*****

"Holy shit, is that you, Samantha?" Felix asked.

"My God, Felix?" the tall thin woman asked. She moved around the bar, grabbing a hold of Felix. Half her head was shaved and the rest long. Tattoos covered her entire body. She was wearing jeans and a dark gray shirt, some metal band. Her brown eyes gleamed.

She kissed him on the cheek.

The guys sat at the bar, she came around and leaned down in front of Felix.

"Why haven't you come in here sooner?"

Gavin looked at Felix and back at her. "You know this guy?" Gavin asked.

"Yes, he told me about this place years ago. We were…close friends, twelve, thirteen years ago, now," Samantha replied.

Gavin smiled mischievously. "I'm sure you were," he replied.

Felix caught the guys' looks being shot from along the bar. "What?"

"Why do I get the feeling that half of these fuckers know you?" Chris asked.

"Samantha and I were engaged once. But things just didn't work out, wasn't in the stars, and I was young and dumb. You lived over here, didn't you?"

"Yeah, I just moved down here shortly before it all happened. I was about to work at the Naval station when everything went to shit."

"Irony indeed. Know anything about that place?"

She shook her head. "No, and you're not the first person to ask me that either."

Felix leaned back. "I figured as much."

She shot Felix a funny look, changing the subject. "What you boys drinkin'?" she asked, popping up from the bar and walking down the line.

Once everyone had their beers, Felix was already on his third. She leaned down in front of him again with another ready to go.

"You been assigned a woman yet?" she asked. Chris choked on his beer, hitting his chest with a closed fist. Gavin smiled evilly.

"No…" he said.

"Good, you need to come by tonight then, so we can catch up," she said, writing down her building and room number in the hotel. She handed it to Felix.

"Better be there tonight, I get off around midnight."

That night Felix stood outside the door. He reached in his pocket to make sure that he had the right door, but instead he felt the photo, and pulled it out.

"What am I doing?" he let out a sigh and walked down the hall.

Samantha sat there waiting for the man who never showed up again.

"You two getting married or what?" Alex asked impatiently.

Felix was drifting off into space as the other and him, all sitting around a small fire in his back yard. He didn't hear him; he was looking out past the fire into the moonlit trees that cut out black against the dark blue ocean littered with stars. The moon hung low just above the black pines.

"Felix?" Alex caught his attention again.

"What's up, bud?"

Chris looked at Felix with a raised eyebrow.

"When are we getting the wedding invites?" another asked.

Beer bottles were piled up in tall stacks, some fell and spilled over the back porch. The grill open and cooling from dinner. The group all reaching their limits for the night. Considering they went through a few cases.

Felix chuckled. "What are you guys talking about?"

"You two have been together for over a year now, longest relationship I've ever seen you in." Alex replied. His sandy blond hair was popping out under the bill of his green multi-cam hat. An American flag sat in the center of the Velcro. He lifted it to comb his long, parted hair with his fingers back up into his hat. His blue eyes danced with reflections of the fire as he looked at Felix across the fire pit.

"I don't know, man, one day maybe."

"Well, we are all waiting patiently for it. You two going to be alright while you're gone?" Chris asked.

"Yeah, I hope so. I'm convinced she's the one, we are just taking it a day at a time," Felix replied.

Chris, with a heavy hand, patted Mark who was sitting next to him, on his back, hard. Mark comically acted like Chris broke his shoulder. Chris pointed at the cooler. Mark opened, dug in, producing a can of beer for him.

"Yeah, man, we are waiting on babies. You don't even hang out all that much anymore, you slowed on drinking, smoking, you are a changed man," Chris stated as he leaned back in the chair. Flipping his luscious black locks out of his face. His thin dark eyebrows on his large brow scrunched as he took the whole beer in one gulp. He stood, a massive man. His tribal tattoos that reached and twisted down his muscular arms almost matched the shadows of the fire.

"I'll marry you two, don't worry," he said with letting out a burp. "I'm licensed to, after all."

Everyone laughed. "You're going to have to get in line. Isaac has dibs," Felix replied.

"You want a gay black man to marry you?" Chris asked, his eyes shifting as he brought his head down and bringing his ear closer.

"Why not? He is like a paradox for his religion. And to be honest, he is the only real priestly type in our group, plus he offered a while ago." The group was laughing. Chris swatted Felix's comments away as if they were a physical thing flying around.

"I'm crashing on the couch," he said opening the door, stumbling into the house.

The group said their goodnights, hugs of old friends were passed around. Their girlfriends and wives who didn't drink all that much continued to sober for this very occasion. Once everyone had gone, Felix and Alex sat outside.

"How is you, boo boo?" Alex asked in a playful manner.

"I'm alright, man, just a lot of nonsense going through my mind."

"Yeah, like what?" he asked as he sat there playing on his phone.

"I'm done, I'm done with all of it, it's time to go. I wanna be happy for once, you know?"

Alex nodded, shifting his attention to Felix. Metal music played low in the background.

"But we knew that after we got here, hell, you were done before you got here. Just wanted to see if the grass was greener on the other side, just like the rest of us."

Felix laughed. "Yeah, but we all know that the grass is never greener on the other side, that shit is burnt."

Felix got up. "Alright man, I'm headed out, got an early day tomorrow."

Alex got up, and with his same closed mouth smile, he stuffed his phone in his pocket, giving his friend a hug. And as Felix turned to walk through the sliding glass door, Alex patted him on the ass, giving him a good game.

"Hey, when are you moving completely out of this house?" Alex asked.

Felix walked into his room, Alex followed, leaning against the door.

Felix grabbed his keys off his bedside table and his coat that was laid on his bed.

"What are you talking about?"

"She gave you a key, you basically are already moved in, you just keep your shit here."

Felix and Alex walked across the front room, passed two of their friends passed out on the wrap around couch.

"I don't wanna leave. I'm happy with her, and I have to go, as soon as I find someone."

"Well, you did it to yourself. I'm sure you two will be fine, just be sure to remind her why she is waiting on you," Alex replied.

"You still taking over this house, when I leave?" Felix asked, standing with the front door open.

"Yeah, how much time we got, before you leave us all?" he said, mimicking breaking down in tears.

"Soon, man, a few weeks."

"Well, you know you will always have a home with us. Even if you are chasing deployments without all of us," he said hugging Felix.

Just like that Felix was gone, to go home, to see Sasha.

Chapter 19
Bite the Hand That Feeds

"This is insane," Gavin protested.

The colonel said nothing.

"You want us, two of us, to cause a distraction, while you send a convoy with that thing you captured, to the north?"

She nodded.

He laughed sarcastically. "This is the dumbest fucking thing I have ever heard of in my entire life. What the fuck are you thinking? Are you trying to kill us, did we do something to you? Why is this our task? And why is there only two of us?"

"You don't understand the importance of this, the North will not send an asset this way until we remove the specimen. You and Felix are the two most violent people here. I just need you two to attack them here," she pointed on the map, to the north-western-most part of Hampton.

"If you two can distract them for 30 minutes, we will have a chance."

Felix spoke now, "This is suicide. Even if we did, and we happened to get out, what the fuck about the teams? We don't know the full complexity of these creatures anymore. It isn't like it was five years ago. Between the winter and the fallout, and the fact that they were just acting like animals, I can see this being successful, then, maybe. But they don't act like animals; she thinks, she plans, she gives commands, and communicates with them. We are dealing with something that we don't fully understand yet. This is not an intelligent plan, and I don't think you're the one pulling the strings on it."

The colonel stood up. He was right and she hated him for figuring it out. His rant, although calculated, had a hint of passion in it. "I have no choice. And if you don't do this, they will kill the people you care about."

Gavin stood from leaning against the window seal. "What the fuck did you just say?" His eyes were fiery sapphires.

"This organization will do anything it can in order for it to succeed. When you were allowed to stay here, it was a binding contract. These people are, after all, the USOAR government, and they will outlast us all. You do this for me, not them, you will help me save lives. I need you two out there, you two are the only ones who have a chance to survive the task I'm now asking of you."

Gavin and Felix looked at each other. It was merely a moment before Gavin spoke his piece, "After this, we are leaving. Last job. No strings attached. But this is it, we are done, and whoever the fuck you answer to, you might want to get out of whatever this shit it is you are involved with. Because they will fuck you, and leave you out to hang for all the world to see. The infected, the alphas, and now the queen. You are playing with the Devil's toys, and like his father, he is a very jealous creature, he is going to come looking for them, and you don't want to be caught playing with them."

Gavin stormed out. Felix nodded, his friend, no…his brother had always had an interesting way with words.

"What about you?" she asked.

"I'm done too, and if I have any say in it, I'm taking everyone I can with me. This shit, your superiors, are going to get you all killed, for their knowledge, their progress, their future, that's what it's all about, right? To see how well their product did, how well their solution worked."

Felix grinned as she stood there. He saw it finally sink in. He didn't know if it was his words or Gavin's, but she finally got it. Maybe this would fix everything, maybe she would make some real changes. But the point hit her like a brick. Now, would it sink in deep enough for her to make a change?

Felix stopped and turned. "We are going to get a ship, and my invitation will remain open. In three days, we are taking a destroyer and loading it with supplies and everyone who wants to come, and we are leaving this shit hole. You should put that out to all your people, because we will, regardless, behind your back if we have to."

*****

Gavin and Felix stood outside of their vehicle, a heavily armored and modified car. Who knew what model it once was. The interior was torn out, just two seats, metal reinforced floorboards, a steering wheel with a panel on it with a starter button. A shifter and an emergency break. Three racing pedals, five-point safety harness. Bullet proof glass windshields. *They left the touch screen radio in, thank god,* Gavin thought. Can't bring the hate to the infected without good music.

They reached in; Felix set his shotgun in the rack behind Gavin and Gavin set his behind Felix's seat. Felix sat in the driver's seat. He started the machine up. Its diesel engine roared before coming down to a low purring idle. The two turned to one another, giving a nod of acceptance in the hard war machine.

"You ready to go fuck these things in the face?" Felix asked.

"Yeah, War Turkeys!" Gavin proclaimed. Felix laughed and gave his most ridiculous turkey call.

Chris and Alex standing next to Mitch watched as their friends drove off.

"What's the plan?" Felix asked.

"Let's cause a distraction, we going to that building she wants us to?" Gavin replied, opening a bag in the floorboard.

"Fuck, no, we are going to drive straight through, lead them out of the city." Felix shifted, slamming on the accelerator. The turbo wines and the exhaust roared, echoing through the city.

The queen was sleeping, her large ears perked up, her head swung in the direction of the engine and screeching tires. She rushed to the window in her building. She barked, all the sleeping infected and alphas began to stir. The vehicle roared by, she whipped her large head, barking, more like roaring, that rattled glass and drove everything into a frenzy.

"Did you hear her?" Gavin asked.

Felix checking his mirror nodded with a grin. He slammed on the breaks, sliding to a whipping stop. The queen leapt from her floor, she had to have been several stories up. The two men watched her falling gracefully. Shards of glass glimmering from the breaking dawn to the east, sending beams down the street at them. She landed. Standing tall; proud. Her horde fumbled to follow, realizing they could not survive the fall. Felix made eye contact. She stared, not paying attention to the crowd of infected surrounding her, trampling the ones that fell.

Gavin's weapon was aimed out the passenger door.

"Yeah, come on, motherfucker," he taunted as an infected man slowly and curiously edged his way closer. There were several behind him as he came out of a store front entrance. They were not acting like their normal frenzying selves. The sidewalks quickly filled with them. Most of them shed their human clothing; now, mutated bodies sporting the characteristics of their infector. A parted sea of pink pale, dark, olive, hairless, hairy, mutated people.

Felix hit the accelerator, the crowd around them jumped back, then slowly crawled, carefully toward their vehicle. Gavin was surprised, they were acting like curious animals.

"What the fuck is happening?" Gavin asked. Never taking his aim off the creatures next to them. Felix began to look around, they were, in fact, in their city. Surrounded.

"I don't know." Felix and Gavin took a quick glance at their watches. As if it were planned.

"It's time." And if not more than irony, the queen cocked her head, closing her panting smiling mouth. She turned, looking back.

"I think she knows what the fuck we're up to," Gavin said.

"Fuck it. Let's do it live," Felix replied.

Gavin laughed.

Felix threw the vehicle into 1st gear; Gavin tossed a grenade out his window. They sped off toward the queen. The infected drew closer to the baseball-size object, sniffing. Before their alpha could realize what that thing was; the grenade went off. Everyone, every alpha and infected human flinched. Several of the infected dropped, some lost a limb or two. Their screams from shock and loss echoed. And over that, the queen, she roared. Like a swarm, the creatures began chasing them, like dogs chasing cars.

Gavin tossed a grenade out the passenger window with every turn Felix made. And just like that they killed a few more. They were headed west; on what street they didn't care. Just so long as they could keep them distracted. The queen turned to an alpha; it, he rather, was similar to her. His coat was nearly intact, a mix of gray and dark circles. His tail though was almost complete bone. His claws were long and jagged. He was smaller than the giant hyena queen. She nipped at him, and he took off. She let out a roar. And just as Gavin dropped another grenade, the streets began to empty. The infected began filling back into buildings. Felix slammed on the breaks, sliding to a stop.

They looked at each other. Then back to the emptying streets. Like a herd running from a predator.

"There is no way they have come this far to uttering commands," Felix spouted in wonder.

The galloping was fast-paced and could be heard from over their engine. Wide-eyed, the two men watched as the odd alpha came around the corner, tearing up pieces of the road as its long, jagged nails tore into it for grip. It leapt, Felix accelerated toward it. Taking the right from where they came. Gavin looked back through the small rear windshield. Infected started jumping from buildings on top of their vehicle.

"Holy shit." Gavin began laughing, the sound of the thudding and shrieks as they bounced off the hard metal exterior of the vehicle made him giggle. Gavin started shooting into every window he could, from where he expected them to leap from.

The alpha chasing them jumped from building to building, through a large window and into another. The only reason Felix noticed it was the crash of glass, and shadow that glided across the front of them. The queen saw through the whole ordeal, she had already posted herself on top of another building. Howling, rallying several hundred of the infected and an alpha to lead them. The alpha had very long jaws, several rows of teeth, and a tail three times the length of its body. It was longer than a city bus. Lanky and thin, once upon a time a greyhound.

The convoy transporting the pregnant feral turned north and began to accelerate once the rest of the nine-vehicle convoy made that turn. They didn't make it far, hundreds of infected blocked the road. They had to turn into the city. And once they did, the firing started. Quickly the vehicle was engulfed by hundreds of infected. The creatures tore the soldiers from their seats. The alpha swiped its tail, ripping a turret off a modified Humvee. It was like watching ants take on beetles.

Gavin's radio started blaring. "War Turkey, War Turkey, this is base, over."

"War Turkey here."

"Return to base, mission failed, I say again, mission failed, do you copy?"

Gavin's face twisted in a snarl. "Copy, returning to base, going to need some heavy fire. Because we are going to be dragging everything out here with us."

"Roger, we already have the heavy guns staged," the woman replied.

Gavin tossed the mic onto the dash. He stuck his rifle out the window and continued firing. The two sped through the city.

The queen inspected the empty truck; soldiers were firing in the building behind them. Another vehicle was on fire, a few had turned back to head to base. She growled as the shrieks of her pack came from within the building. She leaped through the second-floor window. Tearing the wall down, killing a man, cornering two more soldiers. They screamed in fear and began to fire. She bit one, tossing her out the window. She was dead before she bounced off the side of the tipped tractor trailer.

The other attempted to run but was stopped by the infected slowly crawling up the stairs. They filled the stairwell. She fell back against the wall. The queen stood over her, sniffing the soldier. She shook from fear. She looked up and with her last breath, spoke to the beautiful giant.

"One day, someone is going to come along, and destroy all of you filthy dogs."

The queen cocked her head, ears perked. And for a moment, the soldier saw the queen grin with her panting. She turned and leapt down onto the street. The creatures crawling up the stairs flooded onto her, tearing her apart. She couldn't let out so much as a scream.

Felix and Gavin are headed straight for the road leading to Fort Monroe. The alpha chasing them from building to building crashed down on top of their hood. The front right tire blew out. The alpha rolled, its bone tail crimped a burnt shell of a vehicle clean in half. Gavin and Felix slid into the curb, the vehicle bounced. Felix whipped the wheel, but it was too late, the wheel under the weight of the armor snapped and folded under the front of their vehicle.

"Motherfucker!" Gavin yelled. Felix tore the steering wheel off as he attempted to control the sliding vehicle. The two men looked at each other and began to laugh. The sparks subsided as they finally slowed to a grinding stop.

Gavin pulled the radio mic from the dash. Felix threw his door open; he grabbed his shotgun from behind Gavin and began shooting at the greyhound alpha. The alpha flipped up right. The heavy slugs sparked and bounced off its thick skull. Leaving deep cuts in the skin of its face, leaving behind the path of the slug. The beast charged, Felix leaped out of the way, running into a building, and the alpha followed in. Felix dropped a grenade; the beast got stuck in the doorway for a moment. The grenade went off. Felix jumped out of a window, the rear of the alpha slumped in the doorway. Its tail twitched.

Gavin got out. "Let's go, they are meeting us at the end of the road." Felix nodded and the two began running down the center of the street.

"Why aren't we being chased?" Felix asked.

"That," Gavin said as they slowed to a walk and stood there.

Standing before them, blocking their way. Spectators of the infected all in buildings and doorways and windows, watching. The beautiful hyena stood there. The queen was blocking their path.

Gavin patted Felix on the shoulder, he shot him a smile. Gavin held out a smoke for Felix, who handed Gavin the lighter. They lit their cigarettes as the queen began walking closer. Her ears pinned back; her tail was straight. They were fucked.

"Did we do it right, brother?" Felix asked.

"No one can tell us otherwise."

Felix nodded. They stood there waiting for their end. It wouldn't be a bad one.

"What are you going to say when you have to answer for everything you've done?" Gavin asked.

"There's nothing to answer for if God is all powerful. He made us this way, after all."

Gavin laughed; Felix laughed.

The two checked their weapons, reloaded what they could. Pulled pins on their grenades.

"You know, man, I'd do it all over again with you, and all of them if I could," Felix said, his cigarette flopping around with every word.

"Me too, brother, me too," Gavin replied.

The sound of another vehicle racing from behind the queen caught all of their attention. It passed by the queen who with perked ears had leapt out of the way. It slid.

Chris bent toward the passenger side. "What the fuck are you two sluts doing?"

Gavin laughed, tossing his grenade nonchalantly into a building doorway. The spoon flung and bounced like a spring off the concrete.

"Getting ready to die on our feet, what the fuck are you doing?" Gavin asked.

"Get the fuck in," Chris yelled. Felix tossed his into the next building. Gavin's grenade went off. Killing a few of the infected. The two men jumped in. Chris spun around and accelerated straight for the queen. She roared, and the streets filled up with angry infected and alphas.

One of the alphas drew its head back. A round struck it in the side of the face, the beast spat or coughed something at them as they passed by. The mucus hit the back of their truck like plaster. Felix and Gavin started firing at everything as they sped through.

Just as they passed the queen, his dark eyes and her bright yellow eyes met. And time almost stopped. She followed his, and he followed hers. He didn't shoot. The infected chased the group until right about the beginning of the barriers. Before the towers started shooting and the trucks' guns began cleaning up the creatures. Just for a second, Felix and Gavin witnessed what looked like the creatures wincing. As if something unseen had hurt them. One, before it slumped to the ground with half a face, went so far as to attempt to hold its head.

Felix turns to Gavin. "Did you see that?"

"Yeah."

"What was that?"

"I think it's the reason why we haven't been overrun yet, there is something here keeping them from getting too close," Gavin replied.

Felix patted Chris on his large shoulders. "Have I ever told you what I love about you?" Felix asked.

"What's that?" Chris joked.

Felix replied, "Not a goddamn thing." The three laughed the rest of the way back into Fort Monroe.

The queen stood there looking at the fort. The infected began to disappear back into the buildings. She turned back once more. Ears pointed upward, one rotating slightly then back. She growled and continued down the street. Sniffing the dead.

Felix and Gavin got out. And something caught their nose. Chris was soon to follow.

"Ugh, what is that smell?" Chris asked with his face twisted in disgust.

He came around to see what Gavin and Felix were now looking at. The three stood there awestricken.

The back-right corner of the truck's bed was melted. Looked like an acid burn, the metal looked like melting paint that cooled. The rear tail light was gone, the corner of the bumper, and part of the bed door.

"Im-fucking-possible," Gavin said.

"This is more than just a pandemic," Chris voiced.

Felix turned, looking down that road into the city.

Alex strolled down from the corner of the Fort's walls where he was laid up with his large rifle.

He saw what all the fuss was about.

"I wasn't sure what that crazy dog was about to do, so I shot him anyway. He took a 338 like a champ though, almost didn't faze him at all," he nonchalantly stated.

Felix held out his hand. Alex looked down under drawn eyelids.

"Put that hand away, we hug around here," he said mockingly with pressed lips.

The two hugged it out like brothers, laughing.

"You two are fucked for helping us, you know that?" Gavin said aloud.

Alex put his hand up, rocking his head with attitude. "I don't know if you're tracking, I fuck that shit so good, she won't lift a finger toward you guys."

Their laughter was broken when the queen howled fervently into a stressful laugh. It echoed through the city. It could be heard on the floating city. She was making it known that this was all hers. And she intended to keep it. And she will come and claim them. Pay it forward, so they say, and in all the killing of their kind, Felix and Gavin, Alex and Chris, and all of them, they were about to be paid in full.

*****

In the colonel's office.

"Ma'am, the floating city to the east has taken the Destroyer."

256

Monica pressed her fingers to her temples, massaging slowly.

"Okay, we will have to wait before we can act on that issue."

"Yes, ma'am. Also, it seems that all the infected in this region are now within a hundred miles."

"I'm moving to Georgia," Felix said with a heavy sigh.

"What?" Sasha spun around.

The kitchen smelt of rosemary and parsley. Felix set the knife down. She sat on the counter in front of him.

"When were you going to tell me?"

"I just found out, I have a few months, but I have to start packing up here soon though."

"New orders?"

"It was a special assignment, probably the only chance I have to finish out my career. It will be for a few years, more than likely a deployment, maybe two, but after that I'm done."

"Felix, do whatever you have to do, it's your life."

"Thought I should let you know, no one else knows, I planned on telling them tonight."

"We will be fine; we will take it one day at a time."

Later that night, the two sat on the couch, he was massaging her feet. She was leaned against the corner of the couch nestled in the cushions. Felix's hand began to slowly run up her leg softly. She pulled away for a moment, relaxing. Her eyes met his. She could see the intent in his eyes. And she wanted him just the same.

She began to breathe heavily, from the excitement of his touch, or because she was nervous. For some reason his heart was pounding rapidly. He didn't know why. He just let his hands do the work. His hands made their way onto her inner thigh. She began to burn with desire. He got up over her. Kissing her lips. She was starting to lose herself.

His hands continued down to her shorts, finally touching her where she yearned for him so deeply. Her body was hit with a jolt of lightning. She began to develop that lustful taste in her mouth. His tongue slid in, and she took it. As he pulled away, she bit onto his lip. He kissed down her neck. Pulling her shirt up, kissing her hard stomach, and pulling her shorts down slightly kissing her pelvic area. Her hips thrust toward him. The hair on her arms and hands stood up.

"Let's take this into the room," she finally got out through her heavy breathing.

She got up, taking his hand and leading him to the bedroom.

She began taking her clothes off as he took his off. She was more than happy with his figure, a soldier, certainly. She couldn't have been more beautiful, her shyness shown through. He was more than satisfied, she stimulated him in so many more ways beforehand, and now, they were going to take each other, as they had wanted to for some time now.

He was kissing down her naked body, a nibble here, a nibble on her nipple. She jolted in excitement. He continued to learn all of her, as she welcomed it, even if she tried to hide it, her body was giving it all away. Finally, he begun to lick her. Her eyes nearly rolled back as she pulled at the sheets. Then running a hand through his hair, he pushed her thighs from around his head. She had no control; the sensation was so intense her strong legs tried to crush his head. Her moans were telling him that he was hitting all the right spots and she was ready for more. The sheets soaked from how wet she was. He got up, crawling up over her. Kissing and licking his way to her lips. Her hands were around his strong shoulders. Pulling him in.

"You ready?" he asked just above a whisper.

"It's been a long time, be gentle, Felix, please."

"Of course, sweetheart."

He kissed her once more, before they fell into each other. The entire night, he didn't go home, and she didn't want him to go, both now, and then.

Chapter 20
The Dog Whistle

"Colonel, why are you no longer sending reports on Felix?" the doctor simply stated, no sign of irritation in his tone, only of fact in his words.

"Sir," she began to explain, but abruptly quieted by his interruption.

"I don't want to hear your excuses, Colonel. You have continually failed to deliver the specimens that you have obtained. Not to mention, you have let him run amuck within your area of operation, he is reaching full maturity. There is little you will be able to do in order to stop him. Might as well send him out for the sake of our species. Alone if you have to. And now, seeing the thermal readings from your area, there is no longer a window to send a convoy north. You have allowed the infection to accumulate in your area to the point where you are completely cut off from the west."

"Sir, the convoy is being prepared as we speak," Monica interrupted, only to be cut off, again.

"It's too late for your simple excuses. I will come down there myself. Collect the specimens, and Felix. Do keep a short leash on him this time. And if I were you, I would start hardening your current defenses, the infected that have accumulated in the city just outside your very walls, is sizable. You in fact, may have called every infected human, and alpha in the United States to your door. I expect your defensive plan and counter attacks ready and actionable upon my return."

"Yes, sir."

"*Auf Wiedersehen,*" Doctor Steinberg said while waving with a limp hand.

The video cut out. Monica, with a heavy sigh, fell into the comfort of her large office chair.

Major Thompson was called in from the hallway.

"Doctor?" Doctor Anderson called, poking his head in through the doorway.

"Yes?" Doctor Steinberg replied, spinning in his office chair, legs stretched out like a child. His coat tails flowing from the turn, he held the front of the seat as it slowed to a stop, facing the doctor in eerie perfect timing.

"I propose we destroy the infection seeing that it willingly accumulated in one location, the entire country is clear from the reports we have received. Due to the outcome of the last false attempt to move the specimen, these creatures have become more intelligent than we anticipated."

"Yes, yes. In due time. I want to see what Felix is going to do, and I want to know what the queen is going to do now that she has without a doubt found the location of one of the other specimens. Not to mention, I will not be destroying young Number 13, Felix. I must collect him, we are going to leave that specimen in place, the young colonel cannot send a convoy out, and things are only going to get worse. Unless of course, we lend them a hand." His tone was gleeful, and as matter of fact as it always was. As if any other thought other than his own was merely wrong or flawed.

"Then what is the next phase?" Doctor Anderson asked, coming fully in the office, leaning against the desk.

The doctor laughed in his high-pitched obnoxious laugh. "Tell the general we will be taking an aircraft out, we have a message to deliver and an asset to retrieve, and if she wants more reason than that, tell her that she will need permission from the Overseer in order to know the full extent of this collection."

Quietly, Doctor Anderson nodded and left the room.

*****

Felix pulled the smoke from his mouth, taking a healthy swig from his beer. *It's cold, and nice, refreshing,* he thought.

He pointed, and Gavin turned to look. "What the fuck is that?" Felix asked.

"I don't know. The lighthouse has always been off limits. Old Point Lighthouse."

Felix's wheels began to turn, and so were Gavin's. They concluded at the same time it seemed, because no words were exchanged. The two got up from the wall and walked toward the small lighthouse.

An hour later.

The door flew open. It slammed against the wall, startling the colonel.

"Why the fuck didn't you tell us about the giant frequency amplifier you have in the lighthouse?"

"Because, that is a secret that I can't trust with just anyone, especially a bunch of grunts like you all. Who, in fact, wanted to leave just the other day."

Felix waved his hand. "We changed our minds, this is not just your problem, this is everyone's problem."

Gavin continued. "We could mount that motherfucker, and use it to push the creatures back."

"Do you have any idea how much power that thing uses? We are pulling what little we can from the grids while they still are somewhat operational. Not to mention, we have generators running non-stop to ensure that it stays running. If it goes out, then we will lose this Fort."

"Then get another one from those Nazi motherfuckers you work for."

"That one we have right now is a prototype, the others aren't developed or anywhere near completion."

"All part of the plan? So, pulling all of the infection here wasn't just dumb luck, after all, it was on purpose. This place is a testing ground, am I wrong?"

"You are becoming a very dangerous group of people. You figure things out almost too fast for any of us to keep up."

"What's really going on here? Come on, Colonel, what's the master plan?"

"I don't know."

"Might wanna figure that shit out. Because if you are the only one that has control of that machine, then we will be alright, but if someone else does, like the cocksuckers you work for, we could be experiencing some technical difficulties, if you know what I mean?"

"I have work to do. Are you all finished? If so, get out of my office."

*****

Gavin and Felix lit up smokes at the same time as they stood there outside on the steps that led into the Headquarters building.

"I wonder if a dog whistle would work?" Felix pondered out loud.

"Like, an actual fucking dog whistle?" Gavin asked.

"Yeah, like an actual fucking dog whistle, we might need to test this one day, might disorient them long enough to escape or used to taunt them. Yeah, we need to hit a pet shop."

"Leave it to your ass to figure something so goddamn simple out," Gavin replied.

The two had presented the idea to Major Thompson, and she immediately sent word to the colonel. She had accepted the request, but only Gavin and Felix were to go on this adventure. Due to the many objections, she decided otherwise and decided to allow others to accompany them.

The next day Felix heard a knock on his door.

He opened it, Major Gloria was standing there in full gear.

"Good morning, Major," he greeted.

"Morning," she said, pushing her way through.

"Come in," he said shutting the door.

"Get dressed, we are heading out as soon as you're ready. Gavin is already at the docks preparing the boat."

"And where are we going?" he asked.

She was trying her best not to check him out as he walked by, opening the closet, and producing clothes, tossing several weapons on the bed, holsters, magazines.

"We are going to the local Pets-Mart to test out your theory. Someone brought it to the commander, and she is interested in your idea. So, we, you, my team, and Gavin are going to test it out."

"Interesting," he said and he got ready.

He caught her staring at him. And he feared that she had made her choice for a partner.

It was only a matter of time. Certainly not the best-looking man around, but desirable due to rumor, or rather a tangible legend surrounding this man.

"You have a lot of scars, and that is an interesting tattoo," Gloria stated.

"Yeah, since the pandemic, I've fought more people than the infection. Even freed a camp of sex slaves once. That was the worst I have ever seen of the human condition. No idea where they ended up. That was just being in the right place at the right time, I guess."

"And the tattoo, were you a Satanist or something?" she asked, standing to look at it.

"No, yes, maybe once; this merely is a reminder of everything we lose in our lives, and the simple fact that, we do not deserve paradise, other than the one in this world."

"You think this world is a paradise?"

He sat on the bed putting his boots on.

"The only one I know of. You?"

"I've seen a lot of bad in this world, and everything we have suffered, I will never believe that when the world ended, it became a paradise."

"Fair enough. I would disagree. Wholeheartedly."

The two heard a knock on the door. Britney pushed it open.

"Hello?" she called.

Gloria walked to the hall. "Who is… Oh, Britney, long time."

"Nice to see you too, Major, what are you doing here?"

Gloria walked with her back into Felix's room. "Just getting this asshole ready to go on a little mission to test out his wild theory."

"I see," she said. The two stood there as he put his shirt on.

"It's starting to become a party in here," he said as he turned around, grabbing his bag.

"I put this together for you. I know you asked a while ago for some medical supplies, so I hope this helps." She held out a kit.

"Awesome, thanks," he said, taking it from her. He stuffed it into his bag.

"Be careful out there," Britney said. He turned and she surprised him with a hug.

"I'll be fine, thanks to you, so don't worry. How about dinner one night?" he said.

Gloria shot them both an ill-hidden look of disproval.

"Sure," Britney accepted.

She left and Felix finished packing up. Gloria and Felix both left.

On the docks, Gavin was leaning against the railing on the top of the boat. Smoke carried from his mouth like a steam engine.

"There you two are, did you get your quickie in before the mission?"

Felix laughed; Gloria pushed Felix. "He wishes, but we got interrupted by some nurse."

Gavin grinned.

"This is my team; Francisco, Bonnie, and Chantel. This is Felix."

"We know who he is, ma'am," Chantel replied. Her accent placed her around New Orleans.

Felix took measure, they had to have been the strongest looking team he had ever seen. Very fit. They were a team of fighters, judging from their stance and stature. Francisco was a short Spanish man, Bonnie was his partner, or more appropriately he was hers. He followed her like a little puppy. She was a redhead. Very pale skin. Chantel, she was mixed, Asian and African-American, very pretty, Felix thought. But she was tiny compared to the other two. Gloria being the fighter that she was, it was no wonder this group looked like small brick shithouses.

"Good," Gloria said as she walked past them all.

"How was it, Felix? You know she has beat every man's ass she has ever come across, not one has ever lived up to her standard," Gavin called down laughing.

"Let's go," she roared.

The boat pulled out and began their trip south.

*****

263

It took a few hours to arrive at one of the many docks near Grommet Island Park. The city looked quiet. No one or nothing could be heard. Just slight gusts of wind carrying rubbish through its streets. They were quick to find a map and oriented themselves. The lush life had begun to reach through the streets of the city. Spilling over the concrete and sidewalks. The buildings crawling with vines, and flowers and green. Felix and Gavin were awestricken with the beauty of it.

Virginia Beach, they were near I-58, which was to the north almost a mile, head west and eventually they would hit the shopping center where PetSmart was located. Gavin had a car battery in his pack. Once the team had found a suitable vehicle, Gavin set in the new battery. After a few attempts, the truck finally started up. Felix hooked up the mini air compressor he was carrying and filled the tires. They seemed to hold up decently, only a little dry rot here and there. Chantel poured in a fuel stabilizer and a few gallons the team carried.

The shopping center was empty for the most part. Only few vehicles in the lot, after all the pandemic spread through the night. Hence the open roads and empty lots. The crew was inside the store with ease. They walked down isle after isle. Felix was standing outside, and for some odd reason, he felt as if they were being watched.

He decided to step inside as Gavin was waiting for him.

"So, did you rail her out, or what?"

"You know I didn't, and you know why I won't."

"You won't have a choice if she chooses you for partnership. If you don't, she could have you executed, or do it herself."

"Yeah, right," Felix said, still looking out the wedged open sliding glass doors.

Gunfire prattled off in the distance. The rounds crashed through glass. Gavin and Felix ducked, sliding through register counters. They scurried around behind them.

"Status!" Gloria yelled from the back.

"We're good," Chantel yelled further in.

Bonnie did the same, as Gavin did.

"Where did it come from?" Gloria called as she ran toward Felix and Gavin.

Sliding next to Felix, she placed her hand on his shoulder peering over the check-out counter.

A convoy of heavily armored vehicles were pulling into the parking lot.

Two prison busses, and several trucks of various types. Men spilled out running toward the opening of the store. They were a rough looking bunch. They stopped short when Gavin and Felix without warning stood and sent several rounds flying from their ARs. They dropped several men dead in their tracks.

Fire begin picking up from the rest. Someone yelled out to the men to cease fire. The man approached. Felix could hear him bitching out the men for not heeding his orders. That he spotted several females, and Felix didn't need to hear anymore after that to know. That it didn't matter who these fuckers were, that whatever they were there for, it wouldn't be good for the girls if they were captured.

"Hey, ya'll in that there store. What is your business in our fine town?"

Gavin looked at Felix, Gloria responded. "None of your goddamn business," she yelled.

Gavin smiled, Felix stepped back with his rifle out, ready to stand and fire.

The man outside had given hand signals. Gavin spotted it. The men split into groups lining the outer walls preparing to spill into the front doors from both sides.

"If y'all tryin' to get those dog whistles, don' even bother, y'all just call 'em to us. So how 'bout you come on out now, and we can talk about it. Civil like."

"Bullshit, cocksucker! You and your hillbilly friends just get in your busses and get the fuck outa here before we decide to be uncivil-like." Gloria yelled.

Felix looked to the crew behind him. "Were any of you ever cops or soldiers?"

Chantel shot him a confused look. "Why the fuck does that matter?"

Felix laughed. "Because I need you to be good at killing people, not feral or dogs right now."

Gavin started chuckling.

Chantel responded, "Hey asshole, my father was a cop, and yeah we are good at killing people, especially at killing psychopaths like you two fucks."

Felix turned back with a Cheshire grin. "Now that is the right mentality."

"Go get 'em boys," the man yelled.

Gavin stepped to the side, his rifle barely clearing the cover, he took a shot. The round ripped through the man's head. Gavin took notice, they were all wearing old military uniforms.

Bonnie, followed by Chantel and Francisco, slid to a stop behind another check-out counter.

"We got the whistles," Chantel gleefully reported.

"You motherfuckers killed Jim'bo," a distraught man screamed.

"Hey boss, they got the whistles. What do you want us to do?"

"Kill the men, take the bitches, alive this time!"

Gavin and Felix pulled smoke grenades from their battle belts.

Each pulling their pins and chucking the dull gray canisters.

"Need you guys to watch our six, find another way out of here."

Gloria nodded, she grabbed her team. Felix slid over behind Gloria. "Give me one of the whistles. I'm going to see what the fuck these assholes are talking about."

Francisco handed him one. "Alright, get the fuck out of here. We will try to hold these assholes off, until you give us the signal to bound back."

Gloria nodded. Felix turned and slid back over to Gavin. The smoke had bellowed enough. Men had begun coughing. Felix and Gavin stood, weapons up. They each turned out the doors, firing. Sporadic fire smacked into concrete. Bodies fell hard. Weapons bounced off the side walk. Gavin's weapon bolt locked. He dropped it to the side, drawing his pistol he continued to fire.

Felix did the same. When his 1911 went empty, he drew his revolver, the blast echoed off the walls. Once the fire stopped. The men all waited for the smoke to clear, nervously, they were shaking. Gavin and Felix reloaded their weapons as they ran back indoors behind the cover of crates of dog food.

The smoke cleared. The men were scattered across each lengths of the building. Blood spilled over the side walk staining the green and gray in bright red. The men began murmuring in fear. Some in a rush of rage began firing into the building. Machine guns and rifles, pistols, shotguns, made short work of the glass. Felix and Gavin were hunkered low.

"Holy fuck!" Felix yelled. Gavin was smiling, even though his hatred was starting to poison his thoughts.

Felix got dog food in his mouth; spit it and chuckled. "Goddamn that taste like stale grain, dogshit with a hint of salt. I can't believe we fed this to our animals? No wonder why they turned against us."

The two men laughed as Gavin grabbed some and ate it, equally making a face of disgust.

The firing stopped, Gavin checked, and Felix saw Gloria waving at them, signaling that they were ready to move. Felix held up his finger, gesturing to give them a few more seconds. Felix pulled his last smoke grenades from his belt. He pulled the pins and threw all three of them. They skipped and rolled across the concrete lot toward the group of men. Gavin did the same.

"Put your gas masks on," one of them yelled.

Felix took his kit and belt off. Gloria began to run toward them. "What the fuck is he doing?" she asked Gavin as Felix disappeared out the doors.

"No idea," Gavin said turning and picking up, trying to get an idea of what was going on outside.

"He left his rifle, why would he do that?" she asked. Gavin turned to see his gear sitting on the dust covered tile floor.

Screams, random shots, followed by more screams. Gavin saw smoke dragging from something moving very fast within the thick clouds of yellow, purple, and white smoke. A man bounced hard off the ground out of the cloud, dragging with him a trail of blood.

Gavin took a shot, the man's head rocked back, red mist sprayed onto the ground. Another, Gloria had this one. A shotgun flipped onto the concrete from the smoke. A crunch, and another man's violent cries rang out. More random gunshots. This went on until the smoke cleared. Gavin and Gloria slowly stood and walked out. Felix was standing in front of the folding doors of the bus. Fearful eyes and every man in the bus was pilling everything they could against the doors.

Gavin and Gloria had their weapons up as they stood on either side of Felix. He was grinning at the men as they were trying to start the bus. Felix kicked the door, rocking the whole bus. The men inside began to cry out in fear. Blood dripped from Felix's right arm all the way down his blade. He was splattered in their blood. Some of them witnessed his work in glimpses through the smoke, and they could see it on their faces. He brought them real fear like the pandemic had. Like they had; that the rest of the team would soon find on the other bus.

"Shoot out all their tires, hit the engine blocks. I got something for these motherfucking cannibals," Felix said coldly as he stuck the knife into the front right tire. Like a hot knife through butter. The tire made a moaning noise as the air escaped.

Gavin and Gloria both noticed it. Bodies were hanging from hooks in the back of the bus. Parts of flesh had been cut away. The second bus had several females in cages, chained like animals. Dirty, bloody, used, beaten, hopeless.

Gloria rushed into the other bus, breaking locks off the cages as carefully as she could. The eyes of the girls were dead. They were gone, drawn so far back from themselves to deal with the suffering they were subjected to every day. Gloria helped them out as understandingly as she could; although pressed for time. Chantel and Bonnie held their hands to their faces as they watched the young women stumble out of the second bus. They too, understood.

Felix put the whistle in his mouth. The men in the bus began to beg. Gavin watched a hellish smile split Felix's face as he drew in a deep breath. He began to blow. His eyes were dead, Gavin thought. They weren't brown anymore, they looked black to him.

"Gavin, keep your weapon ready… Chantel, get in that truck and park it right fucking here."

She snapped out of her shock and ran to the Humvee he was talking about. She jumped in, after looking over the console she figured it out. She parked the tan tattered vehicle in front of the bus doors. Gloria pushed the girls to Francisco and Bonnie who loaded them carefully into the back of their truck. They pulled jackets and clothes off the dead and gave them to the girls. Noticing Felix's horrific work. Legs and arms were severed, faces smashed in. One man was folded in half in the parking lot.

Felix heard gurgling from someone still alive. He walked over, stuffing the whistle into the man's mouth.

"Tape, get me some tape," he called.

Gavin pulled some electrical tape from his D ring on his belt. Tossing it to Felix, he then wrapped the man's face. Taping his nostrils shut and sealing his mouth around the whistle.

After dragging the man by the leg to the front of the bus, he lifted him up and set him on the hood, careful not to damage the tape. He made eye contact with every one of the frightened faces watching him. Once they noticed what he had done, they couldn't take their eyes off the whistle.

A glass rattling bark, and screeches drew near. They were close. The cannibals, slavers, remnants of the old into the new world, were trapped.

Felix walked back inside to get his gear. The men all cried and begged and screamed, some of them began firing out of the windshield at the man. The bullet proof glass kept their bullets at bay. They were trapped. By their own protection. But were they safe from that of the infected, or themselves?

The group took off. Felix rode in the back of the truck with Gavin, sitting on the tail gate. Gavin was flipping them the bird. Felix was laughing as he fought the wind to light a smoke. Gavin handed him a flask.

"Well, at least it was worth something, after all."

Felix played with another whistle between his fingers. They could hear men screaming through the empty streets of the city.

He laughed hysterically. Gavin looked at him with thin eyes. "Just desserts, I think," Felix replied.

"How is that?" Gavin asked.

"The infected are human, the cannibals are eaten by once-humans. Therefore..."

"Just desserts," Gavin answered.

Felix was nervous, and Sasha could tell. She's trying not to show that she found it cute. The waiter arrived, asking the two what they would have. Felix being polite turned the waiter toward her, because one, he still was attempting to decide. She ordered a wine he couldn't pronounce and a salad that he took plain due to not hearing what she said.

"You know you could have ordered a dressing for your wheel," she reassured him.

"Babe, I had no idea what I was walking into here. I thought this was a normal restaurant."

She giggled. "You've never been to a place like this, have you?"

"No," he said. Trying to hide his embarrassment. She couldn't see it, other than his nervous constant watching.

The dining room was all but empty. They were the only two in that side of the restaurant. The kind you wore a dress, suit and tie to. The tables had real cloth on them, silverware, the wine glasses were real crystal. The napkins were almost silk, folded into a spikey fan with a thin ring around it. Chandeliers hung from the ceiling. Probably fucking crystal too.

"We probably are the best dressed people in this place," he spouted as he watched wealthy older couple get seated with their three grandchildren. Silver spoon fed family. Clean haircuts, straight backs, suit and tie. Felix looked down at himself for a moment.

"They probably are confused that we just walked in and asked to be seated. We are in shorts and T-shirts." She giggled. It didn't bother her in the slightest. She was having more fun with the sight of Felix being uncomfortable.

He hid behind his menu trying to figure out what he could eat. In the end a steak was all he found. The waiter was back with their wheels of lettuce. To Felix's surprise, it was in fact a wheel of lettuce. He sliced a piece and took a bite. A beer was set in front of him. Her wine glass was filled.

"Here, try some of this. It's like a whipped cheese topping."

She spooned some onto his dry salad. He took a bite. "I should have just told him I'm having whatever you are having."

She giggled again. Covering her mouth with her hand. She was sitting straight up, well-mannered. Napkin in her lap. She ate the salad with a knife and fork. Felix could only take it all in. Their meals came and went, very enjoyable to both of them.

The man sat the check in front of him. She snatched it from the table before Felix was able to look at it.

"I hate that," she said.

"What's that, babe?"

"Because you are the man, they automatically assume you are going to pick up the tab," she replied, placing her card in the fold. Setting it back on the table, she finished her glass of wine.

"Don't know what to tell you. But, why are you picking up the tab?" he asked picking up the bill.

His eyes widened. "Holy fuck," he said setting it back down.

"You made a few comments about you not expecting this place to be that expensive, so it's my turn to pick up the check. You have spent plenty already on us."

"Okay, hunny, I won't complain, but I certainly feel bad."

"Why?" she asked.

"Because, I invited you."

She giggled. "You don't have to pay for everything. It's my turn, I'm more than capable of picking up the tab."

"Well, you are a strong independent woman, who don't need no man."

She giggled. "Well, then, what do I keep you around for?" she replied.

He leaned in. "Oh, yeah?"

"Yeah," she said leaning the rest of the way for a kiss.

"Let's blow this popsicle stand."

"Let's."

Chapter 21
Matriarch

Felix took a long swig, like taking medicine. He put away five fingers like a shot. Pouring himself another; he put that one back just as quickly.

"As I look back, and think about how shitty our lives were before this, I always thought then that we were focusing on all the wrong shit."

"Like what?" Chris said, packing a can of dip.

"Like technology, celebrities, fashion, politics, shit music, people's feelings. All the scandals that would pop up as soon as someone who could do some good was about to take power. There was so much garbage in the world that it is absolutely surprising that we ever came this far. Between the weapons bans and the terrorist organizations founded by worse people than the people we were fighting in other countries. It was hard to ever want to stay in the army and fight for this country, when in all reality we were fighting for someone else. Ungrateful, worthless, fucks."

Chris nodded, "Yeah, I think near the end, we were all waiting on the civil war. Bunch of pansies who couldn't figure out their own lives, but wanted to throw you to the wolves, tell you how to live your life, preaching tolerance and equality. But they can take away religion, make people felons for standing up for what they believed in, it was all just a circus," Chris replied.

Felix continued, "Parents having to ask permission to change a diaper or breast feed, their fucking spawn, their own goddamn children. People lost their minds because they didn't get their way. When they lost internet, when we were getting ready for World War III, everyone all of a sudden started calling the military Nazis because fighting for your country was white supremacy. What the fuck was it all worth? Nothing, it was all worth horse shit. Everyone wants to stand for something until it came time to see what your life was worth. No one deserved the lives of soldiers, except for those willing to stand in front of our barrels. Our enemies did, because at least they believed they were fighting for something."

"White privilege," Chris said, nudging Felix.

They both laughed, "Yeah, what in the fuck is white privilege? I wonder if anyone ever figured out that our bones are all white? Our blood is all red, and we all had something in common; the will to survive. Too goddamn superficial to realize it was what is on the inside that counted. Doesn't matter. We are far better off now than we ever were," Felix said as he finished his second glass of bourbon.

"How is that, bro?" Chris asked, enjoying the conversation.

"Let's see, I have traveled back and forth in this country several times, when it was full of people it was sickening. Now that it's empty, the cities are quite; gorgeous. The roads beautiful, I can hear the world once again. Before you would have to travel hours to get away from everyone. Just to quiet your mind that was poisoned by the idiot box, cell phones, the news. Other opinions, although many were intriguing. Fuck, movies were losing any worth and imagination. How much regurgitation can you stand before you say enough is enough?"

"You really hated it that much?" Chris asked.

"It's easy to. Especially when you read through history. Did you know that progression killed off probably the only chance we had at actually being a part of this world?"

"What are you talking about?"

Felix cupped his lighter around his cigarette.

"Hunter gatherers, about the happiest we could have ever been, we were a part of the land, our women equal to men, our children learned to survive and respect the world. We hunted and foraged for our food, we lived short lives, but they were good lives. Nomadic lives. Then came the agricultural societies, key word – society. Convenience, they grew in numbers, rapidly, and swallowed the hunter gatherers, destroyed the forest, and as time marched on, slavery, religion, exploration, technology, and then we land at what we used to be. It disgusted me for so many years, watching people argue against fact, blame another race for their self-imposed problems, tell boys they should not be men because men are bad. Tell other people what to do because you want to be able to control them. Our world was infected with progress, it was infected with something that could only be cured by our extinction."

"Jesus, fuck."

Felix turned toward Chris, "Since the world has reset, haven't you noticed?"

"Noticed what?"

"It's perfect now, children are receiving a real education here, save for the feminist mentality and religious aspects, but they aren't hunched over staring into a phone. Parents are actually teaching them, not forgetting about them or letting the television raise them. People are getting along again, learning traits, not how to line their pockets. We are turning back into hunter gatherers."

"Now that you put it that way, it makes sense."

Felix leaned back, taking a heavy drag, "Granted, we are still pillaging from the old world, but eventually, there isn't going to be anything worth taking from those graves. The lessons maybe; books, but that is really about it."

"You know what makes me most happy about this world?" Chris said as he looked around.

"What?"

"All the bangin' primo babes with guns around here, oh my god, bro!" he exclaimed. Felix laughed.

"Not wrong, it's hard to be fat on rations, and the need to be able to run for your life, use a gun, build a fire, lock pick, hot wire a car, cook, hunt, march on. This is what paradise looks like. The infection should be called the cure, not the sickness."

Chris nodded. Gavin sat down with a bottle and his own glass.

"What are you cocksuckers talking about?"

Chris patted Gavin on the back.

"Oh, you know, just unraveling the universe," Chris replied.

"Story time with Felix; haven't heard you spin a web since the last time we were in Afghanistan."

Felix chuckled. He held his glass up. Chris and Gavin followed suit. The candle seemed to dim around them. Passersby walked wide around the three sitting in front of the bar.

"By bullet and blade, we live and die, by tooth and nail we will abide."

The three took their drinks in one shot. They sat at their table, quietly for a moment.

Gavin broke the silence with what was now heavy on his mind, "Do you hate them?"

"Who?" Felix asked.

"The dogs, the feral, whoever caused all of this?"

Felix drew in a long drag, smoke rolled over his face, "No, because we are like dogs."

"How do you mean?" Chris asked.

"We are all the same, we came from something greater, now we are watered down breeds bred for coat and temperament, used for a purpose which we don't understand, but benefit the powers that be. Because, a being standing over us says a few words and we understand those sounds, because it is associated with a reward, if for only a moment. Except, that thing is no longer

273

standing over us. Just like the dogs that no longer can be domesticated, we turn back to our former greater selves. We are just like the dogs, segregated into packs, loyal only to our own, and separate and attack the weak, to eventually overwhelm the mass. Without control, we become feral, without obedience we exist only because of basic survival instincts."

They sat there for a moment.

"Well, that was deep as fuck," Chris replied.

Felix continued, "How can I hate something that is a reflection of myself?"

"How could you not hate them, when they took everything from us?"

Felix and Chris turned to see who that lovely voice belonged to. They were all surprised; it was one of the female Special Forces group team leaders. She was strong, and caught Chris's eye entirely, some would challenge to say, that she caught more than just anyone's eyes.

"Look, what's your name?" Felix asked.

"I'm Lieutenant Rachel Cunningham."

Gavin pointed at her, "I've heard of you; you're one of the women who destroyed a sex slave trading post a year ago. They called that mission the Spring Run. With a team of four or five, right?" She nodded. Chris was staring at her, mouth agape.

"That's right, we lost our vehicles and basically walked the whole way back," she said, turning back to Felix with a scowl on her face. "I wanna know why you don't hate those things out there?" pointing directly at Felix.

"What did the dogs take from us?" he asked. She was dumbfounded beyond belief.

Without missing a beat though, she replied, "How about, everything? Our families, our friends, it turned the survivors into monsters worse than the infected. We barely survived during the three-year winter, and if we could find something to eat, someone would find us, use us for sex, sale us, eat us. It was all the dogs' fault."

Felix listened carefully. He replied nonetheless, her reasoning to him was frivolous at best.

"I agree, however... I blame the dogs for uniting us, destroying an onslaught of social control and brainwashing of your society. I blame them for resetting the earth to a much-needed era. I blame them for showing people what is truly important in this world. I blame them for rekindling faith, as dangerous as that weapon is, it has its good and bad." Rachel was shaking her head in disbelief and disagreement. Felix continued, "I blame them for ensuring our survival. Because...if it wasn't them, then it would have been something worse, like creatures like us continuing to eat each other in the name of whatever sounded good at the time. Equality, was usually the favorite flavor of division back then."

"What are you talking about, they killed everyone, and the ones unlucky enough to survive had to deal with other survivors who were just as, if not more, evil than the dogs."

Felix huffed, "Humans were always this way, we just needed to be ripped from convenience to realize how terrible and great we could be. The dogs took nothing from us we didn't need, or weren't planning on taking from ourselves in the first place."

"I don't follow this idiotic prattle you are going on about."

Felix leaned forward, maliciously, methodically sliding his glass and bottle out of his way. He looked up at her, his eyes dead as he folded his hands in front of him on the table.

"Your world… Civilization; if you could call it that, was attempting to ban religion, guns, freedom of speech, and patriotism, not to mention the American family, and self-sufficiency. Civil war was at our doorstep, just a little push and it would have exploded into chaos. Not to mention all the racial divide. The inaccurate statistics in order to prove a point built already on a foundation of beautiful lies. Feminist, the fake ones, not the real ones…crying for equality until it was time to be equal. Terrorists masquerading as movements crying about one race but failing to mention any of the other races or the fact that their particular race received more government funding and grants than any other in the country. To include but not limited to, Affirmative Action, entire clauses and regulations within the workplace that protects everyone for being different, college grants out the ass, all black schools, activities, police legitimately avoiding these communities for fear of reprisal or gang violence if they should have to defend themselves…so on and so forth. Because in all reality, the entire movement was designed to in fact enslave another, and spin a lie while they looted and destroyed their own town instead of maybe looking at each other and saying, well, maybe we shouldn't burn down our own town, block freeways, threaten anyone different, send a list of demands that honestly wouldn't fix anything, or slander an entire generation that have nothing to do with slavery, just like they never experienced it. People demanding for all of us to accept who they are; mutilating themselves to be, when that person couldn't accept who they were born into the world as. Because, it was a mental disorder, that needed to be helped and studied further. Not try to change biology when literally the category they fell under was again a psychological disorder. Playing on the illusions was actually causing more damage than helping those poor individuals. To include high suicide rates, even more of a reason to divide individuals. Yet; it was being celebrated and called brave and courageous. And again, persecution of one's sexual desire, this time though, it wasn't the gays being hit with rocks, they were the ones casting them. Did everyone not realize that straight people make gay people? So how is it anyone's fault? No one was being born in a test tube yet. So just like everyone else, they deserved to live. If your god didn't want them to exist; *It* wouldn't have allowed them to in the first place. Just like good old evil. It; evil is meant to be there to balance out the disgusting side of morality. But that wasn't good enough. Everyone wants to be special and something unique. The truth is, none of us are. We are all carbon copies of garbage. The last time our species was great was when we only got fire from a lightning strike in a fucking tree while we danced around like frightened animals. But; all of you just fucking ate that shit up, staring into the idiot box, wide-eyed and mouth a-fuckin-gape." Felix's sarcasm was striking a chord with her, he could see it all over her face.

"I don't like your fucking tone," she replied.

"You asked me, so here it is. You wanna have a conversation, then fucking have it and realize that people can think for themselves. I'm one of those kinds."

She was taken aback yet again. *Who the fuck does this asshole think he is?* she thought to herself.

Furthermore, to her surprise, he outstretched his hand offering her a seat. Because it honestly didn't matter what he believed, nor her beliefs. They were going to have a conversation, that more than likely was going to turn into an argument, and end with either of two outcomes. They would hate each other, or they won't. Her soldiers or friends were all standing there anxious to be anywhere else.

She sat. Her hair was dark, pulled back tight, braided down her back. Her eyes deep blue, even in the yellow light of the street lamps. Her skin was a light brown. The group was sitting in front of the bar, around the small circular tables on either side of the steps leading into the main entrance.

One of her subordinates put a hand on her shoulder, "Rachel, let's go, we can report these assholes later, you don't have to entertain them, they are fodder and breeding stock, not our superiors."

Chris and Gavin looked at each other. Rachel shook her head, never breaking eye contact with Felix, "No, I'm going to crush this asshole right here right now."

Gavin nodded, "Good for you. But you two..." Gavin said directing his attention to the two girls on her flanks. "Only the best, the strongest, the most intelligent are allowed to be breeding stock in this fortress. Think about that, before you say we are *just* anything."

They paid him no mind, they simply disappeared into the bar. But his comment stuck with them the entire night.

"Alright, you're going to crush me, so my question to you is, what the fuck about your world makes you think it was better off?"

She didn't miss a beat, "Are you serious, is this a serious question?"

Felix nodded, "Ab-so-fucking-lutely."

She had a look of searching, desperately for how to answer this question, there was so much in her head. She was trying to collect her thoughts and present her case. This conversation was turning into a question-and-answer debate at this point. If she wasn't careful, he was going to manipulate the conversation in any direction he wanted. It unnerved her.

Suddenly Rachel gestured, rolling her eyes, throwing her hand up as if it was common knowledge as she answered, "How about civilization. Being able to go to the store whenever you need to, and not running the risk of getting killed or turned? How about being able to wear normal clothes instead of combat shit all the time? How about being able to eat whatever you wanted. How about technology, being able to order anything from your phone and have it shipped to your door. TV, music, fashion, education. Everything that you said is what was wrong with the world before it ended, was not what was wrong with it. Wanna know what I think was wrong with the world before it ended?"

Felix gestured for here to continue, "By all means."

"It was white supremacist sexist narcissistic assholes like you, that hated anyone not like you, that would rather have guns instead of safer schools. Who would rather the entire system be tailored to you? Above average income, always got that promotion, always got his way."

"Oh, is that right?"

"Yeah, everything you said was just a bunch of bullshit. Which is why I don't understand how you could not hate the dogs when they took everything from you, not us, we were all fighting to change the country to something better."

Felix let out a hysterical laugh, Gavin and Chris did as well.

"Better," he started through his laugh. "Who is *us* exactly? Because you and I have a completely different memory of how society was tailored for everyone except those who wished to be self-sufficient and loved this country, because I can assure you, that until all these movements for equality and police brutality started, it was nowhere even close to as bad as everyone was making it out to be. Make it better, tell me how looting and burning down your own town makes the world better, or how celebrating a mental disorder that states that a person is not biologically the gender or sex that they were born as, that cannot be proven in any way other than through a psychologist? Tell me how it was common in this country to compare us to every other country in the world, when those motherfuckers didn't want immigrants, who were majority Anglo-Saxon white descendants; who have a worse history of murdering their own people compared to anything our country did as a whole? Some to wit; the holiest of holy motherfuckers; have such a horrific history of murdering innocent women and children of almost every race on the face of this planet for not one; but nine motherfucking crusades, in God's name."

Rachel shook her head, "Then how about you explain to me," Rachel pointed to herself with her thumb as she leaned forward, "why you think it wasn't that bad, when black people were being killed every day by cops, and how women were still being oppressed, families being torn apart for crossing the border into this country."

"Are you religious?" Felix asked.

"Yeah. I am, but what the fuck does that have to do with anything?" she answered crossing her arms and her legs. Posing a closed off position that Felix could read all too well.

"Humor me, we are about to go down a deep dark hole, to which no rabbits nor little girls should ever venture. So, Christian, Catholic, Southern Baptist, Muslim, Buddhist…what?" he continued to pry, and that he did. He didn't need to have a crowbar in hand for anyone to know what he was about to do.

"Christian."

Felix nodded as he pours himself another drink. "Okay… Religion, a lot like everything in the world, sounds better out of someone else's mouth."

"What do you mean?" she asked.

"Your God is all-knowing, all-powerful, omnipresent, all that happy horse-shit, right?"

"He's everyone's God, one, and yes."

"Okay, so from your bible, he loves everyone because we are all his little children?"

"Right, come on what are you getting at, spit it out," she demanded.

"You follow the interpretations from a book written by men, translated by languages to the best of their ability although inaccurate, missing chapters, so to protect the people from truths that overarching powers wish to maintain hidden, about a being that is all-powerful and all-knowing yet needed to rest, proves that darkness existed before the light leading one to believe that God is an afterthought of something much older, and that it is not all powerful for having to rest on the 7th day which until the sun was created there could not be a day from the point of view of man, that did not exist yet. Not to mention created a woman from a man; leading men to believe that women are unequal and an afterthought only put on earth in order to serve men for the purpose of continuing the species like the dumb animals your God had started us out to be. Apparently in its all-knowing and all-powerful benevolence couldn't see the future nor care to stop the curious woman and spineless man from becoming more than just animals in a garden, the woman to always suffer the gift of life, and man to forever be powerless against the female, regardless of how you look at the world. Tempted by an angel, that somehow has human emotions and rebelled against his creator. Should I go on?"

"I have a feeling I'm going to regret sitting here now. I'm getting nowhere with you," she replied, gesturing with her hand for him to continue his rant.

Gavin interrupted, "Further than most. You are actually sitting here attempting to understand and reach a common ground, something most of you never understood. Cheers to you." He raised his glass to her.

Felix continued, calling her eyes from Gavin back to him, "You follow a contradictive being, with split personality disorders on a cosmic and unfathomable level that would fuck its own child in order to bring forth into this world its divine son to die at our hands, for sins that the child's creator designed us to commit. Because God has a plan for us all, right? Man was meant to beat his brother to death with a stone because, after all, we are made in the almighty's image. And, God will continue to play this fun little game of testing us with help from its favorite angel, Lucifer. So, what kind of belief is that to follow, if not one designed to maintain the hope of desperate hungry slaves, when spun the right way?"

"We are done with this conversation, I wanna know why the fuck you…" she pointed at him, leaning toward him violently, "…don't hate the dogs, because that is insane, but I'm thinking you are fucked up more than just your empathy for them. It seems there is a lot of mental issues with you, that I'm starting to see could be a serious problem for my people that are good god-fearing people trying to survive the end of the world."

"God-fearing people?" Felix laughed, "I watched your god-fearing people sentence a woman to be forcefully impregnated because she turned out to be homosexual. Forcefully impregnated translates to rape whether clinically induced, or otherwise. Because it is still against her will, by the way. Once she has that child, you then exile her, am I wrong? Not to mention, you all go around here with the authority to challenge another woman for the rights to breed with her partner. Tell me; how you are good God-fearing people? Except well, if you look at the way I view your beliefs, then it certainly can make sense. Beat your brother, your sister down, right?"

"You have a fucking mouth on you, how the fuck is you even allowed to be a part of our new world?"

279

"For saving several of your women, and other reasons to which I believe are meant for someone else's benefit, and means to my end. And I mean death, not my benefit, such as all societies are usually designed," Felix replied, lighting a cigarette.

"You think you can talk shit about our sanctuary away from the infection outside these walls? You sit there enjoying a good life while people are starving out there, most of them froze during the Three-Year Winter. You think you can openly badmouth our ways, we are the only thing keeping you from suffering a worse fate out there," she pointed toward the west.

"Trust me, out there is far better than the suffering all you are unknowingly experiencing within these walls, I promise you."

"What does someone like you, white male, know about suffering?"

Felix exhaled a thick cloud with his answer, "Enough."

She laughed, "I wanna know. You strike me as one of those preppers, gun rights activist, republican supporters, immigrant hating white privileged alpha assholes who used to talk about how your opinion mattered because you were a has-been soldier."

"Whoa, there you are, that's the activist college student from back then, am I right?" Felix asked.

Gavin, Chris, and Felix all started laughing. "There were a lot of them in our time," Chris started, "but that asshole right there wasn't one of them."

Gavin patted Felix on the shoulder, then pointed at her, "I like how fucking violent and hateful you are, you are our kinda person, good for fucking you," he said, still laughing. His comment cut her deeper than she thought.

Felix nodded, "I'm enjoying the shit out of this," he exclaimed. "I'm guessing you are referring to white privilege?"

"Yes, white male privilege, I experienced it all my life."

Felix chuckled, "Oh yeah, did you? First off, I still don't know what the fuck that means other than a term used to divide people even more. First used by some social terrorist organization that sprung up under the beautiful illusion of equality and police brutality yet…destroyed their own town and looted their own shops and stores and caused more damage to their own people than the cops. Point in fact, more white males were killed by cops than any other race, due to the police feeling more safe dealing with white fucks, compared to the possibility or being called a racist or being shot by a possible black gang member. Not to mention, most cops have to stay out of black neighborhoods for fear of being threatened, beaten to death, having their cars burnt to the ground by these so-called activists."

"Not true."

"Most violence committed by any one race in our time before the dogs were done by their own people. These great powerful brave activists in that particular movement, legitimately gave a list of demands, like terrorists, that basically stated that if you are white, give your shit to only black people, not anyone else. That group also focused on only one races lives instead of everyone, and slandered everyone who was white, singling them out who had nothing to do with anything that their great grandparents suffered or police brutality or whatever fucking nonsense they used for a reason to burn another one of their towns down."

"Everyone knows that white people are better off than any other race," she responded.

Felix continued ignoring her, "But hey, racism only happens when it's a white person talking, right?"

"You have no idea what you're talking about. This country supported slavery for so long."

"Yet, somehow, if irony was the more hilarious fuck that she always has been, most races that were oppressed once upon a time clung to that political party who were the ones that wanted to continue to enslave their ancestors."

He threw his hands up, she shook her head. "Not true. White people wanted to keep slaves."

"Alright, before we get into this, do you have any idea where you are sitting, what this place was?"

Rachel shakes her head. "No, should I?"

"You are mixed, half black, half Asian right?"

"What of it?"

"Slavery pretty much ended right motherfucking here. Not to mention, I'm about to blow your fucking mind, you ready…" he said making his point with his finger. "Let's put slavery as a whole in perspective. In all of recorded time, 4500 years I wanna say, I'm probably wrong, it was longer, slavery existed since pretty much the dawn of civilization. In all of that time of human existence, Americans were the first ones to crush the trade globally, kinda weird, right?" Felix said coldly.

"Not true," she quickly replied.

"One of the first slave owners in all of America was a black man, who fought in court to gain the equal status of his family compared to white people. To which he maintained his slaves for a long while thereafter. Also, even before the dogs, years and years later after the global trade was crushed. Guess what, black people were still being enslaved by their own fucking people, Asians enslaved Asians, Spanish enslaved Spanish, and money enslaving civilization. Tell me how our country oppresses anyone other than with that good old debt; when literally it wasn't until the early 2000 that certain African governments stopped fighting to keep laws that allowed them to possess slaves."

"You have it all figured out, don't you, just another stereotypical white man who thinks he knows everything," she said.

Felix lifted his glass in her direction, "Careful, you're starting to sound like white people," he stated sarcastically. "Get an old soldier drunk with like-minded people, and they will solve the mysteries of the universe in one night, and not remember it the next day."

"Just because you think that you saw combat and killed people before the end of the world, that you know more than everyone else," Rachel started, only to be interrupted.

"Yeah, isn't that the thought process of all those activists and movements? You didn't suffer the way I have, so your opinion and point of view doesn't count. Reality check, everything that one person suffers is because of what they did or failed to do. Take responsibility for it, and move the fuck on."

"So, it was black people's fault?"

Felix set his glass down. "It was everyone's fault once upon a time. It's the cops' fault for allowing corruption. It's black people's fault for allowing their communities to be full of crime and hate amongst their own people. It's white peoples' fault for spreading across the world so quickly. It's the government's fault for trying to control us. It's the parents' fault for raising shitty fucking children. It's convenience's fault for making us stupid, weak, and greedy. You wanna know how you fix all of our problems we supposedly had back then?"

Rachel waved her hand, palm up, "Not like it matters now. But let's hear it, since you've got it all figured out."

"If you want equality then get rid of welfare. Get rid of social security, get rid of abortion, get rid of race-only schools, get rid of all the government funding designed to keep the people reliant on a failing systems designed only to cater to one people. Get rid of the system that makes it to where having a job makes you less comfortable than a jobless unmarried woman with eight kids. Or…"

Felix started laughing. "You end everyone's little worlds. You reset the system; you take away everything and make them all desperate. You get this, where we are now. Free; well, not while under the control of your little regime."

"You're insane."

Felix continued, "Equality, make everyone adhere to the same standards, instead of picking and choosing what works for only one people."

"It doesn't work like that."

Felix wrenched his head toward her. "How does it not? You tell me, you can do anything a man can. You can do shit we can't. Your race suffered more than ours so you deserve more, blah blah blah. It was all just a bunch of bullshit. Leading to my point. When your world ended, it was the greatest fucking thing that could have ever happened to us. Nature is the only thing equal in this world. And we are no longer anywhere at the top of the food chain. What fixed all of our problems, what fixed everything…was your world ending."

"We will always be at the top of the food chain," she replied.

"Only because of the shit we make, our intelligence maybe. But if you didn't have that gun, do you think you really have a chance to overpower a man? Especially in the society you say is better than this world?"

"Well, I…"

Felix interrupted her, "The only thing that makes us physically equal is your ability to take a life compared to mine. The only thing that makes us biologically equal, is our differences. You hold the egg; I hold the seed."

"I can agree with the biology, but how does this gun make us equal, when up until the world ended, guns were killing people all over the place, in schools, churches, everywhere. Nowhere was ever safe because of them."

"That gun makes us equal in the predator prey spectrum of nature. But that was one thing that was nearly actually banned, because of the theory that an inanimate object could operate on its own and take a life. You think that just because there were laws, that people actually follow them? No, everyone is only kept honest because of either two things… How they were raised, the morals that were instilled in them, or the simple fact that if they fuck up, they die. That's it. Guns were never the problem, it's only ever been people that are the problem. This world would go on without us, beautifully and terribly."

"Sounds like a terrible life, full of fear."

"Fear, pain, suffering are the greatest teachers. There are always evil people in the world. And no matter how many laws you put in place; reality cannot be challenged."

"I don't follow."

"That we follow the same laws of nature as any animal on the face of the earth."

Rachel slammed her hands on the table, "So you're telling me it's an animal instinct to act the way we do toward each other now? How about before, when families were literally being ripped apart by the government and put in prisons. Sexism has been a major part of our history for a long time, and if we don't help those wishing to be helped from terrible countries than who in the world will?"

Felix sat back, "Yes, sexism really has, probably because most governments all followed the interpretations of a religion or faith. Some of the biggest failures in an entire society is their culture based off of their religion. Something that was starting to be rectified in our country before everything that happened."

"Fuck you, I remember in school that religion was taken out, unless it was the Muslim faith."

"I recall that too, Felix, I have to agree with her, religion isn't as bad as you make it sound. I'm an ordained minister after all, so I'm going to have to say that religion was not the cause of sexism in the country," Chris replied.

"Oh okay, like Christians around the world weren't being attacked and murdered by Muslims and other people simply because of their faith. Our country was getting rid of it and replacing studies of the Muslim culture into schools without any of the parents' knowledge. Sounds an awful lot like an interesting societal transition attempt to me. To make the youth into something different for the next generation, more obedient, needy little leaches on the government so they cannot fend for themselves, less likely to fight the government and more likely to fight each other. Make American women want to follow the same shitty lives as most Muslim women. Or they could have attempted to make the youth culturally aware, but if that was the case, then why only focus on one of the most devastating faiths in the world?" Felix asked.

Chris sat back thinking about it for a moment. Felix turned back to Rachel, "What else do you got?"

"You make it sound like all other cultures are dangerous to our way of life," she replied.

"Which side are you on exactly? Just because you look like you are mixed doesn't mean you can act like you grew up in a different culture than an American one."

Rachel crossed her arms, "And just because you were American doesn't mean you can act like we weren't wrong, and unsympathetic to all the problems of the world. Immigration, starving children, civil war, we're taking kids from their families who were just trying to take their kids to a safer place."

"We're American, regardless of what the world is, this is the product that was produced," Felix replied gesturing to himself. "So, with that statement, are you siding with the ones that ran from the problems in their country, knowing full well that their children were probably going to be raped by cartel fuckers, and maybe even not survive the journey to get across the border in the first place? Or, those that put them in holding centers until a logical decision could be made? I'm confused here. The world needed to help themselves; instead of relying on us to fix things."

"Our borders were literally destroying families."

Gavin replied just before Felix did. "Pretty much everything on a TV or through your phone was destroying families. Culture shift and blending was destroying families. Subliminal messages and the constant grind of ridiculous work hours and false concepts of needing money to enjoy your life when by the time you retired the best years of your life were over."

Felix continued, "Agreed. The country that they were fleeing from was destroying their families, not our borders. What are we supposed to do, go to war for them too? Maybe they should stay in their country and make it like ours if they think ours is so great. If everyone runs away, then when is it time to start fighting, when is it their turn to do something, and not run to America asking us to throw bodies at it and make all the bad people go away? We should only meddle in another country's problems when their problems start spilling into ours. Not because we want to set up another bank or reap the resources still left buried in those mountains. But hey that's a completely different topic. With the number of immigrants that would flock to us from around the world just leads you to believe that maybe if we started turning all of them away, all those civil wars that should have been fought, would finally put someone in power that actually gives a shit about their people. But instead we would rather take them in, and turn the fucking cheek at the reality of the situation. Blame our people for everyone else's problems."

"Oh yeah, and what is the reality of the situation?"

"Everyone in the world expects Americans to fix all their problems. And not only did we give the majority of the force to fight terrorism which was a problem for everyone, especially the countries that took in Muslims, but it got to the point that Canada asked us to not take any more immigrants in because they didn't want their streets turning into England or France where their people, mainly the women were being raped and beaten by immigrants. Guests sheltered from the war that they should be fighting for or against, shouting that this host nation change their ways for them or they were going to start rioting and blah blah blah. How the fuck does that make sense?"

"That wasn't happening."

"How the fuck do you know? You were probably watching the news instead of questioning it. If you did come across the border, your parents would have done nothing to stop you from being gang banged as payment to get them into a better country."

"Fuck you, you don't know that."

"I do. Because that is exactly what was happening. Contrary to popular belief, blame was reserved only for those trying to do something right. Never the ones that were actually the problem. Those kids' parents for instance. Or how about the cartel fucks who brought them over, they are the ones who tore their children's lives apart. Or, how about an entire government under the influence of corruption bought and paid for by drug money? Pretty sure they are the reason their people are fleeing."

"Everything is always a conspiracy with you old fucks."

Felix laughed, "Oh yeah, when was a conspiracy not proven to be correct? Because last time I checked every time secret information got leaked, it turned out to be just as bad as everyone thought. Or, all the scandals ended up being correct, or all the horrible shit no one wanted to believe, ended up all being true."

"Name one."

"Okay," Felix said, gleefully leaning forward. "Cell phones and the majority monopoly companies such as Facebook, Google, Amazon, Microsoft, Walmart, and other large companies were all selling data to the CIA in order to maintain a psychological collection of trends and societal normality. To the point in fact that their CEOs faced severe legal actions due to the misconduct and soliciting of information, on the fucking nation, if not the world. Not to mention, Facebook, everyone had it, was one of the first globalized attempts at communication, or in all reality, tracking and monitoring, always watching, always looking, but not for your benefit, for theirs."

"Poor example. Just another conspiracy theory."

"Got another one; one of my favorites, in fact. Our government comes out and apologizes to the Guatemalan Government for human testing, and the sterilization of their people or injecting them with STDs, I forget which, it happened in the 60s or 70s. Anyway, it was funny because it was the Guatemalan Government that helped them, so why apologize if they were working together? Sounds an awful lot like a martyr attempting to make amends for shit that was encouraged by the fuckers we were apologizing to. To look good to the people that won't waste any time of their busy lives to actually look into what happened."

"Don't believe that one either."

"Testing on the civilian population has been done for a very long time. Cigarettes, STDS, cell phones, propaganda, population control by sterilization, truth serum, hell if information wasn't leaked back in the early 70s, I wonder how long our government would have continued their testing on the mentally ill, imprisoned, soldiers, poor communities, and at the time, minorities?"

"What information was leaked in the early 70s?"

"The Tuskegee syphilis experiment…"

Gavin replied right after Felix, "Project MKUltra…killed a civilian…CIA testing in order to combat spies within our government, using LSD, physical and sexual abuse, not to mention blackmail of senators and officials to keep the money fund rolling, and you don't even wanna know what they did to blackmail them…"

"Ohio state penitentiary from like the 50s to the 60s injected inmates with cancer to see how it develops," Chris added.

She was dumbfounded by all of them. Still wasn't convinced, merely surprised at how all of them believed these things that she had never heard of.

Felix continued, "No worries, just think of it this way, getting to my point here…"

"Thank God," she interrupted.

"Our people, the good ones, who gave a shit about humans regardless of race, creed, or religion, had to make up laws to protect the people from their government, and scholars, educators, doctors, and scientists. Supposedly the epitome of the human race; average people needed to be protected from them. And to this day, none of them would have apologized for what they did, or that they were even wrong to have killed so many people, caused so many birth defects, sterilized thousands and thousands of minorities. If things didn't come out, didn't get leaked, secret files meant to be destroyed got sent to the wrong office, whatever. No one would have protected us, the people. The Government will always find ways to progress, and find even better ways to spin that lie that sounds good, because of all the data they have collected over the years. They send some planes overhead. Chem-trails release a little obedient matter into the air, and then the next tragedy happens. They spin some more lies, and people believe it. And start hating each other, and not those in power. We were always at the verge of civil war, but never fully went into it, why? I think because we were all being drugged, made to be tamer, made to be obedient, because the scientists already figured out how to control us a long time ago."

"Do you know that for a fact? Not everyone is evil, like you are making them all out to be," she replied.

"A religion was written by man in order to control a populace used for labor. In that religion, God had to give rules written in stone so that we would stop fucking up. Governments create laws as needed, only when it matters for fear of the populace, and if the populace fucks up, God wipes them all away. What do you think governments do to people they don't think are worthy? Sound familiar? If all of the evil shit we did to people didn't come out; how long would it have gone on? How many more lives would have been ruined or ended in the name of progression? How much is still going on? Right now, at the end of your world?"

"People are generally good, and people like you is the reason why there were institutions who deal with problems like yours. Fucks like you were the reason we had to start thinking about banning weapons and watching people."

The guys all started laughing again. The look on her face was of complete annoyance. She thought they were all idiots.

Felix laughed, "Problems like mine? The ability to look at something from a different point of view is only a problem to those wishing to hide it. People as a whole are easy to control. The individual, however, is very difficult. But, an organization or group of people can overwhelm or overpower the individual. Our greatest mistake was believing that the people above us, placed into power by us, had any real power in the first place. The few govern the many. Like a shepherd tends its scared stupid flock, meant to be sheered, milked, and led to slaughter. The fact that we used an analogy about wolves being evil goes to show that everything was spun in order to keep people like the sheep and not the wolves."

"I don't follow, not even a little bit."

"Sheep are worthless other than taking their wool and meat, maybe some milk, but humans really shouldn't have milk anyway, especially if you're religious, which in yours I think you are technically only supposed to eat fish and berries and shit. Anyway, just like law, it's changed or written to suit the current riot mentality. I'm getting off subject here, where was I?"

Rachel replied, "You were at the part where you were telling us how much of an asshole you are…"

She was serious, Chris and Gavin, were dying laughing as they tried to drink.

"…oh, that's right…" Felix continued, completely ignoring her comment, "do you even know anything about wolves?"

"No, I don't. All I know is that all dogs were turned into these things that infected people and now go around eating us."

"Well, you really should, it would probably help your tactics a little more when you start realizing where military tactics come from in the animal kingdom, and it will all start making sense."

"How do you mean?"

"Infiltration is a tactic of a snake in the grass. Flanking, separation, and segregation is a tactic of the wolves, who, in fact, due to their pack mentality actually care for the pack, mate for life, and protect their weak. It's where the saying three to one starts to make sense. Overwhelming numbers and swarming attacks come from bees, very mirrored to the technology we were getting very good at in drones. Ants represent the infantry almost beautifully, just good little soldiers fighting for the queen, marching along carrying heavy shit on their backs, day in day out. Every now and then they get to fight each other to see who is worthy enough for a night with the queen."

"You are one insane fucking person," she said.

"Hardly. Continuing on… Wolves, packs, which you know, most mothers always protect their children, but only in the pack mentality of the wolves is it the entire pack's job. So, the point here is, that being a wolf, not a sheep dog, because the sheep dog keeps the sheep in check, being a wolf should have been praised. Not spun in such a way to give the odd subconscious notion that all of you little dumb deaf and blind fucks should stay needing the Sheppard, God, Government. While the sheep dogs; police, military, anyone in bed with those that control the population, keep you easily distracted and lead your astray asses back in with the rest of the herd. You all should have been wolves in sheep's clothing. Blending in, until the right moment when you eat the shepherd and free the rest of the sheep."

Rachel was wide-eyed. Gavin was nodding as his cheeks were turning red and his eyes were beginning to twinkle. Chris was drunk, so much muscle and a knack for eating as healthy as he could made him somewhat of a lightweight.

"I've never thought of it that way. But if the sheep don't have a shepherd or a sheep dog, they will be someone else's prey regardless."

Felix shrugged his shoulders, "The idea is to turn the sheep into wolves, but I have to say, I like your reply."

"Why are there so many people like you? Even when I was young there was always people like you around, but you rarely ever saw them on TV, you all just sat there, never really doing anything, just waiting."

Felix thought on it for a moment. "Everything is subliminal messages; you can't have someone who would give a good one. Everything that we saw, heard, and were a part of until your world ended, was all leading us to this. Right here right now. Where I'm sitting in a bar on the edge of the country, openly carrying a weapon, in a regime like government military that has females defined as the dominant species on this Earth. Fighting against an infection that affected two species… Only two. If it were Mother, she would have balanced it out. But it isn't, it's man-made, because it only focuses on something as if it was designed to. How was it spread? How much of the world is infected?"

Rachel replied, "The entire world is."

"Now, well, that's easy. Swarm technology drones, simultaneously spreading a biological or chemical agent throughout the world all at the same time. Easy to figure out. We have been testing unmanned aircraft for a long time. Weaponization for projectile applications was old news. Biological and chemical; now that is something to be proud of. Letting civilians have this technology makes a lot of people whistle blowers now, even if unintentional, wireless connections are the easiest to hack. Cellphones are wireless technology, easy to hack, easy to watch. We were all the reason why your world ended. We failed ourselves because we all forgot that we put those evil fucks in power. We were brainwashed into thinking we had it all figured out. When those wanting to ban weapons actually sold the most. Those doing good were actually doing the most harm. And we were too busy hating each other in order to realize that if we wanted change…we needed to rise up and destroy our government and place people in power who are good. Crying about it, marching around, free speech, that was all a bunch of bullshit. It was never going to change anything."

"You are a scary fucking thing. You still haven't answered my question, I've sat here and listened to your bullshit, now… Why the fuck do you not hate those things out there?"

Felix leaned back, taking a long drag. "Because, we are all just like them. I see beings just trying to survive. I see packs of dogs trying to eat us and protect their own. I see the result of being a sheep in a world designed for the minority. I see nothing but victims across a sea of what this nation used to be. Once upon a time it was great, but now, because of those beautiful dogs out there, we can finally become something greater than we ever thought possible."

"That is just about the stupidest fucking thing I've ever heard," she replied.

"You're a good god-fearing strong independent woman who don't need no man, except for to continue the species and keep our species from inevitably becoming extinct in a world where God had a plan… Then, tell me what sense it makes to hate what your God intended to happen all along?"

"I hate the way you talk shit about my faith, it's the only thing that has kept me going at the end of the world."

"Oh yeah? I'm pretty sure it was that gun," Felix pointed at her pistol on her hip, "…and your ability to run and hide that has kept you going, but I could be wrong, I too fall under an illusion of hope. It could be food; we need to eat to survive. A loved one, because you know there is nothing on the other side."

"A man like you doesn't know the first thing about hope," she replied.

"Probably, besides the point, you asked, I answered." Felix gestured for her to continue.

"This entire conversation you said a lot of shit that I don't understand, but one that stands out the most is. You keep referring to my world, our world. It was your world too, bitch."

Felix caught movement out of the corner of his eye.

"I want you to pay attention to something, child." Felix flicked ash from his smoke.

She turned, searching for what he was pointing at, "What?"

She saw it immediately, and he didn't say anything because she saw exactly what he was talking about.

The woman unslung her rifle. Taking a knee to greet the sprinting child with a warm embrace.

"Mommy!" The young girl wrapped her tiny arms around her mother, the woman stood with her daughter.

"Hey sweetie, how was school today?" she asked as she walked over to her husband who took her bag from the other shoulder. Her son hugged her leg. She placed her hand on his head. Her man kissed her deeply. The kids said "Eww" simultaneously.

"School was good. Mrs. Kendrick taught us about bees today."

"Did she now?"

"Yes, about the good things that bees do to the planet. I just thought honey was yummy, I didn't know that it can help you get better, and even help you heal booboos."

"That's good, hunny."

"Tomorrow, we are going to learn about farming…"

Felix called Rachel's attention. "Do you see that?" he said pointing with his hand, a cigarette clutched between his middle and forefingers.

"Yes, what is your point?" She turned back.

"What color was their skin?" Felix asked.

"He was black and she—"

"Who gives a fuck? Understand, that's how we grow and become something greater. You asked me why I don't hate the dogs, that is why right there. Because just five years ago, I watched a woman come back from getting fucked by three men, for a can of fucking beans. To feed her family, husband, and three children. That, couldn't open the can without beating it against a rock. We did that to ourselves, not the dogs. They stopped the illusion and gave us ourselves, good, bad, or indifferent."

"That's, terrible. I don't understand what that has to do with this," she shook her head, eyes wide with confusion.

"That is what the dogs gave us. Equality, freedom, happiness, true purpose, they gave us paradise. Skin color, race, religion, sex, doesn't matter in the wake of existence, the universe, *she* is fair, and so is *Mother*."

She shook her head, but continued to watch. The man wrapped his arm around his woman and they walked home together as the daughter continued about her day.

"If they weren't here, they would be hunted like varmint, or hunted for slavery, the children would starve, the woman would more than likely be raped, her husband killed," Rachel attempted to argue, making a point that was weightless to the table.

Felix cut in, "Like I said, humans caused that. The dogs will either eat them, turn them, or they will survive. That is it, there is no other way about it. They are a balance in this world that has not been known for a very long time. Now, the world is benefitting the most from it. The forest is taking over the cities. The animals are coming back in full force, human population is now no more a threat to the planet than our ancestors were before our rapid growth and consumer mentality. That is what the dogs gave us... A real future."

Racheal watched as the family went out of sight. She turned, and Felix could see it on her face, that he was getting through to her, that she was starting to see what he was talking about.

"Hasn't it ever occurred to you that recently you started living your life fully, instead of just trying to prolong it outside your normal survival instincts? You for once in your miserable life, exist. The moment you suffered and lost yourself, lost your loved ones, the world you once knew. Taxes, debt, TV, cell phones, poor inaccurate opinionated education no longer exists. The dogs only took away what you think you needed. They were merely wants; learned from a lifetime of growing weakness due to convenience and technology, in turn, they gave you what was needed."

"Our loved ones, we didn't need them, did we, because they were weak, right?" she snapped back.

"Mother Earth is fair, you either live or die, but you are able to affect that by surviving. The infection is merely a flood, that is washing away an overpopulated species on the earth, much like nature itself tends to balance itself back out once in a great while. Like deer, or hogs, or fish, predators exist to maintain that balance, so the ones that eat leaves, don't eat too many. Understand?"

"Not really." She was now just attempting to save face at this point.

"Before your world ended, were you happy?"

"Of course, I was, what kinda question is that?"

"Did you even know your parents? Or were they as drowned in their phones as you were, how much of the world did you see for yourself, instead of looking through those poisonous devices?"

"I..."

"You weren't happy, you were accepting. The day your world ended was the first time in your life you finally started living."

She had a look of confusion painted on her face, but nonetheless she heard his words clearly. "It wasn't just my world; it was your world too."

"No," Felix laughed hysterically, "my world was one that only ever existed on the battlefield, behind a gun, in front of one, teaching young women and men how to survive the rigors of combat by means of fire and maneuver. My world was the fall of society, it was the end of civilization…"

"You're insane."

"…it was having to regress back into our basic human instincts… It wasn't my world that ended… It was yours… It was of people like you, those who didn't question, that just marched on like good little brainwashed worker bees. Do you even remember what was going on before all this? The race riots, the closed off black only communities, the rise of the all-black militias, the start of the Eastern and Western lines? Do you not recall how bad things were getting? I had younglings, soldiers barely nineteen years old attacking each other because of all this bullshit. We did this, not just white people or black people, all of us. We all played along because someone profited from it. Because somehow, slavery that was abolished back in Lincoln's time needed to be paid for by people who never owned slaves. What was it all worth? Not a goddamn thing. Every monument destroyed showed the world how weak we really were because we couldn't stand there and look at our failure. I wanted to see it, I wanted to know how wrong our world was. Not just white people for buying slaves from brown people who bought them from black people or white or tan or who gives a flying fuck? It's amazing to think that back then, they all believed that their ancestors weren't sold to the Spanish and British by their own African brothers and sisters. I wanted to know how evil we truly were, because deep down that is what we are. We are all evil terrible fucking things. You right now, your little military, is just like all of them. We did it then, and you are still doing it now. Segregate and separate yourselves. That is the game, even in your little fort, I am lesser than you because of your laws and your faith and your wanting of equality that is all just illusions and bullshit."

Rachel felt the weight of his words. She sat back, no longer looking at him, she was now focusing on the bar. She saw the happiness on people's dirty faces, guards coming off of shifts, families greeting each other and walking their loved ones home. Everyone had a weapon, but no one hated one another. For a moment the world turned into an array of color clearer than a blue sky on a summer day.

Felix continued, "It was my world that began, and I'm not sorry you grew up into a fearful, intelligent, fit, young woman, who only needs a weapon, and a direction, to survive, and even then, you probably don't even need those things to carry on, because you are here, now."

She stood up, "I can't accept that, and I will never see it that way." She walked away, knowing full well that she did lose, and he was right.

"Then you will be nothing more than 'a once upon a time,'" he spouted, stopping her in her tracks, "because once those children grow up, they will only have ever known my world. They won't look back to the old ways for guidance, they will look back to what their parents and what we did here, now, to continue forward. Your world is gone, and for the sake of our species, and the future of Mother, you better hope we never become like our old selves."

"Without a purpose, we don't have a reason to exist," she replied, only turning her head, her back facing Felix.

"Our purpose is to ensure that those children don't find their way back to your world. Only way we do that is by showing them how evil we all were once. Teach them the truth of everything, stop retarding it and manipulating it. Teach the younglings that the apple is in fact the orange."

She turned. Face twisted with emotions, snarling almost, hate, directed at Felix and his terrifying words.

"What a sad life you must have lived to believe that."

"I just started living for what my life was truly worth."

His grin, his cheers to her, so arrogantly sarcastic. She quickly turned to escape, into the bar, to drown in the bottle, to search for something within herself to forget meeting that man.

*****

Gavin laughed. "Weak before the fall of civilization, barely able to stand on their own two legs after. I like that…"

"What?" he asked, packing his pack of smokes.

"*It wasn't my world that ended!* Gives me chills."

Felix laughed. "You know, I often thought about that concept…"

Gavin poured Felix a glass of whiskey, "What concept?"

"The sun doesn't set on the Earth, the Earth turns away from the light, to give her a chance to rest."

"Interesting…" Gavin replied.

Felix was staring at the moon, leaning back in his chair, smoke bellowing from his mouth.

"I'm going to need another glass for this." Gavin smiled.

Felix snatched the bottle, and poured a glass for Gavin. Britney sat down next to Felix, then Samantha on his other side.

"We heard that some asshole was out here making girls cry, and when we saw you, we knew immediately," Samantha said shouldering Felix.

"What are you boys up to?" Britney asked, sipping from her glass.

Gavin leaned back, "We are about to dive into Felix's mind in his wonders of the universe."

The girls both took long drinks, "It looks like we are going to need a few more drinks for this, aren't we?" Britney replied.

Felix laughed, then continued, "The universe is a beautiful woman. The beginning of everything, all things, and their end, is the black dog. The sun is the Christian or Catholic or Muslim God, pick one, pick all. Certain faiths are the ideals that we all must love each other through respect. Lucifer, the devil, is just another entity that the light needed in order to guide the curious woman and the spineless man into a true paradise, one not like Heaven. Such as this world, which in my opinion is nothing short of paradise."

Gavin nodded, "Go on, you've been talking about this theory of yours for years."

"I haven't heard you talk about this in a long time," Britney replied.

Felix continued, completely disregarding their comments, "What if, our beautiful Mother, Gaia, is telling us she is sick, the volcano was the fever, and the dog was the antibodies administered a moment too late. We are the cancer cells; we made too many, because we outgrew her immune system?"

Gavin sat there; Chris was wide-eyed.

"But the volcano exploded because of a bomb," Samantha replied.

"We don't know that, we do know the largest cities were attacked by nuclear devices, besides…can a volcano be set off by a bomb? Anyway, when I traveled through that area, there was no fallout, could have been because of the ash, and snow, but the particles would have stuck around much longer than the projected months that it would take for the winds to carry the fallout away. I'm no expert, but the material that the particles stick to really dictates how long the radiation sticks around. Such as Chernobyl, if that metal was chipped away at, turned into dust, and allowed to be taken with the wind, the area could be inhabited. But due to the material that is irradiated, we can't move it, or reduce it in any way that would make sense."

"Nope, too much for me, you crazy," Chris said as he stood up. Some gorgeous woman caught his eye and he was now on the prowl.

Felix continued, "It's funny how this government comes out of nowhere after the spread of the feral. The dogs were manipulated by a chemical or biological weapon, spread by swarm technology. I'm pretty fucking sure.

These people here all work for the very ones that caused all this. One day, I'm going to thank them."

Gavin looked over at Felix who was holding up his glass. The candle's flame danced around, throwing the shades of something beautiful through the glass.

"Her hair is like looking through a glass of whiskey with candle light dancing behind it."

"That was fucking beautiful," Gavin replied.

Samantha and Britney both looked at each other across Felix.

Felix starred at the glass, in a trance, mesmerized by the hint of her, his memory of her.

"You still with me, brother?" Gavin asked, searching through thin eyes for Felix to come back to reality.

Felix laughed, "You know what I like about you?"

Gavin slammed his glass down. "No, what?"

"Not a goddamn thing, you piece of shit."

The two burst into laughter.

"You haven't changed a bit," Samantha said. Britney agreed.

Felix looked at her, making her slightly uneasy for a moment, "Why would I change when I'm given a world where I can be who I was always meant to be?"

Britney giggled, "Kinda like John Milton's *Paradise Lost*."

Felix nodded, *"The mind is its own place, and in itself, can make a heaven of hell, a hell of heaven, what matter where, if I be still the same…"* Felix nodded, "I so do love that work, one of many of my favorite lines from that epic tale. It's funny that a blind man, an old soldier no less, can see further than any of us."

Everyone sitting at the table could tell, Felix was getting drunk.

"What are you going to say when you have to stand in front of the black dog, and answer for every fucking thing you've done?" Gavin asked.

Felix pondered for a moment. "You know, I'd probably just answer with a question."

"Well, what question, motherfucker?" Gavin comically demanded.

Felix laughed, "Why am I answering for all the wrong that I've done when *It* designed me to be the wrong that I am?"

Gavin nearly spat whiskey everywhere attempting to hold back his laugh.

"What about you?" Felix asked.

"It really depends on which God we are talking about, because the old God that created the earth was 'Eye for an Eye,' then within the last hundred years, he all of a sudden became, 'Turn your motherfucking cheek.'"

"Don't care, what would you say?" Felix asked.

Gavin nodded, his smile faded to a serious look, "I'm not here to ask forgiveness any more than you are willing to give it."

Felix nodded with approval, holding his glass up, toasting, "By bullet and blade we live and die; by tooth and nail we will abide."

*****

Rachel came storming out of the bar. "By law!" she yelled. "This man is a poison and needs to die!"

Everyone at the table turned except for Felix. He sat there staring at his glass. Suddenly he heard the barrel clack against the back of his head.

"You need to die. I cannot in good faith let you exist here. You mean to destroy this place. And I cannot allow that to happen."

Felix took a drink. Setting the glass down slowly. His group was slowly backing away, hands on their guns, ready to gun her down if she decided to pull the trigger.

"You know, kid—"

"Shut the fuck up. You don't get to talk anymore. You will die by my hand right here. Right now."

"Not a bad way to go, getting killed by a beautiful woman."

She shook her head. "You're fucking insane."

No one said anything, they just watched as she stressed the tension of the trigger. Soon even her thoughts were quieted by gunshots, fast rates of fire, front gate machine guns. Everyone outside stood looking in that direction. Felix and Gavin did as well. Rachel stepped away. Felix shot her a look with a grin that frightened her.

"Should have pulled the trigger, youngling," Felix said coldly.

She headed back into the bar to find her team. People started stepping out of the bar. Facing the parade field, the guns seemed to continue on, until their belts ran through empty.

"Infected Breach, barricade in place. I say again..." the loud speaker continued the message for a moment longer.

Britney hopped to her feet. "My boys," she said, she was off within a second.

Samantha stood, yelling for everyone to get inside the bar.

People started moving, frantically finding somewhere to hide or seek refuge in a hard structure. Soldiers on guard and patrol all readied themselves. Radio chatter could be heard from several of the ones running by.

"An alpha?" Felix asked.

297

Gavin looked at him with a smile on his face. "You wanna go help the main gate to the fort?"

Felix finished his glass of whiskey. "Yeah."

They both checked their weapons; Gavin checked his M4, and Felix checked his AK.

Rachel and her team sprinted across the parade field, headed for the Headquarters building. The gunfire stopped, and everyone, inside and out, heard a menacing bark, or howl, a laugh. It echoed toward them, almost coming from every direction. The group stopped. Gavin and Felix stood there, crimson red burning from the drag of their cigarettes.

They could hear something, cutting against the wind from her leap over the walls. She landed in front of Rachel's small group. The girls screamed, Gavin, in a brash burst of rage, sprinted diagonally from Felix as he went right. The two began firing, three rounds from Gavin, three from Felix, they talked their guns almost beautifully. The queen paid them no attention, their rounds barely penetrated her fur, if at all they were stopped by her skin. She lurched forward, biting one of Rachel's girls. with one whip of the massive beast's head she was tossed screaming into the darkness. Her heavy wet thud touched the walls and then coming to a crunching halt on the wet grass.

"Hey, motherfucker, right here!" Gavin roared, changing his mag. He pulled from his belt pouch a grenade, telling the two remaining girls standing there to move their fucking asses. He tossed it. They did as he asked. The queen jumped back; the grenade went off. The queen rushed after Rachel this time. Felix rushed. Rachel turned as the heavy thudding of the queen drew near. The beast's mouth was about to bite her in half.

Suddenly, she was sent tumbling to the ground by the force of something. A loud nip, sounding of bone clacking together. Rachel got to all fours, realizing Felix had pushed her out of the way. She had slid at least thirty meters across the grass.

Felix swung his rifle, smacking the beast in her face. His rifle broke at the butt-stock, the spring and piston went flying into the darkness of the night. His rifle flipped and landed in the grass. He inspected the broken wooden stock. "Motherfucker, I just got this," he said, annoyed, lazily tossing it to the side.

The queen slowly turned, growling, lowering her head. Baring her teeth, her short tail straight back, ears pinned the same. She cautiously started walking toward Felix. Gavin was empty, he immediately switched to his Long Slide Smith and Wesson M&P 40. Dumping a mag, reloading, sprinting, and repeating. The bullets didn't seem to have any affect as they smacked against her thick hair. She only cared about the predator in front of her, if even she saw him as that.

"Run! You stupid motherfucker!" Gavin shouted.

Felix held up his hand toward Gavin. Gesturing him with great intent to *shut the fuck up.* Gavin knew. Felix never took his eyes from her gorgeous yellow rings. She was frightening as she was gorgeous. She, the queen, had maintained almost all of her former self. The Brown hyena, the rarest of hyena species. However, she had spots and stripes that were a black against her matted and blood-stained brown coat. She was just massive; her snout was just a little longer. And her smile, it was inviting, and full of teeth that could rival any prehistoric predator.

"What do you want, girl?" he asked calmly, soothingly.

She continued to growl, low, the very sound was felt through the ground. It resonated in his very chest. Her breath was hot. She barked, and it almost knocked the wind out of Felix. All around the two, Felix and the queen, soldiers were setting up crew-served weapons. .50 caliber machine guns, 240s and 249s. Vehicles were now parking in position. She paid no attention to the vehicles, the commands being screamed from leader to subordinates, nor the cries of realization from onlookers standing over a severed woman.

*****

Inside Monica's office, she opened the door, the colonel walked down the hallway. She threw another door open, scaring the life out of a few of her young office clerks. Some sat behind their computers and monitors and a small command center, the rest were crowded around the window. She barked orders to all the wide-eyed, dumbfounded group. "Turn up the fucking whistle. Order the soldiers to fire as soon as the power is at max, ensure the alpha can't escape."

"Ma'am, that is the queen," one of the frantic war room clerks boasted.

"Kill her," Monica said without hesitation.

The command center group of young females and soft-handed men began working frantically. Typing in codes on a touch screen monitor. Another on the radio to the Lighthouse, yelling at them to crank the power on their Dog Whistle. Another, calmly giving orders to the soldiers on the ground to be prepared to engage.

The queen's ears perked up, Felix turned his head toward the lighthouse, both of them could hear it. Her ears shot up, for a moment as the ringing in their ears became a low hum. She knew she would not be able to bear it any longer, and now looking down on Felix. Felix turned back, and now knew exactly what she came for. The dog whistle. These creatures were so intelligent that if they didn't stop them, they really would be history. But Felix could

299

admire for a moment longer. This beast, by fate, or engineering, or God's plan, as all of the worst disasters of epic proportions are, had become an amazing thing. But, if man made it, then it should not exist, and if God made it, then they had to kill it, because that is the cycle of life, according to history, according to the Bible. But if God made this beautiful thing, wanted it to exist for that one reason, then it would succeed, and there was nothing they could do.

Felix thought to himself, *What does a man do, when standing in the face of his maker's request for humanity to no longer exist?*

She shook her head as the frequency began to grow, ringing in her ears.

"I guess God isn't turning his fucking cheek anymore," Felix spoke, in a laugh.

The power reached maximum output, the queen's head rocked down, she attempted to cover her ears with her front legs, in vain. It was just too strong for her now. Screams from the city began to ring out, and from the hospital. Where, one of the infected was being held. The queen, with all her might, nipped at Felix. He narrowly dodged, drawing his 1911 from his right hip and shot wildly. Her head wrenched back and attempted to bite at him again.

She lunged; Felix wasn't going to dodge this one. He dropped his pistol and caught her wild bite. She began to growl as she bared down. His feet were dug in as he held her mouth open. She was staring at him. His face twisted in stress as he gritted his teeth. He was using every ounce of his strength to hold her large jaws open. She swung her head, throwing Felix into a tumbling frenzy across the grass.

She turned. Everyone snapped out of their shock and awe, and began to fire. She was already over the wall and gone into the darkness of the city. Felix stood, listening to the rumble of hundreds of thousands of footsteps moving further from the fortress. They could no longer stand the power of the dog whistle and had to move. Their howls could be heard echoing through the city. It was eerie to everyone in the Fort. Hearing the sound of hundreds of thousands of feral outside their sanctuary. If anything, the terror of their sheer numbers would be enough for people to start giving up.

Rachel walked up to Felix.

"How-did you?"

Felix picked up his pistol, changing mags and holstering it.

"How, how, there's no way..." she continued, wide-eyed, watching him lighting a cigarette, trying not to pay her any attention. He stuffed his crumpled pack into his jacket pocket. The bent cigarette threw a small orange glow onto his unsurprised and without fear expression.

"What the fuck?" he asked to himself as he wiped mud off of his pants and sleeves, still not giving her any notice.

Finally, she grabbed the collar of his jacket. He turned and walked away, she had to let go or she would have been pulled with him. He didn't even budge from his direction. As if her weight meant nothing to his movement.

"What the fuck are you?" she finally got out of her mouth.

He smiled as he turned his head, lazily pointing toward the city.

"Just like them; a product of your world coming to its end," he said, and she looked toward the sound of the howls.

Everyone watched as he walked off, headed to the hotel. Smoke trailing him in puffs with each exhale. Even Gavin was surprised. No one had ever seen anyone do what he just did. He held his own, physically, against an alpha, the alpha. The queen.

*****

The story spread like wildfire. Becoming a small legend quite quickly. This report never got sent to the doctor. But his drones were watching the whole time. The Fort's occupants though, began to speculate, and rumors already seeding in their minds. For Felix, he didn't care, and for his friends, they would always remain loyal, because that's just what they did. But now, if it ever was a secret, it certainly wasn't anymore, before the night chased the light around the world into morning.

"Anderson! Did you see that? How he swung his rifle like a bludgeoning weapon, take note of that, see if you can't base the weapon and equipment designs off of this odd behavior."

"Sir? Why is it odd, he clearly isn't trying to shoot the queen, and it happened to be the thing that was in his hand."

"Anderson, just do it, design a few rifles and some pistols that can utilize big bore calibers. I want the long guns built on monolithic frames designed to beat a hardened object with. Now go."

"He tried talking to it, just in case you missed that, he is starting to slip into the psychotic stage of his lifespan..." Anderson replied in a condescending tone.

The doctor paid no attention to Anderson's statement. He continued with another statement about weaponry as many ideas were rushing through his head all at once.

"Anderson?" the doctor called out. "Take note of his arsenal, I want you to build me some prototypes, based off of the weapons he tends to carry. He has

301

an assortment, time to make some future upgrades for when we implement the program for the next stage of the operation. I want these soldiers to be able to fight one-on-one with a mechanized threat, chimeras, and anything we have yet to perceive from our enemy's current developments. If they can beat that old coots' crazy idea of pilotable robots, then we will have won. Besides," the doctor was now talking to himself, "these soldiers need to be able to kill off what the infection fails to."

Anderson did as the doctor demanded; he would do anything to walk away from this mad scientist of a doctor. Besides, he had more important things to attend to, like the mothers.

"Sergeant Martin?" Gavin called.

Felix didn't answer, he had his hand on his gun staring at some Iraqi soldiers tossing puppies over the wall.

"What are you looking at?" Gavin said, placing his hand on Felix's shoulder.

Gavin then saw it too. The two men were dumbfounded. Their faces split with grit teeth.

"I'm going to fucking kill 'em," Felix and Gavin almost said simultaneously.

They began walking with furious haste toward the soldiers laughing and giggling while they touched each other.

Mitch was doing his checks around the small outpost when he caught the scene about to unfold. "Oh shit, not again," he said as he started to pick up pace to head them off.

"Hey you dumb motherfuckers!" Gavin yelled as he came up pushing one of the small men off his feet.

Felix picked up the remaining puppies and moved them away.

"But, mister, dirty, dogs are dirty."

"Motherfucker, no, no goddamn way. You filthy fucks, makes you feel real big picking on innocent animals, doesn't it?" Gavin leaned down about to strike the soldier.

"Whoa whoa, calm the fuck down!" Mitch yelled, catching hold of Gavin's arm. Struggling to pull him off the frightened man.

The scene attracted quite the attention, to include the outpost commander.

"Go cool off, you trying to get us killed?" Mitch yelled at Gavin. Gavin stormed off, throwing something.

"Fuck them!" he yelled as he disappeared into a blown-out train station.

"Felix, take them out of here, leave 'em at the front gate, and go wash yourself off."

Felix did as he was ordered. He walked out, in full armor, helmet, rifle. Arms full of puppies. He walked them to the front gate and let them go. They scurried off.

Later that night, Felix and Gavin stood at attention in front of a shitty desk in a plywood box.

"Really?" the officer started, rhetorically. "Over some goddamn dogs?"

"Sir, these motherfuckers were tossing them into Constantine wire. Living animals, it wasn't like they were shooting them."

"I don't fucking care. It's already bad enough, we run the risk of them killing us here, giving away our patrol times to the enemy, or poisoning the fucking water supply. They already shit in our showers. What else do you guys want, huh, not happy until we have an insider threat. A suicide vest? You two motherfuckers are making it real goddamn hard to keep the peace around here over this shit."

"Sir," Felix spoke. "We had to; we couldn't just stand by while these cocksuckers hurt those animals."

"I don't give a fuck, you two motherfuckers keep pulling this shit, I'm going to separate you two. I can't have you causing problems out here over the fucking wild life."

Gavin spoke this time, "Then fucking fire me, if we have to give up our morals just to get along with these fucks, then what the fuck is the point?"

Mitch shook his head. "Oh, my god, just shut up and get out, Gavin."

Gavin left, slamming the door. Felix stood in there.

"You need to talk to him. I got it; we all know you two fuckers care more about animals than people. But this shit needs to stop."

Felix shook his head. "I have to pay it forward."

"What does that mean?" the officer asked.

"It's because of the wild life out here that we even knew where the enemy was. If I wasn't watching what those dogs were doing, none of you would have been able to move from that spot. So just out of respect, we owe it to them. That could have been a bad day."

"Get the fuck out of my office, fucking goddamn platoon full of criminals and zoologists. What the fuck is going on here. You know what, Dr. Doolittle, you're on tower guard the rest of the night, you smart ass."

"Yes, sir."

Mitch tried to hold his laugh back as Felix left the office.

Felix climbed into the tower, relieving one of his soldiers. Gavin found him soon enough with food. He climbed up into the sandbag stacked rickety tower, handing the overcooked chicken to him. They sat there watching under their night vision for any movement.

"Hey, where's the fuck on guard with you?" Gavin asked.

Felix turned and pointed down.

Gavin looked, the Iraqi soldier was curled up in a ball sleeping in the corner.

"Yeah, no wonder why your country is fucked. Goddamn garden of Eden my ass."

Felix laughed.

"You know after that last bag and tag we did?"

"Yeah?"

Felix lit a smoke. "I'm failing to see the point of any of this."

"Me too, man, but; we will never change, and probably never get out either. Our country will kill us, just like the other countries will kill their own people."

Felix nodded. "As long as there is war, there will always be a place for people like us."

Chapter 22
Play Dead

The Osprey landed outside on the small airfield to the North of the Fort. Men, armed with weapons that were new to any onlooker, their gear robotic, looked like crude Knights with rifles. They spilled out in rows and made their way, running easily even with all that gear. They were inside the base within minutes. Another Osprey landed in the center of the parade field.

Felix was standing at the front of the Headquarters building watching everything that was transpiring. He lifted his shades, the blades winding down. A man in a white coat stepped out taking measure of the night before, his smile was sickening. He walked, with a detail of four men in heavy knight-like robotic suits. He walked right past him. Felix felt it, everyone that had come out to see what the commotion was, felt it. The man in the coat was smiling at Felix.

Felix saw Mitch coming out of the Clinic. Felix moved away from the building. As he did, he could feel the eyes of the armored soldiers watching him.

"Looks like the USOAR leadership is losing patience with the colonel."

"Does it have something to do with her attempts to move that feral locked up in there out of here?"

Mitch nodded, adjusting his glasses. "These people are morons, I would watch your back around them, they will shoot you in the back. Especially after the stunt you pulled last night."

Mitch simply walked back inside.

"Say 'Hi' to the wife for me, will ya?" Felix said as Mitch got to the top of the steps.

"Yeah, man."

Before Mitch could go inside, he paused to watch the Osprey lift off and land over by the other aircraft on the small air field.

"What are these fucks up to?" Felix asked aloud.

"Felix?" a familiar voice called to him from the window on the second floor.

He turned, looking up, shielding his eyes from the sun, even with his shades on, they did little at that angle.

"Cynthia?"

"What are you doing down there?"

Felix looked back, pointing, "Just watching all the commotion. You recovering well?"

"Come on up, Room 27," she called down.

He did as she asked.

*****

In the colonel's office.

"Doctor Steinberg…"

"Monica," he replied, sitting in her office chair. She walked in and took a seat in one of the other chairs set in front of her desk.

"You have been a naughty little *schlampe*…" he said, lazily pointing his finger at her.

His smile made her adjust herself in her chair. Uncomfortable his smile was to her; as his accent and very demeanor was.

"Tell me, how is Felix, how is the specimen? And how is our little device running that has kept you decently safe for the past year?"

"What are you doing here?" she asked.

"Come, now, *Fraulein*, you knew I was coming. I have to check up on all my experiments, personally at times."

"He is developing well."

"I don't know this, you don't write anymore, you haven't even so much as called," he replied, smiling like a fiend.

Before she could say anything, he stood. "It's simple. I'm going to take him and the specimen if she is ready. Any objections?"

"I thought you needed him to fail," she replied. He walked around behind her, putting his hands on her shoulders.

She did her best to not cringe at his touch, her body did nothing to hide her discomfort.

"I…have changed my mind. He needs to come in for, let's say a checkup, but don't you worry your little head. He will be back before you know it."

"Why are you telling me? You can simply just go take him."

He spun around looking at her. "I would prefer to not cause any more bloodshed than necessary. If you convince him, or have one of his companions

306

say, recommend it…then we could do this peacefully. I fear that if I were to approach him, his reactions would be most hazardous to my health."

"Are you afraid of what you did to him?"

He leaned against the desk in front of her, crossing his arms, still grinning. Monica could not sink into the chair any deeper. No matter how hard she tried, she felt as if his very look had a disgusting weight to it.

"No, no, *Fraulein*. I just wish to not have to kill one of my assets nor lose any of my men, and if he doesn't comply, then he will die. Regardless, if a conflict should occur, it will more than likely lead to an unnecessary amount of bloodshed. He's smart, unfortunately, I think he figured out last night everything as he drank himself to sleep."

"You and your men won't leave here alive if that happens," she replied.

"Why is that? Hmmmm."

"If you kill him, you will be dealing with every single person on this Fort, he is quite popular, saving several of our people, and females at that, and you know what this Fort was designed for. You are the one who implemented the concept behind males as the lesser sex. A male who goes out of his way to protect women becomes very desirable around here."

"I did, didn't I? I had forgotten. Don't worry, the male superior experiment failed too, the women actually killed them all in their sleep, it didn't take long, the ones who developed Stockholm syndrome were killed too, but the ones who survived are now enslaving men. It was an amazing outcome, we all become what we hate. You should have seen the reports on the superior race concept, those yielded interesting results, to which my hypothesis was correct and fueled the Board's motivation to allow my next project to mature."

"It didn't work here, most of the women have accepted the men as equals. It's hard to instill oppression when we educated everyone here the same. There is only a small minority of my officers who think men are lesser. One of which, due to last night's events, has now even requested that your experiment be her partner. We are functioning the way we should. Your experiment failed here, the men that basically interact with the majority of my girls long before this, already had the right idea."

He waved his hand quickly. Eyes closed; he was trying to swat away the compelling conversation.

"We have gotten off subject. Do what I ask, you have three days to comply, until then we will need a place to set up. Also, I will need to see the specimen. Immediately; she is about due."

*****

307

Felix was sitting in a chair; Cynthia was sitting upright in her bed. Crutches laid in the corner. The room was white, a few paintings on the wall of flowers and bowls of fruit. Graphs of the human anatomy, a small tray with a plate on it, from breakfast more than likely. A typical recovery room in an average hospital, even before the pandemic.

The two talked for a little while, seeing how each other were doing, small talk. She adjusted herself, in pain more than likely. Felix offered his flask. She politely declined.

Suddenly, her expression changes, and she broke the growing silence, "You know, I hate you?" she said as she looked out the window. Tears began to roll down her face.

"Yeah…I know."

"You killed my entire team. I've had to sit here for months, and all I could think about was that day. I wish we never came across you."

"If I wasn't there, you would be dead."

"That would've been better," her voice was cracked from holding back that lump in her throat.

"You are a completely different person when you drink, you didn't drink that day, did you?" she asked, sniffling and wiping her face.

"No, I was going to kill all of you, until the alcohol set in sometime after the shooting started."

She nodded, wiping tears from her eyes, "You're not normal, are you?"

He shook his head, "No, there is something wrong with me, and I think it's all connected to the infection, to those lab coat motherfuckers down there…"

She looked at him for a brief moment. Then back out the window. He stood up, walked over to her, placing his strong hand on her shoulder. She said nothing. He walked to the door.

She stopped him. "Did you ever find what you were looking for?"

"No."

"What a sad life you live," she forced it out through her sobs. Wiping her nose again.

"The one that was dealt. Take care of yourself, Cynthia. I'm sorry for everything."

"You wouldn't be if you were sober," she replied.

He walked out, putting a smoke in his mouth. *She's right, I wouldn't care in the slightest if all of them fucking died,* he thought to himself.

Someone in the hall, a nurse maybe, uttered words that he didn't hear. Something along the lines of 'Hey, there's no smoking in here.' But it didn't matter, he lit it anyway as he just got to the door. He took in a long drag. His face was in a scowl as he blew a thick cloud of smoke out. He walked down toward the Headquarters building. She watched from the window. He had the walk of a man who wasn't good, she could see it.

*****

People had gone about their day, but the curiosity was still in the air. Most of them had never seen anyone come from the north. Especially, someone as heavily guarded as this individual in the doctors' coat.

Felix knocked on the colonel's door. Alex opened it, Gavin and Chris were sitting next to each other. The colonel in her chair. They were all staring at him.

"Come in," she muttered finally, with a heavy sigh.

The others didn't speak, or even say 'hello.' Whatever the topic was that he walked in on, was heavy on all their hearts. It was about him and he could feel it.

He stood there next to Alex, both leaning on the table that sat in front of the window. The blinds were drawn, the curtains closed. Monica let out a long sigh again.

"Alright, what's up?" Felix asked.

"The doctor wants you to go with him."

"For what?" Felix demanded.

"For the reason you are so strong and able to take on an alpha by yourself. He believes you are the key in the next stage in evolution."

"That sounds like a trap," Chris blurted out.

Alex spoke next. "Do you trust him, is he good peoples?"

She looked at him. Shaking her head.

"What is going on, Colonel?" Gavin asked.

"He is a head scientist in the USOAR, he is in charge of researching the infection, he designed the dog whistle that's in the light tower. After what happened with you and the alpha, the one you call their queen, he wants you to come with him for a few days, check out your DNA, and maybe use some of it. You have three days to decide. But let me warn you, this man, he will do whatever he has to, in order to get what he wants."

Felix crossed his arms, staring at a painting of an old navy ship braving the swells of an angry ocean.

"No," Chris said.

Alex and Gavin agreed with a simultaneous "Fuck no." It wasn't even an option to them.

"What will he do, if I don't go?" Felix interjected.

309

"He will shut down the whistle, kill everyone here, set a bomb off, kill everyone you love. His power is so vast within the USOAR, I don't even know the full extent of his position. I've heard, he is one of the founding fathers."

Everyone was looking at Monica. "I'm sorry, but if you don't go, they will kill whoever they have to, maybe even kill you, and just take you."

"What are our options?" Alex asked.

"Not many," Monica replied.

"Better to die on your feet than live on your knees," Gavin said. And that statement had them all in silence for a while.

Felix nodded and began to walk out.

"Where the fuck are you going?" Gavin asked.

"I've got three days, I'll make my decision by then, I don't like handing myself over to the people that did whatever this is to me…" and just like that Felix left the office without another word.

*****

Gavin found Felix sitting on a bench under a tree looking out onto the parade field. Gavin sat next to him. Felix offered his flask. Gavin declined, producing his own from his jacket pocket. The two men clunk the tin flasks together and held them up, toasting to what those two always toasted to; memories, the dead, the soon-to-be hereafter.

Before they drank, Gavin began to speak their toast, "To those like us, to those that want to be us, and those that came before us. Fuck everyone else."

Felix laughed. "You know, that is my favorite toast, I remember when you first said it. Fuck that was what, eight, nine years ago?"

Gavin smiled, nodding as he swallowed his mouthful of whiskey.

"What are you going to do?" Gavin asked.

"We are truly free, the world finally has a chance now. Do you think I wanna stand in line again like a good little soldier, a good little robot, yes sir, no ma'am, fuck that, and fuck them," Felix replied.

His look became intense. Gavin watched as he continued.

"I'm going to kill them," Felix said with a grin on his face. "All of them. But I'm going to need your help, Alex, Chris, anyone else that wants to kill these fucks. Motherfuckers are probably responsible for this whole mess, too."

"Mitch?" Gavin asked.

Felix shook his head. "He has his woman here; all of us, we don't have anything accept each other, so let's keep him out of it."

Gavin agreed with a subtle nod.

Felix continued, "Three days."

310

"That's a long time to prepare," Gavin replied. His blue eyes shining, even under the shade of the tree, they had that sparkle in them.

Felix's eyes drew thin as his eyes raked left to right, taking measure. He nodded, laughing a sinister short moment. The one that he had been told was creepy, because behind it, evil intent always danced. Evil to those that were in its path.

*****

Second day, Felix sent instructions and a message through Chris to the people on the boats. He needed answers for several of his questions. His instructions would be the end state, the plan to save as many as they could after Felix finished what he was about to do. But plans in war, battle, a fist fight, never pan out. They lie as they fell, no more, no less.

*****

Three days later. The doctor had not been seen once. Rumors circled that he had been in the Clinic in the secured section operating on a feral. Rumors said that she was in fact pregnant, and from there, the stories were so wild that none of them could be held accountable for accuracy.

Felix stood tall on the green grass of the parade field. His pack on the grass next to him. Smoking a cigarette with a determined haste. The doctor stood before him, soldiers in their mechanical knight armor, that made them menacing, faceless robotic soldiers, surrounding Felix and the doctor as they spoke to each other.

"You don't plan on doing anything foolish now, do you?" the doctor asked, as his Ospreys propellers began spinning on.

Felix didn't answer. He was standing there gritting his teeth. Breathing as calmly as he could. It seemed like a task to do so. He was starting to shake, his muscles vibrated. And the hate that was flowing through him became an ocean of silence.

The doctor leaned an ear toward him, cupping it with his hand, waiting for a response. The doctor looked back at him, stepping closer, holding out his hands. Showing that physical gesture of not possessing a weapon. But knowledge and manipulation were this man's weapons.

"Felix, I know why you're so strong. I can help you become even more. I can offer you some interesting toys. If you will only come in so I can study what is happening to you."

311

Felix didn't answer. He just glared. It started to make the doctor nervous. As well as his guards, who started to posture in an offensive manner.

"Felix? You're shaking, are you alright, *Heir* Martin?"

A decent crowd was formed, Samantha watched from her bar, Britney watched from the hospital, as did Cynthia, and in Dana's office, Mitch stood watching.

"Felix came in the other day to have his blood tested. Britney came and got me immediately. Just for the fact that none of the needles broke his skin. We had to take blood from his tongue after he bit into it," Dana said.

"Wait, what?" Mitch asked.

Dana got up from her chair and walked over next to Mitch, watching the field with him.

"That man did something to him. His body is something I have never seen before, the fibers of his skin are weaved like metal, his entire body has become so dense that when we did X-rays, the machine could barely penetrate his muscle density, forget attempting to see through his bones. His blood is an odd mixture as well, it's almost not blood anymore, it's like a liquid conscious in itself, there was large amounts of silver and other metals in it. To include what I think are nanites, but they were produced from his body. His heart has developed a formation of outer muscles, allowing itself to increase the blood production and flow. His synapses fire in a way I've only heard are similar to that of sharks. I don't know how, but those scientists have done something horrific to him. It explains why he is the way he is now; his aggression is elevated unless he is intoxicated. Due to the odd chemicals release by his blood; it's like his body is producing PCP on its own. He has been drinking to keep his chemical balance leveled out. However; he stopped drinking last night."

The crack and crash of an explosion caught everyone's attention. Felix, however, felt free. The doctor and all his guards turned to watch as the plume of black smoke rolled into the sky. A dark tower, of what used to be the second aircraft.

The doctor turned, yelling, "Take him!"

Felix moved with murderous intent. His fist slammed into the closest guard, the helmet cracked and the soldier skipped across the wet grass, slamming into a parked vehicle.

Next one, Felix drew his 1911, firing while running out of the surrounding circle. The rounds sparked and bounced off the armor. The doctor quickly made his escape toward the aircraft, escorted by two of the armored knights. Turning back at the rear ramp, to watch Felix leap into the air, landing knee

312

first onto an unfortunate soldier. A heavy crunch and the knight lay there lifeless. Their helmet was crushed under his knee.

"Motherfucker," he spouted, calmly, hellishly.

The crack of gunfire.

He ran dodging a volley of fire that chased after him by one of the knights, who no longer cared if he was taken alive.

A bystander was hit with a stray bullet, she folded in half and slumped to the ground. She lay only a few feet from her cover; her man was hiding behind it, wide-eyed, in shock as she lay lifeless before him. The crowd immediately dispersed.

Mitch attempted to walk out of the office, stopped by Dana grabbing his arm.

"Don't, Felix told me to stop you in case you came out there. He knew you would."

"I can't leave him by himself," Mitch jerked his arm away.

Isaac, Britney, and a few men and women walked into the room.

"We can't let you go out there, Mitch," Isaac said.

Felix drew his .44 magnum from his shoulder holster. While in mid-stride, circling the knight, Felix took aim. Firing all six rounds, every one of them impacting the chest of the soldier. The rounds knocked them over onto their back. Not one round made it through but the sound of a vibrating gong rung out. He leaped, pulling his blade from the leather sheath mounted to the small of his back. Before the soldier could get up, Felix landed hard, both of his feet pinned the soldier's arms down, leaving imprints in the grass.

Felix thrusted his knife in the seam of the helmet and neck armor, it glided inward. Blood pumped out in pulsating pours. Choking, coughing, and eventually nothing sounded from the helmet. He pulled the blade, spinning around. He was onto his next target. The knight fired a wild burst, Felix stepped to the side, barely dodging the run of bullets as they smacked against a house behind him. Felix stepped once more, leaning his shoulder into the knight. The knight caught his full force, yelled out in pain as they were sent across the parade field, tumbling. After thirty meters, they slid to a stop, and could hear Felix's heavy, quick footsteps as he ran at them.

"Oh my God," the knight yelled out in utter fear.

Felix leapt into the air. The onlookers watched as he climbed further and further, had to have been twenty feet. He landed on the knight's chest, the armor cracked, and so did the knight's ribs. Felix stood, kicking the knight's head, another muffled crunch, the knight spun on the grass to a lifeless stop.

Felix walked toward the aircraft, breathing heavily, he pulled from his bag that lay in the grass his shotgun. Two soldiers rushed him. He swung his

313

shotgun like a sword. Easily as a pipe, he clacked it to the knight on the left. He butt-stroked the next in the side of the helmet. The stock cracked, the knight's head wrenched to the left. With all of his might, the knight grabbed a hold of Felix's arm. Felix widened his stance, drawing his left hand back, he punched as hard as he could, the blow landing in the side of the crude armor. The armor dented, the left side of it cracked open from the force of the blow. The knight lost grip, falling to his knees. Felix turned, searching for his next target, but instead, turned to a gun pointed at his head. The knight fired. His head violently rocked back, a dark reflective mist sprayed into the air. He slumped to the ground.

Everyone was stunned, onlookers were stricken with disbelief.

The remaining soldiers that were hiding from him, shook away their fear and hurried over and picked him up. He was brought into the back of the loading ramp of the dual propeller aircraft.

Mitch darted outside, gun fire from onlookers picked up, chasing after the Osprey as it climbed. Soon there was no chance that anyone was going to hit the bird as it turned and left.

"Goddamnit!" Mitch yelled.

Alex, Chris, and Gavin watched as the aircraft flew overhead to the north. They jumped in their vehicle and drove toward the fort. The osprey was still burning from the explosive they had set off. Compliments of Mitch's explosives he had built and stored over the years.

The vehicle slid to a stop.

Mitch approached their vehicle as the men got out.

"What happened?" Gavin asked.

"They took him," Mitch replied as the entire fort watched the aircraft disappear into the sky.

"No fucking way," Gavin replied.

"They shot him, and took him, he's fucking dead!" Mitch yelled in Gavin's face.

With heavy hearts the men stood there, quietly. Gavin turned, punching the glass out of the truck's window.

"It's time we took this place over, and got everyone the fuck out of here."

*****

Felix was cuffed, restrained, and placed into a black metallic box with viewing ports on three sides. The doctor sat there in his seat, staring at the box, at Felix. Blood pooled around his head. It looked like liquid onyx with a silver sheen.

314

The soldiers were breathing heavily, some in shock as they pulled their helmets off. Blank stares, sweaty matted locks of hair, men and women. Looks of despair and fear painted their faces as an aftermath of what they had witnessed. Doctor Steinberg crossed his arms and his legs, his right foot fidgeted impatiently. He let out a dissatisfied grunt, almost yelling. Surprising everyone in the carrier.

"HOW IS IT THAT YOU CAN KILL SO MUCH, AND SURVIVE EVEN THE DOGS, BUT YOU GET SHOT IN THE HEAD WITH A TEN MILLIMETER AND YOU DIE? WHAT KIND OF ABOMINATION ARE YOU?"

He sat for a moment longer. Pulling his phone out, he unlocked the touch screen, then scrolled through some contacts only identified by number codes until he got to Anderson.

The phone rang, Doctor Anderson picked up.

"Anderson speaking."

"Prepare the table, we need to salvage what we can, get a cryo-box ready as well, this Neanderthal got shot in the head."

"I take it your trip did not go as anticipated?"

The doctor started fidgeting more frantically. "Just get it done, we will be there in a few hours." He pressed the button, stared at the phone, then threw it.

"I hate these cell phones; how can you hang up angrily when you have to press a button!" He walked over stomping it wildly.

The soldiers all watched while he stomped away at what used to be his device on the floor of the aircraft.

*****

Outside of Fort Monroe.

The queen howled, and so did all the feral. With heavy hearts, and utter disbelief, Fort Monroe watched the aircraft disappear into the distance. Sasha and Kim and her kids all watched from Sasha's boat. John jumped on her boat. "Sasha, it's almost time, Kim…get the kids back to our boat, get them ready, we will be moving to the destroyer."

Sasha woke up, her head was pounding from the night prior. She drank way too much, and next to her, Felix was snoring. She wanted to get up, pondered what had happened last night. She didn't feel like she had sex, she still had her clothes on, but she was wearing his shirt. That she remembered. She had spilt wine on herself, it soaked her entire shirt. Felix had let her pick a shirt out from his closet, and she chose his favorite.

315

She was questioning everything at this point. But the pounding in her head took over any confusion of what happened last night. He stirred. She noticed the tattoo on his back. It was a giant upside cross, from the top of his spine to the bottom. A ring around the center of it. Written crudely, as if he got it in a prison. "We are but a teardrop in the Eye of the universe, and how She weeps so."

Her soft hands ran down his back. Her head pounded harder. She was hung over badly.

"Why did I drink so much?" she asked.

He woke up. Turning his head, his hair was spiked up in the front, different than his normal parted, combed over he liked to wear. She liked it. It was cute, she thought.

"Good morning," he said, running his hand across her tight stomach.

Her hand was still on her head. She replied but it was through pain. He got up, almost without word. He walked into the bathroom, grabbing a bottle of peppermint from the cabinet, a glass of water, and sat beside her in bed. He ran his fingers on her temple and forehead with the oil. Almost immediately her headache was gone. He seemed to have quite an array of tricks up his sleeve. She liked it very much.

She sipped on the water, for fear of vomiting.

He laid down on his side of the bed and started running his fingers over her body. She welcomed every bit of it. His touch, even though his hands were rough and strong, was very soft on her skin. She let out a satisfying "mmm" as he traced her stomach and legs and neck. He kissed her. She had almost forgotten about the hangover entirely.

The two laughed and joked the morning away. He made breakfast for her before she had to go home and get ready for work. As she sat in the living room sipping on water, he brought her a small glass with some off-greenish liquid in it.

"What are you trying to give me now?" she asked.

"It's pickle juice. My cure all for everything from dehydration to hangovers, and around this house, we are mainly drunks. And you, you being a sophisticated and intelligent woman, this will help you recover, seeing that your body isn't used to it."

She giggled. "Yeah, I haven't drunk like that since college. I'm sorry for anything I did last night."

"Why are you apologizing?" he asked from the kitchen.

"Because I probably said some things I shouldn't have or did something I shouldn't have."

"You did exactly what you wanted to last night, except for me, I couldn't let you, believe me, I wanted to. It took every ounce of who I am to hold myself back. But I want to do it right with you, so we will address that at a later time. For now, drink."

She took the entire glass. Her face twisted in disgust. "Oh my god, that is so nasty."

"You'll survive," he said, sitting down next to her with two plates of a rather well put together spread of breakfast food.

She dug in, as did he.

After breakfast.

He walked her out to her truck. "When do I get to see you again?" he asked.

"I'll let you know, I'm not used to this, you surprised me, I surprised myself, I don't act like that."

"You seen what you wanted, and took it. I just didn't let you go all the way. We can do that another time, I want something real with you, so let me do it right for once in my life. Deal?"

"Deal."

She kissed him. Backed out of the driveway and disappeared down the street. Felix lit a smoke. The garage door opened, and Alex was walking out to him with a smoke in his mouth and another beer for his friend.

"She's a keeper, man," Alex said walking from the garage out onto the driveway.

"Yes, she is."

"I heard you two giggling this morning. You two knocked boots, didn't you, you dirty schlampa."

"No, actually, I didn't, I put her to bed. And I went to bed, and now I'm wondering if I missed my chance, or just proved to her that I'm not a piece of shit."

"More like proved to yourself. She wouldn't have ever come, drank as much as she did, if she didn't feel like you could be trusted. Think about that for a minute, boo boo."

"Fair enough."

Felix stood in the driveway, sipping his beer, watching the sky roll by.

"What are you doing, Sasha?" she asked herself as she nearly missed her turn onto the highway.

"I can't believe I drank so much last night; I can't believe he didn't have sex with me." She thought about it for a second.

"He probably thinks I'm that kind of woman. Fuck, fuck, fuck." The sun hit her eyes like stones. She fumbled, finding her sun glasses.

"He didn't take advantage of me when I was throwing myself at him. There may be more to him then I thought."

Chapter 23
Bad Dog

"So, this was the entire plan then? This Fort really was a testing ground. Why the fuck did they pick Felix?" Gavin asked, standing over Monica.

Whatever she had in her hands was scattered across the room from Gavin, back handing it from her clutches. Chris, Mitch, Isaac, and Alex were all standing in front of her. Rachel, Cynthia, Mitch's wife Dana, Samantha, and Britney were all crowded into the room as well. Not to mention the onlookers who had scurried into the hallway to see what the commotion was all about.

"You fucking knew this whole time, why didn't you tell us? We could have stopped this whole fucking thing from happening, you stupid bitch," Gavin was so mad his face turned a shade of red. "You going to say something or just sit there, like you've fucking done all your goddamn life?"

She tried, the colonel tried her might, but in the face of this raging beast, she had nothing to say, or simply was fearing for her life if she did speak.

Cynthia spoke this time, calling everyone's attention to her. The whole room shifted their gaze, except for Gavin, "You knew from the beginning, that he wasn't normal, and you let him in here?"

Their heads all shifted back to Monica.

"He's dead now, nothing we can do," Monica spat out.

Gavin lifted her up by her neck, out of her chair, pinning her against the wall.

"You stupid cunt."

While she strangled, almost no one cared to come to her aid.

"I should put a bullet in your head right here, right fucking now," Gavin proclaimed.

Gavin dropped her. Pulling his pistol out, putting it against her head, "Why not send him some fucking company then?" She looked up at him, clutching her immediately bruising neck.

Gavin continued, "You can deal with his ass when you get to hell, I'm sure he will be waiting for you with a fucking smile on his face."

It took every ounce of effort for her to force the words out. She coughed, still clutching her throat. She mustered the strength to stand. She sat back in her chair, leaning onto the desk, coughing once more. Gavin's weapon followed her, his eyes peered down at her as he stood off to her right side, his weapon still pointed at her.

"Why did they want him so badly that they would kill him just to get it? Never occurred to us before, because a lot of things don't seem to quite fit together these days, but I find it odd that someone could take so much interest into a nobody," Alex stated. Chris tapped his arm with the back of his hand pointing at Monica and agreeing with his friend.

"You better start talking, or I'm going to send you to hell with a few more holes to fuck," Gavin spoke coldly. His very statement brought chills to the spines of everyone in the room.

"Felix was something else, but there are more like him. He was one of many experiments. I didn't choose him; he was chosen long before he ever got here. Part of a Forced Super Soldier project that had seen many failures. This fort was part of the Last Stand Operation against the infection. Once we found that they, the dogs, were communicating and started to become a functioning species instead of a rapidly advancing biological weapon, it was too late. Now they were brought to the edge of our gates for observation, further testing, and to test the latest of the Super Soldier projects. Felix. Once it was complete or he was killed, then, the Northern Research Facility would send a missile here to destroy the remnants of the infection. Our forces would then be sent in to finish the survivors. Thus, the dogs will be extinct, they technically already are."

"Just like a bunch of new-aged fucking Nazis. Any of you read history? It all makes sense now," Gavin said moving around the room, holstering his pistol. Monica opened her computer. He almost knocked Chris and Alex over as he ripped the laptop off the desk and threw it crashing through the window.

"Motherfuckers. What are you going to do now? Felix is fucking gone, and he was the only one that we know for a fact could stop those motherfuckers. We don't have enough bodies to throw at it. And we don't have enough ammo. They outnumber our weapons upward of two hundred to one, they outnumber our bullets, about two to one. There's no fucking way we can stop what's coming. It's time to move the fuck on."

Mitch placed a hand on Gavin's shoulder. "This place, the bridge, and several of the larger buildings are rigged to blow. I put them in when I first got here, during our first shipment of explosives. Couldn't trust them to protect us. Had to ensure that we had an out."

"Clever motherfucker," Gavin said, his face was still red with rage but his expression subsided to a form of relief.

"The floating city is bringing the destroyer here in two days. They will have their boats at our docks in two days, so that means we have two days to get everyone ready to move."

"We are offering you the chance to save your men and women, Monica, take it. Don't sink with this ship," Alex stated. He had no intention of comforting her, but she knew he wanted her to come with them.

She rubbed her neck.

Gavin turned, ripping a cigarette from his mouth pointing at her. "She should fucking go down with this ship; she fucking sank it."

Rachel and Cynthia both stood there, anxious to hear her answer.

She looked at them. "Spread the word, bring in the rest of the team leaders. Reinforce the barricades, prepare our ships. Everybody pulls a shift, everybody carries a weapon, I want ammo stacked and ready at every entrance, fallback position, and escape routes. You all know what to do. Pull everyone from the outposts to the floating city, send them with a message, we will move to South America, and reestablish our base of operations there."

Everyone nodded and exited the room. Gavin, with a twisted face of hate, broke from his locked gaze on the parade field. He was gone out of the room. Wide-eyed soldiers stared at the group as they left. Gavin yelled at all of them to get the fuck back to work, asked a few, what the fuck are you looking at, and shoved some small framed pretty man out of his way. The usual violent soldier he used to be was now back. For all their sakes, the best side of Gavin they could have, now that Felix was gone. Felix once called him 'The Violence of the Infantry.'

*****

The Osprey landed, and the doctor got out, irritated to no end. Only to be met by Anderson, waiting at the edge of the helipad. His hands stuffed in his pockets. Steinberg walked past him; the young doctor quickly caught up to him.

"She's pissed, you know that. You wasted an aircraft, and lost how many soldiers? She wants to speak with you right now. You don't have a choice."

Steinberg didn't even acknowledge Anderson. He was fuming with a mixture of disappointment and thousands of ideas flowing in and out of his head. What could he do to salvage the work he had, what were the statuses of the other subjects, how could he recover them? What could he do right now to save face? Many more wrapped around his head, almost blinding and deafening his senses with thought.

"Sir, let's go." Four heavily armed men, sporting beards and very sophisticated military equipment. They had no affiliating marks or name tapes. Just camouflaged uniforms of the military prior.

"If you refuse, we will kill you, doctor," another one said.

The doctor was merely talking to himself in blind fury, until one of the strong arms reached from reality and pulled him out of his own head. Steinberg was surprised, shocked even. How dare they touch him? Who were these inbred Neanderthals putting their dirty hands on him? He turned, one stuck a gun in the doctor's face.

"Don't care who you are, you are going to the general. In a body bag or not."

He complied. They walked him back out of the main underground facility. Stuffed him into an SUV with blacked-out windows and they drove him off.

"Doctor Anderson?" one of the robotic armored knights called to him.

"Yes, soldier?"

"Where are we going to put him?" she asked, pointing to the box.

"Is he alive?" he asked.

"No, gunshot wound to the head."

"Bring him into the operating room, I'm sure the doctor will want to take samples and dissect him when he gets back."

The soldiers did as he said. They brought his box into the lowest level of the facility. Wheeling him past the many creatures produced from the doctor's gene splicing and forced evolutionary experiments. They brought him through another wing of the facility, the door held up a sign in its archway. *Super Soldier Project, Human Gene Manipulation Division.* Subordinates of the doctors in clean rooms peering into microscopes. Machines whirling as they dropped liquids into rows and rows of vials.

Several giant black boxes with numbers painted on the centers of them. Caskets with a very sci-fi styling about their sleek designs. A total of twenty of the boxes sat leaning against the wall hooked to machines that lay quiet. Empty, all of them.

The next long rectangular window the soldiers passed by, suits like theirs were being shot at, hit by machines redesigned for testing. One was being pounded by a metal bending machine. Others were set on fire. Some shot at by various high caliber weapon systems.

The next room. Weapons were being tested by worried scientist. The soldier stopped for a second to watch. A large man in a lab coat readied himself. Ear muffs covering his large ears. Clear safety goggles on his face.

An assistant, much smaller than he, handed him an odd revolver. His right-hand shaking, he took it. He took aim, and fired. Even through the sound muffling room, the blast was loud. The gun almost jumped from his bear-like hands. He handed it back to the assistant, shaking his hand out. Clearly in pain. They continued on.

Finally, they arrived at the operating room. They moved the casket on to the table. Nurses flooded into the room, pulling his heavy body from the case. Removing his clothing. Laying his things out on the table. His bag was next. They began cataloging everything he had on him. Type of clothing, type of weapons, type of ammunition, his two knives. They even cataloged everything he had in his bag.

Lock picks, a beanie, ammo, water purifier, three canteens full of alcohol. They all looked at each other oddly as they continued to catalog his belongings. Food bars, rations, paracord, grenades, fragmentation, and smoke. A map, a small taped up clipboard with luminescent tape on both sides, a pen tied to the spring clip. Flashlight and batteries, matches, magnesium block, Bic lighters, several packs of cigarettes, a Kukri, and gloves. Bullets, lots of bullets.

"Jesus, why do they always have the exact same shit on them?" one of the nurses asked.

"Because they were survivors. That's why the doctor picked them all. They possess the same mentality."

"Which is?"

The nurse sighed, "To survive."

"Well, it wasn't very good at it now, was *it*? Picking a fight with our soldiers."

"I bet he didn't last a minute against them," another said.

One of the guards, the very one who shot Felix in the head, broke the laughter of the nurses, "He almost killed all of us. We got lucky. It took a ten-millimeter point blank to the head to put him down. Go ahead, check the rest of his body, we hit him several times. Not once did the bullets pass through. Show some fucking respect for him. He didn't choose this."

The nurses all looked at each other. One of the younger ones replied, "Yes, ma'am." They looked down at Felix, finding small red marks on his skin from where the rounds skipped off his body.

"Jesus, she's right," another said.

*****

Doctor Steinberg sat in a chair in front of a large oak desk. An older woman sat before him, a scowl on her deep lined face. Her eyes almost as gray as her hair. Her fingers folded in front of her as she stared at the doctor. A video behind her on a large flat screen played. Showing the soldiers in the prototype armor being killed by Felix.

He said nothing. They watched and listened until it was over, and Felix was shot in the head, ending the fight. The screen then clicked over to a slideshow, by a few clicks on the general's computer. Graphs, of various recourses and expenditure reports. The doctors' various projects were all in the red, power usage, loss of life, fuel, assets. It implied that he was costing more than he was worth investing any of their patience, and resources further.

"Doctor, far be it from me to understand the attraction or wool you have pulled over the eyes of our founding fathers, but this, this is now getting out of hand. That, right there…"

She pointed to screenshot of Felix holding the queen's mouth open. "Do you see that?"

"Yes, and?" the doctor replied.

Irritated, wide-eyed, she spouted off, "That is a fucking monster. That you created, and couldn't control, one that you chose, who was a soldier once, with a will to survive, and a love for the end of the world, is that not insane?"

"Well…"

"Is that not insane? I don't know who is more of a liability here, the things that you are creating or you?"

He began to make excuses through his fidgeting, she held her hand up calmly, continuing, "I'm about to shut your science project down. I do not believe your subjects are worth the loss of current assets to further our progress into the future. You have done nothing but render many of my soldiers useless against these monsters. We don't have many to begin with, to conduct future operations overseas in order to purify the rest of the world of the infection and the uninfected remains of the dying civilization. Your colleague, Doctor Chin…his weapons are nearly ready, and only has cost us some fuel and salvaging missions that have produced results he, and I for that matter, believe are ready to combat even your so-called super soldiers."

He attempted to interrupt again, to be quieted by her wrinkled hand again. "Now, Doctor, I am starting to lean my recommendations toward all of his projects, the prototypes and weapons that he has produced yield promise. And their capabilities are far more applicable to land, sea, and air, which yours are not. So, now you may talk, and do be quick, you are already intruding on my time as is."

His body was clearly oriented away from her, his legs crossed, foot wildly fidgeting. He was leaned into the corner of the large leather chair. The four large men stood around him, ready to kill him at any sign of hostility toward the general.

"It seems you have been spying on my efforts. Did you know he single-handedly killed one of the alphas, with hand weapons, of all things. He, head-to-head, held off the queen just the other night. He has become what we have been hoping he would. And you and I both know that regardless of what weapons we employ, it's the soldiers on the ground that make the difference. Smart bombs, mobile robotic suits that are piloted, aircraft, they all take human beings to operate, remotely or otherwise. So why not just make them like Number 13. He was a success, and you and I both know that AI is a tragedy waiting to happen, unreliable and irrational when left unattended by human meddling."

The general interrupted, "He was killed with a single gunshot wound to the head, how the fuck is that a success?"

The doctor closed his eyes, fidgeting more violently with his foot. "As a stone cast from a mere man onto a giant brought the great beast down. As all heroic tales end. The project needs a few more trial runs but it will succeed. And we can produce more humans than we can machines. Soon there will be only what recourses we can salvage from recycling. People, we merely need to produce perfect people. And we are reaching that capability as well. The first human processing incubators are currently being tested."

"And what of your other projects?"

"What other projects?"

"The creatures you spliced to make those things you call children. What are they, and why are you trying to hide those things from the Board?"

"They were an accident, but not in vain, they possess many qualities that need to be studied, they may one day outlive us. They are not things, they are beautiful, and could be the answer to our future we are striving for."

She waved it off. "You're not convincing me, nor have you convinced the Board, nor the Overseer. They are giving you one year, more time than I or any of the others recommended. You and your little circus of abominations have one year to produce results. If you cannot, you will be shut down, all your work will be seized, and more than likely destroyed as long as I am in command, and you will be executed for your fraudulent misuse of recourses, not to mention your crimes against not only humanity, but Mother Nature herself. They may have faith in you, but I, however, do not. I find that even with what we have done, you are spitting in God's face, and will pay for your sins in this life or the next."

"*Fraulein,* you are in charge of the remnants of a military that was responsible for releasing the pandemic into society in the first place. How can you sit there and tell me that I will be punished for my sins, when as long as we wear these symbols on our shoulders, we are the guilty, the murderers, the sinners, are we not? I find it amazing that even you, after everything that has happened, still believe in something as ridiculous as an omnipresent being of light."

"One day, He will forgive us," she spoke it with conviction that even the doctor could respect.

"Only when we succeed. Now if you are finished with me, General, I have work to do, and only a year to do it in. You want to see results, I'll show you a spectacle that will never be forgotten in the history of humanity."

"For your sake, Doctor, I hope so."

The doctor was escorted out of her office.

*****

Felix's eyes opened, the intensity in his expression brought a weight down on the young nurse she didn't understand. Nor the fact that this man, who was shot in the head, was looking at her, his eyes almost black, even under the light beaming down on him.

The Nurse backed away from Felix, dropping the forceps and the malformed 10 mm. He sat up.

"Se-s-sedate him, now!" the nurse yelled. "Sound the alarm!"

Felix's eyes slid to his nearest target. His face twisted in hatred as he immediately gathered the environment into his perception.

Felix caught a man, lunging at him with a needle, by the neck. The man dropped the syringe, and begun clawing at Felix's arm. The nurse jerked and wrenched, letting out a short grunt that was silenced as his windpipe was crushed.

Felix stepped onto the sterile white floor. The nurses were all back against the wall, frightened. The alarm began blaring, lights flashing from LED rectangular boxes down the halls and around the facility.

Guards rushed down the halls. Armed with rifles and side arms, full body armor, like the armored knights that first subdued him. The nurses all ran out, shutting the giant blast doors. They watched from the large bullet and blast proof glass. Felix put his clothing on. Collected up his things, loaded and holstered his weapons. The soldiers arrived at the blast doors, he couldn't hear them but the shocked pale nurses all were pointing and from what he could tell, telling the soldiers that he had risen from the head. Dried blood was still crusted to the side of his face and head. His shirt and jacket were dry now and it was beginning to flake off of him in silvery specks.

The doors slid open. The soldiers entered the room; the nurses heard a crunching thud. One was sent like a rag doll, sliding out into the hallway. Gun fire rattled off, a few screams and crunches and the nurses bolted from the corridor. Felix walked out, checking his new commandeered rifle. Out of the corner of his eye, something caught every bit of his attention as it stood there. That evil thing, the black dog, taunting him with a smile. He turned his head, breathing heavily, that thing made him nervous. But it was gone, only two people in lab coats stood before him, frightened stupid looks on their faces, holding an odd pistol, and several odd weapons laid out on the table before them.

He walked over to the door, kicking it clean off its heavy reinforced hinges, it slammed into the large overweight scientist, killing him. The door sent sparks down the long indoor gun range, trailing a thick streak of blood with it.

The smaller one, she was young. Backed against the table, she felt a gun under where her hand fell. He advanced toward her, she brought it up pulled the trigger. It clicked, empty. He had her wrist in his tight grip. He towered over her, grinning as he stared into her eyes.

"You wanna live?"

She choked out a stuttering "Yes!"

"Good, what are these awesome toys you have here, and how do you operate them?"

"The-they were made for the super soldier project, based off data collected from the field on Number 13."

"Interesting."

He pointed everything out on the table before him. Two under barreled revolvers in .454 Cassul. Thick framed, black, with rubberized smooth grips. Hexagonal style cylinders, holding six 300 grain shells. Each of the two revolvers sported six-inch barrels that were sleeved in a large recoil dampening rectangular slab-slide steal sleeve. Both had shoulder holsters made of leather. Next to them, a sleek semi-automatic shotgun. Its receiver was solid, running all the way to the end of the shot tube and barrel. The charging handle was spring loaded into the side of the bolt, it was pulled out from a small smooth cut, meant for a finger to open the latch and charge the weapon. A large button for a bolt release, and another for a bolt forward lock. The bottom length of the receiver starting from the loading port running to the end of the weapon, triangular in shape, forming an edge along the bottom of the shot-tube. Felix inspected all three of them, deciding very quickly that he liked them.

"What is this for?" he asked, referring to the dull edge.

"It was designed so that the user can use it to strike opponents when in close quarters combat or out of ammunition."

"Interesting. It's not sharp?" he said, further inspecting the weapon.

"So, it maintains strength and longevity, it's not meant to cut anything. Can I go now?" she forced it out through her nervous shakes.

He swung the weapon, it struck her in the neck, with such force it lopped her head rigidly off. Her body rotated sideways slamming into the concrete floor, splattering blood across the side of the room.

"Not meant to cut, my ass," he chuckled to himself.

He was about to leave when something had caught his eye. A black case that held several twelve-gauge shells in it. He picked one up, it was metallic, black, and a glass dome rested where the shell would normally house a slug or be folded to retain pellets or BBs. He flips it over.

"Charged Particle Battery" was stamped into the bottom of the casing.

He stuffed the shells into his pockets, the speed loaders ready to go with 454s. And he then loaded his shotgun with yellow shells. Small diamonds with the iconic explosive symbols were panted or stamped onto the shells. He gathered that these would probably be his best bet. As he gathered what he could, he noticed a sheath, not a sling, that looked like a sword sheath for the shotgun. He slung it over his shoulder and sheathed his new shotgun. It buckled around his chest to insure stability. And the sheath was magnetic, due to it pulling the shotgun into it the rest of the way.

He picked up the rifle he had earlier and shouldered it, peeking out of the door way. Heavy machine gun fire began raining down on him. Sparks flying, bullets bouncing off of metal. A well-placed throw landed a grenade right in front of the door. Felix, crouched, stepped back, plugging his ears and opening his mouth. The grenade went off. It wasn't as bad as he remembered. He quickly picked his rifle up, ready, and stood clearing out of the doorway. The smoke from kicking up dust off the concrete was enough for him to move freely into the open. Something he would have never done in the past; for some reason, he felt it deep inside that these fuckers won't get to kill him. After all, *she* was waiting.

He fired, picking up speed and running into the next room. The door blew in. He landed, rolling back onto his feet. It was an armor testing room. Sharp shields, knight style armor, oddly sleek designed swords and spears were dropped where the testers once stood. Scared of the alarm, and more than likely the gunfire and screams that followed suit, everyone had evacuated from this particular room.

He peeked from the door, never getting near the frame with his rifle, he leaned, took a well-placed shot. One soldier dead. He crouched, leaned again, took another shot. Semi-Auto fire was much more efficient than automatic fire, even with his new-found strength, forced manipulated strength. Chemically or otherwise, he didn't know nor did he care.

This time he side-stepped, skipping into the open, taking three shots, then disappearing into the room he had just came from across the corridor. Dragging a vortex of dust with him. Three more soldiers slumped lifelessly. Bleeding from their faces which were not armored; they had forgotten their helmets in all the commotion. The deceased were pulled from the now staggering formation down the massive hallway. The soldiers seemed to continue to pile in, until an intelligent leader barking orders through a slew of curse words, told them to stay the fuck back. *Wise choice,* Felix thought. He drew his shotgun, leaned, one-handed, took aim, and fired. The round screamed like a hellish creature. It exploded in the chest of their leader. The blast was powerful, it rocked the entire corridor. Sending pieces of armor, limbs, a few bodies in all directions. He loaded another shell, and sheathed his weapon.

Felix checked the mag of the rifle, only a few rounds left. He loaded it back into the M4. He stepped out with it shouldered, taking aim, stepping over soldiers in shock, bleeding to death. He tossed the rifle and picked up another, checking the chamber, and the mag. Suitable. He started heading toward the main stairwell. Stacked with more unfortunate souls that were about to meet their maker, by his hand.

*****

"Is this what you were talking about?" the general asked, clearly irritated. Even nervous, some would say.

Doctor Steinberg was giddy with excitement as he was brought back into the room.

The two were standing there, staring at a blacked-out screen, 'no video' blinked white in the bottom corner. She turned and typed a few key strokes, a series of camera feeds jumped onto the screen.

"Do you see? He killed them all," the doctor proclaimed.

The general was not amused... "It; a thing you designed, with weapons, YOU designed. Can he be killed?" she demanded.

"Yes, of course."

"How?" again demanding.

"Well, we know a bullet can knock him out, we just need to keep shooting him until we destroy his brain or heart. If he bleeds out. Missile strike, a bladed instrument. Yes, yes, a bladed instrument. The Knight Program, we can test the full potential of the Knight Armor assets."

"I'm initiating the MADD Protocol, I'm calling Professor Chin, maybe he can correct your mistake."

Doctor Steinberg laughed. "Hardly, my entire project was designed to combat that very concept. Due to his production methods mirroring our enemies across the world, I had to ensure we had a means within our own ranks to combat each other."

"We will see. If I lose any more of my men due to your failures, I will personally see to your execution."

Steinberg paid her no attention, his eyes were wide and he was terrified, she could see it all over his face. But he was terrified because of his monster. Not her threat.

Soon everyone in the room was called to the attention by a furious woman who came barreling in. "Where the fuck is he?" she demanded.

Beatrix found her target and began beating and slapping the doctor wildly. It took three men to pull her off and throw her out of the room. The door was then shut in her face and locked. She stormed down the hallway in utter fury.

The general spoke to her defense, "I should have let her finish."

*****

Felix stood in a video room. A woman was in the fetal position in the corner, sobbing to herself as he was pulling up files on the pandemic.

"Chimera" was the name of the file he accessed.

He observed. Watching a pup, a hyena. Young, taken from its mother. Infected with a disease. Humans and animals of all kinds tossed into the cell. Its progression through the ability to infect humans and then lastly, the dogs.

He watched as several more people had been tossed in the cell. Bitten and turned. Then he watched as they were observed. Over several months they watched as the infection changed them. Their bodies slowly resembling that of the queen. Then they were all killed.

He cringed. Saw her face as she felt her children being slaughtered. "Poor baby girl; they really did a number on us, didn't they?" he asked out loud.

They, the general, and everyone in her office watched as he watched those video catalogs. They saw his sympathy and empathy for her and what they did to her.

Finally; in the records. Felix watched as the beast was released in New York, and thousands of drones launched all over the world. Another element simultaneously set up nuclear devices throughout the major cities.

He believed it. And it merely smeared his face in a smile that even unnerved the general as she watched him watch them do what they did. Felix

330

turned, and killed the woman cowering in the corner with one shot. He didn't even look down his sights.

He left the observation room and was now on his way. To where? They would all soon find out.

*****

"He found the Garden. If he kills those two, everything that we have worked toward will be lost," his voice was shaky. He fumbled, pulling his phone from his pocket, scrolling through to Anderson.

Anderson picked up.

"Anderson, we need to protect the children. If he kills them, it will be years before we can produce another pair."

"Understood, want me to send in their Guardian?" Anderson asked calmly.

"Yes, do whatever you have to, just save my children."

"Sir, she isn't ready, nor is the armor, she hasn't matured anywhere near Number 13. Even with the armor, I don't think she is capable of succeeding in a head-to-head conflict with Felix."

"I don't care if she is not ready. Just send her in, right now!"

The phone hung up. Steinberg stood there chewing on the tips of his fingers in a nervous fit. Eyes wide, sweating profusely. The general sat at her desk, talking on the phone, she gave directions to initiate the MADD project and not to enter the facility, wait for him to move outside before engaging... "Yes, the threat is extremely hostile, and don't be fooled by the fact he is merely a man... Yes, he is one of Steinberg's abominations, proceed with caution." She hung up the phone.

She calmly told one of the many colonels standing in her office to go tell everyone on ground to pull back into the safe houses. No one was allowed to engage Number 13.

*****

Felix passed by two extremely large blast doors, it stopped him in his tracks. His head wrenched left. The doors were two stories tall. He walked over to a normal-sized door at the far-right end of the giant sliding doors.

"What the fuck is this?" he asked as he looked up to inspect it. He tried to open the door. *No luck, it requires an access code, biometric scan, voice recognition, probably a fucking urine sample to open the motherfucker.* Felix was becoming irritated quickly.

He stepped back, and ran at the door, slamming into it. The entire door shook. He did it again. The smaller door buckled. He was becoming so blind with rage he forgot what he was doing for a moment. He rammed it once more. The door broke free, bouncing off thick grass, slamming into something, somewhere in the gorgeous forest that he had now found himself in. A tree fell, rustling thick bushes as it crashed down from the door cutting crudely through its base.

Alarms of a different tone had begun going off. The entrance was sealed with a thick, quickly hardening foam behind him. He turned back. "What the fuck is going on here?" he asked as he took a leisurely stroll. An artificial sun drifted through a pleasantly clouded blue sky. Birds and other animals scurried about through the forest, and Felix couldn't tell if they were real or not. The sun looming overhead certainly looked real as it shined from the dome-like screens.

The rain forest, or jungle, whatever it was, it was beautiful. The small path led him to a glass house, three bedrooms, two baths, a kitchen, a library, several flat screens, medical equipment, monitors, a clean room. He could see through everything, including the latrines. Only one room looked lived in. As he drew closer, he noticed a mirror running the length and the height of the entire garden.

The room that he noticed, now his attention was back to the glass house, was fit for any average child. He stepped closer, as he noticed pictures around the room.

Felix heard something, no louder than a soft whisper. He turned, drawing his pistol, turning with coordination and speed that was no longer human.

He was stopped dead; it almost took his very breath away. He holstered his pistol. "Holy fuck," he said, gasping in awe.

And standing before him, holding hands, scared but attempting to show bravery, were two children. But they were not children. Felix slowly kneeled down. His face holding back his disgust as he looked into each of their yellow eyes.

They reminded him of snakes. Skin smooth and glassy. Printing of spirals running down their scaly bodies. They were dressed in T-shirts and shorts that matched. Nails black and pointy, functional, Felix presumed. Their equal length hair was long spines, hers was blue, and his was red. Slits for pupils. Their faces and noses, fingers and toes, bodies were in the form of humans. Their tails laid still behind them.

"Hello," the girl spoke.

Her brother squeezed her hand tight. She winced, pulling away.

"Hello," Felix replied, bewildered.

She stepped closer. "Are you hurt?" she asked.

"What?" Felix replied. Realizing he was covered in his own dry blood, and fresh remains from the unfortunate soldiers who crossed his path.

"No, I'm fine, this is from bad guys trying to hurt me. What are you doing here, young lady?"

"I live here with my brother, Adam."

His eyes drew thin. "What's your name, sweetheart?" he asked, knowing full well what she was going to say.

"Eve."

He laughed, unbelieving; hysterically.

"Eve," her brother pulled on his sister, "stop talking to him, you know we're not allowed to talk to strangers. He's a very bad man, look at him. Do you not smell the blood of so many others on him?" Adam pleaded out; pulling himself to his sister's side.

"Why do you laugh, mister?" Eve asked. "Are our names funny to you?" She continued curiously, ignoring her brother.

Her eyes bright yellow, not once wavering as she awaited his reply.

He stood. "No, my dear. Only ironic. You and your brother remind me of a story I know of, one that starts as bad as it ends."

"Why is it a bad story?" she asked.

"Because, it's one of the few books in the history of mankind that only sounds good when someone else talks about it."

"What book is it, I wanna know?"

"The one I know of is the Holy Bible. But most faiths or religions will do."

"I don't know that story, mister."

"Good, it is a book meant for the chosen, and most of us are not the chosen ones. Better to think for yourself. That's where us humans went wrong, we allowed people who didn't care about us, think for us, and they gave us the world we have now. It's not a good world for good children. It's a world for people like me."

"Father says me and my brother are the chosen ones, and one day will re-pop...you...late...and save the world. I don't know what repopulate means, but I would like to save the world, I think."

"That's a tall order for children. I hope you succeed one day. Until then, weep for us, my dear."

"Why are you hurting people?" she asked. He was surprised almost, even shocked, that she jumped back to that. She sniffed the air. "My brother is right; you smell of death. Not just one, but so many I don't know the number."

Felix chuckled.

333

"Because it's what we humans were born to do," he spoke through a sigh as he lit a cigarette, wondering why no one was chasing him or preparing to breach this place. Might have something to do with these two younglings before him.

"That's bad. You shouldn't kill people. Father says we are going to live in a peaceful world, where no one has to hurt anyone, and me and my brother will be the first ones to see it."

His head turned, looking down at the little girl. She was doing what kids do, swinging back and forth; her brother, timid, like most boys are at that age. She was humming to herself. *They may not be human, but they sure play the part well,* Felix thought. Searching around with his eyes as something caught his acute hearing, even over the muffled alarms.

He knelt down once more, eye level with the girl. "How do we get out of here, sweetheart?" he asked.

"I don't know, we are never allowed outside, not until the world is cleaned of all bad things. Father is afraid we will get sick if we go outside now."

"Right..." he said, standing.

"Why are you so dirty?" she asked, touching his left hand that clutched his new pistol. It was covered in carbon from the bullets he'd fired. He jerked his hand away, wondering when he drew his weapon again. Looking down at her bright big beautiful eyes. She didn't once flinch. Only the look of a curious girl staring back at him.

"Because, my hands are always dirty, my dear."

"You should wash them. That's what I do to clean them."

Felix laughed, wholeheartedly. "If it were only that easy, my youngling."

A small creature scurried in front of the two kids, hissing at Felix. Felix merely raised an eyebrow at the big strong protector.

"Don't be scared, Snickers... He's our chimera, I named him after our favorite candy bar. Uncle Anderson brings them to us when we are good." She reached down and snatched the beast up.

She held it up, like a child hugging a cat that clearly is annoyed. The beast, like the two children, Felix had never seen before. Its thick blue fur covered legs reached straight out. Its cat-like head pined back against her chest, the eyes were deep green; pupil's a deep purple, slits. Its ears long and thin. Black stripes ran down the length of the creature's body.

"Where do your parents..." his eye twitched, "...come from when they come to visit you?"

Eve looked past the glass house to the left corner of the giant mirror. Fumbling with the beast and trying to point. It reminded him of all of his friends' kids. He supposed no matter what, the innocence and bond of people and animals even reached through the side that which we should have never gone. Artificial creatures, humans, even Felix wondered what special place in the forgotten spaces of Hell they would all go for doing what they did. But, even with that, the doctor was very clever in naming the two children after the spineless man, and the curious woman. And then it hit him, there was no sin, they were doing exactly what they were all meant to do. In the image of the creator. What a vile creature God must be.

"Alright, kids, I'm headed out, you can come with me, but I won't promise a safe world for either of you."

"No, mister, we are not allowed to go with strangers."

Felix laughed, nodding in agreement.

"Smart girl," he said.

"Are you going to clean the world for us then?" she asked innocently enough.

He paused. He thought on it for a moment. Kneeling down to her. "Maybe. Maybe I just might do that," he said.

Her brother stood in front of him. Blocking Felix from his sister. Hissing.

"Maybe, your names are not fitting, after all?" Felix then said. Cocking his head slightly.

"Be gone from this place, monster," the boy said.

Felix stood. Grinning like the evil he was now portraying in that old story.

"Take care of yourselves then," he said. Before he could move, a round screamed toward him. With wide eyes, he pushed the kids out of the way. But it was too late.

The round struck the ground in front of them. Adam and Eve, and their big strong protector, Snickers, were blown to pieces.

Felix was almost unscathed by the blast. He stood there, his fists balled in rage covered in their blood, and fragments of bone. He picked his hands up, they were heavy, staring at them for a moment, pieces of flesh clung to him. His eye twitched. He grinded his teeth gripping his revolver tighter.

He wrenched his head to the right. "Who fucking dares enter the garden I wish to tarnish?" he growled out through his whisper, ever so coldly.

*****

The giant was standing near the entrance to the Garden, in front of the giant mirror that acted as a one-way viewing window. Fidgeting with a malfunctioning shield that sported a 60 mm cannon running out of the pointed end. Felix was gritting his teeth. He stepped. The giant knight dropped the shield low, no longer aiming, cursing a slew of words Felix couldn't hear. His rage was deafening.

"I'm going to slaughter every last one of you insignificant creatures," he spoke. Fog puffed with every word.

He slammed into the knight. The eight-foot-tall robotically sleek, feminine plated body, accenting her womanly features, red and black armored monument of robotic success, was grunting as she caught his fist. He didn't look surprised, he jerked his fist away, stepped and delivered a devastating side kick. The crunch of the armor cracking vibrated into her helmet. Her heads-up display flickered off. It turned on just in time to catch Felix swinging his new shotgun.

She blocked with her shield. It split in half, jaggedly, throwing sparks. The crude dull blade of the monolithic receiver of his shotgun left an indent in her forearm. She swung, pushing him away. He landed on his feet, and charged like an animal. He attacked her left and right, a spinning kick, a right hook, a back-handed swing of his one-handed shotgun. He skipped back, fired. The round impacted into her chest, sending her out of a cloud of dust and dark smoke. She bounced off her back, landing on her hands and feet.

The gears and machinery powering the suit whirled wildly, more like screaming, from the stress of keeping up with Felix. Her battery was already low from the power it took to defend against him. *He is just a man, even being enhanced, it is physically impossible,* she thought. But then again, their previous model armor didn't hold up against him earlier that morning, merely attempting to take him alive, even dead, wasn't worth the loss.

"Dear lord," she said aloud.

He walked out of the smoke like a ghost. Loading another shell into his shotgun. He fired several more times. The rounds impacted. She tumbled; her suit was breaking under the stress. The screen went black, the suit lost power, and she was on her back against a wall or maybe one of the trees. She didn't know. She no longer could lift her body. The crackling of circuitry catching fire was all she could hear over her heavy breaths. Her chest was starting to burn from the hot metal.

"Oh, please God," she stuttered out.

A loud thud, and something was pulling at her head. His fingers found their way into the metal, he squeezed once more, crumpling the face cover. He pulled harder, at first, she was being lifted, until finally, the metal broke free. She fell back onto the ground. Frantically gasping for air, she couldn't make any other sound, only the brightness of the artificial light loomed over head. His blacked-out figure against the light, and the wetness of sweating profusely, running all over her body gripped her.

He leaned down. His face was expressionless, and that scared her more than anything she had ever faced. Even against the hordes of the infected, the mutations of the malicious dogs, and the very people she worked for.

"You're just a man," she cried.

This normal, average looking man before her, his dark eyes full of evil she couldn't begin to understand. He sheathed his shotgun, he looked around. Noticing a spear lying in the grass. It was hers, he walked over picking it up.

"What are you going to do?" she demanded.

He was back on top of her, she was trying to be brave, but it didn't matter, with one swift move he shoved it through her chest.

"There is nothing on the other side for you," he whispered to her as the blood rasped coughing had gargled from her mouth.

"Except for when I get there. One day, I'll be there in that nothingness to hurt you in a way that even Hell doesn't have a level for such punishments yet, do you understand?"

She was gone. Felix turned back to find his revolver.

*****

Doctor Steinberg was on his knees in the general's office. Sobbing, frantically shaking, snot running down his nose, tears down his face. He was incoherent, after witnessing the greatest of his achievements destroyed right before his very eyes. By the hand of another of his own achievements; *It must be how God must feel looking down on us all,* he thought.

"Jesus, Mary, and Joseph. Doctor, compose yourself," the general spouted. Looking on, admiring the monster she witnessed on her monitor.

"Maybe, you might have something here," she said.

*****

Felix reached the surface.

A long concrete pad, forest all around the area. Jets and planes, helicopters and military vehicles all parked under an endless row of covered hangers. A control tower stood watch over the area. He squinted at the sun that shined brightly overhead.

The alarms continued to sound. He took in a deep breath. Exhaling, he turned and walked toward the open flight line from the giant bunker entrance he had just blown open. As he moved further out there, he realized that whatever the odd new weaponry standing before him was, it wasn't like anything he had seen thus far.

337

It was about thirty feet or so in height. White, very sleek fighter jet like body structure. Reminded him of a video game with pilotable robots. He was right to associate it with such a thing, because the design features were very much inspired by the cartoons and video games that sported giant robots. The engineer that built this amazing prototype, clearly was a fan of the pop culture, anime, and video games.

"Surrender or we will use lethal force," the gorgeous voice said. *It seems that this government likes to utilize females to do all their dirty work,* he thought.

"You have three seconds to drop your weapons—"

Felix drew his weapon, fired a grenade into the sharp triangular head shutting her up, destroying one of her cameras.

"Fuck you, cocksucker. You and all your kind. I will show you what the Devil looks like."

Luckily, she had several other cameras to work with. Felix was impressed with the simple weapon he had employed.

"Hmm," he grunted as he looked his weapon over. "I wonder…"

Taking out one of the few particle shells he had, he decided to load it into the tubular magazine. It was the next round. The pilot engaged a small targeting switch on one of her joysticks, and a large targeting gate outlined Felix on her wrapped screen. She pulls the trigger. A chain-gun's three barrels spun and began to spit lead fire as it walked its heavy 20 mm rounds toward Felix. He side-stepped, dodging the first strafe. He fired again, one handed, as if the weapon had no recoil. The round struck the head of the machine again. Taking out another camera. She flipped another switch, going to her last camera.

He was nowhere to be found.

"Where the hell?" she said as she leaned forward squinting her eyes as if it would help. Searching her monitors, vigorously.

He was already at her flank; he had extracted his charged particle battery round, decided that he didn't want to use it just yet. He loaded several explosive shells; one into his breach and three into his tube. He fired several times, the rounds impacted, exploding. By the fourth round, the left arm was sent crashing to the ground. The machine, by the impact of the fifth round was sent over on its side. The auto stabilizing gyros were too damaged by then to spread its leg and keep balance. It fell like a drunkard who had reached their limit.

He loaded his weapon with five more shells and sheathed it. He was on top of it, beating his fist into what looked to be a side entrance hatch, where the left ribs would be located, comparing it to a human.

A few moments and he was wrenching the door open. The metal screamed as it was twisted from its heavy hidden hinges. She screamed, but there was nowhere to run, nothing she could do. He crawled into the cockpit. She punched and beat against him, but he felt harder than the metal of this robot.

"Please no, please god, someone… HELP ME, I'M SORRY, IT WASN'T MY FAULT. THEY MADE US THIS, THEY DID THIS TO ALL OF US, YOU DON'T HAVE TO DO THIS, PLEASE. I-I-I-"

Slowly, he pulled a knife from the small of his back. That same cold expression, the entire time he pressed the knife into her neck. She kicked and screamed, used every ounce of her strength to stop his hand from pushing it in. He wasn't even trying, and she was powerless with all her might. She choked and gargled; the knife separated her spine within an instant.

"I'll show you as I will the others; the evil that not even the Devil could appreciate."

Felix popped out of the hatch and walked toward the flight line. Wiping his blade off on his thigh, he sheathed it back into its horizontal faded leather sheath. He stuffed his bloody hands into his pockets finding his crushed pack of smokes and made his way.

*****

The General's office was quiet. They heard the entire event, the pilot's pleas for mercy right before her cries were silenced by the blade sliding in, gargling of blood, and the popping of her spinal cord as the knife separated her vertebra.

"Ma'am…" one of her many officers said aloud, breaking the silence. "What in God's name are we dealing with here?"

The general pulled Steinberg's head up by a fist full of hair. She back-handed him into reality.

"What the hell is that thing?" she asked, pointing at the monitor.

He gave no response. He merely stared blankly; like a man without purpose.

"Ma'am?" that same officer asked.

"I don't know," the general responded.

She looked at her cabinet of leaders in the room, letting go of the doctor. She let out a sigh, pulling a handkerchief from her uniform pocket and wiping her hands off.

"He is going somewhere; we either shoot him out of the sky, or wait till he lands and salvage what assets we can from this incident."

339

Anderson was listening in the back of the room. "He's going back to Fort Monroe. More than likely to continue the search for his woman, and to kill the infection now that he understands, somewhat, his capabilities."

"You're one of this dribbling idiot's subordinates. Anderson, right?" the general replied.

"By the state of Doctor Steinberg, I am no longer a subordinate, ma'am."

"You know that thing out there?"

"Yes, the last surviving Super Soldier, the other twelve committed suicide; why he hasn't, we don't know. I recommend we take advantage of the situation here. We have the rare opportunity to reduce the infection, and Number 13. We have enough data to continue the project, and with more control measures to insure a retainable product. 13 is a failed experiment as of right now, so I recommend that once he arrives at Fort Monroe, we launch, killing the infection, and the first generation of the Super Soldier projects, and once the dust has settled, we send in teams to clean up any potential infection, thus wiping the US territories clean. The southern borders are now being walled off as we speak, so it should be a matter of time before we can continue to rid the world of infection."

The entire office turned to watch as one of their aircraft, in which Felix held a gun to the head of an unfortunate pilot, lifted off the airfield. He was headed back to Fort Monroe.

Felix sat in the copilot seat, his large under barreled revolver pointed at the pilot's head.

"You plan on keeping that thing pointed at me the whole time?" he asked.

"If you don't want to die in the most horrible way you could fucking imagine, you will take me to Fort Monroe, and I will let you go."

"That easy?"

"That easy."

Felix had no intention of letting him live.

He thought about Adam and Eve, and it dawned on him, he was the snake in the Garden. He was happy for them; they didn't get a chance to grow and see the world they would inherit. And like the Adversary or the Accuser, Lucifer, Satan, Iblis, the Bearer of Light, the Enlightened One, he merely was there for a reason, pose a question, temp them, force the question, but in his case, they died. And for that, he wondered, if he was like them, and no longer human, where did the soulless go, if our very self were to be manipulated by man?

*****

Fort Monroe lost power, the occupants in Hampton finally lost to the infection and thusly the generators were destroyed. The generators that powered the dog whistle were holding strong. But they knew, soon the infected would figure out that the generators don't push enough power to keep them at bay any longer.

Monica stood on the stage; the fort was gathered onto the parade field, everyone who could be out there was waiting for her to say something. Alex, Mitch, Dana, Chris, Gavin, Samantha, Britney, Isaac all standing up there with her.

"What is going on?" a woman in the crowd asked.

The crowd began agreeing, mummering, and yelling the same. Monica held out her hands, quieting the mass. They all stood waiting for her to say anything.

"You all know that our military was formed from the USOAR, and they currently hold a research facility in the North. They have been conducting experiments in the wastelands for years now, since the beginning of the infection. I'm sorry I have lied to you all. They have even implemented the idea behind our partnership structure in order to produce worthwhile successors to continue our species. But I believe they have abandoned us, because they wanted something that we had, someone you all know and have come to call your own. Felix. Now that they have him, they no longer need this location, and more than likely will send their weapons to destroy us, or just let the infection destroy our hard-fought sanctuary."

"What are we going to do?" someone in the frantically mummering crowd asked.

"We are going to fucking fight!" Gavin yelled.

"Like Felix did?" someone in the crowd yelled out, everyone got quiet.

"Now he's dead!" another yelled.

Gavin stepped forward. "Yeah, he is, and you know what, he fucking died fighting for something. He filled his fucking boots."

"What about the rest of us?" another in the crowd called out.

"Yeah, we didn't want this fight, we have families we have to look after, the dogs and the feral are enough, now this?" another said.

Gavin continued, ignoring their comments, "We will harden our defenses, and prepare to leave as soon as possible. Felix may be gone, but we are still here, and we will not let our friends and families die in vain for the powers that be, that don't give a fuck about you. It's time to sink or swim. The floating city has acquired a destroyer, big enough to house all of us. Their boats will be waiting at dawn to start transporting everyone to the ship. Those of you that can fight will stay until the very last person is on the boats. We will lay out the plan, and start preparing right now, we will not die for those motherfuckers."

"How do we know they are not going to leave us to die here?" someone else asked in the crowds.

"Because we have been sending them supplies for weeks now, more than enough for all of us and them. Some of our own are on those ships, waiting for us. Friends and family, good people just trying to survive like all of you."

The crowd began to mummer again, this time the comments seemed to be favorable.

Gavin continued, "I need fighters, you will link up with Alex, Chris, and anyone else who wants to set in. I need you all to lay down your weakness and push forward. I need boat drivers, I need a group to start moving supplies to the docks, pack up your kids, grab your guns, it's time to live on your fucking feet."

One, there is always one. "We didn't ask for this fight. If you all didn't let that monster come into our home, we would still be fine, and the North wouldn't turn their backs on us!"

Gavin turned and walked down the steps toward the crowd.

"You think they would have come to help when it really mattered? You think that this new government isn't like the one before them, they came from the same people, with that ultimate goal, with that need to reduce and control all of the stupid and weak. This is it, you wanna come with us, then find your fucking intestinal fortitude and pick up a gun and protect your fucking family."

"What do you know about family! This military is outfitted with robotic armor and heavy weapons, we can't fight against that!"

Gavin started yelling, "I lost my fucking family like most of you, I had two kids and a wife once. The only reason I am even fucking here right now was because these cocksuckers were the ones who killed them."

The crowd turned to each other and looked back at Gavin. His eyes were becoming glassy as he continued.

"Yeah, most of you don't know. But that unit symbol on most of your shoulders ravaged the country. They killed a lot of people that weren't infected, capturing and conducting experiments on the rest. While all of you were hiding, turning your fucking cheeks, this is the reality. This military was responsible for the fucking infection! They set it lose, they probably infected the entire world. How's that, you all wanna help us put an end to those responsible for the end of the world? Or just say fuck it and give up?"

The crowd began looking at each other.

"You wanna continue to exist, spit in the faces of those who would bring us back to our shit ways? Then come with me. We can defeat anything. Those

342

people need those sophisticated machines to combat this. We just need some bullets and gunpowder. The machines they have will fail, this infection will end, and we will be the only ones left standing because we fill our fucking boots," Gavin yelled in a furious and motivating voice.

The others followed him.

The crowd was being sorted into groups led by Gavin, and the others. Monica watched as the entire fort was being pulled together by these men and women. People started working immediately and without issue. Before long the parade field was empty, but vehicles sped in and out of the fort, word was being pushed out to the front gates to start pulling back. They were preparing for their last stand.

The fire was dying down in the fire pit. Crimson coals glowed as they took soothing breaths of the cool summer's night. She was intoxicated, and Felix could tell. Everyone had long sought their beds, and now they were finally alone. She was sitting next to him, singing along to a low melody by Ella Fitzgerald. Her voice was soothing as the warmth of the fire pit was. Warm and inviting, *he thought. She leaned over, taking the cigarette from his hand. Taking a long drag.*

"What are you doing, Sasha?" he asked with a curious smile on his face.

Since they met, although they were still very new to each other, she had mentioned frequently that she hated his smoking. And yet, she was taking another drag. He knew she was drunk. She let all her insecurities go, she had no care in the world. It was welcoming.

She didn't answer him, she just rocked slowly with the music. Leaning against him. His large hand reached down touching her inner thigh. She was burning with desire, but he couldn't tell, she wasn't giving him any clues that she wanted him right there and now.

She laid her head to rest on his shoulder, pulling herself closer. She handed him the smoke, he threw it in the fire pit, because she was getting up to sit in his lap. She did just that. She wrapped her arms around his shoulders as she rubbed herself against him. She leaned in. Felix met her halfway. They kissed, long, deeply. As two so very deeply in love, it lasted. The world had fallen away.

After a few moments of making out like young lovers, they decided it was time to go to bed. She pulled herself off him, yearning still. He stood, and was met by those plump luscious lips once more. His hands feeling her strong back as they slowly reached around her tiny waste.

They couldn't get any closer than they were, not without taking their clothes off. At this point, he wouldn't have minded, and she wanted it so very badly. It burned inside of her. Like a fire that had been dormant for so long, choked by lack of oxygen, and here this man stood. Pouring gasoline all over her heart and setting it on fire.

They held hands as they walked inside. She nearly stumbled into the sliding glass door. She turned to kiss him once more. He pulled her away for a moment, looking at her in her big emerald eyes.

"I want you very badly, but I can't, not while you are this intoxicated. I want you when you're sober."

She was shocked, she certainly had been thinking about this all day. Through their adventures, the lunch they laughed and joked through. The whole car ride to his house, after the dinner they had made, and even when all his friends and their wives or girlfriends pulled her away to get to know her. This beautiful intelligent woman that had caught all of his attention, was the guest of honor. She couldn't believe it, that he was really willing to pass on this opportunity right now, when she was so ready to go. She was dripping with anticipation.

"I'll get you a pillow and blanket, and you can sleep on the couch. We can wake up and then try this later, but I want you to want it, not in an altered state of mind, Sasha."

She leaned in; seriousness written all over her face. "I'm not going to bed anywhere, except where you are."

He sighed, with a smile. "Okay, come on."

She held his hand as they walked into the bedroom. The light clicked on. She walked over to the other side of the bed, furthest from the door. He laughed. She didn't take anything off, she just pulled the covers back and snuggled into bed.

"Why are you laughing at me?" she asked.

"Because I sleep on this side, so that is perfect."

"I sleep on this side at my house," she started to slur and sound dreamy.

Felix took his clothes off down to his underwear. She turned to sneak a peek at the sound of his belt clinking and clanking to the ground. He was clearly yearning for her as well, she couldn't help but notice what was printing through his boxer briefs.

"You have a V cut, that is sexy," she said.

He laughed again.

"Well, that was a very nice compliment. Thank you."

"Do you need anything, water, something, are you done with the light?"

"I'm fine. Thank you."

He shut the light off, turning the fan on. He climbed into bed, wrapping his arms around her. She accepted them gladly by putting his arms where she wanted them.

"Sweet dreams, Sasha," he whispered into her ear, kissing her on the cheek.

"You know?" she asked.

"What?" he said muffled as his face was nuzzled in her thick brown hair.

"For a man who uses 'fuck' like a comma, you're very sweet sometimes."

They fell asleep in each other's arms.

Chapter 24
Loyal as a Dog

The night had been long. Preparations for the oncoming storm were almost finished. The walls were lined with every weapon they could find. Explosives littered throughout every road and passage. Vehicles were parked at the main gate ready to react to any part of the small island that could get hit. Tanks sat at the main gate acting as an armored gun blockade.

They were going to push everyone to the boats at dawn. But the air smelt of war, it smelt of a final battle. The soldiers and anyone who could carry a weapon felt it too. As the sun began to rise, the boats' engines all started up. Gavin was standing tall at the main gate, stacked high with barriers and sand bags, the entrance looked out into the city of Hampton. As always, there was no fear in his eyes.

Soldiers walked by. "Sir, the colonel sent me to inform you that the boats have started moving."

"About fucking time," Gavin replied. He said nothing else, and for an awkward moment, she waited for a real reply, when it didn't come, she left.

Since the power went down, they had been unable to charge their radios for short range communications. Runners were now being used to deliver any messages and orders, which had been a very delayed and timely strain on all of the soldiers and leaders of this now rag tag team of survivors. With the power down, the dog whistle was running off of fumes from a diesel generator. They had an hour maybe, before their protection failed, for good.

A loud howl echoed throughout the city. Gavin knew it all too well.

"It's her," he said with a grin on his face.

He pulled his flask from his back pocket, he was dressed in a plate carrier, mags in a neat row of eight lined his abdomen. His rifle slung across his body. His pistol sat ready on his hip. Grenades in pouches along the back of his battle belt.

"You ready, brother?" Chris asked.

Gavin with his wide smile and deep blue sparkling eyes never looked so happy as he flicked his cigarette into the mote down below.

Mitch and Alex were escorting loads and loads of people from the small walkways that were the only pedestrian entrances to the fort from the east and south side. They followed them to the marina that merely took a few minutes each turn. The issue now was the boats. Their rickety hauls were black against the sun rising behind them. They were nearly there. But how many could they fit? Alex only counted two. Mitch counted three. Unsure, until they got closer.

The ground began to rumble, with the sound of thousands and thousands of infected once-human creatures, marching sluggishly toward them. Alphas leading small elements of their own. But the queen, she stood atop the remnants of a toppled building, a sign of nature over-throwing man's weak monuments. She barked, this time though, it was a roar, a horrific long growl that shook the remains of the glass around her. She was their warlord. Their queen. Marching toward the sun, to finish off those who had wronged her, she was now the flood.

"Why us?"

Gavin looked at one of the soldier kneeling before him, facing out with her machine gun propped up on sandbags atop the old walls.

"What are you going to do about it, the why does not matter, as much as we try to understand it, what are you…" he said as he poked her in the side of the helmet "going to do about it? It's all there, our world, and here we are, hanging on to the edge of it, because something better than us pushed us to the edge of the cliff. So what? What are you going to fucking do?"

She looked up at him nervously. "I'm going to kill as many of them as I can."

Gavin grinned, turning to leave. "Be safe, sir," she said.

Gavin turned, "Be violent."

*****

Felix's eyes opened; his hand was still in the air holding his weapon to the pilot's head. They were near and he could see it, that Fort he had become so very accustomed to. Radio traffic screamed through the pilot's headset. Felix couldn't hear it. The General's orders to the pilot were to crash, kill Felix, and that he should aim for the lighthouse to take out the dog whistle.

Almost every living soul looked toward the sound, toward the sky. Out of the sun that consumed the shape of the aircraft, it shot out to the south. The Osprey drew near, and immediately more fear spread to the masses. Mitch, Alex, Chris, the colonel, Rachel, Cynthia, all of them, begun to poison their realities with hope. They just had a feeling, that it was help from the north or maybe a defector. Gavin did not, he thought they were about to be fired upon.

The Osprey began to pick up speed as it circled back toward the north, back toward the Fort, and then, the pilot nosed the aircraft downward. Felix realized what he was doing and shot him in the head. He holstered his weapon and immediately grabbed the sticks, but it was too late. The bird crashed into the lighthouse, bounced off the ground coming apart in the air, and splashing into the water.

"Fuck!" Gavin spouted.

The queen let out a hellish roar. And the infected all screeched and screamed in reply. Their war cries echoed, like a stadium full of hundreds of thousands of fans. It almost broke the very will of the soldiers of Fort Monroe. Except for those who longed for this day. Gavin paced up and down the length of the wall, his eyes watching the sea of their enemy that crawled and ran, and marched on, toward them.

"This is your motherfucking day, those things out there ate and murdered your families, your loved ones. They infected your brothers and sisters; they raped their fucking souls. So, let's set them free. Kill every fucking thing with a heartbeat. This is where your life is worth something. So others may live on. Let's go to hell like real fucking men and women, with a goddamn smile on our fucking faces!"

The sea of creatures began to funnel into the narrow highway headed toward the gates. Mitch heard a single shot, the flare reached high, shinning like a dying star. He pulled from his backpack a large controller. Flipping a few switches, a small claymore clacker was wired into the box along with a battery pack and antenna tapped all together. Locations of each set of explosives were scratched under each of the switches. He clacked the device.

The whole bridge exploded, sending rock and rubble into the air, splashing down into the water. Raining like hail onto the hunkered down soldiers. Body parts of the infected, even two alphas were thrown into bloody pieces. The creatures began jumping into the water, swimming for the cove. The western wall began picking up fire once they noticed the water was now packed with frantic swimming infected. They were on the shore fairly quickly. Claymores and several other explosives were set off by trip wires, and command ignitions set on the walls.

Felix was swimming toward the island as fast as he could. A boat rumbling behind him slowed as he turned to take the ride. The sun was blocking the figure, but he could tell it was a female. Her long thick hair was blowing in the breeze as the sun climbed the horizon behind her.

She pulled him onto the boat with much difficulty. Water splashed around them. She had tears in her eyes, speechless, and although Felix was sober, he lost focus to his task. He had longed for this day since the first night all of this started. Now finally, she was there in front of him. Her face pressed against his chest, her arms wrapped around him tightly, as if she was never going to let him go.

"You're alive," she choked through tears.

"I am now," he replied. She pulled away, looking him over.

"You have more gray in your hair," she giggled, running her fingers down the sides of his head.

She ran her fingers over his scruff, "I always liked your scruffy face."

He wrapped his arms around her. "I've missed you, horrifically," he said softly.

She stood on her toes to kiss him. The entire world fell away. The gunshots were small pops in the background. The explosions, little thuds, the only thing he could see and hear was her. He could stay like this.

It was the howl that called him back to reality. They pulled away from each other and looked on. Tracer rounds skipped off of concrete and buildings, in and out of the feral and alphas.

He turned, holding her face, looking deep into her eyes.

"Take me to the docks, I have to kill her. If I don't, then they will have won."

"Who will have won?"

"The people that started all of this."

She nodded as she broke into tears. She kissed him once more. He wiped her tears from her face with his thumbs. He followed her into the cabin, she rocked the throttle to full and they sped toward the docks. After all, she had to start transporting people off the docks to the destroyer. The boat butted up to the docks, and Felix jumped off.

"Felix!" she ran after him as impatient families rushed onto the boat. He turned, and she leapt at him. One more kiss before he left her again.

"Promise me, you'll come back," she said.

"I'll be back, babe. And after this, we can disappear somewhere away from everyone and everything."

She beat her fist against his chest, it was marble to her callused hands. "Promise me."

He gently put his hands on her cheeks looking into her eyes.

"I promise."

He turned, and disappeared through the crowd. She ran back to the ship, spun it around, looking back, fumbling. One of the men on the boat with her took the wheel and drove the ship. She sat against the wall, her head buried in her knees, trying to pull herself together.

"That was unfair of me to ask him to make such a promise," she wondered.

This was the first time in nearly six years that she had heard anything about him, or even had a chance to see him. She had thought for many years that he probably got killed in a fight. After all, this was the world he ultimately wanted, and rarely ever backed down from an adversary. As crazy as it sounded to her, she never thought that he would actually get it. This world. He probably found a younger, stronger woman, had a few kids, and forgot about her. But none of that mattered. She just wanted to know that the man she loved, who loved her in return, no more and no less, was alive.

And he was. She smacked her cheeks, wiped her tears away, and took the wheel.

"Was that him, the man you had been waiting for?" the man asked, standing next to her.

"Yes."

"You two have to be the only ones I have ever seen reunite since the world ended."

She didn't respond, she was having enough trouble as-is keeping her emotions together. After all, she had a job to do, and she would do it, as he would do his, and after everything was said and done, they would leave, together. As they wanted long before they were torn apart. She just hoped that his love of this world wouldn't take him away from her again. Deep down, she had a feeling that it would.

Samantha and Britney looked at each other, then walked toward Sasha.

"You know, Sasha, it's been a long time."

Sasha turned. Spotting Britney and Samantha.

"You two were in Fort Monroe the whole time?"

"I feel terrible, I'm so sorry I didn't know you were just across the water this whole time," Britney apologized.

"It's okay, we need to get these people to safety, we can talk about this later," Sasha replied.

"So where are we going?" Sasha asked.

Felix was dumbfounded by her. She's in a sundress with an interesting print of vines and flowers. She pushed her glasses up the bridge of her nose. Her hair was brushed and straight, coming down to just the small of her back. A small leather woven belt for no reason other than accessorizing the dress, tight to her small waist. Her strong legs looked so inviting that he just wanted to touch her. The dress came to just above her knees.

"You going to answer my question, or stand there like a weirdo?" she said after a few moments. She knew why, she thought it was cute. Such a hard man so easily distracted, but why was he so distracted by her? What did he see in her that she didn't? It really didn't matter.

"Wherever the road takes us," he finally replied.

"Did I lose you there for a moment?" she asked as he opened the door for her.

"Yes, you did. You look absolutely gorgeous, Sasha; I honestly have no words for it."

"You're being ridiculous. This is just an old dress I got while I was in Vietnam with family."

"Culturally sound too, starting to sound like the complete package, well-traveled, independent, beautiful, and a smart ass," he replied. She laughed. He closed the door and skirted the front of the car, jumping in.

They pulled out of the driveway. It was getting close to midnight by the time they stopped for gas. They had to have seen several small towns, everything was closed so it was just a late-night sightseeing trip. He jumped back in the car; she was singing almost every song he had playing from his odd mix of music. He couldn't believe it; how many she knew and was harmoniously enhancing. He loved her voice. It soothed him.

"So, this is your plan, still trying to take me out into the woods and leave me?" she teased.

"Still going on about that?"

"Just know, if you do, I'll come find you and dump you out here."

He laughed, she laughed.

Felix started to slow down. "Look at that," he said.

"Yeah, the dog?" she replied. He shot her a curious look, eyebrow raised, and a hilarious smile.

"The dog?" he asked.

"You know what I mean, the deer."

He burst into laughter, as they slowly continued down the back road somewhere in central Texas. They had to stop; the deer were spilling onto the road. There had to have been a hundred out there. She grabbed a hold of his arm and leaned her head on his shoulder. They watched for a good while, content, the radio was low, and the moon was bright. The deer moved across the street from each side of the thick forest.

"What a perfect night," she said with a sigh of content.

Chapter 25
Hellhound

Gavin was firing from cover, nearly exhausting his combat load. Magazines, shell casing piled up at his feet. The smell of carbon, burning flesh, blood, dirt, it put the biggest smile anyone had seen on his face since Felix showed up months ago.

The feral are being cut down by the heavy machine gun fire from the fortified positions along the north side of the wall. Hundreds of dead floated in the bay, serving as buoyant platforms for their pack to crawl over. The water once blue green, was now red. Their blood filled the bay as the guns sent heavy streams and walls of led into the horde. Their bodies began to fill the bay, making it easier for the creatures to get across since the bridge that was now but rubble ruins protruding from the red glassy surface.

An alpha leaped over the wall. The beast's jaws sagged with skin; steam rose out of its mouth. A group of soldiers slowly stepped backward as the beast flinched from the bullets barely piercing its thick saggy skin. The alpha, sprints at them, sliding to a grinding halt, vomiting all over the poor souls. The acid that washed over the group like a waterfall, burnt and ate at their very flesh. The screams were muffled by choking gargling sounds of their *own* flesh as they slumped over, sinking into a pile of yellow red and peach soup.

Gavin's face was twisted in disgust. He ripped a grenade launcher from a nearby soldier who just loaded a round. He took aim and fired. The round exploded, throwing the limp leg across the street. The beast screamed as it crawled with its two front legs. Whimpering, crying bloody murder as it dragged its intestines across the concrete behind its exposed hips and skin torn right leg.

Gavin tossed the launcher back to the young man, just barely a teenager. The boy watched as Gavin pulled a grenade from his belt, he pulled another soldier from the wall. She was scared, picking her helmet up off her sweaty forehead. He pointed with the grenade.

"Take this, and go shove it up that thing's ass, stay away from its fucking fluids, they are acid."

She nodded, taking the grenade from him. She hopped down from the wall, falling on her side. Once up, motivated by Gavin's mocking and irritated derogatory terms toward her, she ran over to the screaming beast. She pulled the pin, threw the grenade, and then scurried back toward her original post.

The sea of feral started piling up around the walls. The living creatures were now having to scale the dead wall in order to get to the Fort's strong old walls. The moat around the fort was now filled to the brim with dead, making their attempt to infiltrate that much easier.

Isaac was helping boat load after boat load of people. They seemed to never end. Mitch waited on a ledge over the pedestrian walkway for more signals to initiate their final defensive measure. He was stricken with awe, the numbers alone made them seem like angry ants rushing another anthill.

Oh my God! was all Mitch could think.

Alex was next to him; taking impressive shots down the road as some of the infected got past their barricades. Every round he shot from his .338 Lapua killed their target. Impressive puffs of pink mist shot out of their heads as the infected rolled to a bloody stop on the pavement.

"Nice shot, man," Mitch said laughing coldly at the impressive skill.

"I try," Alex replied sarcastically. Taking another shot. Killing another infected.

"Alright, Mitch, I'll see you at the docks, I need a better position."

Mitch went to shake his hand. Alex pulled him in for a hug. And just like that Alex ran down the eastern wall to set up.

Chris was yelling commands to the soldiers on the western wall, now that Gavin was on the northern wall. The creatures had split into two advancing formations. Flanking them to the north where the main effort was. The queen was in the middle of the massive group. She sat patiently watching the infected attempt to overtake the wall. Still hundreds of thousands at her back waiting to move on her command. For one reason or another, she kept them at bay, when they could have easily washed over the fort by now.

*****

The colonel's cell rang. The number read "Unknown." The hallway was empty as all her subordinates either left for the docks or were on the walls holding off the infection so that the rest could escape. The hospital was nearly empty. The food storages and medical storages had all been moved during the night onto the docks. Along with anything else they needed that could be transported.

She answered the phone.

"Monica?" the voice called to her. A familiar voice. It was the general.

"Yes, ma'am."

"You have 45 minutes before impact, consider it a professional courtesy. Also, be advised to stay away from the north, there is an armada standing by to capture your destroyer. I would head south if I were you."

The general hung up before Monica could utter the words to her. But Monica assumed she knew what she was going to say. Taking a risk to warn them like that would certainly sentence her to death. Monica set the phone down on the desk and walked out of the office. A detail of her finest soldiers stood by, alert, fearful, waiting for her.

"You ready, ma'am, we are nearly finished with the evacuation."

"Send out my last order as your commander to everyone left alive."

"Ready, ma'am."

"We have 35 minutes before the missile hits, get everyone to the boats. Have Mitch initiate the final defensive measure in fifteen minutes or whenever the opportunity if the infection should reach the docks."

The four soldiers scattered, running in four different directions. They each found their marks. Yelling up to them the time left, which was about 27 minutes now. Mitch started moving down to help with the last of the medical personnel. The boats on the docks had made several turns. All eight of the boats were now waiting for the last group to board.

*****

Monica yelled to Felix as she noticed him running toward the northern wall.

He slid to a stop, looking for the origin of the voice.

"Glad they didn't kill you," she yelled.

"I don't have time for your shit right now, what do you want?"

She looked at her watch. "We have about twenty minutes until a missile strike reaches us. Don't fuck around with them too much. We will all be waiting for you."

Felix gave her a lazy thumbs up before continuing to move toward the north wall. He noticed that the soldiers had started bounding in large groups off of the walls. All running past him. The feral slowly made their way over after them. Gavin was still on the northern wall on a machine gun. Chris was next him, the .50 caliber barrel nearly melting off.

"You ready?" Chris yelled in between their burst of fire.

"Go ahead, I got you, fucker!" Gavin replied.

Chris tossed grenades and fired from a revolving cylinder grenade launcher until all six tubes were empty. He tossed it. The rounds landed in the sea of raging infected, throwing splashes of body parts and blood from the explosions.

Felix rushed, leaping onto the wall, landing next to Gavin. Chris didn't see him jump over him on his way down.

"Thought you were dead!" Gavin roared as Felix fired from his shotgun.

"You will be if you don't get the fuck out of here!" Felix yelled back. The two were laughing.

"Not yet! I'm not done yet," Gavin replied hatefully.

"Let's go. Fuck them!" Felix yelled after reloading his shotgun. Gavin tossed grenade after grenade into the rising pile of writhing infected as they climbed the walls.

The two jumped down and sprinted toward the walkway at the south end.

Alex was positioned by Mitch once again, the last of the soldiers had made it down toward the docks. The last of the people were now out of the base. All of them running toward the south eastern walkway.

"Is that Felix?" Mitch asked.

"I can't believe it, he really came back, he was shot in the face, how the hell is he alive?" Alex asked as he pulled the trigger, killing another feral that made it over the wall. To his disgust in the fact that he merely was doing little to nothing. "This is fucking useless," Alex said tossing the rifle into the moat.

"Hey, Chris!" Alex yelled pointing.

Chris stopped, looking back. Gavin and Felix were running as the horde poured over the wall.

The infected were surrounding them, Alex and Mitch climbed down, Chris yelled to Gavin and Felix to hurry their fat asses up. Chris turned and ran through the walkway.

"Chris!" Gavin yelled.

Chris turned back.

"Blow it, tell Mitch to blow it!" Gavin yelled.

Gavin slowed down breathing heavily, realizing that they weren't going to make it. Felix slowed with him.

"Drowning, right?" Felix asked, lighting two cigarettes.

"Yeah, fuck it, it has been our time for a long time. They deserve to get on that ark, not us."

Felix handed Gavin a lit smoke.

"You know, man, I would do it all over again. Maybe, would've come to find you guys sooner."

"Did you see her?" Gavin asked, finally catching his breath. The feral had slowed their assault from the sound of a horrific roar that echoed from the north.

"You knew?" Felix asked.

"Yeah, she came with the crew to meet with Monica this morning. I'm glad you finally found what you were looking for," Gavin replied.

Felix laughed, patting his friend on the back. "Yeah, looks like I have to break my promise again. And it would seem, we have become worth the attention of the queen."

"What?"

Felix nodded to the north. Gavin turned to see her leap effortlessly over the wall. The feral merely following underfoot like a bunch of aimless puppies. The queen walked out into the open, staring down the two men. She huffed a low growl. One of her alphas sprinted for the hospital, crashing through the building. Moments later, Gavin watched the alpha appear out of the smashed building with the pregnant feral female. She looked as if she was about to go into labor right there. The queen never took her eyes off of Felix. Nor did he take his eyes from hers.

"I thought they took that thing to the north when they took your dead ass?"

Felix laughed, "Guess fucking not. It seems we have some snakes yet to deal with in the garden."

Felix began to walk toward that beautiful hyena.

"Where the fuck are you going, fuck face?" Gavin demanded.

"I'm going to fuck her in the face with this badass shotgun," Felix stopped and turned toward his friend. "I need you to do me a favor, will ya?"

Gavin walked over to him; his very steps demonstrated his irritation.

"No, motherfucker, you don't get to go to hell without me."

Felix laughed. "Alright, man, when Mitch blows the shit out of this place, I'm going to shoot the pregnant one, and the queen is going to come kill me. Just do what you do best. Kill everything you can, try not to die on your knees."

"Let's go, then, cocksucker," Gavin replied.

Felix laughed. Gavin didn't know, but Felix had no intentions of letting him die today.

*****

Mitch, Chris, and Alex were running to the docks. Mitch flipped the rest of the switches and pressed the ignition. The explosions never came, he clicked

356

the button several times producing no effects. Chris saw several feral standing in the middle of the street; it scares him. He reacted with firing several rounds into the creatures, killing a few by pure luck. The rest did not react or even care, they were moving toward the walls now. Dumbfounded, the group slowed to a stopped. Several people were still waiting on the docks for the last turn of the ships to arrive. The previous eight couldn't hold anymore, and there was still about 20 people left.

"What the fuck is wrong with it?" Alex asked spilling his irritation through his tone.

Chris took it from Mitch, flipping randomly and pressing every button on the controller. Nothing was producing results. Mitch snatched it back out of Chris's tired hands.

"The battery is dead."

"Fuck!" Chris replied.

"We gotta get to the boat, we can wait for Felix and Gavin there. If they are still alive."

*****

Felix and Gavin passed a flask back and forth as they came to terms with the situation at hand. They could hear the rocket's engines popping and crackling in the distance. They had a few minutes max before it hit, they were not getting out of this alive.

Felix took aim, when the pregnant infected fell onto all fours, catching his attention to full interest. He lowered his weapon as the beast screamed and moaned on the parade field. The entire horde seemed to draw in to see, to watch the miracle before them. The queen walked over, nudging her with her large nose, like a mother checking her pups.

The feral woman, no more a woman, rather a werewolf if anything. Hair covered her entire body; a small tail had been produced some years ago wagged nervously. Her snout was elongated several inches further from her face than most, and her legs were very similar to a dog's. She was the most mutated infected they had ever lay witness to.

Blood and amniotic fluid spilled from her uterus, and out a screaming thing plunged into the world. Felix and Gavin stepped closer, attempting to gain a better visual of the birth before them. The noise coming from that thing pierced their ears like needles.

The queen rose her head and began to howl, and so did the horde. It was teeth rattling. The people on the docks started whimpering, crying, the sound was so frightening that even Chris, Alex, and Mitch had to pull back.

357

"I guess they finally reproduced. After only six years."

"Well, what are you thinking, brother?" Gavin replied.

Felix shook his head. "I'm starting to think, my friend, that maybe we should just let them be."

*****

"No, Felix, we need to stop it all."

Felix nodded with grin. "I just wish it wasn't these things, I could've been at peace if it was just humans. Not these things that don't have a choice, they just are." It began to war within in what they honestly should do.

The boat crept into view, still several hundred meters away. Only one, the others were nowhere in sight. The howling stopped, and the missile drew near. Felix looked at everything, really looking, breathing it in, if sight was a breath.

Gavin stood there next to him, ready to die, whatever resolution he had come to was settled. His oldest friend. His best friend, even after so many years they were still like brothers. He looked at the queen, the hyena, and saw the reason. Why, after all this time? It was never really about what it started as, the pandemic, the people who set off the bombs. It wasn't just some infection that continued to eat away at the very people who created it. They were all safe in bunkers, it wasn't even about the creatures killing the humans. It was about the pack. The family. The queen was attempting to protect her own. Her children. As any mother would.

It dawned on him, an epiphany if anything. He nodded as the thought rolled through his mind. That they were now just trying to exist. Just like them. Maybe it really was time that the humans lost, and just let Mother Nature have this world. For all their writhing and suffering they were very powerless against themselves and her. That's what was happening before him, their own attempts to control the world and Mother Nature, playing God, it was their biggest downfall.

"You wanna save the world. Or save the human race?" he said out loud.

Gavin squinted his eyes at Felix, attempting to figure out what madness was coming over his friend.

"To save the world, you eradicate humanity; to save humanity, you eradicate Mother. And then, we both die. It's a lose-lose situation, no matter how we look at it," Felix answered his own question.

"What are you thinking?" Gavin asked.

Felix walked around in front of his friend, his back to the creatures, the infected, the future. He put his hand on Gavin's plate carrier, taking hold of both of the shoulder straps.

"Brother?"

Gavin saw the intent in Felix's eyes, he began to pull away, but was powerless against Felix's strong grip. After all, he wasn't normal anymore.

"No, you motherfucker, you don't get to have this, you are not taking this away from me!" Gavin punched as hard as he could. It was like punching a marble wall. His knuckles were bleeding after the second strike.

"They need you, brother, they always needed you, you are the one to lead these fucking people, just do one thing for me."

"Fuck you, you piece of shit!" Gavin yelled at his friend, now attempting to buckle his strong arms.

"Tell Sasha I love her, and always have, and I'm sorry."

"Fuck you. Tell her your fucking self!"

"Goodbye, brother, we had a good run."

"No!" Gavin yelled. Felix stepped to the side, turning a full way around whirling, throwing Gavin toward the water.

Gavin flew through the air, screaming obscenities toward his brother. Calling him everything under the sun, except late for dinner. Gavin disappeared over the old wall.

Felix nodded at his well-placed throw; satisfied as it looked to have cleared the land as well. "Alright, now that I don't have to worry about his ass…"

Felix cracked his fingers by wrenching each hand as if he had claws, then his neck.

"Alright, girl."

*****

Gavin splashed down, and for a moment as he looked up into the sky through the dark water, he thought to himself how much he hated Felix at this moment. The sun was cutting through the water in glorious beams of light that he admitted was beautiful. But his hatred for the moment wouldn't let him for a second enjoy it. He felt betrayed, and didn't know what to do anymore. What could he do, Felix saved his life, but did he really save him in the end?

Get on the Ark, or drown in the flood? played in his mind, and he hated Felix for not letting him drown in the flood.

*****

The queen looked up toward the missile, it was nearly there now. She barked so loud that every single feral and alpha left alive could hear her order. Like an angry mound of ants, they began piling on top of her and the new born creature. The entire army of feral began building a living dome on top of their queen and the other surviving alphas. Felix watched as it grew higher and higher. Within a minute it was already a squirming mountain of living creatures. She was truly something else, he thought. She just used the entire infected army of mutated humans to shield her and the others from the missile.

"Well fuck." Felix laughed out, plugging his ears with his fingers.

The missile struck. Felix watched it. The explosion was powerful, knocking him down and back. Bodies shot out in all directions, hundreds of thousands of them. The people on the docks were knocked over. Waves jarred and jerked the boats on the water violently. The pillar of smoke rose and rolled into a gorgeous mushroom cloud as it snaked its way high into the sky.

Bodies began to fall into sloppy messes with wet thuds. Blood began to rain down, painting the entire ruins of Fort Monroe in crimson. The water was now slicked with blood and dead pieces of the fleshy shield. Felix crawled from a pile of dead. He spat up blood. His vision was blurring, his head was splitting like a log under a heavy axe. The concussion from the blast definitely damaged his organs, and if he was lucky, he may be able to kill her and the newborn before he bled to death internally.

He stood, drawing his weapon. He fired at the remaining pile of living infected. The small explosions threw body parts and pieces from the still sizable shield, although most of their insides were mush from the blast. He loaded the particle battery shell into his shotgun. Pressing the bolt locking mechanism, he took aim. He could see her head rising from the pile, infected bodies fell from her like rag dolls. He pulled the trigger. The shell whined like a turbine. A full three seconds went by, nothing had produced from the cartridge other than noise. He unshouldered the weapon to unlock the bolt. The weapon fired. The beam, thin and brilliantly neon green, walked violently across the ruins of Fort Monroe for a fraction of a second, catching the grass and ruble on fire.

Felix strained to keep hold of the weapon; even though it lasted for not even a second. Smoke rolled from the end of the barrel as its glowing white metal began to cool to its black metallic self once more.

"Holy fuck," he said out loud.

He looked up, the queen's ears are pinned back, her massive teeth were bared as her growl shook the ground. Her pack, even the alphas scurried in fear from her path, the few that still lived anyway. Her ears suddenly picked up. She sniffed, her head began to move back and forth as she frantically searched the piles of dead around her. She nudged with her nose, throwing dead piles over like a wave. She found what she was looking for. The new born. Lifeless. She nudged the pup with her nose. The creature's gray and blue fur was matted with its mother's blood. The pup was dead. The queen let out a whimpering cry that Felix nor anyone had ever heard. He could feel the sorrow in her call. The infected all around her began to whine and express the very emotion she was portraying.

She began to draw in a deep breath. It sounded of a furnace and light began to flicker from within her jaws. The crackling of thunder exploded through the air. The sky was bright and clear and beautifully blue. She heaved, and a brilliant white beam lit the ground before her, on fire, crashing the world with thunder. She heaved again, and another steady beam cut into the ground. Everything in her beam's path caught fire just the same as Felix's weapon.

"No fucking way," he said in disbelief. She looked up. And for a moment, Felix felt he saw her smile at him. As if she understood what she just did. The smile, that grin, quickly became hatred as she roared at him.

The walls of Fort Monroe were blown over, buildings were reduced to rubble around him, trees were knocked down. A few buildings and vehicles were on fire in the distance. Felix loaded the next shell. Now that he knew how to use it, and hopefully this one did more than just flicker and catch some shit on fire. Maybe this time, he would actually fucking aim it properly, he thought to himself.

The queen barked her orders once again, whooping as hyenas do. The horde, like a stampede, charged Felix in a very convenient funnel. He loaded his last shell in the tube, he sheathed the shotgun and drew his two pistols. He let the remaining few get closer. Only a few alphas and maybe fifty feral survived the blast from what he could count. The alphas looked badly injured and didn't pose that much of a problem to him for the moment.

Felix fired, his two revolvers sounded like a machine gun as their heavy rounds tore through the faces and chests of the infected. Each round yielded at least two deaths and injured another behind their screaming shields. He reloaded with the speed loaders. Firing again, they were within arm's reach now. He drew the shotgun. He spun, chopping and lopping an infected's head clean from its body. He wielded the weapon like a club. He swung, breaking another's neck. He kicked another, sending it skipping across the ground. He stepped forward, striking another in the chest, the sternum cracked and the creature let out a hellish cry. He backhanded another. He elbowed the next. He drew his pistols once more, firing wildly. Every round hit their mark. He took off running. Holstering one pistol to reload the other, then doing the same, until both guns were up and ready once more. He slid to a stop, firing. Two alphas knocked the remaining four or five infected down. Charging for Felix, he jumped out of the way. The beast's thick bone-like armored skull rammed into a pile of rubble. Felix pulled a grenade and tossed under the beast's hindlegs.

Several seconds later; that beast was slumped to the ground, head still lodged in the concrete.

The second alpha bit onto Felix's legs and whipped him into the air. The bite hurt, but luckily, for some reason, the beast's bite didn't penetrate his skin. Felix dropped one of his pistols as he hit the ground hard, rolling back onto his feet he stood ready as the giant beast chased after him. The ground was being thrown in clumps as the giant's large paws pressed off the surface, lurching the beast toward him. Its long tongue flapped to the side of its long thin snout.

Felix took aim, firing, the second round struck the beast's eye. It missed its footing on the forward step, crashing hard onto the concrete, biting its own tongue off. The beast writhed and thrashed about, throwing splashes of blood. The blood wet out a fire burning from a vehicle's engine. Felix tossed another grenade; it landed rolling under its head. The grenade went off, the beast fell limp.

"I'm running out of time," he said, spitting blood.

The sound of heavy footsteps coming fast from behind caught his attention. Felix turned; the hyena, the queen, jerked her head to the side. With one swift movement, Felix was launched from the ground a hundred feet, crashing down, bouncing off the concrete into a pile of rubble.

"Motherfucker," he said as he winced, struggling to his feet.

She was already on top of him, coming down with her feet. She stomped him with both massive paws, once, twice, the ground was cracking as he was shoved into the broken street. Blood coughed up from his lungs. He was running out of time, indeed. She barked; her breath was like a gust of hot air from a tornado. It pushed rubble and debris from around them. She began to press her nose into his chest as she growled louder and louder. Blood was spilling from the side of his mouth. Her jaws began to flicker, he could feel the heat. He could smell his clothes about to catch fire.

He pulled a small push knife from his belt and stuck her in the nose with all his might. She waivered for a moment. With much difficulty, Felix managed to raise himself off the ground and punched as hard as he could. He landed the blow on the top of her nose. Her head bounced off the ground as she buckled from the force of the blow.

Felix fell to his knees. She was back up onto her paws, she nipped at him. He rolled away, narrowly escaping. He picked up a sprint, drawing his shotgun. She chased after him, nipping as if she was after a cleverly agile cat.

Felix landed on top of a large pile of rubble and saw the last of the people rushing onto the boats. Through the smoke, he saw his woman helping them on to her boat. She was the only brave one to come back for the rest. For a moment he recalled one of the many reasons why he loved her so deeply. She was a far better person than he ever was, she showed him things about himself that he never knew. *And there she is, still waiting for him. But it can't be, after all this time, and he was so close, he could just run to them. He could just say fuck it and leave with them.*

He turned and could see that the hyena, the queen, had noticed something. The way he was looking at the people on the docks. She no longer cared about Felix, and had set her brilliant sights on the only thing that could hurt Felix now. The very thing that she lost; she would take from him. His future.

"Wow, this place is gorgeous." Sasha said.

"I thought our first date should be a hike, I really suck at dates, so I'm sorry if this is not your thing, but I like it, so I gave it a shot," Felix said, shutting the door on his car.

"No, I would rather do this than go to some restaurant or movie. It's beautiful out."

Felix laughed.

"What are you laughing at?" she asked.

"We are wearing almost the same thing," he said.

"Oh, god, I didn't even realize that, why didn't you say something earlier?"

"I just noticed it," he said as he continued to laugh, she joined in for the moment.

The pair were dressed the same. Both wearing shorts, hers tight against her butt, and he was doing everything he could not to stare. She was wearing a black tank top. He was wearing a black T-shirt.

They pressed on, walking through the trail into Chalk Ridge Falls. Only few people were on the trail this early in the morning. It was quiet, and peaceful. The two didn't talk much as they treaded the trails in search of the waterfalls.

No need to, they were enjoying the air, the forest, the small streams they treaded over. Before long, their twists and turns landed them somewhat lost. But they didn't care, or at least Felix didn't. He was busy enjoying her beauty.

"Aren't you supposed to be some smart army guy," she teased.

"Who, me, nonsense," he replied.

"Can't you find the trail back to where we started?"

"You wanna head back?" he asked.

"No, I'm enjoying myself, but it looks like it's going to rain. So, if you don't mind following a woman, I'm going to take lead."

He held out his hand, stepping to the side, gesturing her to lead the way. She walked on, head held high.

They trod through brush on a small trail. It began to sprinkle, and then soon it turned into rain. They crossed a stream, and headed further into the forest.

"You take me on a date to a park, and then get us lost, just so you can leave me out here stranded. I see your plan. Can't fool me, mister."

Felix laughed. "Oh yeah? And what reason would I want to strand you out here, what gain would I get from that?"

"I don't know, seems plausible to me."

"And what do you mean I got us lost?" he said. He could hear her giggling up front.

She turned back, and caught his eyes looking at her bottom.

"And what are you staring at?" she asked with a crooked smile of perversion on her face.

"Nothing, just daydreaming," he replied, knowing full well he was caught.

"How about you take the lead, Mr. Army dude," she said, comically gesturing for him to take the lead.

He did, and they continued on, further into the forest, they were both soaked, but it was warm, and beautiful. A sun shower had washed over the green and made the colors of the forest more vibrant. The two had forgotten that there was a waterfall somewhere in this park.

Felix scaled a slippery hill impressively, Sasha thought. He stood on top of it, holding his hand out, waiting to help her up. But he didn't know, she didn't need any help. So, she darted up it, impressively, Felix thought. Just before he turned to press on, she began to slip back down the steep slick hill. He turned, catching her hand, and with one stroke he pulled her up, into him. She hit his chest hard, and for a moment, they were holding each other.

"We should get out of the rain," she said.

"Agreed," he replied, letting her go.

The two continued through the forest. They lost track of time, talking, laughing, slipping down hills, the two were covered in mud and wet from the warm rain. Felix admired her comfortable nature, in nature. She had mud smeared across her face, and he said nothing. He didn't know that he did too, and she wasn't going to tell him.

They finally reached the edge of the forest to find that they had walked so far out of the park, they ended up on a hill overlooking a plot of land. They skirted the forest until they found an open break to the other side.

"Oh my god," she said.

A rainbow cut the sky; the rain drowned it out. They were standing on top of the cliff face overlooking the entire park below. She climbed down to the edge and sat on a rock. Felix slowly walked down to her, sitting on the other side of the rock, next to her. They sat there quietly, peacefully. The rain finally stopped. The cactus all around them was brilliantly green, its white and yellow spines pointing in small clusters.

The climb down was quick. They made it back to the car, Felix looked at his watch, she checked her phone. They had been hiking for three hours.

"Do you have a shirt or something, I think I have cactus or stickers all over my shirt," she asked.

"Hold one minute, I think I have something here."

He checked the back seat, the trunk. He found a green and black large head wrap.

"Is this a headwrap, like from Afghanistan?" she asked.

"Why yes, yes, it is. Very useful piece of fabric, very survival friendly, and right now, it will be put to a far better use I think," he replied.

"I haven't used a bandana as a top in so long, I probably can't even do it anymore."

Felix turned around as she pulled off her shirt. Lighting a soggy cigarette. She smiled as she tied it around her. She stood up. He turned to see, and he couldn't believe how something so simple could look so good.

"Alright, what's next?" she asked.

"I don't know, this is all I really had planned, this and lunch, where would you want to go?" he asked.

"Anywhere is fine," she replied.

"Alright, fatty food it is."

"First we need to shower…separately. And you have mud on your face," she said.

He laughed.

"So do you."

Chapter 26
Good Boy

"Is this everyone?" Sasha called out to the gracious passengers scurrying aboard the tug boat.

The boat was rocking harshly against the docks as she stood there after the last person boarded.

A man out of breath called her attention. "No, we are waiting for Felix!" Alex yelled.

She turned, searching frantically. The boat started pulling away. One of her crew began to drive away, he didn't care if everyone was on board, just that they needed to leave before they were all killed.

Alex realized who she was, wide-eyed, he limped to her, grabbing her arms before she could jump off the boat. "Get your hands off me!" she snapped back, jerking away in vain.

"He said he was coming; he will be here. Sasha, it's me, stop, stop it. It's okay," Alex attempted to calm her. But it only made her more furious.

"Get your hands off of me!" she yelled, pulling her weapon from her holster.

Alex backed away, his hands up.

A flickering green beam cut out of the fort and through the city to the south of the bay, buildings, trees, the very rock caught fire. Everyone was murmuring in shock, disbelieving onlookers could only stare, it looked like something out of a *Star Wars* film to most of them. The buzzing noise echoed through their ears. A tall building in the city toppled over as a few more buildings deeper inside along the path of the beam followed suit. Dust and dark, thick smoke rose from the Hamptons; all of it, south and west were on fire, and Fort Monroe was merely ruins. Second and third explosions continued along the path of the beam.

The boat was drifting further and further away until they picked up speed, headed toward the destroyer. She saw it, as she white-knuckle gripped the side of the boat's railing, tears of anger streaming down her dirty cheeks. The queen was sprinting full force, sliding to a stop. Clawing up parts of the deck as she nearly slid into the water.

The screams and cries of fear had warned the driver of the boat to speed up, but as he cranked on the accelerator, the tank ran empty. The crew, the scared passengers started murmuring in pity for themselves. Some prayed, some sat speaking of hopelessness.

Standing on the docks, the queen knew it was too far for her to leap. Instead, she drew in a deep breath. The fire danced behind her, ash rose into the air, reminding everyone of the first days of the end of their worlds. The driver of the boat rushed to the back to pull fuel cans from their cages.

The roaring of a furnace grew as the beast was about to throw her white-hot beam across the water at them. There was nothing any of them could do. Sasha relaxed and watched, Alex, Chris, Mitch stood around her. The world fell quiet.

"He never stopped searching for you," Alex said.

She nodded, tears rolling down her puffy cheeks as she waited for their end. She wiped them away, sniffing, standing tall.

Cowards jumped over the side of the boat, swimming away. Only one swam toward the boat. Furious, cursing the whole way. Not even sharks possessed as much violence that this man was dragging with him.

"You should know he kept a picture of you two with him everywhere he went," Alex continued. She held her composure even though the tears continued to stream down her face like liquid diamonds.

Suddenly, she heard him yelling, flying through the air, the dog fired her beam. Felix crashed down, hard; his body landed on her head. He had her by the ears as his legs swung and planted on the deck, ripping her head to the side with great difficulty. As if he was trying to wrestle a bull to the ground.

The beam boiled the water along its path, drawing a steaming line in the ocean toward the floating shanty of boats. Several boats exploded in small fireballs, setting several others on fire. The beam burnt some of the swimming crew members headed for the floating city.

Felix grunted; the dog's beam discharged and flickered out. Felix gripped tighter as she hopped on the deck from side to side, shaking with all her might. He was lifted off the ground, but he never let go. He managed to land a perfectly timed kick into her leg, she flipped to the side as her front legs spun out from under her. He pinned her down. She growled viciously. More and more infected began to slowly stir from the ruins of the Fort onto the beach. Survivors that were just knocked down from the explosion. It would be a matter of moments before he could do nothing, Felix knew.

He looked up, and he could see Sasha. Standing on the end of the tug boat. She was watching him, that was his woman. The waves rolled under the boat. She stared back at him.

"I'm sorry, babe," he said aloud. The beast's eyes never shook from his, Felix looked down at the beast's, meeting her eyes.

"I can't let you take them," Felix grunted as the queen roared and jerked. "WE ARE FIGHTING THE WRONG ONES!"

*****

"That motherfucking piece of shit, goddamn that cocksucker, I'm going to kill him when I see his ass again!" Gavin roared in anger as water splashed off of him as he climbed into the boat. He violently pushed away the people helping him. He snatched a weapon from an awestricken bystander pushing them to the side. He saw Sasha and pushed it against her. She took it without taking her eyes off of Felix and the queen.

Gavin grabbed another weapon from another man. "How about you stop being a bitch and fire, motherfucker!" Gavin roared in the scared man's face, punching the man, breaking his nose, Gavin spat in his direction before shouldering the rifle.

"Fucking shoot something!" he yelled again, this time at everyone else on the deck.

Machine gun fire picked up. Gavin, Chris, Alex, and Mitch had taken weapons from the people on the boat and began firing at the creatures running down the beach; attempting to aid their queen. Magazine after magazine were being handed to the four men firing.

Sasha shoulders her rifle and exhales slowly. She takes aim, standing, holding it as steady as she could. "My crazy man," she whispered.

She fired.

The round struck the queen right between her eyes. Pink mist sprayed into the air. The bullet skipped off her skull.

"Nice fucking shot," Gavin yelled through the talking of their fire. By now, everyone on the deck had begun firing into the crowd of infected survivors as they ran for the docks.

Felix released the grip from one side of her head with his right hand. In a blur, he drew the shotgun, he had one shot since she was stunned from Sasha's bullet. He swung downward, cracking her in the side of her skull as she attempted to right herself up. The deck buckled under them, barely holding their weight, she whelped. He stepped back, pulling the trigger. The weapon began to whine that high-pitched noise. She lurched forward and bit down on his arm holding the weapon. One of her teeth punctured his artery under his arm and he felt it.

The weapon fired. She whimpered in a hellish screech, her head turned back, the beam cut along her mouth down the left side of her body. It cut deep, her fur burnt and smoldered. She swung her massive head back, rolling it sideways and she clamped down on his torso. Her teeth punctured his neck, chest, and thighs.

*****

Justin and his family watched as the beam flickered through the morning sky just out of the mouth of Subtropolis. Bill and Monique sat on a porch drinking coffee as it cut into the reaching blue. John and his family on the boat, they all watched the beam. Mesmerized at the green thin flash that was gone as quickly as it had come. People, survivors, the facility to the north, everyone watched it cut across the sky who were outside that morning. Kids playing in a walled-off community all stopped to gawk as their parents frantically called for them to come inside. The sky for a moment was a mix of blue, yellow, and green. The beam hit the Moon before finally disappearing, the morning was quiet again. The Moon began to turn, and with it a piece was cleaved from it.

*****

Felix and the queen fell on the deck; her on her side and him on his back. Felix bleeding out, the queen burnt and fried on one side, bleeding and breathing heavily. The weapon bounced off the broken wood into the water. Both looked into each other's eyes as they lay in their own blood. He rolled onto his side and crawled toward her. She rose her head, but it was so heavy, she fell back onto the deck. Blood soaked the side of her thick matted hair.

Felix pulled himself up turning to sit back against her. She allowed it, she was tired, content, and ready. He watched the boat drift further and further away, another boat in the distance was advancing toward the stranded tug boat. His right arm felt her matted fur as he gently petted her. He ran his fingers through her fur as if she was his dog. As if he were there to comfort her through her last moments.

"Good girl," he whispered soothingly as his head fell back, resting against her.

He looked up into the blue sky, "What a life we lived?"

Her breaths faded, as did his.

The infected went into a frenzy, screaming and attacking each other. Gavin, Alex, Chris, and Mitch stopped to watch. The creatures were killing each other, when they turned their attention to Felix. The world seemed to fade into a deafening nothingness.

Sasha didn't turn away. She watched, yearning for him for so long, only to see him die to protect them.

The boat was anchored to another, pulling further and further away. She swore she saw a black dog sitting over the two as they lay in their own blood on the deck. It bent down, smiling as its ears picked up, its large head with long horn-like pointed ears rose slowly. It unnerved her, sending chills across her entire body. It looked at her. It saw her. For a moment she saw all three of them walk away.

Soon the island was small and the fire smoldered, sending a long thick black plume of smoke into the air. Letting anyone for miles know that this was where they killed the horde, they killed the alphas and their queen. They survived. For everything that was sacrificed, for everyone who was lost in the name of preservation. Here they lay, in their blood, a human reduced to the state of his ancestors, and an animal risen to the state of hers. Man, and that species' best friend. No more enemies, their blood as cold as the other. Peaceful, resting for eternity. What a fitting way to go for a man who loved animals more than humans.

"I love you, my crazy man," Sasha whispered.

"Who the fuck is that?" Felix asked, pulling a poor soldier violently by the collar over to him, just trying to get to his crew with his stuff for the training exercise. He dropped his helmet from Felix rattling him for answers.

"I don't know, Sergeant, she just showed up this morning. She's some civilian," the young soldier replied.

Felix pushed him away. "You're useless," he roared in his sarcastic voice.

Chris walked up. "Hey, brother, looks like the investigators are interested in this whole program they implemented. They sent a psych doc down here to profile all of us, to ensure we are the right kind of people for allowing females into the infantry."

Felix almost didn't care that no one knew who that beautiful creature standing in front of him was. He was determined to find out for himself. He shook his friend's hand and walked right up to her.

"Ah, perfect…" the lieutenant started as he pointed lazily behind her, "this is the man right here you want to talk to."

She spun around, and to her surprise he was right behind her. He was taller than she expected, and fierce, his eyes dark. He almost lost whatever words were rolling around in his head by the sight of her. She could tell, even though it was cute that his intense look softened almost immediately when their eyes met.

"Who are you and what are you doing here?" he asked in his best attempt to hide that he thought she was the most beautiful woman he had ever seen in his entire life.

"I'm Sasha, I'm here to monitor the integration of females into combat positions in the military."

He almost didn't hear anything after she said her name.

"That's a beautiful name, I'm Staff Sergeant Martin, but you can call me Felix, nice to meet you."

They looked each other in the eye as they shook each other's hands. He thought she was so very beautiful. And she thought he was ruggedly handsome.

"I guess I'm with you then?" she asked.

"As you should," he replied.

Chapter 27
You Can Teach an Old Dog New Tricks

Two soldiers dressed in green escorted a black box down a very long hospital hallway. They passed through a corridor; creatures screeching and clawing and roaring as they passed by those fortified cells. A familiar scene to those that were connected to such atrocities. On to an elevator where Doctor Steinberg waited impatiently with joy.

"Yes, you brought him back to me..." he proclaimed, leaning down, intimately clawing at the box. He continued, "Thought you could get away, but you can't escape death, none of us can, silly little soldier."

"Yes, sir," one of the young men replied.

"And what of the report?" the doctor asked with excitement, pushing through his demand.

"Right here, sir," the other soldier escorting the black box replied, handing over a metal clipboard.

The doctor snatched it from the soldier. Opening it as quickly as he could. His eyes scanned as he whispered the words inaudibly to himself. He paused, throwing the clipboard into the air. He turned, his coat struggling to catch up.

The nurse took a step back, surprised with an odd smile upon her face.

"His cells are still alive! Nurse?" Steinberg roared, shaking the poor young woman.

"Y-yes, Doctor?"

"Quickly, we must operate, and then, I think we will put him on ice, his tissue is very valuable. We cannot wait, just in case he decides to come back to life, like last time."

"Yes, sir," she replied again in an almost monotone voice.

The doctor spun around once more, patting the box. "Oh, Number 13, you were the one. After all these years, hundreds of thousands of lives lost... NO! Even more just to create you, and out of all of them, you were the one to survive it all, and even kill a chimera. I hope you found what you were looking for. But your sacrifice, involuntarily of course, will begin the biggest purification ever conducted. War, famine, the plague; hell, even the dogs will pale in comparison. Sleep well, young friend."

"Glad to see you are back to your old self, Doctor," Anderson spoke in admiration, and a hint of antagonizing. "What of Adam and Eve, and the other projects?"

"We will rebuild, they are all just the beginning, we will change the face of the entire world. Next, we will begin building safe havens for when these soldiers are matured enough to cleanse this filthy world."

The doctor was humming to himself in absolute cheerfulness as the smile he wore upon his face couldn't be any larger than it was. The elevator disappeared further into the shaft, as his laughter echoed and faded into the darkness with them. The heavy clank of the locking braces echoed through the shaft that they had made it to the bottom floor.

The group turned to be met by a tall man.

"Sir?" The doctor was surprised.

The soldiers, even Anderson, stood at attention as the man approached, placing his hand on the casket.

"What a shame..." the tall man spoke, softly and quietly.

"What is a shame, sir?"

"That a worthy adversary met his end before I could challenge his conduct of war."

"He was only a success in that he will lead our way into further progress, sir," the doctor replied, his voice was shaky, riddled with fear.

"Was he?" The tall man turned his head slightly.

"He was hardly worthy of your attention," the doctor exclaimed.

"In perspective... This man, although not a man anymore, product of manipulation of our Father's creation, had caused you so much trouble. Killed so many in his wake, stood against hellish beasts cast forth from the immense challenge to the existence of God, science, and withstood the most devastating weapon in the existence of mankind. And you would tell me that he was hardly worth my time? Who are you to suggest that my opinion of a soldier is wrong?"

Doctor Steinberg was shaking physically. He couldn't answer, and dared not to further bury himself in his replies.

"Rest well," the tall man said, turning his head toward the casket. "I pray that your wrathful soul finds that unending battlefield. I, too, will one day find you there. That's the only place for those like us."

The man walked onto the giant shaft elevator. The soldiers wheeled the casket off. Doctor Steinberg and Anderson stepped off, turning back to watch the elevator begin to lift; but who pressed the button? The man was dressed in a unique dress uniform that Anderson thought reminded him of the uniforms of the Luftwaffe from World War II. His hair was silver, well-kempt as it was combed precisely to the side, his eyes cold, brilliantly blue. His beard was dark and thick. His skin was tan, possibly a descendent of the middle east. A good-looking man of middle age but his stature and posture would suggest a life of war and military etiquette so deeply ingrained it was discerning. A large sword hung at his left hip, a dagger at his right, a red sash was tied around the sword. The only thing out of place was how old the sash looked, it was burnt and frayed, barely holding itself together by its weak threads. He also didn't have a firearm on him at all. In this day and age, bladed weapons. He was an oddity, demanding of respect in the expressionless face he wore with pride.

One of the soldiers turned to the other one, "That was him."

"Who?"

"The Overseer."

"What a scary motherfucker," the soldier whispered.

"Shut your mouth, impudent fool!" Doctor Steinberg spat out as he spun around.

"Yes, sir," the soldier blurted out, merely out of muscle memory.

Doctor Steinberg moved toward the soldier rigidly, still riddled with fear. He backhanded the young man in a flash. Surprising to all the onlookers, save for Anderson who merely watched the swirling yellow warning lights disappear into the shaft.

"Overseer Samuel Dudael. You should forget him, if you value your life."

The soldier was shocked at the statement. The nurse chimed in, "Dudael?"

"Yes?" Doctor Steinberg wrenched his head toward her, with a burning intent in his eyes that made them all uneasy. "You know that name?" he asked maliciously.

"I was a theology major, Dead Sea Scrolls, Dudael means 'Kettle' or 'Pot' in Hebrew, it was said to be the imprisonment of the fa—"

The gunshot rang out, the casing clanged against the metal floor.

Both soldiers were dumbfounded. Doctor Steinberg fired two more times, killing each of them. Letting out a sigh as he stood over their bodies.

"What a waste, she was intelligent, and so far more intelligent than I'm willing to risk," the doctor exclaimed.

Anderson shook his head, "Now we have to have this mess cleaned up. Can you not kill everyone who learns of him? It's getting annoying."

"No worries, young doctor, come on, we've wasted enough time!"

The doctor turned to find her standing there. Aiming a pistol at him, shaking through the determination in her eyes.

"Oh?"

"I can't let you have him," Beatrix said.

A gunshot rang out, followed by a heavy sigh. Anderson tucked the pistol back into his coat.

"Shall we, Doctor?"

"What a shame, she too was a waste."

The two men walked past her has she gargled blood on the cold metal floor.

Standing on the deck of the destroyer, they all looked out into the ocean as they sailed south. Standing around Isaac and Sasha, and next to her Gavin. Everyone was there that once knew that man. With heavy hearts they all listened to Isaac, almost the entire group of survivors of Fort Monroe were standing there listening to his words. For he was indeed their minister once upon a time.

"I met Felix a long time ago; and honestly I judged him, I saw what he was and it frightened me. But I looked to the lord and found resolve. This man, who was every bit a soldier and low-life, once upon a time a criminal, accepted me for who I was. It didn't make any sense, he even claimed to be a Satanist when I met him," a few giggled in the crowd. Isaac continued, "I didn't understand why he was the way he was. He brought so many of us together and called us his brothers. This man who seemed so closed-minded, so irrational, so hateful, ended up being the only reason some of us came together and became family."

Isaac turned to Sasha, holding her hands. "When he asked me to marry you two, I was shocked. You know that? He hated religion, but he loved me and respected me enough to ask me to be the one. He always said that 'a gay black minister, his brother, is the only person who deserves to marry him to the woman he loves.'"

Sasha held back tears.

"You know how that made me feel?"

She shook her head.

"Like I was a part of this family, his family. All of you. He may have had his flaws; but he was a good man."

She sobbed; Isaac continued.

"Let us pray."

Gavin spoke in a whisper from red eyes and tears as Isaac prayed for Felix's soul.

"Farewell, my oldest adversary, my dearest brother."

*****

The weight was almost unbearable, it felt like a sea of chalk, a dusty blanket that pressed in all directions. It smelt of nothing, there was nothing in the air. No wind, it wasn't cool nor hot, it was emptiness.

Felix woke up in utter darkness, sitting as he was moments ago, leaned against her head. Felix stood, looking behind him to find that beautiful adversary. He reached, stopping only an inch above her head. She pressed against his hand. Accepting his greeting as she too stood.

The sound of children laughing echoed through the dark, off of what? Made no sense due to the overwhelming emptiness. Before he knew it, the queen, the hyena, as gorgeous as she was, was running into the nothingness whooping low. You could tell by the tone she was happy, chasing the laughter of two children.

"Welcome home," a young boy said.

"We've missed you," a gleeful young girl added.

Felix turned to find them standing in the distance. They waved. The queen turned her head to acknowledge his presence once more. Before he could wave back, the children turned and ran off; the hyena, the queen, playfully chasing after Adam and Eve. Their laughter echoed into silence, fading with their figures blackening against the darkness, completely out of perception.

"What the fuck? Where am I?"

Felix turned, finding another before him, standing tall as it sat on its hindlegs. All six eyes staring at him. The beast towered over Felix as he stood there unafraid. The only light in the vastness of darkness seemed to be shining from under them as if the darkness was letting it go from its chalky grips.

"I used to think I was crazy when I first seen you."

"Saw..." the beast corrected him.

Felix laughed. The beast laughed in its deep and echoing voices.

"Are you ready to answer for all the wrong you have done?"

"Why would I answer for what I was designed to do?" Felix replied.

The beast laughed horrifically... Maniacally. "It would be very hypocritical of me to honestly impose such a question. However," the beast chuckled once more "...you're accurate in your reply. Only if the rest of your kind looked at it in such a way. Your laws and regulations, your self-imposed restrictions and appointed self-righteously misguided power over you in hopes that their will, will lead your fragile worthless worlds into the byproduct of disorder, war, suffering, genocide...the illusion of peace."

"Are you my God?" Felix asked.

The black dog cocked its massive head, his tail twitched in ghostly excitement. "Yes... Older than this world's creator. However, we have all the time in the universe, and one in particular cannot wait to meet you. For now,

376

we have work to do, because the youngster has started something he cannot stop. And I wish to bring balance again. However, the road is long, and your dirty hands will be forever unclean in it."

"Is it time to go, then?" Felix asked.

The beast let out an even louder, more obnoxious laugh. It stopped suddenly, fiercely moving its massive head toward Felix. Felix reached for his gun; it was not there. And he was naked. Fear started to settle in like cold hands on his back.

Its six eyes, all different shapes and sizes, all sinister, clustered in threes on both sides of its face. One of the universe, sparkling as it slowly spun, one of white, one of black, one of a cat, one of a dog, and the last, one of the ocean but not like any he had seen. Felix could only fathom. With that, he was baffled by it, didn't know which ones to focus on, as all of them were making eye contact. The black dog made it easy for him by rotating its large head, eerily stressing one eye at face level. His grin ran all the way to its long, pointed ears.

Without its giant, shark-tooth smile breaking once, it spoke. Its voice coming from every direction in a series of different pitches and tones. The only one Felix could understand was that of its sinister voice, it sickened him to hear it, but it was the only one he could make out from the weight of the sounds.

"You will live and die generations at a time. Time to go has gone, you are no longer bound by it, other than where I place you in order to disorder it."

"Why me?"

"Because of your answer to a simple question…"

Felix waited for longer than a natural pause would allow, "What question is that?"

"…did the world end?" the beast asked curiously. Eagerly; even though Felix could tell it knew the answer.

"No," Felix began. "It finally started existing for what it was truly meant to be."

The beast's smile disappeared as it sat up, its long tail switched sides around its massive paws.

"Are you prepared to measure the weight of your existence against the Light, Darkness, and all that which lies in between?"

"Will she be alright?"

"You are dead to them, best to leave the past where it lies, she will always remember you, that you can be sure of, and her memories of you are the best she ever had. However, not the best she ever will. For that, be thankful. You only ever were merely a catalyst in your own world, and now, in my beloved universe. Besides, you did something that will bring you a joy that will surprise you in the future."

Felix's expression changed to that of relief as it sounded through his reply, "Good," he nodded as he stared off into the darkness, "...she deserves far better than me; all of them did."

The beast leaned down once again as his smile split his face.

"You didn't answer my question..."

"I do not deserve such a thing," Felix replied.

"You were one of the few that could see me in your world. So, this is your choice now, will you aid the universe in her existence, or be that teardrop she shed, like the rest of your filthy species born of such a whimsical thing as light?"

Felix smiled. And through a sinister deep growl, he said, "We are but a teardrop in the eye of the universe, and how she weeps so."

The black dog's grin widened.

"She didn't weep for you, child... But she will, in time... For all of her children."

Felix turned and looked off into his future. The void merely stared back. And that thing behind him watched.

"You know?" Felix started.

"I know, but go ahead anyway." The beast chuckled.

"A child once stood before God, and they asked that thing of brilliant light...the child said, 'why did you create evil, if you are all good, if you love all the little children of the world?' And God answered, 'Because, child, I am.'"

Felix chuckled; the beast chuckled. It rose into hysterical laughter between the two, and then there was nothing.

"You know what I'm afraid of?"

"What?"

"I'm afraid that one day...I'm going to wake up and walk away from this world..."

"..."

"That day will be the day...that I truly am free... Until the blade whispers my name, and I know the bullet's truth."